THE DEFINITION OF NORMAL

E. S. CARPENTER

Published by Quesylis P H

Cover by Courtney Lopes

CHAPTER ONE
ASSOCIATION

It sounded like a tank coming down the street. Little Jake had heard his new neighbors were moving into their house today and he leaned against the back of the chair, face glued to his front window…looking…waiting. He didn't wait long as the gigantic light blue and yellow moving truck broke the silence of a quiet August Saturday morning. The engine revved loud, though it was going very slow, and as the driver spotted the house, he pulled closer to their side of the street, breaking a few hanging branches on the two mature elm trees guarding the curb. The wheels started screeching and more limbs cracked as the monster-sized truck came to a halt.

Three men in dark green coveralls lumbered out of the cab and went about setting up for the unload. Jake was mesmerized and strained his head almost sideways against the window, trying desperately to see every detail of the unfolding events; too young to realize he could just go to his side kitchen window and have a front row seat.

One of the men started pushing and pulling levers that made the neatest sounds and moved the big hydraulic metal platform from against the back of the truck. Loud clanks echoed as the men released the back doors, pulled out their long metal ramp, and threw it on the hilled front lawn of the house next door.

Then Jake saw a silver car slow up and start to turn toward the drive between their houses before he lost sight due to the restricted view of his choice of windows. He pushed hard against the sill and propelled himself away, spinning in a single step, dodging an end table, and raced to the family room.

"Dad, I think they're here!"

His father glanced up from the sports section of the local newspaper on his computer. "That's great, Jake." He stood up from the thick leather sofa, and called out, "Morgan, our neighbors are here."

Jake's mom came down the hallway and reached for Jakes hand. "Want to go say hi?"

"Oh, yeah, Mom."

"Chris, you coming?"

Jake's father placed the computer on the glass top coffee table and followed Morgan and Jake toward the side kitchen door.

As they opened the door, a single woman moved around the car on the far drive. Still, only the driver side door was open, but there were things jammed against every other car window. The car was packed. As Jake and his mom descended the side steps, the woman opened the far back door, and leaned inside. A moment later, out stepped a small four or five year old boy. Jake immediately let go of his mom's hand and ran to the back of the car, popped out on the far side and stood there, making no further approach.

He gave the little boy a big smile. "Hi. I'm Jake." He stepped one large step forward and stretched out his arm. "Welcome to the neighborhood."

The boy immediately grinned and timidly took Jake's hand with amazing limpness and they shook. Or rather, Jake shook the smaller boy's arm as if it was a piece of cooked spaghetti.

"I'm Steven."

"Are you going to live here?"

"Yeah."

"Too cool! I live right there." Jake pointed over at the house on the other side of their shared driveways. "Wow, you guys have a lot of stuff!" He turned and yelled, "Mom! Can I help Steven move his stuff in?"

By this time, Chris and Morgan were standing next to their new neighbor, smiling as they watched their children meet each other. With a wonderfully warm smile, Jake's mom turned to her new neighbor, "Hi. I'm Morgan and this is my husband, Chris."

And with a soft voice and equally warm smile, the woman replied, "Hi. I'm Genavieve Blair, Steven's mom." She extended her hand. "My husband Connor should be pulling in any minute. He *was* right behind me." She glanced at the street, then back to her new neighbors. "Oh. Everyone calls me Genna."

All three turned to watch the two boys again. They had each taken something from the car and were walking to the side kitchen door. Genna was noticeably delighted. Before her son even reached the door for the first time, he had made a friend. Without taking her eyes off the boys as they disappeared inside, she whispered, "Oh how adorable."

And Morgan responded just as softly. "I agree."

Moments later, Connor's car turned into their new driveway and stopped four feet behind her car. She could see his instant smile as he noticed her standing there with the two strangers. He exited the car and immediately walked to them with his hand out well in advance. "Hi."

Chris took it. "Hi. I'm Chris Harrison and this is my wife, Morgan, and our son, Jake, is inside your house. You seem to have inadvertently recruited a moving helper. He's been dying to see if you had any kids his age."

Connor's eyebrows rose. "Steven already has a friend?"

Genna replied, "How fantastic is that."

Connor chuckled. "Pretty fantastic."

Genna turned to Chris. "Is it okay if Jake and Steven play *move in* together today?"

With a slightly concerned look, Chris replied, "I don't want him to be in your way."

"Well, Steven making a friend here was Connor and my greatest concern and I already think your son is amazing for the way he's welcomed his new neighbors. Would you let him stay?"

Morgan lit up and replied for Chris. "If you don't think he'd be in the way, I know Jake would like to, but if it gets to be too much, you can send them over to our house. In fact, why don't I set a break for you by telling them their lunch break is at our house, and we can let them play video games or whatever, in our family room or yard. This way they can do something else when they become bored *moving you in*…What do you think?"

"I think that's an excellent plan. Is Jake an only child? Steven is."

Morgan nodded. "Yeah."

The women made eye contact and smiled at each other, and Genna continued to encourage their new connection. "Can I give you my phone number since it looks like we'll each be taking turns watching them today?"

Morgan's smile grew deeper as she pulled out her phone. "Sounds like a great idea."

The two men were equally pleased with the new friendship. "I'm in construction," Chris told Connor, "so don't hesitate to ask for some basic help if you have a problem with your new house. After all," he pointed over his shoulder, "I have its sister."

"Thanks Chris. I appreciate it. Are you a carpenter?"

"Commercial carpenter."

"Oh. Okay."

The two boys came running out of the house at full speed. Jake made the turn at the top landing outside the kitchen door and took the steps two at a time. Steven did his best to keep close, but far less daring, negotiated each step individually. Each grabbed a small something, then turned and disappeared as fast as they showed up.

Genna spent the morning answering movers' questions and trying to make sense of her kitchen, as the boys continually ran past her, in and out the side door, helping unload her car.

"…playground isn't too far and it has three baseball fields…"

"…and Justin has an older brother and sister…"

"…it's gigantic and has really cool windows you can look out and see really far…"

She listened and constantly smiled as Jake sold the neighborhood to Steven while they unloaded. She wondered where they were putting everything, but she wasn't concerned. She was quietly thrilled Jake was there for Steven. She'd find and fix everything in due time.

Morgan spent the morning making the Blairs a casserole and waited till eleven-thirty to dial Genna. "Hi. It's Morgan next door."

"Hi."

"I was thinking maybe you could use your break and I can feed the kids?"

"That'd be perfect. Jake's delightful! He's selling us on the neighborhood. I now know where the playground is and where I need to buy our groceries."

"Oh, thanks. He's not being too much trouble?"

"Are you kidding? He's making Steven's day. I was dreading how bored he was going to be today, but I didn't want to leave him with his grandmother on our first day. I would've hired a boy like Jake if I knew it was going to be such a terrific way to make Steven feel welcomed his first day in his new house."

Morgan smiled. "I'm happy it's working out."

Genna continued, "You want me to tell them to head over for lunch?"

"Whenever you want."

"Look for them any minute." Genna's voice reflected great appreciation. "Again, thanks so much."

And her gratitude pleased Morgan. "Oh, no problem at all."

Moments later, the boys came running into the Harrison house, Jake leading the way.

"Hi boys, how's your day going so far?" Morgan looked down at Steven. "How are you doing, sweetheart?"

He drug out his answer like a five-year-old child, breathing heavily from the dash next door. "Good."

"Are you hungry?"

"Yeah."

"Well, I have pizza and French fries, but I also have peanut butter and jelly, or cereal. What 'cha want?"

He gazed up at her with big, soft brown eyes. "Pizza?"

She smiled and patted the top of his head. "Sure."

Jake was already seated at the kitchen table. "Sit here."

Steven turned to him, and went right over next to him.

The food was already in the middle of the table. She fixed them each a plate, and a glass of chocolate milk. "Chris. There's pizza in here if you're hungry."

Seconds later, Chris turned into the kitchen. "Hi boys. How you making out?"

"Good, Dad."

He looked at Steven. "How you doin'?"

Steven looked up and softly replied, "Good."

Chris gently motioned toward Steven's plate. "How's your pizza?"

With the same little voice, Steven answered again, "Good."

Chris grinned.

Morgan leaned back against the counter. "Will you watch them for a quick bit? I made them dinner and I want to bring it over. Okay?"

He grabbed a piece of pizza. "Sure."

Morgan cradled the loaf of bread and bag of noodles under her arm, lifted the covered casserole off the counter and opened the outside kitchen door with the edge of the dish. "Be right back."

She could see Genna from outside the other side door. "Hi. I have some things for you."

Genna noticed her arms full and hurried to the door. "Hi. What…"

"I made you dinner." She walked over to the stove and put it down. "Here's a loaf of bread and a bag of noodles."

"Oh my, Morgan, that's awesome. I got so into this, I forgot all about dinner."

Morgan turned from the stove to face her. "I remember how hectic it was moving in and we didn't have Jake yet. Okay, have to get back to the kids. They're eating pizza and French fries. Chris is watching them."

"Thanks so much. You're great."

Morgan opened the kitchen door. "Call me if you need anything."

"Okay. I will."

Morgan was immeasurably touched. The two families had taken less than a day to form what seemed like a significant bond, based on the instant friendship of their two only children.

By the end of the day, both boys were exhausted, having spent their time laughing and playing between the inside and outside of both houses.

As Morgan tucked her half-awake son into his bed after his long and busy day, she asked, "Did you have a good day, love?"

Jake used his last bit of energy to answer. "The best, Mom."

"Good." She kissed him softly. "Sleep tight, love. I love you."

"I love you too, Mom."

In the house next door, Genna tucked Steven in, and asked the same question but with completely different words. "So, how do you like your new house so far, sweetheart?"

His little voice filled with exhaustion. "Good, Mom."

Steven was a more reserved child, but Genna could read him through the connection that only comes from having created him. She smiled softly, and caressed his forehead as he lay under his covers.

"I love you, sweetheart."

"I love you too, Mom."

She leaned over and tenderly kissed his forehead, shut out his light and left the room.

~ ~ ~

Jake and Steven formed a friendship only two young people could have. Each shared their talents as much as they shared their young hearts, and their ever-increasing bond helped four parents fall in love with two children.

Chris tiptoed toward the kitchen as he heard Morgan come in from work. He waited for her to drop her purse on the seat closest to the kitchen door, then semi-whispered, "Morgan. Come here."

"Why. What's going on?" She watched him walk gingerly in front of her to their bedroom, then hold out his arm so she wouldn't walk too close to the open window and catch the children's attention.

He whispered, "Jake and Steven."

She bent over slightly to get a better view of them in the backyard, and whispered, "What about them?"

"Jake is teaching Steven how to catch a fly ball out back. I've been listening for half an hour. It's fantastic. Listen."

Jake extended both arms toward Steven. "But you will get it. That's why we're practicing. If we keep practicing, you'll get it."

Steven stood twenty feet away, facing his friend, with an oversized glove on his right hand and his shoulders hunched forward. "I'll never get it."

Jake was softly adamant. "Yes, you will."

Steven matched Jake's adamancy with dejection. "No, I won't."

Jake stood near the fence between their yards with the baseball in his right hand. "How bad do you want to stop being picked last?"

"A lot." Steven's voice now had a pleading tone.

"Then I can help."

Chris smiled at the patience and determination in Jake's reply.

Morgan whispered to the back of Chris's head. "I didn't even know Jake could catch one,"

"I've been working with him. He's gotten pretty good. But what amazes me is, he's a better teacher than I am."

She peered around him and studied Steven's diminutive frame in the distance. "Steven isn't going to get hurt trying to learn, is he? He's so small and frail."

Chris sat on the floor against the far bedroom wall facing the yard and eyed Morgan. "He'll be alright."

He heard his son's voice, and turned his head toward the open window.

"Okay, let's start over." Jake ran closer to Steven and tossed the ball with just a small arc. Steven held up his glove and the ball stuck in it. Jake smiled at Steven's success, though he was too young to understand Steven's small hand wasn't developed enough to control the baseball glove, and Steven was too young to understand, to make the argument.

He awkwardly tossed the ball back to Jake. "But then we're studying together. You help me ...I help you."

"Okay, okay! But we need to work on this first. *This* is important!"

CHAPTER TWO
PROGRESSION

Living next door to each other created a natural and wonderful connection between the boys. They were in the same grade throughout school, and for the most part, even the same class. They played together constantly and continuously, everything from alone together, to unorganized street games with their other neighborhood friends, to little league baseball on the same team. They always seemed to come together and leave together. And escorted by one or the other set of parents, went to sports games and other events, much like they were brothers who lived next door to each other, which naturally made the parents feel somewhat related. By choice though, which at times made the dynamic more special.

Even their houses were related, just mirror images of each other. Craftsman style ranchers built in the same year by the same builder, with side kitchen doors that faced each other across their driveways, big backyards and an identical hill on each front lawn, setting each house at the same distance from, and level above the sidewalk. Each even had two large elm trees at the curb.

Steven and Jake were in each other's house as much as they were in their own. The only difference was, everything was just switched around to the opposite side. They both thought it neat actually. The boys even decided they wanted the same bedroom in their respective houses, but Jake's father made their extra bedroom a playroom for both of them, with all the electronic hook-ups and shelving to make any game player or media user very happy. And they played for hours at a time with no trouble at all.

Both sets of parents joked that they wouldn't get along this well if they were actually siblings, and were grateful for their children's relationship, nurturing and rewarding it as they grew together. The only thing they seemed to regularly disagree about was whose house to play in. They each liked the other's.

They grew closer as the years passed. As they grew though, they started looking very different. Jake became very masculine as he matured. He became more athletic in high school, and even played third base on the junior varsity and varsity baseball teams. Steven never missed a game and was his biggest fan. By the time Jake was ready to enter college, he was six feet tall with wide and impressive shoulders, muscular thighs, strong arms, and a man's voice.

Steven's hormones led him in a different direction. He was always thin and frail, and matured far less masculine than his best friend. He had tiny shoulders, soft skin, very little facial hair, and his legs and bottom, though thin, seemed to have a somewhat feminine shape and tone. His jawline never tightened. Even his hands were thin and delicate. He reached five foot seven by ninth grade and by the end of high school, had not grown a fraction of an inch taller or a pound heavier.

Steven started feeling different before he started looking different and he started looking different before he was old enough to understand what he was feeling. Though the changes started appearing early, neither friend saw it as a concern. Both gave every indication their longstanding relationship could withstand any new changes being noticed.

They each had what anyone would consider a good childhood, but Steven's differences caused difficulties beyond Jake's awareness. His physical appearance invited its share of abuse from friends and strangers alike. He had his share of grade school and neighborhood bullies, though all seemed smart enough not to intimidate him in front of Jake. Most of the harassment was too subtle for Jake to recognize anyway, and even when he shared it with his best friend, Jake never saw the issue for its depth of injury. Jake's age prevented a true understanding, and Steven never conveyed the true level of damage. His ability to express the hurt he felt was as foreign to him as the concept of hurting someone for no reason other than physical differences. And for some odd reason, he thought explaining it in deeper detail would diminish Jake's view of him.

The subtle abuse Steven endured growing up was also well ignored by other significant people. For as much as the grown-ups around him loved him, they equally overlooked things that needed to not be overlooked. There were times when life found him alone and even strangers took passing swipes at him.

The small tortures existed and the abuses happened, but he did his best to bury the occurrences deep inside. He could pull up examples at will if he wished, but he didn't have to. They seemed to rise into consciousness on their own, all too regularly. He fought them, but when he lost the fight, he chose to conclude that those instances were just part of who he is. He had to look at them that way. It was the only way he could look past them.

It was little consolation, but he also knew he wasn't alone. He was sure people like him were singled out, and he was equally aware how far down the wrong side of that continuum he stood. People abuse who they can, for every reason imaginable, but best of all, for no reason when no reason is necessary. Opportunity being the only reason needed for those who have the ability and the notion, and those instances cut him almost as deeply as his own mind did when he registered how different he was.

He adjusted the best he could though, and fought the battle his mind insisted he fight, but the impulses controlling him were stealthier than even the bullies. He remembered the first incident. It was a completely random occurrence, but it was the first time his differences caught him off guard, and significant enough in his young mind to remember vividly. He found a girl's clothing catalog in the mail. He always collected the mail after school and one day accidentally discovered one and started paging through. At first, he had no specific agenda as he looked, but he wasn't looking at the young female models, he was looking at their clothes. The catalogs would be innocent enough, just girls in cute things. Girl clothes were always prettier and softer looking.

But the first time he found a lingerie catalog in the mail, his heart pounded at a level he hadn't previously experienced. The clothes were incredible. He stared in amazement, though he had a slight pang of guilt studying the catalog. Was it wrong looking at these pictures? How could it be? They came in the mail for anyone to see. Steven kept the catalog concealed and studied the pictures on occasion, hiding it away in the zippered side compartment of his video game bag.

The next unintended experience was equally significant. He accidentally found a wardrobe cabinet filled with feminine clothes in his grandmother's basement while she babysat him one summer, and spent a series of visits excusing himself to play down there. Just putting his hand between all the soft fragrant material was exhilarating. He had to try something on. He could feel his heart race as he tried on one particular dress. He registered the way the outfit made him feel as he moved. Though it rubbed his skin in a way his boy clothes wouldn't allow, the inner feeling was far more meaningful. The sensation was like a drug, creating an unparalleled response throughout his entire being.

He grew out of the need though, or at least grew strong enough to break the desire to continue this secret exercise. The fight went on like this for years, but never fully registered in his awareness. He never put a name to the activity. He was only curious and it was harmless. The desire would eventually all but disappear and he would go lengths without an associated thought. But something always seemed to trigger its awakening without notice or warning and he would spend another period of time consciously thinking about wearing girl things and being a girl, and even being a girl in front of Jake.

Some time had passed before Jake found Steven's hidden catalogs. Steven thought they were well hidden in the private zippered side pocket of his video game bag; never thinking Jake did anything but look in the main opening for a different game to play when the mood moved him. When Jake initially found the first lingerie catalog, he wanted to look at it with him.

"Where'd you get *this*?" Jake jumped on the bed next to him.

Steven did a double-take and his heart jumped, thinking Jake would know why Steven kept it. "It was in the mail."

"Really! I got to start getting the mail." Jake laid stomach down next to Steven on Steven's bed, placed the catalog in front of them and opened it. As he paged through, Jake commented on the models and which ones he thought were pretty, while Steven focused on the soft feminine clothes.

Steven didn't know why, but while they looked together, he experienced strong new urges for Jake. Why was looking at a catalog filled with sexily dressed females making him feel like he wanted to explore Jake? He had a strange desire to ask Jake if he wanted him to wear something like this for him. He would if Jake wanted. He couldn't seem to sum up the courage to tell him, but what would be the harm? He paged through with his friend and the more Jake commented, the more Steven yearned to wear these things, but he decided mentioning it might cost him his best friend, so he remained silent. Fear still greater than desire.

This confusion would ebb and flow in Steven for the next period of years. Its presence never strong enough to cause anguish but never weak enough to be considered non-existent. His feelings for Jake seemed to come and go also, and they always seemed to coincide with the whole girl confusion in his mind. As he got older, the feelings became stronger but never strong enough he couldn't dismiss them. In fact, the older he got, the more he was sure nothing good would be gained by Jake becoming aware of these thoughts and that reason alone was good enough to sustain his efforts to repress them. Admission would only ruin his and Jake's friendship, he was sure.

But what if he could tell him? What would it be like to share his biggest secret? What would it be like to be a girl in front of his best friend?

As he matured, the confusion became even more complex. He didn't think he was attracted to other boys. He didn't look at them that way. He didn't know if he would look at them if he was a girl, but he wasn't attracted to them when he felt like a boy, and he only felt like being with one boy when he thought about being a girl. In fact, when he was a boy, he thought he liked girls. Well, not one in particular. Not even a whole one. He liked their clothes though. Searching for girls in pretty outfits became a secret hobby, but he didn't have to work at it. They were everywhere and even watching television became more enjoyable. But he had no interest in the rest of the girl, or the rest of whatever female classmate he was secretly studying.

He did wonder about Jake's body though and nothing made him more excited than secretly thinking about his best friend's body, but not when they were together. He had very little to no desire when they were actually with each other, unless they were wrestling.

These thoughts were unbelievably confusing. What did they mean? How could he get them out of his head?

Schoolwork became that answer. Schoolwork helped immensely. He also tried to obsess about other things. One summer, he decided to learn as many stats about baseball and baseball players as possible. The activity worked for the most part, for almost an entire summer. Then he innocently went to a discount store with his mother one Saturday and she made a detour to shop for some intimate things. Feelings he thought were all but gone resurfaced as he discreetly studied a few items in the next aisle.

The fight was inside him to stay though he was too young to comprehend its entirety. He fought it when he could and even won the battle, always up to that point. But high school caused the battle to increase and the new level of inner conflict caught him by surprise.

From the first day, he and Jake walked into the high school together every morning. In a short time, Steven developed a habit of secretly observing people noticing Jake. Especially girls. After all, he was already more mature than his young age and already a rather physical presence.

Everything they were experiencing was new and far more overwhelming than either anticipated and Steven's feelings of inadequacy were growing at almost the same rate as Jake. Jake couldn't see what Steven was noticing nor would he think there were any issues with their differences, and Steven understood. The shortcoming wasn't Jake's. Steven knew Jake couldn't see what he was experiencing, and Steven was aware enough to be able to recognize his unique viewpoint.

And though Steven knew differences like his were well within the parameters of development, the realization didn't stop him from feeling inadequate, especially at his age. Inadequacy in one form or another was a secret companion to almost all high school students, whether real or imagined, though Steven could argue the lot wasn't evenly divided. It also didn't stop him from feeling he was no longer in Jake's league and through a weak but tangible correlation, Jake's world. He loved his best friend enough to understand he didn't want to be in Jake's way as he reached social heights Steven was quite aware were beyond him.

His schoolwork though, continued to be his only equalizer. Otherwise everything he looked at pointed back at him and told him he was inadequate. The way Jake matured, the way every female matured, the way no pretty girl ever talked to him except to ask for an answer to something she didn't understand, and even the curt way some of them went about that, was demeaning. He wouldn't say anything, but he was intelligent enough to be completely aware.

Jake never noticed the depth of these issues within Steven. Jake never noticed the fight, or the confusion, or even the emotional distress Steven's differences caused. His new world was also far more complicated than a short time ago and he was as buried in its new complexity as everyone else, including Steven. He was blossoming into a young adult like almost all his peers and keeping up with everyone else was its own full time activity. Did Jake notice Steven was a little behind physically? Of course, but it didn't bother him. Jake cared for him like a little brother and treated him even better.

Their first high school year, Jake ate lunch with Steven every day, but each made their own friends, since they were in separate classes and social groups. Jake also made friends at a different pace than Steven—noticeably different friends. Steven noticed the students in high school seemed to divide almost by physical maturity, with very few exceptions, and it made their lunchroom table distinctly peculiar. The two halves looked completely mismatched and though they all ate together, the contrast between each group was nothing short of amusing.

Their different friends and classes started a natural separation but it wasn't Jake who separated from Steven. It was more the opposite. Steven started withdrawing from Jake. He saw the differences. He saw almost all of them with wide eyes, and more than a few times, a lump in his throat.

They had a good run together and it wasn't like they were strangers. Jake treated him dearly when they were together, but Steven was sure he was holding his best friend back. When Jake started playing baseball for the school, his popularity rose again and Steven loved Jake's success. He watched his best friend closely, though the more he watched, the more he was sure he was in the way. Could he separate completely? No. Steven sat quietly at every game, whether Jake actually played or not, and since the games were after school, they always went home together. They were both baseball fans and they used that common thread to keep connected when both thought their connection was waning.

Steven didn't try to separate for Jake alone though. He didn't know why, but when Jake was with a girl, it was depressing. He never registered a reason other than he knew he was no longer as close to his friend as he once was, and no situation brought that more to light than the assumption of the intimate relationship of a girlfriend. He knew a girl would most likely come along and take his place someday. That was the way life was supposed to be. It depressed him, but he understood. But sometimes he couldn't watch. Actually, most times he couldn't, and the easiest way not to have to watch was to not be there.

But after the initial whirlwind of change high school created, Jake came to miss his dear friend and spent the time and effort reintegrating Steven back into his world, and though the repercussions were subtle, Steven was aware of the turmoil his decision caused. The faint undertones weren't hidden completely, and the resulting disorder divided Steven's heart. He didn't want Jake to lose his social standing, so he fought Jake's efforts; feebly declining all the initial reintegration invitations, and making excuses his best friend immediately disregarded.

When they were alone though, time seemed to revert back to how their friendship once was. They played together, playfully torturing each other, physically, mentally and emotionally, like they had always done. Nothing made Steven laugh harder or feel less different than when Jake teasingly tormented him, and Steven knew in his heart Jake enjoyed this game as much as he did.

But this time in their lives had higher than previous highs and lower than previous lows and these fluxes affected Steven more than Jake. Steven had far more angsts filling his brain and the burden of those extra concerns only added to the pile every young adult deals with and the regular pile was almost all a person that age could handle. And just when Steven would feel like everyone else, something would happen to bring him back to reality, with certain examples bubbling into his consciousness without warning, even against his will.

"Don't shut it."

Steven knew Jake's voice and turned his head away from their shared open locker to greet him. "Hi."

"Hey." Jake gave him a quick glance, then threw his math textbook onto the jumbled pile of books and paper at the bottom and grabbed the social studies book almost at the bottom, turning what was piled neatly on top into an extension of the mess below. Each had their own locker but the school was large and sharing one at each end of the school made the between class logistics much more manageable.

Steven watched him for a second. "Do you have a game today?"

Jake lifted half of the book pile and pulled out a notebook. "Yeah."

"Is it home?"

He shoved the unwanted books that had moved into the opening, to the back of the locker. "Yep. You going?"

Steven stood there, watching. "Don't I always?"

"Jake?"

They both turned and looked at Gabrielle standing behind them with her book against her chest. She was taller than Steven but shorter than Jake with hair that was full, curly and beautiful.

They both said hi but she was only looking at Jake. "Can I talk to you?"

"Sure."

Steven stood by the open locker feeling awkward, not knowing if he should shut it. The conversation was short but out of Steven's earshot. Gabrielle turned and walked away and Jake came back to the locker.

Steven pretended to look for a non-existent something on the locker's upper shelf. "You alright?"

The question confused Jake. "Yeah."

"What'd she want?" He really didn't want to know what she wanted and could hear Jake wished he hadn't asked.

"A prom date."

Steven exhaled. "What did you say?"

"Sure."

Steven's eyes widened as he registered his disappointment, and after a brief pause, feigned indifference. "See you."

"See you."

The locker clanged shut and they each headed in a different direction.

Steven spent the next class in a fog. He hated when Jake's good fortune did this to him. He really did want Jake to be happy. *Then why do I feel this way?* They both met at their other locker after the next class and the Gabrielle conversation continued on their way to the lunchroom.

"Do you like her?"

"Who?" Jake spun his head like Steven was referring to someone in sight.

"Gabrielle."

Jake looked back at Steven, noticeably embarrassed at his eagerness to see who Steven thought was cute. "Sure."

The way Jake meant it and the way Steven heard it were completely different, and Jake's answer—answered nothing. Steven would disappear after events like this, for reasons beyond even his full understanding, afraid Jake would question the connection between his depression and Jake's new relationships.

The emotional difficulties associated with Gabrielle faded over a short time and the lack of interaction between Gabrielle and Jake eliminated the rest of Steven's confused anxieties. Jake didn't go out of his way to talk to her and though he was very friendly toward her and made prom plans with her, he didn't spend any time outside school with her. He never asked her on a date or went to her house. He didn't even go out of his way to be with her in school, while they were in the same building for most of the day. Steven was sure he kept better track of their relationship than Jake, and though Gabrielle told everyone they were dating, everything he recorded led him to believe Jake didn't *like her* like her.

Steven could also see Jake working to keep their relationship as strong as ever, and the more he noticed, the less he could do to separate from him. It was a taffy-pull in his mind though. He loved Jake enough to want him to find complete happiness and the more Jake turned around to pull Steven along, the more Steven wanted him to fly as high as he could without him. It would be fun watching Jake soar; if only he spent more time on schoolwork.

The revelation that thought caused sent pure elation through him. There *was* something he could offer Jake. How could he have forgotten! He used to always help Jake with schoolwork. Steven decided to offer Jake the only thing he thought was as significant as the things Jake did for him. He would do whatever necessary to help Jake with the only thing he was better at—schoolwork. He would carry Jake just like Jake, in so many ways, carried him. This would become his mission, whatever it took. Steven was clever though. No one would notice, not even Jake.

Steven watched Jake open the locker as he approached. "Hey."

"Hey." Jake knelt on one knee and pulled a textbook from the bottom of the pile while Steven waited for access to the jumbled books.

"What subject do you have next?" Steven knew and knew Jake hated it.

"English." Jake's voice confirmed his dislike.

Steven pulled out the two books he needed and stood up. "I'd be glad to help you, you know."

Jake shut the locker hard like all the really masculine boys seemed to do, and hesitated just enough to wait for his friend to head toward class. "You don't have to."

"I know I don't *have* to. What if I *want* to?"

Jake glanced at him as they turned toward their destination. "I'll get by. Besides keeping all A's has to be hard enough."

He adjusted the books in his arms. "Don't tell anyone, but I do less work than everyone thinks." The statement wasn't a complete lie, but it wasn't as far from the truth as anyone presumed. "Would you let me help you?"

Jake's eyes narrowed as he studied Steven. "You'd help me?"

"Jake, I'd do more for you than you know. We're doing homework and studying together starting tonight. First priority…English."

"I really hate English."

The quick confession produced a deep contentment, though the satisfaction quickly turned to unease as he noticed Jake studying him until they reached the top of the stairs and headed in separate directions. Though Jake wasn't even aware of the challenge, he had inadvertently won the main battle between them. Steven would never consciously try to separate from his best friend again. But he quickly had other battles thrust in his direction.

~ ~ ~

Steven woke one cold winter morning with pain in both his breasts. At first, he thought he had slept wrong. The pain would subside, but it persisted for some time. What happened next, first confused, then disheartened him more than anything up to this point in his life.

The change was slight, but very disconcerting. He researched and found out the term is called gynecomastia and he was becoming well aware of the result it was having on his chest. He knew he should have mentioned this to his parents, but he already felt disappointingly less than masculine and this was just too embarrassing to bring to their attention, and as long as the change was almost unnoticeable, he opted to keep it just one more disheartening secret. The embarrassment was compounded by another realization starting to pop uninvited into his head, but the thought was too bizarre to give any credence.

At least the gods were kind enough to extend this new physical burden in the middle of winter, when coats and sweatshirts could hide things as well as keep them warm. But, even the sweatshirts rubbing against him were uncomfortable, so he added additional layers, and realized the more layers, the easier to hide himself.

Steven did his best to hide this new teenage embarrassment from strangers, friends and family alike. He wore oversized sweatshirts in the winter and loose heavier than normal shirts in the summer. It became *his look*. He had learned over time how to de-emphasize his chest and only rarely would he leave himself less than fully covered, even to Jake. By the end of high school, he didn't have much, but what he had was definitely feminine.

He also used this secret condition as his main reason why he had spent his high school years avoiding girls. He was afraid his situation would become school gossip and after weighing the plusses and minuses, decided he could forego a girlfriend to remove the chance of the rest of his high school days and life becoming unbearable.

Steven had all but resigned himself to his differences. He realized he wasn't physically the same as his peers, even though he tried to fit his interpretation of the definition to the best of his ability. He knew he felt feminine sometimes, but he was told he was a boy, so he hoped, even expected to someday get through this time when he felt less than a boy. He used the word *less* in his mind. He couldn't think of a better way to describe it.

He tried to make peace with the idea of feeling less, but these feeling shaped his personality. They made him a quiet and humble young child who subsequently became a quiet and humble young adult. Everyone assumed this was simply his natural demeanor. It was his demeanor, but driven far more by situation, than disposition. He learned well why people like him were quiet. He quickly learned to use quiet to hide and it became his demeanor, except when he was with the person he projected as the center of his young world. He seemed to only find joy when he was with his best friend, though he still never seemed to enjoy unreserved happiness.

Jake, on the other hand never had a gauge for normal. He assumed every young male felt exactly like he did, including Steven. Why should he assume differently? He saw himself as average in all aspects of his life. He had an occasional girlfriend though they were never more than a passing interest. He never initiated the relationship. They just seemed to happen. It was always the girl who declared they were dating but he was easy-going and just went with the flow, more curious about the social expectation than driven by desire.

But he grew to become rather head-strong and confident. Not only developing physically in very masculine ways, but mentally and emotionally as well. His beliefs were gaining a strong foundation in his psyche, partly because he was becoming more and more confident in the way he went about discerning information he perceived wise, and partly because he was the son of a very physical and emotionally confident man.

His father was every definition of masculine, but had this soft and nurturing way with children which other adults admired, not that he cared what other adults thought. In fact, Chris cared very little what anyone's opinions of him were, and Jake, with the flattery of imitation, developed the same mindset. Jake loved and friended all those who either loved or friended him, with no exception. He liked what he liked, which also rarely followed the consensus. He didn't conform to fashion or to peer pressure, though his non-conformity was never in the form of overt opinions or actions which would demean another.

He measured himself in other ways, and one of the things that caught his attention, was the way his male friends portrayed their masculinity. He watched the supposedly rugged personas and when he compared himself to them, realized how different he was. He didn't feel the need to be tough to portray his masculinity. He didn't feel the need to tie his gender to the assumed social standard so eagerly accepted by his peers, and he found quiet comfort accepting his own softer heart. He would catch himself smiling at the idea he was more human, than male, and that thought pleased him. It was one of the many reasons he craved Steven's company. There was no testosterone contest with Steven. With Steven, he was allowed to relax and just be human.

But there were times Jake didn't include Steven socially. There were times Jake didn't feel up to worrying about Steven being present. A small pang of guilt always accompanied the decision, but sometimes the guilt was an acceptable replacement for the effort to watch out for his best friend. Outwardly, they were very different, and sometimes the differences were bigger than the effort to ignore them, even after Jake started realizing he was more like Steven than anyone would have guessed.

His father was above average in outward masculine appearance, and Jake was noticeably one level up the scale from his father in all things visually masculine, and there were times when that led to social activities that were best enjoyed alone.

Jake knew his thoughts were as far from ordinary as he imagined thoughts could be. His were just better hidden in an outer shell that projected *typical* far easier. But his prom date with Gabrielle brought certain well buried feelings to a new and greater level of understanding. Jake noted all too well, the role Gabrielle inadvertently played in his life. Up to his prom date, he had paid little attention to the invasive thoughts that had been sneakily entering his consciousness from about the time he entered high school, passing them off as nothing more than part of the normal confusion that entered his brain every so often without warning or invite. But those thoughts went from confusion to clarity by the end of their date.

He let out a quick snort as he thought about sitting in the car after the prom, kissing Gabrielle. He vividly remembered how happily astonished he was at the time. She was pretty, and obviously eager, and he was amazingly uncomfortable and somewhat bored. He resigned himself to the duties of being her escort, and shut his eyes, but when he did, all he could picture was kissing and holding Steven. He opened his eyes in shock, then quickly closed them, eager to recreate the vision. And with that vision came a feeling that pervaded his entire being.

His mind filled with thoughts of what it would be like to have Steven return his kiss. He refocused and tried his best to concentrate on her. He had only the best prurient intentions toward her, but he was there solely because she asked and he was fulfilling all the requirements expected for the evening. Finding furtive pleasure from the activity she seemed to be enjoying was only fair. Besides, he easily justified his fantasy of kissing Steven with thoughts of how soft and feminine he is. He smiled all too aware the thought of kissing Steven as he kissed Gabrielle with his eyes closed, was giving him the reaction Gabrielle hoped she could give him.

Before the prom date, he assumed he just hadn't met the right girl. *I'm sure I'll find one that makes me feel like Steven does.* He didn't know what she would look like, but he knew what she would be like. She would have Steven's inner qualities. He was calm, smart, kind, gentle, meek, caring. He thought about Steven's eyes. *She has to have eyes like his though.*

He fantasized about a girl like that. At least he always started his fantasies thinking about girls like that, but as he matured, many of his fantasies ended with thoughts of Steven. Many times, the only way he could finish his fantasies were by thinking about Steven.

He knew for a long time he wanted to kiss Steven far more than he ever wanted to kiss a girl. He justified the feeling by convincing himself it was due to how close they were and all the thought meant was they were best friends. It was just a confusion. He had many of them. They were part of his age, he was sure. He was almost positive.

He did his best to rationalize these mixed thoughts, making excuses to appease the confusion acceptance would cause. *I just have to become deep friends with one, that's all.* But one thought scared him more than all the rest. *Will I end up pretending for the rest of my life?* And his only equally weighty counter thought, for the time through this internal argument was—*I am going to disappoint everyone who loves me. I am going to disappoint everyone who knows me.*

But the night with Gabrielle didn't reveal the feelings. It sealed the revelation. Jake had spent enough time in high school ignoring or rationalizing the inclination for all inferred social pressure, but that one night changed his mindset. That one night made him resolute in the idea that the outward pressures which took him so long to reason with were exactly what he would attack next. He spent time studying his feelings; learning their true nature and where they stood within his social structure, and to his surprise, the well-publicized argument, allowed him an ease of access which greatly aided his efforts. And after quickly reasoning that he was more normal than one of the sides insisted, used the information to develop his deep philosophy on the subject. He went from having an indistinct worry that his true orientation made him inferior, to realizing his orientation had nothing to do with weakness, or a curse, or a flaw, or anything but a natural part of the history of every culture ever recorded.

But he still couldn't bring himself to tell his best friend, and there were times he wanted nothing more. There were times when he and Steven were so comfortably together, he came amazingly close to sharing these secrets, only to be totally grateful later, after he failed. These instances led to a lesser and lesser chance he would ever share them without great reason or prompting. He rationalized this also. Steven never shared things as deep, and all outward indications were Steven had comparable confusions.

He wasn't ready to confess anything, but the revelations did change how he interacted with Steven. Thoughts like these caused Jake to be a little more torqued when they were together, and quicker to grab Steven and play wrestle with him. The way Jake would grab him had completely changed though, from a young boy trying to overpower his smaller and weaker friend, to a tender tug and initiation, like a guy would do when play-wrestling with his girlfriend. It was always innocent and plutonic, but their wrestling had become the contrivance he used to enjoy some rather intimate physical contact with Steven, without stirring questions of intent. He had a second motivator as well. Steven did not hide his enthusiasm for the activity.

They reached another level of friendship for their time between the end of high school and college. They sought each other out more than ever in school and spent more time together away from school. Their relationship had come full circle and the tests it endured gave it new strength and meaning.

When the end of high school approached, it seemed like the entire senior class was talking about college. Who was going where and why and though Steven and Jake mentioned it a few times, both were afraid to discuss their future plans in detail, trying to put off hearing the other was heading in a different life direction. Jake didn't want to learn where Steven was headed, not knowing Steven was as afraid Jake would decide to forego college altogether and have his father get him a construction apprenticeship. After enduring the near split in their relationship at the beginning of high school, both felt great satisfaction in their rejoining and both were now equally uncomfortable about the next step in their lives.

Jake knew the offer Steven's grandmother made him. She had full intentions of paying Steven's entire college cost, no matter where he went, as long as his grades were above a B and they hadn't fallen below an A—ever. Jake had no idea what he would do or where he would go if someone had made him that offer, and he knew all too well his choices were between the local community college and the local community college, since he was paying for his own education, wherever he chose.

Steven's grades gave him a wide variety of next education choices. Everyone knew he would be accepted wherever he decided to go, but he was in no rush to make any decisions. He was a homebody, not an adventurist. Certain things like family and loved ones counted more to him than exploring new places. He had plans to spend his time working and studying anyway, so why go through that trouble in a strange place, away from everyone he loved?

Jake saw his education quandary as completely different. His parents hadn't attended college and neither understood Jake's need for counsel, and with their perspective, stayed uncomfortably away from any future education decisions Jake had to make, except to awkwardly ask what he was planning, at amazingly inappropriate times. Jake had no idea what the true nature of almost all careers was. The closest two people he knew that actually went to college were Genna and Connor, and asking them about the subject would most likely open up the conversation he feared most.

But the conversation was inevitable. Time made it so.

~ ~ ~

The curiosity got the better of Steven one afternoon and the subject came up as they sat on the carpeted floor in the converted media room, leaning against the recliner and each other, with video game controllers in hand, concentrating on the TV monitor in front of them.

Steven never turned his head or hesitated pressing buttons. "Are you going to college?"

Jake fielded the question with the same dexterity. "I think so."

Steven's video character jumped and kicked Jake's. "What do you mean, you think so?"

Jake's character hit the ground with blue streaks circling his head. "I guess so?"

"I don't understand." Steven dropped his controller and looked at his friend, then watched as Jake used his momentary lapse to kick his character in the face and put him out for the count.

"I want to, I guess, but I'm not as good as you in school and I have no clue what I want to be. My parents never went. Hell, I'm pretty sure nobody in my family ever went. No one's ever talked to me about it and I'm pretty lost." He lowered his controller. "Are you registered anywhere?"

Steven faced Jake and smiled, hoping Jake would come up with the same idea he had come up with months ago. "No."

Jake turned toward him. "You're just as bad as me."

Steven knew exactly why he wasn't registered. He could go anywhere, but he wanted to go wherever Jake was going. "Not quite as bad as you. I know I'm going."

Jake smirked. "That's so much better."

Steven knew what Jake's options were. He was never told, nor did he ever ask, but he had been part of the Harrison family for over a dozen years.

Jake's next sentence brought Steven out of a quick trance. "Are you going away somewhere?"

Steven shook his head. "I don't think so."

"Why not?"

Steven made an unsure smirk and softly shrugged his shoulders. "What's to go away to?"

Jake's voice rose. "Man. You could go away to someplace warm. With beaches."

Steven frowned and glanced toward the TV monitor. "Yeah. It's a vacation."

There was a short pause as they stared at each other, Jake's bent knee resting on his. Finally, Steven offered a thought that wasn't as new as he made it sound. "Why don't we keep doing what we're doing?"

"Okay, but let's pick a different game."

Steven sat up, trying to sell the idea like he had just thought it. "No, school."

Jake grinned jokingly. "I'm pretty sure we're not allowed back in high school next year."

"You're an idiot."

Jake leaned over from his sitting position onto Steven and pinned him within a second. "You are too. We're a team of idiots. But what are you talking about?"

"The two of us going together. We could work together like we've been doing since kindergarten."

Jake looked down at him, still pinning his hands. "You've been carrying me since kindergarten. Well, maybe not kindergarten. I'm pretty sure I carried you in kindergarten."

"What do you say?"

Jake sighed. "We both know what my only option is. You can go anywhere in the frigging country. There's no way you're going to frigging community college."

Steven's heart dropped as his friend fought him. "But you can't." He did *not* want them to go separate ways, and the significance of the moment made his eyes blur with moisture. Jake's reaction was instant as he released the pressure on his wrists.

It was Steven's turn to continue selling, and he wasn't settling for anything short of a sale. "Come on. We'll study together. We'll still be able to hang out. I'll help you get used to college. You have no one to even talk to about college work and neither do I if we don't go together."

"That's insane."

Steven kept selling. "It'll be fun. Besides, it's only for two years. It puts off any big decisions, and I don't feel like making any big decisions anytime soon." He had other unaddressed decisions floating in his brain already taking up too much room to want to add another and he knew he wasn't ready to step into a completely strange part of the world quite yet.

"You'd do that for me?"

"I'm not doing it for you. I don't feel like picking one place in a thousand right now, and then being miserable because I miss home." The statement was true but it wasn't what Steven knew he'd miss most.

Jake lowered his brow and stared at Steven, just enough to make Steven's face start to flush. Steven responded to end the silent inquiry into the truthfulness of his last statement. "Okay. That's it. That's what we're doing."

Jake smiled. "I can't believe you'd do that for me."

"Stop saying that. I'm not doing it for you."

Jake's face softened. "I can't believe you'd do this for me."

Steven let his guard down slightly and narrowed his eyes. "Are you kidding? For all the things you've done for me, this is nothing."

"This isn't nothing. This is a biggie. A real biggie." Jake stood and pulled Steven off the carpet and into him and gave him a true friendship hug. "This is the nicest thing anyone could do for a friend."

"You're my best friend, and it's not that special. Besides, you've been doing stuff for me for as long as I can remember. You *always* do stuff for me and I hardly ever do anything for you."

"You know that's not true."

Steven finished the sale. "So. Want to tell everyone?"

Jake reached out his hand to Steven again and pulled him in for another hug. "Yeah, I want to tell everyone."

Steven playfully smirked. "Pretend coin flip?"

"Like always." Jake reached in his pocket pretending to take out a coin, and gave it a pretend flip, caught it and looked at the back of his empty hand. "Awwww. I lost."

Steven raised an eyebrow at him. "Are you sure?"

"Yeah, I'm sure. Let's tell them over your house. Believe me, my mom and dad won't mind. They're going to adore you for doing this for me."

"Will you stop saying that? I'm not doing anything special."

"It is. And you know they're going to say it is, so you better be ready. My mother's going to hug and kiss you and cry. You're going to be their favorite person and they're going to tell you they want to do something for you or buy you something. I think they love you more than me."

Steven quickly responded, "I *know* my parents love you more than me."

They left the room, tracked down their parents and told them they had news to share, and everyone agreed to meet in the Blair family room as soon as possible. Finally Morgan and Chris came in and all were assembled.

They stood in front of the TV together, facing their four parents and Jake straightened up. "We have great news." Then he turned to Steven. "You tell them."

Steven eyed Jake, then turned to everyone. "We decided on a college."

All four parents gave some sort of happy approval, and Connor replied, "Where?"

Steven took a deep breath. "The local community college, because we want to go together."

Morgan jumped up and hugged Steven and started crying as predicted. "You are the most wonderful boy in the whole world." Without letting go, she turned to Genna. "He's the most wonderful boy in the whole world."

Jake laughed as his mom inadvertently choked him. "See. I told you they love you more than me."

Steven took a swipe at his best friend and missed. His arm was being restrained by a crying parent.

~ ~ ~

Their time through the first four semesters of college went well, but certain things about community college life were different. Friendships were different than high school. The relationships were enjoyable, but noticeably less committal. Everyone was transient and had their own agenda. This made their relationship that much more important to each of them and subsequently their time together and their closeness increased again.

One typical lazy summer afternoon between their last two community college semesters, as they sat on the carpeted floor in Steven's bedroom, Jake decided his video game character had endured enough abuse at the hands of Steven's and it was time for a little real-life revenge. He reached over, put his arm around Steven's waist and pulled him close to start wrestling, but Steven was in the middle of a video game move and never let go of his controller to get his balance, and as he fell awkwardly into Jake's arms, Jake accidentally ended up with a handful of Steven's chest.

Steven went immediately limp and Jake's heart jumped. And for as much as Jake wanted to let go, his male hormones overrode the desire and he gently cupped the surprising softness for a pause. He quickly gathered himself and moved his hand away, but his heart had begun pumping at quite an elevated rate, so he continued to play wrestle with his dear friend, treating him even more tenderly than had become the norm.

Steven heart and mind became equally charged by the event and reacted nearly the same way Jacob's did, but Steven's breathing was noticeably more pronounced than Jacob's. Steven couldn't believe the pure joy he received from Jake's accidental feel.

They softly wrestled for another few moments when Steven spun so his back was to Jake, hoping it led to another attempt by his best friend, and as if perfectly timed, Jake gently ran his hand once again over Steven's soft chest, under the premise of innocent play. The electricity was equal for both, and though this second *feel* was less than as accidental as the first, Jake sputtered, "Sorry."

It was all Jake could muster, and with a soft pause Steven whispered, "For what?"

"For accidentally grabbing you there."

Steven's reply was soothingly understanding. "It's okay. I know you'd never hurt me. I know how close we are."

A moment passed and they were gently wrestling again.

Steven's soft voice broke the momentary silence. "Can I ask you a question?" Jake let Steven get the upper hand and he straddled Jake's stomach; Jake's arms voluntarily pinned under Steven's grip.

"Sure."

With Steven's heart beating a notch above a moment ago at the anticipation of his question, he asked, "Did you like it?"

Jake's strange smile betrayed his response. "Like what?"

Steven smirked at his friend, making him lead. "The way it felt."

The words were like lightening as they struck Jake, though he tried with all his young might to make it as inconceivable as possible. His smile grew, which went straight to Steven's heart. "Like the way what felt?" trying to delay the necessity of an answer.

But the electricity created by Jake's caress gave Steven more than enough courage to consider exploring a deeper connection to his best friend. "The way my chest felt."

He paused as he let Steven continue to pin his hands, and replied with a reserved chuckle, "Yes. It…" and then stopped, confused by how to tell his best guy friend what he really thought.

But Steven was quite surprisingly enjoying the noticeable shift in control, and continued the inquest. "It what?"

Steven watched Jake's eyes widen as if he had also suddenly realized the potential to explore and destroy yet another façade between them. "It was more amazing than I ever imagined."

Steven smiled. "You imagined doing that to me?"

Jake blushed and hesitated, "Kind of."

Steven enjoyed seeing Jake like this, and the joy was a complexity of feelings Steven himself never expected. Sure, he had passing R rated fantasies about Jake, but he instantaneously recognized the immediate increase in all things possible as the fleeting incident happened, and it gave him an immediate and exhilarating awareness which encompassed every aspect of his being.

That other bizarre thought that had been popping into his brain during his transition from child to teenager was this feeling he wasn't supposed to be a boy. He couldn't describe it and tried desperately to keep the idea locked in the deepest recesses of his mind, but today, those feelings shot up through his being to the point where he was almost overwhelmed by the reaction he was having and now wanted to nurture it.

Jake, however, was a guy and was nervous. His concern though, was mainly based on a worry for his friend, and he had figured out that Steven's chest was a very private concern for him. Jake was his best friend and they had shared many secrets, but not once did Steven ever give any indication that he wished to share this secret.

"You have, haven't you? You've thought about doing that to me."

"Well…yeah." Jake started relaxing. "I don't completely know why, but I'm closer to you than anyone in the world, and I'm a guy, and…" His voice faded off, but he also didn't want this new whatever to simply go away, and he inhaled like he had the life breathed back into his lungs. "I don't understand it completely. I thought about it and I wanted to. And it was better than I ever imagined it would be."

Steven straddled him with his mouth unconsciously open. He examined Steven's eyes and whispered, "Is it alright I liked it so much? I mean….I *really* liked it."

That bigger secret Steven thought so bizarre he didn't share completely with his own conscious mind, let alone Jake, was now front and center, and the confession went right through Steven, lighting his heart and mind on fire and all he could think to do was take Jake's hands and gently place them on his chest.

Jake's mouth opened as his hands were placed. He exhaled as if Steven's chest had taken his breath away. Steven's physical and emotional reaction was even more intense. Not only had they started addressing the biggest secret between them, but the accompanying feelings were far more exhilarating than he would have ever imagined.

This new experience was abruptly cut short by Jake's phone alarm and the realization of the time. Jake had to go to work. With complete panic, they both got up and Jake hurried out the door to change into his work uniform, with Steven's encouragement coming from behind. "Have a good night."

Jake rode his motorcycle just fast enough to make it on time, and though his adrenaline was pumping at the exhilaration of having to rush to work, his heart and mind activity stayed slightly above normal, longer than normal, for a completely different reason. All he could think about was Steven.

After Jake ran out the door, Steven went back into his room to think about what had happened; his heart still racing. He wanted to relive the entire visit, but as he laid face up on his bed, more complex thoughts raced through his head. He oscillated between the physically and sexually charged event and the emotional and psychological reaction his brain was having. First, he would remember the act, then his mind would shift into the morass of his sexual orientation, then back to the feeling of Jake's hands on him which led to thoughts of years of emotional discomfort his chest caused, then back to whether his enjoyment made him think he should consider becoming female and then the thought of the complication and confusion becoming female would cause, to worrying whether Jake could be with him as more than a friend, to whether Jake would even like him as a female.

His time alone wasn't turning out to be the pleasant reminiscence he had hoped. *Why is life so much more complicated than anyone admits?* He sighed, wondering if this is what a girl would feel after her boyfriend left for the night. The thought made him smile as he realized he wouldn't mind being Jake's girl. He undressed and crawled under the covers. Maybe his dreams would be less complicated.

CHAPTER THREE
APPREHENSION

"Steven. Time to get up."

Steven opened his eyes and noticed it was still pitch black out. *Shit. Family reunion weekend.* A smile came across his face as he remembered yesterday, and he popped up like a jack-in-the-box and just sat there. Parallel thoughts ran through his mind. He felt energized and anxious. He would have rather spent the day focused on the events of yesterday, but he knew there was no way to physically excuse himself from this family obligation, not to mention any attempt to do so would crush his mother. This weekend event existed long before he was around and to his mother; it was the single most important whole-family event of the year. Everyone had in-laws, which split attendance for every holiday get-together, but this weekend was made so the entire Blair extended family could be together, with little chance any in-law event would supersede it.

His mom's voice came through his bedroom door. "Come on sweetheart. I want to be on the road in forty minutes." She was noticeably excited.

Connor popped his head in the door, "You okay?"

"Yeah. Dad. I'm up." He felt the strange grin appear and watched his father do a double-take. "You sure?"

"Yeah, Dad. I'm up."

"No, now I'm back to the first question."

Steven smiled. "Yeah." He thought more deeply about the question, "I'm okay."

He didn't need to explain why he was okay, but he was. In fact, he made quick plans in his head to be preoccupied all weekend. Not that this function ever failed to be anything but a complete blast, but at the moment, his entire being was feeling things so new, so electrifying, even this event was not going to interrupt his preoccupation.

He was in the bathroom and about to step into the shower, when he came out of his thoughts enough to realize he didn't even remember getting out of bed. He ran his hand over his chest. Was everything a dream, or did it really happen? Did Jake really feel him up? Even the thought was electric.

His mind raced as the hot water beat on his head. *I need to talk to him. I can't. I'll be in the car. I'll text. What will I say? Ugh. Of all the weekends. I'll call him in my room. It's too early. He's sleeping. I'll wake him. And say what?*

"Hurry sweetheart. I told Nana we would pick her up by six."

Shit. How am I going to text with Nana sitting next to me? It would be at least another three hours before Jake would be up. And in another five, he would be so busy with family, a text or phone conversation would be almost impossible.

Maybe it's for the better. What would he say to him anyway? But he couldn't stop smiling. The thoughts in his head were nothing short of electrifying.

His father knocked on the door. "Want a coffee to go? I made a full pot." It was just his father's way of saying hurry up, but he didn't mind. He liked his father's tact, but he was two minutes from ready anyway.

"Yes please." He slipped on his shoes and walked out of his bedroom all in one motion.

"Hi, sweetheart."

"Hi, Mom." They kissed hello as he entered the kitchen.

"Ready to go?"

He took his coffee from his father as they walked out of the house and into the calm morning air. The closing of the car doors echoed in the stillness and Steven strained to see if there was a response next door. Nothing.

The sun was just starting to peek over the horizon when they pulled up to his grandmother's house and Lorraine met them outside her door with her overnight bag and a big smile. Steven grabbed her bag as Connor kissed her and led her to the car. After a quick loving greeting, they were moving again.

Lorraine examined Steven and with a big smile, softly stroked the side of his face, "Cipolline." It was her pet name for him. He smiled back at her, "Hi Nana." They kissed. "How are you?"

"I'm good."

"How's school?"

"Jake and I are doing great." Steven's heart jumped. He finally said Jake's name this morning and it felt surprisingly gratifying.

The rest of the ride's daydreaming was occasionally interrupted by small talk, and Steven tried his best to be present when requested, but all he could think about was this new desire to explore this new feeling of femininity and the new twist on his and Jake's relationship, and the more he thought about it, the more he wanted to explore being feminine. He thought about Jake caressing his chest and relived the moments over and over, each time feeling more and more deeply about wanting him to do it again, and how he would entice Jake to do it again, and again. He daydreamed about girl things, girl clothes, girl mannerisms, girl everything. Things he never imagined he would allow himself to consider, even as short as a week ago. He kept glancing at his watch, waiting for Jake to be up.

"Are you anxious about today too, cipolline?"

He met his grandmother's eyes and fidgeted in his seat. "I can't wait."

"Me either."

He impatiently waited for eight o'clock and when it came, he couldn't text and his heart raced like it was mad at him. He tried to appease his own heart. *Ten more minutes.* And leaned his head back.

His grandmother reached for his hand. "So have you decided on a school for your four year degree?"

He looked at her. "Not yet."

"When do you have to make a decision?"

"We're going to start narrowing it down soon." She thought he meant the three of them, but he meant him and Jake. It was an inference he was glad to let continue, and equally glad his grandmother appeared to assume it.

"My offer continues and I hear your grades are even improving from nearly perfect."

"Jake and I are working really hard, Nana, but we're having fun. School's fun. It's hard, but it's fun."

"How is Jake?" Steven loved Jake and Lorraine's relationship, and she knew him well. They were extended family and Jake had come to consider her one of his grandmothers. She often joked about loving him for two reasons. He loved Steven like a brother and he loved her cooking!

Steven sat up like his seat had an electric short in it and bubbled, "He's awesome. He's doing great too."

The speed and enthusiasm of his response produced a reaction in all three and Genna laughed, "You two are too funny." She turned in her seat toward him. "But I'm so proud of how you both have made it your mission to do excellent in school."

"Is he thinking about going to the same four year college?"

"Yeah, Nana, he is."

"I have to text him to make sure he knows we have our family reunion this weekend. He may have thought we were going to study together, so I have to make sure he remembers." Steven had his phone already out and immediately started typing.

Jake. I'm 150 miles into our family reunion trip. Did u remembr it was today?

His phone beeped moments later. Yeah. Have a good time

Steven couldn't think of another significant thing to write. *Coming back Sun nite.*

By the time Connor pulled up to the reunion, he and Genna had discreetly acknowledged, Steven was wired. The assumption was; it was the reunion. This was a weekend equal to its billing. Every family member was there and it was an incredible time. The greetings alone lasted hours and the party extended inside and out, including an entire floor of the resort.

Connor came out of their hotel bathroom at the end of the long first day, as Genna pulled the covers over her. "Can you believe Steven today? I've never seen him so…happy. So outright happy."

"I know. It was fun to watch, wasn't it?"

Steven's demeanor was noticeably different all day but no one had a clue why. He was subconsciously jittery and happy, and he couldn't wait for the reunion to be over. He had to get back to explore those events which had made him noticeably different today. He needed to explore the electricity he and Jake had created.

~ ~ ~

Jake put his phone back on his end table and laid back with both hands in fists on his forehead. "Damn." The Blair reunion was the only thing he wasn't ever a part of and though he mostly didn't mind, he was curious what they did. He would ask questions, but he always pictured the event as much more than Steven's descriptions, but with yesterday's happenings, he felt like it couldn't have come at a worse time.

How fast can this weekend end? He rolled over and tried to go back to sleep.

He heard the knock on his bedroom door, followed by his mother's voice. "Jacob, are you up?"

He rolled over in a stupor. He did fall back to sleep. "Yeah Mom."

"Want breakfast?"

"Just coffee and cereal." He loved food but he could live on cereal alone.

A few minutes later he came slowly down the hall and into the kitchen. "Good morning."

"...morning."

His father turned slightly in his seat. "You look like hell. Do anything fun yesterday?"

His father's words were clairvoyant enough to make his heart jump. But he gained his composure, "Just studying." 'Just studying' could be used as a positive answer for almost any inquiry and though he didn't lie often, there were certain omissions in life that were for the benefit of all.

He grabbed the biggest bowl left in the cabinet as his father continued the conversation "What you got planned for today?

It was small-talk but it caused enough of a noticeably negative reaction to warrant an explanation, "The Blair reunion's this weekend."

Morgan chimed, "Can you believe we've never been invited?" Chris laughed and Jake tried to, but the effort made him feel like he was betraying the fact he really did wish he could go. Morgan noticed and let the subject die, and she gave him his space as she went about her Saturday around the house.

Jake moped around the entire afternoon and Morgan got tired watching. "Hey, is there a baseball game at home tonight? Want to go if there is?" She said it from the kitchen while both men were in the family room and Chris perked up. "Sure. Let me check."

"Yep. Seven o'five." He glanced at Jake, "Come with us. I'll buy you a few beers. …Give you an excuse for looking like hell."

Jake's heart secretly jumped again but he only quietly grinned.

For two days, Steven watched his girl and women relatives, mixed with flashbacks of Friday's event, and it refueled old thoughts and desires at an all too new and greater intensity. He went from electrified at the potential of a positive outcome for his fate on Saturday morning, to exhausted and resigned Sunday evening.

All the weekend did was muddle the surety Friday had brought. It also brought back years of mixed emotions tied to secret experiments with different clothes and different feelings that led to secret battles deep inside him, and he involuntarily sighed the entire drive home. The event had taken its toll on him, and the only conclusion he had in the end was, he was in no way a true boy, or a true girl's equal.

Chapter Four
Equivocation

Steven woke earlier than normal Monday morning. The weekend's activities shut him down as soon as they arrived home, but when he awoke, he immediately thought about the Friday before and for the first time in his life, he was uneasy calling Jake. He sighed. *Wonderful, something new that's no longer normal.* He was worried seeing Jake today would be completely awkward and stared out his bedroom window, trying to think how he could delay the meeting for a day, or at least until later. He decided he caught a cold at the reunion and would stay in and rest, and as soon as he had his excuse, he needed to talk to his best friend. He picked up his phone and dialed. "Hey."

"Hey. How was your trip?"

Steven weighed the question with far greater magnitude than intended, and answered honestly. "It was okay…nothing special." He hesitated for another moment. "How was your weekend?"

"We went to the baseball game Saturday night. It was good." Jake softened his voice. "What you got going on today?"

Steven lied as planned. "I'm not feeling too good right now. I think I caught a cold. You?"

"I have work tonight."

Steven heart sank. He had all intentions of not seeing Jake, but as soon as he heard he couldn't, his desire to see him increased, and he immediately sought their next connection. "We can get together tomorrow if you want."

"Sure, if you're feeling better."

Steven's lie now made him insecure about Jake's response, and he hesitated. "Okay. Talk to you tomorrow?"

"Sure."

Steven hung up his phone with a surprisingly heavy heart. The quick call had increased his inner confusion and the confusion was based on his becoming more and more sure what he wanted and what he wanted was not what he ever allowed himself to believe he wanted. This was not only the greatest inner struggle he ever experienced, but also the first time he was ever in jeopardy of losing control of this battle. He was becoming sure it was finally time to lose. He was becoming sure; losing this battle was the only way to end the war inside him.

He spent the rest of the day coming up with what he thought was a concession to his own heart but once he did, he felt some of the weight leave his shoulders. He remembered seeing a very effeminate male in the perfume and make-up area of one of the anchor department stores in the mall and decided to go and at least observe the person. He decided he needed to at least attempt to understand the different worlds he knew existed. He made silent plans for after dinner, and his apprehension elevated from the time he made the decision until he was within eye contact of the gentleman.

When Steven spotted him at the edge of the aisle, not twenty feet from the second floor inner mall entrance, he realized he could walk within touching distance of him, heading into the mall's inner court, and the closer he walked, the more his heart raced. He stopped at the counter across the aisle, long enough to grasp what the gentleman was discussing with the young girl in his make-up chair. He was explaining make-up technique, as he made her up and his gestures made it quite apparent he was effeminate. He appeared very confident though and comfortable with his life, and seemed to be greatly enjoying applying his trade. He was in his own world even though he was on display in front of a constant stream of individuals from all walks of life, as they paraded past his make-up chair next to the aisle.

Steven walked past him and out to the mall walkway and the railing guarding the opening behind it. He sat on the closest of three stone benches, like he was waiting for someone, and quietly observed. The gentleman was demonstratively animated. Not at all like him. But the more Steven watched, the more approachable the gentleman appeared. He was amazingly friendly. He seemed amazingly kind and gentle. He must have been enjoyable; everyone who sat in his make-up chair went from outwardly unemotional to obviously pleased by the time their session ended.

Steven was sure he had met people from all walks of life, but he didn't recall meeting anyone so outwardly open with their differences, and the thought caused a small revelation in him; different isn't as scary up close as it is far away, and he noticed the revelation had a calming effect on him. He felt so calm, he knew he could leave and take with him a mindset different than the one he had before he studied this person. But the most amazing thought in his mind was; this person could teach more than one lesson.

He walked past the gentleman and almost wished he could say thank you. He was glad the man existed. For as silly as it was, he didn't know what he would have done if he wasn't there to observe. But by the time he reached his car, inner rehearsals to try to explain the difference to Jake overtook his thoughts and overwhelmed his courage. But the more he thought about it, the more he was sure of one thing; he had a need to explain it. The courage the man gave him faded faster than he hoped, but the trip did give him some comfort. His mind planned another visit before he started the car.

He spent the rest of the evening and all the next day buried in his upcoming semester's textbooks. He didn't forget to call Jake, but he went the entire day without calling him. He just couldn't. Instead, he sat locked in his room, trying hard to concentrate on the one activity that allowed him to forget everything else.

He knew he hid in his room more than he should, but it was so safe. He had become good at hiding. He could stay alone for days, but he never quite felt comfortable with his abilities to hide in public. The older he became though, the more he realized how impossible it was to live hidden, but his wildest thoughts of bravery never included parading himself, and that was all he could think of when he thought about this make-up person. *He* didn't hide. In fact, he did just the opposite. He paraded. How could he blatantly be who he was…and survive?

He woke the next morning, with full intentions of trying to bury himself further in his studies; falling back on old and safe excuses. His grandmother wanted him to concentrate on school, instead of getting a part time job, and that meant preparing for the next semester's work to the best of his abilities, but as the day wore on, he felt an urge to be with Jake until finally, he couldn't suppress it anymore. "Enough studying." He took out his phone and dialed. "Hey."

"Hi."

Steven felt a twinge in his throat as his next question surfaced. "Want to get together tonight?"

"Definitely. You feeling better?"

Jake's voice seemed more soothing than ever.

"Yeah. A lot better."

Jake interrupted the slight delay. "Want to come over here tonight?"

Steven's heart gave him another noticeable twinge as he answered his best friend. "See you after dinner?"

"Wait."

"What?"

"Mom wants to know if you feel like eating with us. She says you haven't visited in a while."

He softly inhaled. *Being loved is the best cure for everything.* "Tell her, sounds good. What time?"

"I get home from work around five twenty. Give me twenty to shower."

"Okay. See you then."

He pictured where Jake was heading. He remembered the restaurant well. His grandmother took him there all the time when it was hers, but he hadn't been back since Jake started working there. He pictured the dining room and the memory brought a mixed reaction. He loved when his grandmother and grandfather owned it but her selling it was now tied in his mind, to his grandfather passing. She was friends with the new owners though, and asked them to train Jake as a server, and they gladly obliged, but Steven wasn't offered the same opportunity. He asked if he could work there too, but his mother and grandmother insisted otherwise. He mostly understood, but it didn't make complete sense to him. He could handle school and a job just like Jake could. His grandmother gave him weekly spending money and a different job; school. But he would have liked a few work friends.

Steven was quiet during dinner, but he was normally quiet and he knew a little extra quiet was easily compensated by a little extra politeness and offers to help with things like the dishes. He was sure Morgan and Chris noticed. He was even sure Chris had an idea he was going through some things, but Chris never said a word, though he always seemed ready to talk if Steven wanted.

Jake also never seemed to mind what mood Steven showed when they were with parents. Steven was always different when they were alone together...except for today. They excused themselves like they always did, and went to the media room and played a video game like so many times before, but Steven could feel the uneasiness between them, though neither mentioned it, which raised the awkwardness another level. He was quietly distraught by the time he went home, and went straight to his room and curled into a ball under his covers. The most important constant in his life was now also starting to unravel.

~ ~ ~

Steven kept busy the next day concentrating on his textbooks, but before starting, decided on his next trip to the mall, and once he did, the day was amazingly long and boring, offset with intervals of anxiety and despair. He had to try to get a better grasp of at least his immediate future, and at the moment, he was lost as to how or where to find the answers. He impatiently waited for a parent to come home so he could borrow a car, and when he heard Genna's car, marked and closed his school books, and walked toward the kitchen door. He masked his pent up anxiety, and greeted her lovingly. "Hi, Mom."

Genna kissed him as they met between the kitchen and hall. "Hi sweetheart. How are you?"

"Good. You?"

"Good dear." She headed down the hall toward her room. "Are you home for dinner?"

"No, if it's okay. I have an errand to run. Can I borrow your car?"

She replied, "Of course sweetie." as she disappeared into her room.

He wasn't as excited this trip, but he did feel a greater anticipation. He had already spotted the gentleman when he realized he could have as easily been off from work, and the thought startled him. He walked past the man and eagerly took his seat on the stone bench in front of the railing, but the weekday hour and lack of clientele had an effect on the man's activities, and Steven lost sight of him. He was daydreaming with his head down when he noticed the shoes in his eyesight.

"Hi. Are you alright?"

"Yes." Steven answered before he looked up, but when he did, his eyes grew and his heart jumped. It was the man. He cleared his throat, trying to compose himself. "Yes."

The man's voice was soft. "Are you waiting for someone?"

Steven sat up and took a deep breath. "No." And as soon as he said it he realized it was the wrong answer and his heart raced even faster. "No, I'm just relaxing." He could feel his face tell on his own lie.

But the man had a very disarming way about him. "You've been out here for a while."

"Yeah. I know. I'm not a stalker or anything."

The man looked at Steven's frail build, from shoulder to shoulder. "I'm guessing not. But I'm guessing there's more you're not telling me."

Steven raised his eyebrows and opened his eyes as wide as he could. He couldn't think of any words, but the gentleman seemed to understand.

The man reached down and took his hand. "Come."

Steven felt embarrassed and didn't move, but he didn't withdraw his hand. The gentleman looked back and with a slight head nod toward him, repeated, "Come."

Steven stood and followed the man as instructed, and the man held his hand until he was seated in his make-up chair. "Don't be afraid. I'm going to pretend to do make-up on you as a way to allow me to talk to you. My boss gets mad when I'm not working, but never questions me when I'm making someone up."

"Hi. I'm Victor, but all my friends call me Vicky. I hope you'll call me Vicky." The man looked deeply into Steven's eyes as he finished his introduction, and the eye contact seemed to muffle the words. The man's stare penetrated his being and he felt his confusion being conveyed as Vicky silently and simultaneously communicated his years of inner conflict.

Steven didn't know the man had already measured all the outward indicators, including seeing Steven sit for hours a few days before, or how easily he recognized the inner confusion Steven's face expressed, but Vicky's knowing smile confirmed the many times he had seen the same confusions in mirrors throughout his own life. He broke the soft stare, turned and picked up a palette of colors from his make-up table, and held it next to Steven's face. Steven's eyes widened as he followed the palette.

"Are you being beaten?"

Steven answered timidly. "No."

Vicky purposefully straightened his make-up table. "Is anyone harming you in any way?"

Steven studied Vicky's every move and softly responded. "No."

"Thank God." Vicky breathed deep and exhaled. "I'm going to give you my phone number before you leave. You don't have to give me yours, but we won't be able to talk as long or as deeply as I think you'd like, and this way we can talk when we have the time. Is that okay?"

Steven watched intently. "Yes."

"Okay. What's your name, honey?"

"Steven."

"Do you have a lot to talk about and no one to talk to?"

Steven had no idea why that made his eyes well up, but it did. He breathed, "Yes."

"Not to worry, honey." Vicky handed Steven a tissue. "I once had a lot to talk about and no one to talk to too. It will be alright."

He slowly searched through the make-up applicators on his cart as his voice continued to offer soothing comfort. "Do you live at home?"

"Yes, and my parents love me."

Vicky reached for a flat round jar and a brush. "Good. That's real good. You have amazing eyes."

Steven stared at Vicky with permanently raised brows and wide eyes, but Vicky's focus seemed to suddenly divide. "I really can't wait to make up your eyes. Would you like your eyes made up some day?"

"Yes." The answer came quick and without an accompanying thought, and it surprised him, but didn't faze Vicky. His reaction gave him more courage. "I'm not sure what gender I'm supposed to be sometimes."

The new statement also didn't faze Vicky as he rotated the small plastic box of colors now in his hand. "Welcome to the club. In ancient Sparta, they used to kill us as babies. Now they just peripheralize us." He lowered his chin and raised an eyebrow. "We've come a long way." Vicky started laughing and Steven breathed in the humor like it was medicine.

Vicky turned away and reached for another palette of colors. "You're lucky."

Steven's brows dropped and his eyes narrowed slightly in response to Vicky's words.

Vicky glanced at Steven and smiled. "You'd like to think the loose sweatshirt and the baggy pants hide it, but I'm betting you could pull off the change rather convincingly."

The statement startled him. He gathered himself, then made eye contact with Vicky and held it. "I think I have a crush on my best friend."

"Your eyes are gorgeous." Vicky held up an eyeliner pen next to his eyes. "How long has he been your best friend?"

Every time Vicky held a different something next to his face, his heart had a reaction. He brought his focus back to the question and whispered, "Since I've been alive." Then immediately looked up. "Since I was five."

Vicky spoke almost to himself. "Earth tones. Jewel tones would look good, but earth tones would make your eyes breathtaking." He came out of his work trance and waived the brush in his hand. "Well, if you can't tell your lifelong best friend, who can you tell?"

Steven took a breath and followed Vicky's hands, then looked up at him. "Do you think?"

"Honey, you don't?" Vicky held up a set of small squares of color and a tiny tool. "Now tell me about this best friend."

His therapy seemed innocuous but it held more experience, genuineness, and empathy than a paid professional and with his permission, Steven forgot about his own issues and became lost in his favorite subject on a level he had shared previously, with no one.

After he told his story, Vicky softly asked, "Are you glad I came and got you?"

Steven smiled at the sudden awareness of the last thirty or so minutes and softly exhaled. "Yes."

Vicky dropped his arms to his sides. "Would you like a new friend?"

He exhaled again and looked deeply into the man's eyes, and with a slowly growing smile and a soft nod answered, "Yes."

With a promise to call, Steven left Vicky with a new friend, a phone number, a lifeline into a previously unexplored world, and the next level of self-understanding.

~ ~ ~

The night's sleep was more pleasant than expected and Steven woke the next morning in a better mood. Vicky, his initial thought, turned out to be as wonderful as he hoped, and his company was genuinely enjoyable, but the revelations Vicky exposed, uncovered as much anxiety as they answered, and his mood gradually deteriorated. He decided to try to address his oldest and greatest confusion, and went to his closet to retrieve his video game bag. He unzipped his most prized possession and reached under the plastic false bottom. It hadn't been long since he removed the skirt and blouse from its hiding place, but he needed to find out how he would feel wearing them now, with all that had transpired recently. He needed to come to grips with his greatest quandary, and he could think of no other action that would assist him more.

He sighed more than once as he changed, but the biggest sigh came when he turned to the mirror on the inside of his closet door. He stood there and stared. He knew. He hated that he knew, but he knew. He quickly contemplated one last denial, but he also knew how many *one last denials* he had already been through, and they were enough to know there could never be a true last denial. He knew.

He thought about Jake and quietly taunted himself; wishing he had someone as important as Jake to confide in, but he only wanted to tell Jake. He had other friends and he was even sure Vicky would listen, but Jake was his one and only true long-time everything, and the fact he wasn't sure he could tell him was more devastating than the realization that there was no one he loved, who he could tell. He curled up in a ball on his bed, and quietly cried.

He had no idea how long he was asleep and his mind raced the instant he woke, but one thought dominated over the rest. *Jake has no idea who I am.* And the thought made him feel so alone…so isolated.

He swallowed past the lump in his throat. *Maybe if I throw the clothes away.* He knew how futile the thought was. He tried to throw them away countless times before, and even succeeded once, and when they were gone, he never felt so mad at himself or confused at why he felt so mad. It took great effort to get another outfit and the effort added to its importance, and the importance added to his confusion and the confusion added to his realization he couldn't break his need to be who he was, and the more he came to that realization, the deeper his disheartenment. He was exhausted trying to make sense of it all. The best he could hope was to give up trying.

He even wondered if his desire to sometimes be a girl caused his chest to grow. Was it a punishment? Was it a curse? It sure felt like a punishment. He tried to think how he could do better. He wasn't quite sure what needed to be done better, but he would try anyway. He wouldn't wear the clothes. He knew the curse wouldn't go away unless he threw the clothes out, but he couldn't. He promised his own mind he wouldn't wear them again; trying desperately to bargain this torture away.

The silent tears flowed as he tried to reason with the gods who had imprisoned him inside his own being and his eyes blinked continuously, trying to clear his vision enough to stare at the image in his mirror. They were the only movements he consciously made. And through teary eyes, and a broken heart, he exhaustedly realized how futile the fight. He knew exactly who he was. The older he got, the deeper he could see inside. He knew.

~ ~ ~

Morgan's head popped up as the thought broke her temporary focus on the TV. "Any idea where our son is?"

Chris looked up from the computer on his lap. "His door is shut."

She looked at the clock on the mantle and turned to Chris. "Ready for dinner?"

"Sure."

She went down the hallway and knocked on the closed bedroom door. "Jacob, we're eating dinner if you want to join us."

His muffled voice came from the other side. "I'm not hungry."

"Okay, love. Well, there's lunchmeat and there's cereal if you're hungry later." She turned into the opening from around the hallway wall "We might as well eat." and continued toward the kitchen.

Except for the quick trip to the basement that afternoon, for a workout that more resembled self-abuse, Jacob lay locked in his room since Steven left the night before; face down on his bed, head half buried under his pillow, with hands and feet hanging off all sides. He was alone with his thoughts but he was no closer to a solution than when the quandary presented itself. The frustration he felt was unmatched. He couldn't remember a single time when a workout didn't free him of the storm within…until today. But this frustration was dressed with just enough hopelessness to throw him beyond a speedy fix or even a temporary reprieve, and all that realization did was add to the frustration.

Why do I feel things for him that I don't feel for any other human being? How is it possible, he's the perfect fit to my deepest hopes for the rest of my life? Why are my feelings for him so strong?

He pictured Steven in his mind; quick fleeting thoughts …moments frozen in time …sounds…smells…touches that meant more than Steven could ever understand. And the deep craving they caused weighed heavy on his heart. He kept picturing how gentle he was and he couldn't stop associating the thought with his definition of feminine, and he couldn't stop associating those feelings with an overwhelming desire to be connected to him. His heart sank further as the thoughts offered no normal solution. He closed his eyes and hoped for the continued relief of sleep.

The break wasn't long and the questions taking turns in his head came immediately back as soon as he reentered consciousness, but his thoughts were the only difference in the two states as he lay face down, motionless.

His first waking thought was that of the only two choices he could envision for his life, and neither were what he ever thought would define his existence. His first choice was a life with his definition of the perfect person. An inner bliss accompanied that choice. True happiness when they were alone with each other. But with it also came thoughts of an inability to enjoy life openly and without judgment when not alone. He saw future discomfort with the discovery of this choice, for every future casual friendship; even those most understanding. And he saw the ever-present potential for confrontation caused by those who couldn't comprehend...couldn't fully understand what he felt.

Or he saw a deep ever-lingering heartfelt pain at not pursuing what he was sure would be his only true happiness. A happiness that seemed to flow naturally with the core of his being. One that others would consider all too appropriate to condemn. He once again succumbed to the overwhelming thoughts accompanying consciousness and his mind passed again into the relief of sleep.

A deep breath and a realization welcomed him back to sentient thought; his happiness was worth it. Steven *was* worth it. Steven was worth any and all future pain...any and all future awkwardness. *When I see him, when I touch him, it's like no other. He's exactly what I want...exactly what I need.* His lungs filled, followed by a long deep sigh; all too aware the choice wasn't the one society suggest he make, and there was no more the possibility of escaping society, than a fish could escape the wet of the ocean.

But how do I tell him what I'm feeling? Is the chance for something deeper worth the risk of losing him? Even if he's okay, how could it work? Not only weren't the answers coming, but the questions weren't taking a rank of magnitude. One question seemed as impossible to solve as the next; each question posing the same level of frustration as the next and each answer creating more than one additional question. Then his heart jumped and its weight increased with yet another realization. There was no one he could turn to for guidance; no one he could confide in. *How come even these questions feel like they should remain hidden?* It wasn't long before the only recurring temporary solution came once again to his thoughts, and he shut his eyes, hoping for yet another break from awareness.

~~~

Steven's days were ending with more trepidation than normal, but the mornings were filled with far more resolve. He woke realizing it was time to address the most significant conclusion he made the day before. It was time to stop pretending he was anyone but who he knew he was, and start changing into the person concealed inside, and he could think of only one way to bring that hidden inner person out. The thought scared him, but he needed to at least experiment with matching the inside and outside of his being. He faced the mirror on his closet door and whispered. "Time to try to look how I feel. Time to stop lying."

Though his boy wardrobe was extremely limited, he was completely aware of the clothing styles. He had been secretly studying them for years. He gave a single chuckle as he realized he knew more about female clothes than male clothes, and he suddenly realized how temporary he always considered his boy things. His gut grumbled as he decided he was going to do something pretty bizarre, and he smiled at the timing. His belly knew before his brain that he was going to act on the thought.

With his stomach's permission, he planned another private outing. He was going shopping. He didn't dread the idea as much as he thought he would, but the emotional drive was far greater than any intellectual dread.

The outside shopping center was far easier to get to than the mall, and he knew a few stores would have what he was thinking he needed. He had been inside the discount store at the end of the small shopping center enough times to know it had exactly what he wanted, but there was another store he wanted to explore first.

It hadn't been long since he used his bike but the dust on it suggested otherwise. His clunker of a car had died two days after the end of last semester and he had made due without a replacement the entire summer. He just wasn't comfortable asking for another, and though his parents let him borrow either car whenever he wanted, they were only available when they were home from work. He spent a half an hour and a handful of towels cleaning his bike, and another half hour finding the key to the lock, but he was eventually on his way.

The thirty minute bike ride was pleasant enough, but as soon as he locked his bike under the storefront canopy, a dread came over him. How was he ever going to explain shopping for what he wanted to shop for? He sighed and stood there. The fight in his brain made old fights seem childish. He looked in the window.

Not one customer inside. The store looked deserted. *Wonderful. I'm going to be on display.*

He formulated a plan. He'd go in and look around. If someone asks, he'll say he was buying a present for his sister. If they look at him funny, he's outta there. If they're nice, he would shop. If they're real nice, he'd ask for help. He breathed deep and went in. He was immediately overwhelmed, but he began looking around. There were definitely some tops and things he could shop for and definitely some things he wished he owned.

He spotted a rack of skirts. *Wow, are they short.* His heart raced, imagining himself wearing one. He was almost shaking. After casually walking around the entire store, trying to calm his nerves, he found the jeans rack on a side wall and started looking through them. He didn't see the young salesgirl approach and she startled him.

"Hi. Can I help you?

Steven turned. "Hi. I'm just shopping for my sister. Her birthday's coming up."

She raised her eyebrows. "What size is she?"

Steven could feel his face begin to flush. "I don't know, but she's my size. We're twins."

Her excitement increased. "When's your birthday?"

He looked confused then his heart pounded, *What day is it? Wonderful.* "Next Tuesday."

"Happy birthday!"

His response sounded anything but appreciative. "Thanks."

"Can you give her a call and ask her what size she is?"

"No. She's at work, But I could try them on if it'd be alright."

"You'd try on girl jeans for your sister?"

His heart pounded and the effect was showing in his breathing. "Maybe I should come back."

"No. You're here and I'll help you." She looked into his eyes as if she sensed something.

He met hers and then looked away, thinking after a slight pause to turn to the jeans.

She stepped beside him and moved the first three jeans to the left. "Let me see." She removed a pair from the display rack and held them in front of him. "You'll have to try them on though." He looked at her, and wanted to say thank you so badly; the denial of that basic instinct made feeling natural, difficult. He managed a slight smile.

She pointed to the four louvered white doors on the side wall of the store. "Right over there?"

He looked at her timidly. "Okay."

He went in and shut the door and with his heart pumping forcefully again, started changing.

"They might be a little snug. Girls wear thinner things under their jeans."

He didn't register who the young woman was talking to until he heard the second sentence. He had never felt this many emotions. He squinted as his lungs tried to keep up with his heart. *They're only jeans. They're only jeans.*

"Are you doing okay? Do they fit?"

"Yes, I think so."

"Do you want to buy her a top too?" Her voice was soft and almost apologetic.

Steven sighed. She knew. He asked her permission with his answer. "Yes?"

"Wait a quick sec. Don't take the jeans off."

He stood there, then looked in the mirror at the jeans but all he could see was his chest moving up and down as he tried to breathe.

She knocked and he barely opened the door. "I picked you out two, so you have a choice."

"Thanks. Thanks for…" He didn't know how to finish the sentence, so he let it die.

Her response was as soft as a kindhearted young girl could sound. "You're welcome."

He examined the tops she gave him. One was fairly unisex, but the other was noticeably feminine and his heart jumped again. The feeling going through him was like nothing he'd ever felt before. He had to try it on. He wanted to ask himself why a simple top could elicit such strong emotions, but his mind was amazingly without confusion. He slipped the top over his head and looked in the mirror. "Is this me?" He squinted slightly and felt his heart answer. "This is me."

He changed back into his things, almost out of breath. A few moments later he opened the door. The young sales girl was standing behind the register counter, and she looked at him with apologetic eyes as he gently placed the three items on the counter. "Is that all you need?"

He answered softly. "I guess."

She started folding the first top.

Standing still was almost impossible as he watched her fold the clothes. Now that he was done shopping, his entire focus was on leaving, and she was taking so long. He felt like his face was blushing on and off every few seconds, but his brain was now operating completely separately. He interrupted her concentration. "Would the jeans size be the size she would need in skirts too?"

She smiled softly. "Yes. We have some really cute skirts. Do you want to see?"

His chest instantly resumed moving at the previous higher pace. "I guess so."

She noticed and smiled in a way that let him know she understood. She hurried from around the counter and excitedly walked to a skirt rack.

"This would look so good on her." She pulled a cute soft white skirt with purple flowers off the rod and held it out toward Steven. "What do you think? Isn't it cute?"

He reached his hand out slowly and felt the soft material and immediately wanted to let it express who he was; his desire to fulfill his need, now greater than the worry over what the young sales person thought. "I could buy this for her too." He glimpsed at her to see her reaction to his lie. She softly smiled and looked toward the counter.

They walked back to the register and the young girl wrapped and bagged everything. She spoke softly without looking up, as she gathered his change. "My name's Abbie. I usually work days and it's usually dead in here. You can even call ahead and I'll tell you if I'm alone…if you ever want to buy other things for your sister, after her birthday."

Steven stood there, with his mouth unconsciously open, his chest once again showing the need for more oxygen, and softly studied her. She handed him his change, with a look that showed she was now unsure whether she should have shared her last thought.

"This is the first time I've ever bought anything like this for my sister, and I'm glad you were here."

She smiled warmly. "We have an online store too."

His eyes widened again. *Why didn't I think of that?* He exhaled and turned to leave and two feet from the door turned around and timidly walked to a bin with intimates on it, back by the register. She met him there and helped him find what she believed would be his size. She put the additional items deep in his bag and then placed the entire bag in another, handed it to him and offered the meekest smile.

He sighed ever so slightly as she folded her hands on the counter. "I hope your sister's happy with what you got her."

His heart jumped again, but he remained composed and smiled warmly at her, "thanks for all your help" turned, and awkwardly walked toward the door.

CHAPTER FIVE
COMMUNION

The next morning, Steven popped awake like someone shouted his name, and his heart instantly raced. He expected the shopping trip to have taken its toll, but what he felt instead was a curious exhilaration thinking about the event, and that exhilaration fueled his next thought. He immediately decided he had delayed his plan as long as he could. The day had come.

Queasiness accompanied the realization that there would be nothing normal about today. He had woken earlier than normal. The complexity of the last ten days shut him down way earlier than normal the night before, but the night's sleep had renewed his desire to carry his plan through. The plan he had spent almost two weeks developing. The plan he had spent almost ten years studying for.

His first morning thoughts also brought an anxious smile to his face. He was going to let Jake know for the first time who he was, and his heartbeat actually scared him for how strong it pounded inside his small ribcage. Either Jake will be okay or he's going to be mad and that thought scared him, but he had hope. He was still the same person. His rational thoughts were to want Jake to accept him and still be his closest friend. His deepest thoughts were of hope Jake would want to do more than just accept him.

But whatever Jake's reaction, Steven could now understand and accept the reality he could see, and with his own acceptance, came the need to at least share his true inner self with Jake. He had one more quick trip, for some things he remembered in the middle of the night. One last minute trip and he believed he'd be ready for the gigantic step he was trying so hard to keep courage for.

He felt driven by a conscious determination to explore the possibility of becoming closer to the inner being he had repressed for so long. It was virtually inexplicable in his mind, but the need was undeniably strong. What had been an asexual somewhat feminine and confused male only a short time ago had over the last two weeks slowly transformed into the mindset of a young female.

He hurried out of the house. He wanted to get to the local discount store as early as he could. He had a plan but he needed a few more things, and needed to return his mother's car to the drive before she had to leave for work. He hadn't missed his old clunker a bit all summer, but he missed it again for the second time in days. He rationalized the timing of the trip though. He wanted to be home by the time he figured Jake would wake so he could invite him over to share the things going on in his head.

The store was empty when Steven arrived and he went directly to the bath section and examined a few feminine bath products. He held two bath oil bottles up to his nose, breathed in, and placed one in the cart, then remembered he needed a different razor. He quickly looked them over, then placed one next to the bath oil beads in the cart, and immediately decided he needed to get home.

He was the lone customer at the registers and the young cashier treated him with grace and tact, and rang up his purchases without a single quizzical or demeaning glimpse. He double bagged his purchases to avoid anyone casually detecting what he had bought, and headed home with an inner peace he didn't fully understand.

Jake awoke in far less suddenness. But his first thought did make his heart jump. He had an instant urge to see Steven and the thought was both energizing and disquieting. He had done very little but think about his best friend since that incident and their lack of time together had reached Jake's limits. But the separation helped him come to a few interesting decisions. They needed to talk. He quickly rehearsed twenty apologies for what happened that Friday and they all seemed to end with a secret confession. He tried to rehearse the words in his head so Steven wouldn't be scared or confused, but he had to let him know what he had been thinking for quite a while now.

He did care what his dear friend thought though, and Jake had no clue how a serious talk with Steven would go. But then he realized they were best friends and however Steven wanted to treat what happened that Friday and what would be discussed today, was fine with him.

Jake had risen well after Steven, but still early enough to know Genna and Connor were up getting ready for work, so he called their house phone.

"Hello?"

Genna's voice made Jake sit up straight in his bed. "Hi, Mom B. Is Steven up?"

"I think so. Let me check. ...Steven?"

He heard her knock on his bedroom door. "Steven. It's Jake."

He waited anxiously through the pause.

"But he seems to be gone already." Her response echoed her curiosity.

Jake's heart fell, and his mind raced for a second. "Well, okay. Thanks Mrs. Blair."

"Do you want me to leave him a message?"

He made his voice light and unconcerned. "No. I'm sure I'll catch up with him before you see him."

"Okay sweetheart. I'll talk to you soon."

"Okay, Mrs. Blair. Have a great day"

"You too sweetie."

Jake laid back down as if he had just lost his most prized possession. Steven was never out of the house this early. Ever. Where was he? Was he alright? Did he hurt him? He lay motionless and stared out his bedroom window; his heart distressfully heavy.

The phone on his end table rang a few minutes later and he reached for it way too anxiously, knocking into his lamp, and catching it as he read Steven's name on the display. He slid the lamp back in place as he pressed the call accept and inhaled. "Hello?"

"Jake." Steven's nervousness came through. "Hi."

Without acknowledging Steven's greeting, Jake quickly asked, "Are you alright?"

Steven hesitated. "Why?"

Jake sat on the edge of his bed. "Because I called your house this morning and your mom told me you weren't home."

An uncomfortable pause followed. "Yeah, I'm alright."

Jake exhaled. "Are you sure?"

"Yeah….but I think we need to talk. There's something I want to share with you."

The statement fed Jake's apprehension. He didn't know where Steven was headed with the thought, but he had the same need. "There's something I need to share with you too. You can go first."

"I think maybe we should be together for this."

Jake felt the weight of the statement. "Okay. Are you sure you're alright?"

Another hesitation followed. "Yeah." But Steven's tone conveyed a different meaning than his actual answer.

Steven continued. "But I'm kind of lost about how to tell you what I want to tell you. Would it be okay if I maybe explain it in a slightly different way?"

Jake softened his voice, hoping to convey a caring that represented the years of friendship they had accumulated. "Sure, I don't mind. We're best friends, right?"

Steven's voice trembled with a hint of condescension at the idea there could be any question. "You doubt that?"

"No."

"…Don't…ever."

But the idea Steven wasn't home needed further explanation. "Where are you?"

"I'm on my way home."

"Okay." Jake waited for more information.

Steven hesitated, and then his voice quivered again. "Can we get together today?"

"Sure." Jake responded eagerly, but the question sent a bolt of insecurity through him.

Steven's voice lightened. "Good."

"But I have work at five. I get done at ten-thirty though."

Steven's voice dropped slightly. "Oh."

"We have a few hours. What time?"

"An hour, but don`t come till I call you. Okay?"

"Sure…Are you okay?" He knew he had asked the question more than twice and received a positive response each time, but Steven had never put an invitation for a visit in quite this way.

"Yes Jake, I'm okay." He sighed into his phone. "I promise."

Jake heard the car moments after he hung up, but it didn't register instantly. Once he realized, he jumped up and looked out his window just in time to see Steven disappear inside his kitchen door.

Steven ran into the house. He could hear his mother in her bedroom and hurried into his room for fear of being caught with his purchases. He breathed deep as he shut his door, and gently placed the bag in his closet. Then sat at his desk, opened a textbook in case she opened his door to say goodbye, and waited impatiently.

Moments later, he heard his mother walk past his closed door on her way to the kitchen. "Steven? Are you home?"

"Yeah, Mom. In here studying."

"Jake called this morning."

"I know. He got ahold of me."

Okay sweetheart. I'm leaving."

He yelled a little louder. "Love you."

"Love you too."

His heart pounded as he heard the kitchen door shut, and he hurried to the bathroom and started running a bath. He ran back to his room and retrieved the new bag, hurried back to the tub, removed the bottle of scented bath beads and dumped some into the shallow pool of water starting to accumulate. As he waited for the water to rise, he hurried back to his closet and retrieved the bag of items he had bought the previous day, returned to the bathroom, removed a few things buried deep inside and the soft silky material fortified his resolve.

Steam started rising off the water and a soothing feminine smell began to permeate the room. He placed the two delicate items on the sink counter and slowly stepped into the scented water. Its steamy warmth and accompanying fragrance began releasing his tension. He leaned back and let the water envelop him, turning his head slightly to view the unusual intimates he now owned.

It was nearly forty minutes since he talked to Jake and he had prepared himself the best he could. He stared at the two garments as he dried himself, then inhaled deeply before reaching for the first. He had experimented with different clothes before. In fact, he had been experimenting with different clothes for as long as he could remember having access to them, but as he placed his first leg into the delicate garment, a realization came over him. He was putting it on for a completely different reason and both his legs began trembling.

His emotions were beginning to overwhelm him. He wanted so badly for this to feel natural, but everything he was taught told him he wasn't allowed. This wasn't allowed to feel more natural than what he was told were his proper clothes; what he was taught was acceptable. But it *did*. It did feel natural. Why couldn't he have been made so this *was* acceptable? Why was it *not*?

The silent tears began as he placed his other foot in the garment. He was trying his best to accept the disconnection between his heart and his world, but he knew these conflicts all too well. There would be no solace. He hesitated reaching for the second garment, but his inner being softly demanded he continue. His inner being no longer gave him an alternative or allowed him a choice. But he really didn't want an option. He had beaten himself thoroughly, for longer than he cared to remember and he was tired of the fight.

He finished putting the second garment on and then a T-shirt and shorts over them, then went into the bathroom to make sure his eyes didn't look like he had been crying. He spotted his mother's curling iron and decided on a quick experiment and as he toyed with it, his heart once again told him this was who he really is. And with the calm resolve of a person tired of fighting so many things, breathed in and reached for his phone.

He dialed his best friend. "Jake?"

A rather croaky "Hi" came from the other end.

"Hi. ...Do you still want to come over?" Steven caught his words. He didn't mean to manipulate Jake with his question, and was rather embarrassed at himself for the way it sounded.

But Jake handled the volley. "What do you think?"

Jake's answer immediately lightened the conversation and Steven responded in kind. "Well then, what are you waiting for?"

Jake playfully countered. "You…you idiot. Are you on drugs or something?"

"Something. Want to find out?"

"More than you know."

"Then hurry up!"

Armed with permission, Jake left his house at a slightly higher than normal speed. Thankfully, the outer kitchen door opened as he hit the handle or he was taking it with him. He negotiated the five steps outside his door in two bounds and the two adjacent driveways and middle dividing strip in six, then up the other five outside steps in another two leaps. And as he had for the past dozen or so years, walked in the door of his second home, past the kitchen and dining room, and toward the family room…and from out of the hall came an attempt at a blind-side tackle which caught him completely off guard. The hit wasn't ferocious. In fact, it was rather girlish and tender. But he was just blindsided nonetheless by what seemed like a rather cute and remarkably smelling young female. But no young females lived there. He gathered himself and restored his equilibrium, then braced himself against this crazy girl who had a grip around his waist and wasn't letting go. Who was this? Who in this house would unsolicitedly attack him, in such an unthreatening way? Who but Steven? Oh my god, the young girl was Steven.

In an instant and a rush, Jake yelled, "Steph."

The young girl froze and without letting go, stood up from her slightly bent attack posture, "Steph?"

Jake froze. "No!" Backpedaling as fast as he could. "No! I was saying stop and Steve at the same time. It just came out wrong."

"You liar! You are such a liar! You just called me Steph. As in Stephie. As in Stephanie."

Jake continued backpedaling, "No. I swear."

"What do you mean *you swear*? Steph isn't the combination of stop and Steven. Besides…" Steven's voice softened, "It's the best thing you've ever called me."

Jake stood there dumbfounded. "What?" Then he noticeably inhaled Steven's fragrance, and Steven's eyes widened as he witnessed his friend's reaction. "You like?"

He breathed in again. "Yeah! Is that you?"

The hallway wasn't well lit, and though Jake noticed slight differences in his best friend's appearance, specifics weren't clear enough to make definitive conclusions.

Steven ignored his question and took his hand. "Come with me. I want to share a few things with you."

He followed, holding Steven's hand as if he had always been a girl, and Steven held his hand and led like he had always had the power to make boys do what he wanted, and they walked to the more open and better lit family room. He knew who was holding his hand, but as he watched Steven lead, he detected a female and not a male, as his best friend had been for as long as he could remember.

As they moved closer to the room and the light became brighter, he started noticing more things about him. And as they walked onto the plush family-room carpet, Steven once again slipped his arms around Jake's waist and tried to wrestle him to the ground. Jake registered the futile struggle, laughed and gladly feigned weakness from the attack, grabbed his friend softly around his waist, rolled slightly so he would take the brunt of their controlled fall, and with this seeming female safely in his arms, fell as carefully to the carpeted floor as possible.

"What are you *up* to?"

He giggled as Steven straddled him and he once again voluntarily succumbed to his friend's futile effort to pin his arms. He waited until Steven had control, then stretched his arms out to the sides, making Steven's chest drop against his, and breaking his grip on his wrists. By the time Steven recovered and pushed up off him, Jake had wrapped his arms around Steven's back and he could only gain so much control over their distance. Within moments, Jake's hand felt the bra band across Steven's back, and as he did, he stiffened.

They made eye contact again, and Steven spoke softly. "Can we talk about the other day?"

Jake's voice matched the gentleness. "Of course we can talk about the other day. We can talk about anything you want; yesterday, now, tomorrow or fifty years from now. Always." He positioned his arms flat on the floor next to his head and Steven immediately reached for Jake's hands and held them in place.

"Do you see me as a girl sometimes?"

Jake's eyes narrowed as Steven's question registered. He hesitated with his answer, but what he had just felt, led him to believe he could answer honestly. "It's not that I see you as a girl, but we're close. I mean, I'm okay with who you are, no matter who you are. Is it okay though to tell you that you have some feminine qualities I think are really cute and looking at you as something more is something I'd like to do?"

His words brought a comfortable smile to Steven's face, and Steven's smile reassured him. "Do you see yourself as a girl sometimes?"

He felt Steven relax on top of him, and take a soft breath before he started speaking. "I've been fighting some things off and on, for a while. I'm aware I'm not typical or average in some things, and they've been a battle inside me for a long time. Sometimes I have control of the battle. Sometimes the battle starts to win. Sometimes I feel feminine. Sometimes I don't think about it. Sometimes I don't mind hiding my differences. Sometimes I get tired of hiding them." He took a deep breath. "I wanted to be a boy for everyone. For you. For your parents. For my parents. For everyone who knows me as a boy. But sometimes I don't want to be a boy for me. Sometimes, I don't feel like a boy, whether I want to be one or not.

But when you touched me the other day… When you touched me, I felt like something told me I can consider not fighting this anymore; not hiding anymore. Is it okay if I'm tired of this battle? Is it okay if I don't want to fight it anymore?"

Jake's eyes narrowed. "That's a lot."

Steven sighed, leaned forward and stared deeply into his eyes. "Do you fight who you are, to be who you are?"

Jake swallowed as the sentence registered. Steven's words had far more meaning than the question they made, and the implication made his heart drop. It was obvious his best friend was different, but for as close as they were, he had no idea this ever-present conflict was going on inside him.

Steven sat up straight. "Wait. Did you say you like the idea of me being feminine?"

Jake smiled. "Yeah. Is that okay?"

Steven playfully pressed down on both his hands. "Is that okay!"

He watched Steven's delight, and the reaction sent a jolt of pleasure through him.

"Wait." Steven bounced on Jake's stomach and leaned forward. "There's more."

Jake raised an eyebrow as his mouth broke into another slight smile. "Like what?"

Steven took another deep breath. "Sometimes I think I have feelings for you."

Jake leaned his head up and stared directly into Steven's eyes. "You never noticed I did for you?"

Steven breathed in quickly, as if the words went up his nose. "You do not."

He rolled over on top of Steven, pinning his hands on the carpet next to his head and without responding, leaned down and quickly kissed him.

Steven's heart pounded and his eyes widened in response. "Why did you do that?"

"Because I wanted to. Why? Was it awful?" He smiled as he noticed Steven's increased breathing.

"No."

"Are you mad at me for doing it?"

Steven's voice softened. "No."

He met Steven's eyes and momentarily lost all other focus, but except for his breathing, Steven also lay motionless as he stared up at him.

Jake hesitated for another moment, then slowly started sitting up and Steven instantly panicked watching the distance between them grow. "Wait!"

He paused as Steven inhaled deeply, leaned up and kissed him, then gasped, and without recovery asked, "Is that alright?"

Jake inhaled and smugly replied, "Mine was better."

The tone of his statement instantly released Steven's apprehension. "It was not."

He leaned forward. "Yes, it was."

Steven playfully topped his condescension. "No, it wasn't."

Jake calmly topped Stevens. "Yes, it was. And I'll prove it to you."

He lowered his head. "You kissed like this…" Their mouths softly came together and they both held the kiss longer than either of the first two. Then after a brief pause, added, "And I kissed like this…" Jake kissed him again, now longer than the other three.

He paused for a moment and let Steven's reaction fill his senses, then watched as Steven smiled derisively and answer back, "But what I didn't show you was this…"

Steven reached around his neck and pulled him down until their lips met once again, and this time, opened his mouth, and Jake's heart responded with a thump he could feel out to his forearms. He followed Steven's lead; opening his mouth and exploring the next level of intimacy with his best friend.

The kiss softly broke, leaving Jake in a state of unfocused bliss. Then he noticed Steven's reaction and his breathing increased.

He began recovering first. "Told you."

After a momentary hesitation, Steven responded, "Told me what?" His short quick inhales affected his response.

Jake smiled. "That I do."

Steven stared at him as if he hadn't understood. "That you do what?"

Jake's smile increased. "That I have feelings for you too, and that I have for a while."

Steven's eyes narrowed with a confused curiosity. "How come you never told me?"

He let out a deep sigh. "I'm guessing for the same reason you never shared this before?"

Jake knew his feelings were real but he also knew the stigmas they created were just as real, and with far greater social implication. These influences were a large part of their struggle, but neither seemed to be able to fight their inner nature any longer.

Steven finally recovered from his quick trance and softly addressed his best friend. "Jake?"

Jake stared into his eyes and smiled in response. "Yeah?"

"Would it be okay…when we're alone…if you call me Steph or Stephie or Stephanie…and not Steven anymore?"

Once again Steven's words registered as more than just a request. His friend had never opened up like this before, and the emotions Jake felt were amazingly deeper than he ever imagined feeling for his dearest friend, and Jake felt the need to reciprocate the feelings. "Sure. Would it be okay if sweetheart slipped out every once in a while too?"

"Really?"

He could tell by the inflection in Steven's voice that the idea pleased him, and he was all too happy to confirm. "Really."

But even with all these new revelations, Jake was still nervous about asking Steven what this meant to their relationship. All the initial kisses did was make him sure he wanted more, and his desire for more made him uneasy. He moved off his friend, stood up and then reached for Steven's hand and Steven gladly gave it. He didn't take his eyes off Jake for a moment as they sat together on the sofa; Steven's breathing still well above normal. They sat close, but only their closest knees touched, until Jake slowly moved his hand from the back of the sofa to Steven's shoulder, and stared gently into his eyes. "I have no problem seeing you as female. In fact, I'll always see you how you want me to, whatever that is, but I think you're beautiful anyway." He hesitated and became completely nervous. "Do you need space to do this or is it okay if we become even closer as you figure this all out?"

He could feel his heart speed up as he waited for Steven's response. Steven smiled. "Is that my decision?"

He softly nodded. "Yeah. Most definitely."

But Steven had no hesitation reaching emotionally for him. "You mean I have the option of being even closer to you? My option?"

His breathing quickened. "Yeah."

Steven qualified the offer. "You don't have a problem with me not being a real girl?"

Jake straightened his left arm on the back of the sofa behind Steven's head and inhaled deeply. "If you decide you're a girl in your heart, then you *are* a real girl to me. And not only do I not have a problem with it, I'm actually thrilled we can become even closer."

"Would you want me to be *your* girl?" Steven's eyes widened as he finished the question and the look went straight to Jake's heart.

He smiled at her forwardness and offered with no hesitation, "Yeah. I'd love you to be my girl."

"And you'd be my boyfriend?"

Steven's caring interrogation tickled Jake to his core. No one else ever did that to him. No one else knew how to trigger that deep something Jake loved feeling, and he could sense the strange smile it produced. "Yeah. I would be your boyfriend."

Steven's eyes glistened as he stared at him. "Well, don't boyfriends and girlfriends make out?"

Those words made Jake's heart jump, and the right side of his mouth curled into a curious grin, "Yeah. Yeah, they do. But you know, this changes our wrestling matches completely."

Steven leaned his head on Jake's arm and playfully grinned. "I know."

And as Steven studied him, Jake slid his right arm around his waist, leaned forward, and placed the softest next kiss on his lips. And as their mouths came together, Steven fell into her long anticipated female persona with complete joy and contentment. Their lips never separated as each slowly, tenderly and naturally opened their mouths and kissed like new lovers.

Steven shivered with joy as their kiss broke. "Oh my god Jake." Steven's reaction to the kiss was like nothing Jake had ever witnessed. Jake curiously watched in amazement as Steven openly displayed an elation beyond anything he would have ever expected. His heart jumped as Steven reached around his neck and kissed him again, immediately opening his mouth and displaying an eagerness and pure delight that only accompanies first times.

The kiss registered differently inside Jake. He felt the peaceful calm of a secret confirmation. He had been kissed before, but he also hadn't spent years contemplating his emotional confusion every time his best friend had a significant other. Instead, Jake had very clear hidden feelings that were just enthusiastically reciprocated and the kiss went right to Jake's heart. He didn't say anything. He wasn't sure he could explain it even if he wanted to. But he felt a love like he never imagined he would ever feel. Of that he was sure.

The kiss broke slowly and as soon as it did, Steven jumped in his seat. Suddenly he had an unexplained energy that needed to come out and it all seemed to want to come out right now.

He faced Jake. "You really want to be boyfriend and girlfriend?"

Jake touched Steven's hair, his grin now all but permanent. "More than you know."

"So, are we boyfriend and girlfriend now?"

Jake playfully smiled. "Either that, or I'm the greatest liar ever."

He never heard Steven sound more feminine. "Jake. That's not funny."

He felt instantly apologetic and quietly noted how completely his emotions were tied to his best friend's. "Sorry. I was only playing around."

Steven's forgiveness came before Jake asked for it. He was still in the middle of the interrogation. "So we can kiss each other when we want?"

Jake looked into Steven's eyes and shook his head barely noticeably. *If you only knew what you could ask for and get complete permission for.* He breathed in and nodded. "…Of course we can."

"And we can make out?"

Jake laughed. "Definitely."

"And I can be a girl to you?"

He sighed but his smile never lessened or waivered. "You are officially a girl to me. You're Stephanie Blair. My girlfriend."

"But you can get any girl you want. Why would you want me?"

The question made Jake sit up and immediately defend his heart. "Because I don't want anyone else. I want you. I've been trying to find you in someone else for years but my thoughts always go back to you, which makes you who I wanted all along."

He leaned forward and kissed him again as the exclamation to his statement. When their kiss ended, Steven's request for confirmation was softer than either time he asked before. "Really?"

Jake leaned forward and kissed him as tenderly as he could. "Really."

Steven was done his interrogation. He had convinced her, and with that convincing came an immediate desire to let out the person so long locked inside.

"Then I want to show you some things. Can I? Is it okay?"

Jake reached for the side of his best friend's face and softly touched it. "Stephanie, whatever you want."

"Okay. I bought a few other things. Can I show you?"

"Sure."

"I'll be right back. Okay?"

Jake sat back. "I'll be right here."

Steven jumped up and then leaned back down and gave Jake a quick kiss because she could. "Be right back." Then she ran out of the room.

Jake slid his hands behind his head and smiled with an inner peace that included a hint of unbelievable fortune. What he had secretly hoped for; what he was so afraid to admit, was turning out to be better than he ever imagined. He already missed her.

After a short time she reappeared in the hallway, walking toward him as he sat on the sofa, and as she walked into the light, he stared at her in amazement. She had changed her loose boy T-shirt and boy shorts for the little white skirt with purple flowers and the cute cotton top Steven had purchased, and she looked startlingly adorable. His smile broadened and he quickly stood.

Stephanie immediately felt great inner joy from his reaction but her curiosity made her ask. "Why are you standing?"

"Because, because…you're beautiful. How?"

"Really?" She didn't wait for an answer. "But I have to show you what I bought and I can't model for you if you're standing on my runway."

He reached for her and she smiled and playfully pushed him away, then walked up to him, chest to chest…and pushed him so he fell seat first onto the sofa. He grinned ear to ear as he fell backward.

Just as Jake started getting his bearings, Stephanie stood in front of him; her smile showing him the first glimpses of her beautiful female soul and her skirt showing more of her rather smooth, cute legs than she ever shared with anyone. With her derrière arched slightly back and chest pushed out, she asked in a rather feminine way, "Do you like my new outfit?"

Jake sat up, clearly enjoying the playful intimacy she was initiating, but offered no answer; just a two handed reach for her hips, which she was able to evade and asked again. "Well, do you?"

His answer resounded with energy. "Yes."

She tilted her head slightly. "Very good. Correct answer."

She then asked, "Do you like my new top?" She ran her hands over the top and her chest. The excitement she felt as her touch confirmed this breathtaking transition resounded inside her.

He panted, "Yes…" and then grinned uncontrollably. "Very much."

She softly smiled. "So far both of your answers are correct. Now it's time for a few bonus questions. Are you ready?"

He sat up. "Yes"

She pulled her skirt hem sideways with her left hand. "Do you like my new skirt?"

She watched his eyes leave hers and armed with her permission, gazed intently at the cute feminine skirt, revealing legs he now seemed all too interested in exploring, no more than inches from him and all he could muster was a fairly faint and windy "Yes."

She smiled at his short but obviously positive answer, "Very good."

She smiled teasingly, turned her slightly arched back to him, lifted her skirt quickly and showed him an ever so quick glimpse of her white lace panties, and in a softer more seductive voice asked, "What do you think of my new panties?" And before she could turn her head around to anticipate his answer, he had her from behind in a standing spoon and lovingly wrapped his arms around her.

"I love it." He leaned forward enough to kiss her on the back of her neck and whisper in her ear. "Do I get an A?"

His surprise attack stole her breath away. "Yes, so far."

She turned in his arms and surrendered to a kiss, ten years in the making.

Before today, Steven had never been kissed and it was exhilarating to think Jake wanted him. He reached around Jake's neck, immediately opening his mouth and feeling the pure elation of another kiss, and the pure bliss the assumed permission the title of girlfriend held.

She had always loved Jake and even wondered occasionally if she was in love with him, but she felt their kiss so deeply inside that there was now no doubt. There had never been anyone else and no one compared to him. As the kiss intensified, she softly succumbed to a force that encompassed deep and yet still developing feelings of femininity.

His hands tenderly embraced her in her new outfit as their new emotional connection continued to unfold. His hands traced over her, never pausing for more than a moment, never squeezing with more than the slightest pressure, as if she would balk if his squeeze was strong enough to get her attention. But she felt every movement and every caress. Her skin was on full alert and his hands were electric. Every new touch sent a fire through her and fed her heart. And with every recognition came an assuredness that this was who she was meant to be.

They sat arm in arm together on the sofa, kissing, talking, and cuddling, but their physical contact wasn't the most notable change in their relationship. As Jake tenderly caressed his best friend, he started asking soft curious questions that showed a heartfelt desire to understand more of how Steven felt and what he had gone through to arrive here, and Steven opened up and let Jake inside a place neither previously understood fully. Jake innocently asked and Steven innocently answered; neither consciously aware of the true connection this new depth was building, though both felt the new bond being created.

It was now late afternoon. Their parents would be home soon and he had work that evening. They decided to part, so she could turn back into her old self before they arrived, and he could honor his obligation.

She walked him to the side door, holding his hand the whole way. She didn't want him to leave and he definitely didn't want to go, but he turned to her at the door, wrapped his arms around her and as softly as their first kiss, leaned down to her lips and kissed her like only best friend lovers can. The softness of his tongue took her breath away. She knew this kiss would be all she would think about for the remainder of the evening and into the night. What seemed like a moment in time though, turned out to be longer than either expected and Jake's phone alarm went off again. He gave her a look of regret and shrugged. Her heart sank. She had never heard anything so disappointing.

Steven's voice was soft and submissive. "When do you have to go?"

They stood facing each other, holding hands. "Five minutes ago. Five and a half hours. That's it. I'll be right back."

"Yeah, but our parents will be home."

He appeared lost for words. "We'll figure this out." He kissed her deeply one more time. "Five and a half hours."

She needed something more from him or she was never going to last that long. She whispered, "So, am I girlfriend material?"

He smirked, "What do you think?" He cupped her face in his hands, kissed her one last time, and ran out the door.

Steven heard Jake's motorcycle leave his drive, as he buried the shopping bag with Stephie's new things inside, deep in the back corner of his bedroom closet.

~ ~ ~

The sun was up when Jake opened his eyes, but he didn't know for how long. He didn't have enough sleep, but he woke with an instant energy and a smile on his face. Today, he wasn't worried about whether the person he had a major crush on, was anything but his girlfriend. He flashed back to yesterday and instantly decided he needed as close to a repeat as he could create. He decided to go next door for breakfast and quickly showered.

Steven sat at the kitchen table, eating a bowl of cereal when Jake opened the Blair side door and he coughed and choked on his spoonful, immediately trying to hide what he was wearing, but he was wearing a boy T-shirt and boy shorts. Jake laughed at his girlish reaction. "Hi."

Steven hid behind his arms, the table and his bowl of cereal. "Jake. What are you doing here?"

"My parents left and I didn't feel like having breakfast alone. Why?" He looked around. "I do this all the time."

"Yeah, but I…"

Jake paused for a moment, waiting for the rest of Steven's complaint, and enjoying Steven's panic, then shook his head almost unnoticeably as her reaction pleased him to his core.

"Hey! Want Stephie to make you breakfast over your house? Just the two of us?"

Jake rubbed his hands together and smiled. "Sure!" He wanted breakfast, but he needed Stephie.

"Okay, go. I'll be right over."

Jake squinted as he watched him. Steven waved the back of his hand. "I'll be right there."

He walked slowly to the door and reached for the handle as he watched Steven throw his perfectly good bowl of cereal in the sink and hurry to his room. He would have eaten that, if he had asked. He hesitated as Steven disappeared, turned and went back home.

Not long after, Stephie entered his side door with her video bag in hand and shut and locked the door behind her. She was wearing the jeans and the other top Steven had bought and Jake's heart jumped when her outfit registered in his mind. He smiled at how feminine she appeared as she walked toward him. Her soft fragrance, a surprisingly pleasant finishing compliment to her change into his girlfriend.

She slipped her arms around his neck, and gazed into his eyes with a big smile. "Good morning."

He tenderly wrapped his arms around her waist, "Good morning." and then kissed her hello.

The kiss started innocently, but neither could control their new connection long enough to have it end that way, and they immediately fell into a deep lovers' kiss, tasting and exploring each other's mouths; both thrilled the reality was as wonderful as the anticipation. She pulled away and with a little bounce in her voice asked, "What do you want for breakfast?"

He immediately replied, "Eggs over easy, bacon, pancakes, hash-brown potatoes, coffee and juice please."

His food order had the exact result he envisioned. It was like he shot her, and he started laughing. She pushed him, and he laughed harder. "Okay, cereal it is. Well, you know where the cereal and milk is. What are you waiting for?"

He grabbed her again and gave her another kiss, and after the minute she needed to recover, went over to their pots and pans cabinet and removed a pan, then went to the fridge and grabbed a few eggs and the butter, and proceeded to make him eggs. While the pan was heating, she placed a few slices of bread in the toaster, and as she stood at the stove, he walked up behind her and snuggled softly against her. "I could get used to this."

She breathed deep as his arms wrapped around her. "Could you?"

He felt her exhale and take another.

"I was thinking. If we go away to college after we're done this semester and get our own place, I could do this for you, and it would really help me."

He held her and whispered to the back of her ear. "I could get used to that." He felt her hold her breath for a quick moment as she registered his words, then let out the soft breath as she continued cooking.

He watched her finish, and noted how something so simple could suddenly become a new pleasure. Steven had cooked for him before and they had eaten together countless times, but this was different. This was the first time Stephanie ever cooked for him and he caught his own surprisingly pleasant inner reaction. She served him and sat across from him, intently watching him take the first few bites.

"How's your eggs?"

He glanced down at her tightly clamped hands resting on the table and struggled to hide the pleasure her anxiety produced. "Best I ever had."

She smiled. "You're such a liar."

"No. Really." He grinned with a mouthful. "Best eggs Stephanie ever made me."

"You're an idiot."

Her enjoyment of the statement went pleasantly through him and her response made him laugh. He knew. He loved making Steven laugh, even if it meant being an idiot. Making Stephanie laugh was a surprisingly deeper joy. He also loved their little endearment term. They used it back and forth for as long as either could remember.

She shared a few new thoughts as she sat across from him and watched him eat. "I made a list this morning of things I want to do as Stephanie. ...From clothes to school to everything else."

She explained her plans to further become Stephanie, and Jake sat and paid attention like they were partners in the plan.

When she finished, she raised her eyebrows and looked into his eyes. "What do you think?"

"I'm with you. I think we should find a four year college that has a strong diversity program and progressive human development approach, so you can go as Stephanie Harrison--I mean Blair. Stephanie Blair. I'd like it to be close so I can keep my job to help us pay for our apartment, but I can find a job anywhere, especially with the recommendation I'd get from the owners. But I'd like it to be far enough away from here that you and I could live as boyfriend and girlfriend."

As she absorbed his intentions of complete support, she moved over to him, sat on his lap and put her arms around his neck. "You really mean it?"

He softly wrapped his arms around her and nodded. "Yeah."

She held him tight, as he stroked her hair and rubbed her back. He knew there were going to be bumpy roads ahead but he had big shoulders. He was sure he could carry his share of the coming difficulties.

She spotted the clock on the stove. "It's nine-thirty already? Time for me to go. Can we have a date later?"

He inhaled. "My heart jumps when you say that."

She leaned away from him and looked into his eyes. "You really like me being your girlfriend?"

He met her eyes. "More than you know."

She inhaled as his words registered and after a brief pause, hesitantly asked. "See you later?"

"Definitely."

They kissed softly and she went home.

~ ~ ~

The feelings Jake stirred in Steven gave him all the courage he needed to endure things he felt so uncomfortable doing. There were limits to what he could do right now, but he had to see exactly how much she could accomplish. She laid on Steven's bed, and dialed the number he'd stored in his phone while he sat in Vicky's make-up chair at the mall.

"Vicky?"

"Hello?"

"Vicky, it's Steven from the mall. Your stalker?"

Vicky's voice brightened. "Oh, hi! How are you?"

"I'm doing good." Steven sat up. "I told my best friend about me. Actually, I showed Jake. I bought some things and wore them in front of him."

Vicky offered his approval. "That was bold and gutsy."

"I figured it was easier than trying to explain everything to him and I decided I knew him well enough."

"So how'd it go?"

"Are you working? I'm not calling you at work, am I?"

"No sweetie. I'm off. Just sitting around the apartment. So how did it go?"

"We're boyfriend and girlfriend."

"No way! Congratulations."

Vicky's enthusiasm encouraged him. "He told me he liked me like I like him and told me he wanted me to be his girl. I was thrilled and shocked. I hoped but I never thought."

"I'm so happy for you. And I'm so thrilled you called to let me know."

Steven moved the phone from his left ear to his right. "You said you wouldn't mind being friends? I was wondering, can we be friends?"

"Sure. I'd love another friend. Especially one like you. You could be my new project."

Steven's voice perked up. "Like teach me how to do make-up?"

"I'll teach you more than that, honey."

"Really?"

"Yeah! When's the next time you plan on being alone with him?"

Steven stood up. "Today, after I go clothes shopping."

"Would you like company? I'll do your make-up."

"Really? You'd do that for me?" Steven paused. "I don't have a car."

"I do."

Steven's excitement increased again. I'll give you gas money."

Vicky laughed. "You don't have to do that."

"But I want to. I was going to ride my bike to the strip mall."

"Oh, I like your determination. This could be fun."

Steven shared directions and Vicky pulled up thirty minutes later.

"Hi. You ready?"

Steven looked in the car and smiled. "Sure."

They spent the next few hours together, shopping, getting to know each other and becoming friends, and as they drove back to Vicky's apartment, he finally offered the one thing Steven had secretly waited for, the entire trip. "So are you going to let me make up those eyes now?"

Steven's heart instantly pounded and all he could do was look at Vicky with a slightly open mouth.

Vicky glanced at him and giggled. "You are hilarious. How could you possibly be more innocent than girls five years younger than you?"

Steven shrugged his shoulders. "They had a fifteen year head start?"

Vicky nodded in agreement. "I guess they did. But not to worry. I'm going to catch you up plenty fast!"

He unlocked the apartment door and let Steven enter first. "Welcome to my little corner of the world."

"Thanks. It's really cute."

Vicky quickly brought the subject back to his intentions. "I really am excited about making up your eyes!"

Steven turned to him with a look of curious confusion. "But don't you do make-up all day long almost every day?"

Vicky walked past him waving his arms. "I do. I know. I'm sick. But I don't care. I have to do your eyes."

Steven's amusement and curiosity grew with every new level of animation his new friend displayed. "What's so special about my eyes?"

Vicky smiled like he was eventually going to share a secret and his voice suddenly turned serious. "You'll see." Then he smiled the soft soothing smile Steven saw when they first met and Steven exhaled. Vicky was as sweet and caring as he first appeared and the more they were together, the more it comforted him.

Vicky pointed to one of the two stools facing the counter-top below the opening between his kitchen and small dinette area. "Sit over there and face out this way." As Steven turned the chair to face the living room, Vicky picked up the plastic make-up box sitting against the wall and placed it on the counter, then moved the second chair out of his way. The smile on Vicky's face made Steven smile.

Steven sat as Vicky continued. "Now I'm not going to teach today. Today is for me. I'm playing. See, this is my therapy. I make people up every day, but only once in a while do I get the canvas I need to create my own art."

Steven didn't understand and Vicky didn't explain further. Steven narrowed his eyes in slight confusion and Vicky responded. "Remember how you sat looking at me at the mall?"

"Yeah."

"I want to see those high eyebrows and wide eyes again."

Steven fidgeted in the chair. "Are you going to tell me how to take this stuff off so I can go home tonight?"

Vicky stopped dead. "Already you want to remove my art?"

"No!"

Vicky playfully grinned. "Will you relax."

"I can't!"

Vicky reached in the make-up box. "Why not?"

"Because this is the first time I ever sat to have my make-up done."

"And when I'm done, you'll realize this was the first time of the rest of your life."

The statement opened Steven's eyes as wide as they've ever opened and Vicky immediately fell into focus and immersed himself in his art and his therapy. He continually switched from casual conversation, to soft comments to himself as he walked Steven through the process of transformation that had become far more than just his trade.

Steven broke the short lull in their conversation as Stephanie felt the strange applicators on her face. "I've been thinking about something I don't understand."

"What's that sweetie?"

He inhaled slowly. "I've been hiding ever since I started realizing I was different…and you do just the opposite. How do you do that? Aren't you afraid?"

The statements made Vicky take a breath and step back. He stared at Steph and shook his head slightly, but before he spoke a word, Stephanie continued her thought, "You're so comfortable with yourself."

Vicky smiled. "You know your question is complicated, right?" He patted Steven on the shoulder then reached for something in his make-up box.

Stephie followed Vicky's every motion. "I know."

Vicky breathed deep. "I was like you. I think we all start out like you, and many of us stay that way, hiding or semi-hiding forever." He smiled as he restarted the make-up process, and his voice immediately changed back to its soothing tone. "I just couldn't survive like that. And I understand what that meant, but I decided a long time ago that life had too much to offer and the only way I could enjoy it is to be part of it." He straightened up. "But I wasn't born like this. Let me change that, I think I was born like this. But for a short period, my enthusiasm for life was beaten out of me. But I got it back. I had to work to get it back, but I got it back."

His make-up application intensified with his words, and Stephie became a little anxious.

"Does that mean I don't run into my share of assholes? Oh honey! I've been met by young men right in the mall parking lot leaving work." He whispered almost to himself, "It's always young guys."

The words resonated inside Steven and he straightened in his chair.

Vicky paused, smiled and made eye contact with Steph. "But I'll gladly deal with ten assholes if it means for every ten, I can meet someone like you." He dabbed the applicator on the back of his hand. "If we both hid, we wouldn't have met."

He rummaged in the make-up box. "But I'm not stupid either. I no longer leave the mall alone at night…or empty handed."

Stephie questioned meekly. "Why do people have to be like that?"

"We can't go there sweetie. It's too depressing. But…" He made an exaggerated stroke with the brush in his hand. "Voila'! You're done."

He picked up a small round mirror from the counter and held it in front of Steven, then smiled happily at the results he was about to share. "Here!"

Steven's heart jumped. He knew he'd eventually see what Vicky was doing, but the time to look was now. He held his breath as he moved the mirror away from his face, and his mouth unconsciously opened. A look of shock to the point of tears appeared and his eyes started welling up.

"Don't you dare cry."

Steven's eyes opened saucer wide as he looked at his new friend, and Vicky quickly handed him a tissue. "I'll smack you!"

Steven exhaled then exclaimed, "Vicky!"

"What honey?"

"I look like a girl." She lowered the mirror and gazed at Vicky with unbelievably wide eyes. "I really look like a girl."

Vicky swabbed his brushes onto a paper towel and swayed his head. "No, you don't."

Stephanie's eyes narrowed.

Vicky glanced at her. "Girls don't look like you. You're model gorgeous."

Steven filled his lungs. "I wish."

"Dearie, Jake will confirm, don't you worry."

"Do you think?"

Vicky started closing make-up jars and containers. "You have to call me and give me details, okay?"

"Okay." Stephie turned in the chair and faced him as he continued cleaning his tools. "I can't tell you how much what you did for me at the mall the other day, and what you did with me today, means to me. You're wonderful."

Vicky put his fingers to his mouth. "Sweetie, that's a very nice thank you and you're welcome. I'm not wonderful, but I love that you think I am."

Stephanie's chest rose and fell quickly as she stared at Vicky's art in the mirror.

He broke her concentration. "Are you going to have a heart attack?"

"Vicky, I can't believe you made me look like this. Will I ever be able to do this to myself?"

"Yeah sweetie you will, and all too easily." Vicky took the mirror from her. "You ready to go show your beau?"

Stephanie smiled and Vicky offered another insight. "Today's Jake's birthday."

Stephanie responded somewhat confused. "It's in December."

Vicky glanced at her, smiled and shook his head with mock aloofness. "Well it's coming early this year." Stephie inhaled.

He continued to put his make-up away. "Why don't you change into something to go with your new look and I'll drop you off at Jake's. Oh! He lives next door, doesn't he?"

Stephanie looked at him. "Yes."

Her eyes surprised him and he did a double take, then nodded. "Convenient."

Stephie grabbed the shopping bags she accumulated earlier, met Vicky's eyes and motioned to the hallway next to where she was sitting.

"Yeah sweetie. Use my bedroom, not the bath. Second door on the right."

Ten minutes later Stephanie came into the living room wearing girl jeans and a simple cotton top. Vicky examined her up and down. "Much better than the baggy sweatshirt and boy jeans. You look adorable. We good to go?"

Stephie turned a very soft shade of red. "Thanks. Yeah." She paused and met Vicky's eyes. "I had a really good time. You really are great."

Vicky held Stephanie's hands. "I'm going to hang out with you just for my ego, sister. Now give your beau a call and tell him you'll be home in twenty minutes and you have a surprise for him."

She texted Jake as they drove, then quietly sat as her heart pounded with expectation; excitedly anticipating his reaction to her continuing change.

~~~

The mid-day light bathed the family room as Jake sat waiting on the soft navy blue leather sofa. Normally, he loved how the cushions absorbed him. Normally, it was very comfortable. But today, sinking in restricted him just enough to make him feel like he needed to stand; his anticipation making it almost impossible for him to relax. He was like a child at Christmas waiting for her. Yesterday was one of the best days of his life and all they did was kiss, cuddle and talk. That pure pleasure was enough for him to now want more. He definitely wanted more.

He heard the side door open and his heart jumped. He was amazed she could do that to him. When she finally came into sight, "wow" came out of his mouth without thinking. Her soft shape was more feminine than he realized, and he stood. She kept making him stand. He wasn't even aware it happened.

"You look fantastic!" Then as she moved closer, he saw her make-up. "Who did your make-up? You're gorgeous. Seriously, Steph…you're gorgeous."

She walked up to him, slipped her arms around his neck, whispered, "thank you" and kissed him.

He felt each new kiss resonate to a new depth inside him. He reached around her and reconfirmed, "I'm serious. You're beautiful!"

She blushed. "I was hoping you'd like."

She moved to the sofa and looked up at him, waiting for him to sit next to her. He didn't disappoint. He sat and brought her into his arms and they kissed like two young lovers, and as they kissed, his hand tenderly traced over her, exploring his new girlfriend. They continued to cuddle and kiss but between kisses he stared at her, until she became noticeably self-conscious.

She nervously met his eyes. "What's wrong?"

"What's wrong?" He laughed. "You're frigging gorgeous! How the hell did you go from my boy best friend to the most beautiful girl I ever saw? I mean, I always thought you were cute, but damn. What are you, some kind of magician?"

Her face lit up and she bounced slightly in his arms, "I'm not, but Vicky is."

"Who's Vicky?"

Stephie shared the whole story of how Steven and Vicky met and why, and Jake learned more about what his best friend was going through, and the more Jake learned about her courage and fight, the more he yearned to be emotionally linked to his best friend. They kissed and cuddled for hours, joking and teasing; holding and touching in ways that softly revealed another depth of connection. His hands gently slid over her, like a boyfriend who had earned the permission only years of caring earn, pleased by her obvious delight at being lovingly fondled by him.

He slid his hand softly over the side of her hair and broke the peaceful silence. "This is absolutely fantastic and you are definitely a very sexy girl, but you have to tell me how you want to handle this and us, when we're not alone. Have you thought about that?" He switched from relaxed boyfriend to concerned best friend and protector in an instant.

His statement brought her back from nirvana and she sighed. "Yes." She stared intently straight ahead. "Jake?" She turned toward him. "Is it okay if I'm not ready to let everyone who loves us know what I intend to do just yet?"

"Sure sweetheart."

"I love when you call me that."

He smiled. "You are."

Her voice turned serious. "It's just that, this is a big adjustment for me and I don't want everyone involved in it. I kind of just want to have a natural change with you right now and get used to being a girl and being your girlfriend... and everyone else will make it more complicated and maybe even weird...and it isn't... Does that make sense?"

"Of course it does. In fact, it makes perfect sense. I always like the way you think. You already figured this out?"

"I don't have everything figured out but I've been thinking about a lot of things since you put your hand on my chest and I woke up for the next two weeks thinking about it." She playfully hit him on his round protruding shoulder muscle. She continued more seriously, "You matter a lot to me for a lot of reasons and focusing on you helped me come to some different, but really nice conclusions."

"I'm glad I could help, but I do want to tell you. Whoever you decide to tell, friend, family member, or stranger, I want to be with you, standing next to you."

He could see in her eyes she knew what he meant. He had been her protector for years and she could see that role intensifying.

She looked into his eyes. "Can I share another thought I've been nervous about since we decided to be more than best friends?"

He slid his hand over her hair and studied her eyes.

Her words started slowly. "Is it okay if I'm not so good at being a girl in every way? Can you have patience with me? I know you're my best friend, and I know how close we are, but I think so much of you that I'm worried about not being all the girlfriend you should have. Everything is so new to me." Her eyes turned glassy. "The more I think about how great you are, the more afraid I am at not being enough..."

He smiled softly and shook his head. "Your understanding of your imperfections is what makes you perfect. But don't worry. You can experiment with me like I'll experiment with you. I've never really ever been anyone's real boyfriend either."

She wrapped her arms around him and held him. "Well, you're a pretty good boyfriend as far as I'm concerned."

It was hard to distinguish where the friendship hug ended and the dating hug began, but that's what made their relationship so special. It was late afternoon and parents would be coming home soon. Once again they decided to part, so she could turn back into her old self before they arrived. He walked her to the side door, feeling a bit more confident about their new relationship.

He turned to her at the door. "Does Steven want to play video games or something tonight?"

She smiled. "Sure."

He grinned at her response. "I'll text you after dinner." He leaned forward and kissed her and she eagerly returned the kiss. He watched her head across their driveways and disappear into the house next door.

CHAPTER SIX
ADAPTATION

Steven's phone rang on his bedroom end table and he grabbed it without opening his eyes. An excited voice on the other side spoke too loudly. "You up?"

He smiled softly. "Yes, alarm clock. I'm up."

"We meeting outside at seven twenty?"

"Yes, alarm clock, we're meeting outside at seven twenty, just like every school day for the last four semesters." The phone went silent and Steven placed it back on his end table and smiled as he slowly rose out of bed. He wandered still half asleep, down the hall toward the bathroom, and his morning shower.

"Good morning."

He turned around. "Hi Mom."

Genna smiled. "So glad I can see your smiling face more, now that school's started."

"Well, when you find it, let me know where it is. I lost it this morning."

"Very funny."

He wasn't upset school was starting. He loved school. He wasn't upset he had to get up early. He'd been waking in a great mood. He was upset he had to spend so much of his day as Steven and so much of that, in front of Jake, and he was determined to stay functionally asleep as long as he could this morning. By the time he put his back-pack on, he heard Jake start the bike. He quickly grabbed two cereal bars on his way to the door.

He was actually excited the new semester had started again, though way too tired to show it. He had gotten into a rhythm over the last few semesters and school was getting easier. He had also built a good reputation there and was sure the reputation helped with new professors and new grades.

He opened the door to see Jake sitting on the bike and already facing the street; his helmet on, ready to go. Steven slipped his other arm through his backpack as he walked up and took his helmet from Jake. "Man, why are you so anxious?"

"We got things to go and places to do, woman." He turned to make sure no one else heard. Steven put his helmet on and climbed on the back, slid his hands in Jake's jacket pockets and held on.

"Good?"

"Good."

They turned onto the street. Jake in front and Steven right behind him. Sixteen years and certain things hadn't changed.

Though Steven's schoolwork was almost flawless through the beginning of the semester, he was focused more on Stephie's immediate steps toward transitioning, and the more Stephie was around Jake, the more Steven yearned to be the female he finally accepted inside him. Jake's agenda also seemed to have a new focus. He now seemed even more intent on matching Steven's school success and Steven interpreted this new and deeper drive as yet another level of connection between them.

School was once again their primary attention, but they used it like they always had; as a reason to spend time together and enjoy each other's company. But Steven needed less time than most to produce excellent work, and when his schoolwork was done, Stephie found her brain wanting to learn more about the girl so long repressed inside.

Steven sat up straight at his bedroom desk, as he suddenly realized he hadn't registered a thing he read in the last ten minutes and closed the textbook. *I wonder if Vicky's working.* He dialed his new friend.

"Hey girlfriend,"

"Hi Vick. You working?"

"On my lunch slash dinner break. Why?"

"I just wanted to let you know how things went and see when I can come by your work and start learning how to do my make-up?"

He heard Vicky crunch on something. "Details first girlfriend. Details"

"Well, Jake called you a magician. He thought I was beautiful."

"Told you. Mind if I eat and talk?"

"No. Not at all."

"So, you want to learn how to do your make-up?"

Steven answered meekly, "Yes."

"I love your formal yesses. You're like a proper lady or something."

Steven laughed. "I know. I'm sorry."

"Nothing to be sorry about. It'll change as we get closer."

Steven smiled. "I'd like that."

"So would I. You're cute as a button! Make-up lessons can start as soon as you want. I'll send you my schedule by text. Weekdays during the day are my slowest. It's the best time for me to teach. Oh, I told my friends about you and they want to teach you some things too."

Steven's heart jumped at the confirmation; there were other things to learn. "Is any of it scary?"

"You have to be the most timid twenty year old on the planet. No. None of it's scary. Want us to help you?"

Steven answered instantly. "Yes. Sorry. Yeah."

Vicky chuckled. "So when do I meet this Jacob you can't stop talking about?"

Steven sat up straight. "Why don't the three of us have lunch one day this week?"

"Oh, that sounds fantastic, sister! Okay, I have to go."

"Okay Vicky. Talk to you soon?"

Vicky replied in a softer voice. "Of course sweetie. Bye."

Steven couldn't believe how soothing Vicky's voice always sounded. He smiled softly. *Every girl like me needs a girl like him.*

<p style="text-align:center">~~~</p>

The first school week flew by and their first class-free Friday arrived. Steph finally slept in, but when she woke and looked at the time, she sped up. She was thoroughly enjoying her new world and sleeping late interfered with better activities. She paused and listened. She could tell both parents were already gone, so she popped out of bed, skipped to the bathroom, and started filling the tub. There was something about a bath that registered feminine to her, and she loved when her free time allowed her to discover more about her new identity. She poured the bath oil into the water accumulating at the bottom of the tub and enjoyed the smell as she sat with her chin in her hands, smiling at nothing and staring at the slow rising liquid. Finally, she slipped off her T-shirt and stepped into the steamy fragrant bath.

As she soaked in the tub, she decided to pop in on Jake. Steven saw him nearly every day, but there was a yearning growing inside her to see him only as Stephanie. She had even begun to feel slightly uncomfortable with him seeing her as anyone but Stephanie, but they lived too close and their families were too close to avoid it. The feeling did make her want to overcompensate though, for those times he was there but she wasn't and Steven had to take her place.

She primped herself to the best of her abilities and fantasized about surprising him. When she was satisfied, she walked across the drives and knocked lightly on his kitchen door. No answer…and she knew he was home. His motorcycle was behind the steps, and his parents each had their cars at work. She figured there would be no harm going in unannounced. She had been in there alone countless times before. She removed the key from its hiding place and unlocked the door, "Jake?"

She waited, then heard iron clinking in the basement. It couldn't be Mr. Harrison. He never missed a day of work, and if he did, he wouldn't be working out. She walked to the top of the basement stairs. "Jake?"

She heard his voice. "Down here."

She walked down the stairs and into the musky air and instantly spotted Jake sitting sideways on the red plastic weight bench, glistening with sweat. She surveyed the exercise area, a little confused, a little amazed, and quickly becoming a little aroused. "Hi."

He watched her look around. "What's new?"

She noticed to her pleasant surprise, he was glistening with sweat. "I always thought these were your father's. I didn't know you lifted weights down here."

"I'm not as religious with it as I'd like to be." He stood up, grabbed the towel he kept on a crossbar of the bench, and as he negotiated the five steps toward her, wiped his face and chest. He stood away from her, leaned forward and kissed her. "I'm all sweaty."

Her heart jumped. "I don't mind." She watched him lower the towel and stared at it as if it was a secret prize.

He sat back down and nudged the short dumbbell with black metal weights on it between his feet, then bent down, picked up the bar with both hands and lifted it directly over his head. Her mouth unconsciously opened as she watched. Bending only his elbows, he let the bar drop behind his head then raised it straight up, and repeated the movements until he could no longer lift it and the bar became stuck behind his head. Her heart jumped, thinking he was in trouble, then watched him lean forward and drop the small bar from behind his shoulder to the ground. He stood and walked away; sucking air into his lungs, as sweat glistened on every uncovered part of his upper body.

She stood and went over to the small bar covered with black discs and wrapped her hand around the handle. The dumbbell didn't budge.

He watched her and grinned. "That's a little heavy. Be careful."

"How much does this weigh?

He rubbed his shoulder, "About eighty pounds."

He sat back down on the bench, lifted the weight over his head and repeated the exercise. He stood after dropping the weight, sucking air again; grabbed the towel and wiped his face and arms. She stood and held out her hand for the towel. "I'll do that for you."

He looked at her, his face flush red, "It's all sweaty, Steph."

Sure her voice would reveal her true intention. "I know." She didn't hesitate and took the towel from him, and its dampness immediately accelerated her heart. She forcefully controlled her instant need for additional oxygen and began wiping his chest. He sat and let her, and she wiped from his neck to his shoulders and down to the top of his stomach.

She moved behind him as he sat motionless but before she continued, she quickly brought the towel up close to her face and breathed in.

She wiped his back and moved away as he bent toward the weight. She sat down and watched in awe as he performed the exercise a third time, clutching the towel with both hands. If he had walked over to her at that moment and reached to drop her panties, she was sure she would have reached her pleasure threshold on the spot.

He spun toward her after he dropped the weight and offered with more breath than voice, "Sorry I'm not saying much."

"No. It's alright." Then she whispered as softly as she could, "It's so alright…" And as she said it, she discreetly pushed down on her lap, trying to inconspicuously hide how alright it was, but she didn't want to interfere with his concentration. Besides, she wanted this front-row-seat into the future.

"What does that exercise do?"

He smiled. "The back of my arms."

Her brows rose. "That's all?"

"Pretty much."

"When do you do your shoulders?" She calmed down enough to stand and towel off his shoulders again, which for all his body-parts, had the least perspiration.

"That's…" He thought for a few seconds, "…three days from now."

Her heart jumped. "Oh."

He did a double-take. "I like your outfit."

She sat straighter. "Thanks."

"…remind me to attack you when I'm cooled down and showered." He glimpsed at her through the corner of his eyes without turning his head fully toward her.

She replied softly, "It's okay if you don't want to wait."

He glanced at her, purposefully acknowledging her reply but made no further motion toward her. He offered her a consolation. "Seriously, you look beautiful.… What do you want to do today?"

She noticed his breathing increase as he turned to stare at her again. "I was thinking we could maybe watch a movie?" His focus lowered to her outfit and she realized what she was wearing. "Or maybe just listen to it?"

He smiled. "Whatever you want."

"Oh, Vicky wants to have lunch, just the three of us."

He moved to the back of the bench and started pulling down on the bar attached to a pulley with black metal disks on the other end; his chest straining, sweaty, and hard. She quietly sat up, loving this unscheduled show.

He released the bar. "Sure. That sounds like fun! How is he?"

She regained focus. "He's doing good. He's really cute, and we're becoming friends."

"That's great. I'm almost done." he reached for the pulley. "Another…three sets."

Her heart dropped as he said the words. It might kill him, but she could watch this all day. She eyed the towel. That towel was going to disappear.

"So when were you two thinking?"

"Sometime this week if you feel like it."

He grabbed the pulley again. "Sure. Let me know." He dropped the pulley for the last time and sat to cool off for a few minutes. She stood and slowly toweled him off. He leaned forward and kissed her.

"Okay. Shower time."

She sighed softly.

~ ~ ~

It didn't take them long to readjust to the routine of the semester and the natural integration of working the rest of their lives around it. Steven dialed his phone between school buildings as he headed to his next class. "Hi Vick."

"Hey hon!"

"Are you working today?"

"Yep. Eleven to seven."

"Well, Jake and I are free this afternoon. Can we visit and go to lunch together?"

"Oh, definitely! Let's do it! It'll make my day!"

"When's your lunch break?"

"I can take dinner any time between two-thirty and four-thirty."

Steph confirmed. "See you then?"

"Hope so!"

They spotted Vicky at the far end of the store aisle, as he turned and spotted them walking toward him, and he let out an overly enthusiastic welcome. "Oh, look at him. He's gorgeous. You go girlfriend."

Steven laughed out loud. The more he was around Vicky, the more his mannerisms tickled him. Steven could see inside him and for all the outside idiosyncrasies, there wasn't a more tender and goodhearted soul to be found. Jake didn't seem to mind the attention either. He didn't have a problem being found *hot* by anyone. He was confident and mature enough to be able to handle a compliment.

Steven hugged Vicky, then Vicky turned to Jake and Jake smiled and gave him a warm hug. "It's great to meet you."

Vicky gasped playfully. "Oh! That'll hold me for about a month. Oh my!"

He replied confidently. "Remind me to see you monthly so you don't run out."

"Hey!" Steven punched him on the shoulder then turned to Vicky, "Are you free yet?"

"Yes, darling. Let's go have lunch and gab like only girls can." He glanced at Jake. "Present company excluded."

Jake lowered his brows. "What makes you think I can't hang?"

"Oh my. I like this one." Vicky grabbed his bag and the three of them went to lunch in the mall. During their time together Vicky showed Jake, his willingness to help Stephanie for nothing more than friendship, and by the end of their hour together, he also saw Vicky's beautiful heart.

Vicky was becoming Stephie's window into a world which a short time ago wasn't easily accessible, and a friend who shared many secrets, tips and contacts. He also introduced her to a support network, though better hidden than a help group should ever be, and Stephie treasured the guidance, and became happily indebted to Vicky for it.

~~~

Genna stood at the entrance of the family room and slowly examined each nook. Her house was a source of great joy for her, and she liked nothing more than visiting every corner of every room, under the guise of her Saturday morning purpose. She usually spent her Saturday mornings cleaning and straightening her home from the beating it received while the three of them hurried through their weekdays, and though all three Blairs voluntarily assumed certain household chores, Genna of course, cleaned up after the *cleanings* her two men performed.

She tried to hide her inner need to revisit their chores, especially right after they were completed, but this activity had become her ritual. She did love paying attention to their efforts though. It was one of her silly joys. The mirrors they cleaned were never streak free. Bathroom countertops, straightened but not quite empty, and bedroom drawers almost fully shut. The kitchen would be fairly clean but they never seemed to wipe the counter top after the pots and pans were washed and she just couldn't figure out why they couldn't straighten the pillows, wherever they were. They both almost finished almost everything almost always.

She went around to each room. Nothing ever took long to make it a woman's definition of done and their efforts did make her chuckle inside. Her follow up became just another way of expressing her love for them, though she wondered what the place would look like if she wasn't able to add the finishing touches to everything.

She was in the bathroom quietly finishing Steven's latest effort and as she cleaned the clean mirror above the sink, noticed through the mirror, a cute but unrecognized bottle in the far corner on the upper edge of the tub. At first it didn't register and she had to glance at it three times before analyzing the item more closely through the mirror. She turned her head, not yet turning her body, examining further. It was a bottle of bath oil beads, but it wasn't any bath oil she owned. She rarely took a bath and had only one bottle of scented oil to her name; a gift from her niece Kelly.

She turned and approached it slowly, as if the object would suddenly disappear after being noticed, then gradually reached for the bottle. She brought the top to her nose, and tentatively inhaled the soft feminine fragrance. She paused for a moment and her eyes widened as she grasped its meaning, and instantly wished she hadn't picked it up. She inhaled and stared at it as if she was holding the key to a secret she wasn't supposed to learn; quickly turning to the door, afraid Steven might realize what he had left behind and suddenly appear and catch her with the evidence.

She gathered herself, breathed deep, and scanned the entire room, wondering where she should put the item so no one else would know her discovery but quickly realized; wherever she moved it to would be wrong. She looked around again, as her mind now focused on keeping a secret no one even knew she had. *Connor will never notice this exactly where it was, and even if he did, he would think it's mine. Even if he mentions it, I can always say it's mine.* Then she realized Steven would know she had spotted it, if it wasn't exactly where he accidentally left it.

She carefully placed the bottle back, even twisting it to face how she thought she discovered it, then examined the object like it was communicating with her. She inhaled and intently digested its message. It told her she would soon have mothering to do, in all its depths and complexities and she was grateful for the message it shared. The message would help her prepare.

~ ~ ~

Steven went through many subtle changes over the next several weeks, with the help of Vicky and her new network. Stephanie learned more about girls like her and what they can do to become more feminine. They gave her informal walking and talking lessons; even standing lessons. They shaped her eyebrows, and told her about electrolysis. She was letting her hair grow and the network was, by committee, trying different hair styles on her whenever she was around.

She became an expert at doing her make-up. She could do a daytime casual, a work, evening, clubbing, and even a bedroom version and when dressed now, looked like any other young woman out and about living life. But she wouldn't let them pierce her ears or paint her fingernails or toenails, and her refusal to take her new-found femininity to such a simple next level, upset them. They understood, but they wanted these simple feminine indulgences for her, as much as she quietly wanted them for herself.

But the depth of Steven's transformation had an additional, almost unnoticeable effect on another part of his being; his demeanor. The transition had started taking its toll on his psyche. Living unsafely between a male and a female had begun to increase his insecurities, and though he was sure his normal insecurities hid the additional anxieties, he soon found out otherwise as the topic came up in one of her and Vicky's many phone conversations. "Are you enjoying being outside in your new existence?"

Steven's voice reflected complete confirmation. "Of course."

But Vicky seemed to know better. "How come I'm not buying it? When was the last time you went out and did something normal, as a full blown girl? ...No pun intended."

Stephie could tell she was on the verge of a loving scolding. "I go out."

Vicky playfully interrogated. "You lying to me girl?"

She knew she was caught and caved way too quickly. "Well, I don't have anywhere to go! But I make myself up and dress as a girl whenever Jake and I are alone."

"That's your lame excuse? Well, as your teacher, I have your next assignment. You and Jake are going to take your cute girly ass outside, dressed all girly, until you start getting used to being out as a girl."

Steph smirked, then sighed. She knew Vicky was right and she quietly loved how Vicky cared enough to spot things like this.

"And I'm calling him and telling him that's what you're doing. So be prepared." Vicky paused for a second. "Hey. Do you dance?"

Steven's heart jumped. "Who? Me?"

"No! Yes, you! Who did you think I was talking to?"

"Not me." They both giggled.

"The hell I'm not. You don't dance?"

And Steph started whining. "Vicky, are you going to make me dance?"

"No sweet cheeks. I'm going to *teach* you how to dance. Or should I say *we're* going to teach you how to dance."

"Ugh."

"Don't *ugh* me. You'll love it!" Vicky's voice lowered, "Besides. You have no idea how sexy it can be with your man."

That caught Stephie's attention, and suddenly, all she could think about was teasing and rubbing against Jake on a dance floor. "Well, I'm pretty sure Jake never danced in his life either."

Vicky snickered. "How the hell would you know that?"

"Because I've been to every party he's ever gone to."

"Damn, are we going to have fun with you two. Dance lessons start in a week. It's a two credit course, and I'm your new professor."

Steven offered one last plea. "Couldn't I just do a term paper or something?"

"Don't give me no shit, girl! I'll flunk your ass!" They both giggled.

"Yeah, well either I get extra credit for telling Jake, or *you* have to tell him."

Vicky held his ground. "No extra credit and no passing until you're dancing *and* having fun at the same time. Same goes for your hunk."

Steven sung his response. "He ain't going to like it."

And Vicky sung back, "Oh yes, he will!"

For the next two days, all Stephie could think about was dancing with Jake.

Jake looked up from his notes and rested both forearms on the light blue library tabletop. "I can't dance."

Steven moved the textbook from his lap to the table and immediately started selling. "Neither can I, but I'm telling you…he swears it's fun."

Jake playfully pleaded. "Not if you're sure you're making an ass of yourself."

"Oh, would you knock it off." Steven's wide eyes and teasing smirk met Jake's shocked eyes across the table. "You won't make any more of an ass out of yourself than you already are."

Jake pointed at him. "Hey!" They both laughed.

Steven continued to push the idea. "It'll take us like three or four times before we're ok, but then I think we'll like it. I think it would be fun, and I want to do it with you."

"Four times?"

Steven heard the teasing in his voice and playfully begged, "Please? I'm telling you. We can have fun with it. Besides, Vicky's friends are a blast, and this could be something we do every once in a while with everyone." He sat up and softly pleaded. "Jake! We sit home like two old people. We have to go out and *do* something."

Jake shut his book and studied his eyes. "I thought you liked sitting at home."

Steven leaned forward. "I do, but Steven hid inside. Stephanie needs to stop hiding and try things."

Jake countered. "You owe me one."

He lowered his chin and looked deeply into Jake's eyes. "I'll pay you back as many times as you want and you know it."

Jake smiled. "How many times do I have to do it and suck at it before I don't have to do it anymore?"

Steven responded calmly as he lowered his eyes back down into his textbook. "Talk to Vicky."

CHAPTER SEVEN
INTEGRATION

Over the next weeks, Genna began seeing the changes in her child and even noticed Steven not around as much as she had become used to. She watched like a concerned loving mother, torn between wanting him to confide in her, and giving him enough space to do what he needed and wanted to do.

She loved her child, of which there was no doubt. She loved her child unconditionally. No achievements necessary. No requisites. But she had no paradigms on how to address the situation she was witnessing. She started calling Steven on the phone, as a way for them to stay as close as they had always been, and allow him to adjust without either of them losing their connection. His new situation had nothing to do with her desire for an airtight bond with him. In her mind, there could be no disconnect. She would rather be dead than disconnected from him.

She wondered if he worried she wouldn't love him as much, if he didn't meet certain social criteria. *Is he worried I'll see him as anything less than I have always seen him? Ah, children…sometimes they're too young to understand who can love beyond requisites…beyond judgement.* Her love for him existed, only because he existed. Not love because he does something or doesn't do something. In fact, her love couldn't be broken. He could hate her and her love for him would not be one filament less than total. And not one inkling less effort would she give to help him or protect him. Her definition of unconditional and complete had been set in the stone of her being.

Genna removed the baked potatoes from the toaster oven and placed one on each of the two plates on the table, then set the small casserole dish between them. "Connor. Dinner."

Connor turned the corner into the kitchen. "Smells marvelous. Want ice tea?"

"Sure."

He grabbed two glasses, then the ice tea pitcher from the fridge.

"Sweetheart?" She sat and waited for him to sit. "I want to run a thought by you."

He glanced at her as he poured her drink. "Sure. What?"

She smirked. "You know I have a bad habit of prefacing certain conversations."

"Yeah. We've been together a long time." And with a preface to a preface, he met her eyes more than usual as he began fixing his plate.

She started. "I know you love Steven."

He laughed. "Of course I love Steven. I think he's a beautiful person."

"But would you make a conscious effort to show him complete love, if he was less than your definition of a beautiful person, as you've so qualified it?" She knew his qualification didn't carry the significance she gave it. She even knew the answer to what she was asking, but she needed to make sure he was aware of the weight of his words.

He thought for a second. "I'd like to believe I separated the two sentences, but you've made your point." He clarified his statement. "Let me better separate the two sentences. I love Steven. I not only love him because I've found him to have a good soul, but since you've brought it to my attention, I'll add; I believe I have true love for him. Why?"

She smiled playfully. "I'm not done my inquiry. So...you would love him separate from him meeting certain social standards?" She wanted to use different words but thought they would give too much away.

He glanced up. "Yes."

Her tone was casual though her words were substantial. "Would that love include supporting him in ways which would be new to you if it fit his world?"

He thought for a minute, as if to show he was not taking the inquiry lightly. "Yes, I would. I love my child."

She continued. "Which means you would love him through actions, and not just words? You would be part of his world as you've made him part of yours?"

He eyed her deeply and smiled in a way that revealed a greater understanding. "Sweetheart, he's as much my child as he is yours. Yes, I'm a guy, which often makes my focus far narrower than yours, but it's only narrower, not blind. I love Steven. I don't care who Steven is or becomes. He'll always be the baby who brought tremendous joy to us, and I believe he came here counting on one thing and one thing only; that we would be here for him while we could. We brought him into this world without pretense. To make one now would be our greatest failure and our greatest shortcoming." He paused and smiled. "I can still see clear mental pictures of him at certain ages in my head with little to no effort, and every mental picture is pure joy. I could sit and cuddle with him at age twenty, like I could when he was six. It's he who no longer wants to cuddle, not me. But I still have the exact same love. That doesn't change."

Her voice became softer. "It doesn't, does it?" She lowered her fork to the table next to her plate, and sighed. "I miss cuddling with him too. His contact fed my soul." She looked directly into his eyes, "So you've seen the soft changes?"

He met her eyes. "Yeah, I have."

"And you're alright?"

He chuckled. "Yeah, sweetheart, I am."

His assurance sent light goosebumps over her shoulders and down her arms and she paused as they ran their course.

He took another bite and looked at her. "Has he said anything to you?"

"No. And I haven't to him. I want to. I want to take him in my arms and hold him and tell him I want to carry him through all his troubles, but I also want to give him the room he needs, to do what he needs to do, and come to me when he's ready to come to me. It's an awful taffy-pull in my heart."

She breathed deep, then her entire countenance brightened. "But that doesn't mean I can't pave the ground he hasn't walked on yet." She leaned forward. "I'm going to invite Chris and Morgan over for dinner. I think the four of us need to make sure who's on what page, and that's best done when odds favor our opinion." Her excitement grew. "And we're already two against two at worst, so I like our odds."

He met her smile. "You're a wonderful mother, and the love of my life. Thank you for your love of our child. You love like you do everything, which never ceases to amaze me."

She stood and walked around the table, and he moved his chair out to accommodate her. She sat on his lap and slipped her arms around his neck. "I love you the same way."

He wrapped his arms around her. "I count on it. It's my one calm in a world of storm. I love with all my heart, but I know I don't love as deeply as you." They kissed like friends, but it quickly turned into a lovers' kiss. After a moment, she stood and returned to her seat, and they casually enjoyed the rest of their dinner.

During her coffee break at work the next morning, Genna sent Morgan a text. *Hey! Want to come to dinner Sat nite? The 4 of us. Drink 2 much wine together?*
Moments later, she received Morgan's reply. *Hell yea! U got din. I got the wine.*
And Genna confirmed. *7 ish or whatever ...like norm ...k?*
Definitely!
...C u then.

~~~

The date had been set for a week but now that the day had arrived, Steven wasn't as comfortable with the idea as when he agreed to it, and Jake's restlessness wasn't helping. Jake and Steven drove to Vicky's apartment, but Jake and Stephanie were going dancing with Vicky, so both knew there would be a delay before they were on their way.

He handed Steven her all too familiar video game bag, now concealing far more adult things as they entered Vicky's living room, and sat on Vicky's sofa without a word.

Steven and Vicky discreetly made eye contact as they watched him try to make himself comfortable; not realizing he was nervously excited by the idea he was finally going on a real date with Stephanie.

Vicky pointed to the table, "The remote's right there honey. Help yourself." and took Steven's free hand as they walked toward his bedroom and disappeared together. A while later, Stephanie came out looking like a model, in a glistening short gold skirt and matching cowl halter top, perfect make-up and shiny black high heels. And when Jake saw her, he exhaled, as if his heart melted, then smiled and stood up.

Vicky immediately yelled, "Damn!"

Stephie laughed and exclaimed, "I just won us a round of drinks!"

Jake squinted at her, confused, but she offered no further explanation as he approached his girlfriend and gave her a hello kiss.

"You two ready?"

Stephie met Jake's eyes, then both turned toward Vicky but neither offered a response. Jake looked as intimidated as Stephie felt and she felt as intimidated as a twenty year old could feel. Vicky smiled, "We're meeting friends at the club." He studied them and gently shook his head. "Listen, all of this is going to be a little overwhelming tonight, but just try to relax. I promise you're going to have a good time if you just relax, and I promise I'll take care of both of you."

Stephie's heart beat a mile a minute as she sat in the car. She had never been so *feminine* in front of this many people or so close to as many people as she thought she was going to be tonight. The ride was short but right now she wished the place was three hours away. Finally, the anticipation and the car ride reached a release point. "Are you sure I look…passable?"

Both Vicky and Jake responded at the same time, "Oh honey. Yes."

"Sweetheart, you look fantastic."

She turned her head past Vicky, to Jake in the back seat, then back to Vicky, searching for reassurance in their faces as they responded. She felt exhilarated, and so different; elated yet unbelievably nervous. A short while later the tall trees lined against the road opened up and the car slowed and turned into the all but hidden gravel lot behind them, and her heart jumped.

A lone building sat at the back, off to one side of the opening, surrounded by another wall of tall trees that appeared almost eerie in the faintly lit darkness. The strung white lights on the wood porch stretched from one end of the front of the building to the other, making the building glow in the night, and the only other light that could be seen from inside the opening was a single dim street light at the other end of the expansive clearing.

Vicky pulled into a parking spot and three doors opened into the hazy still night. As Stephie stepped out, her lead leg nearly buckled from the anxiety. Jake lurched toward her and reached for her arm. "You okay?"

She peered into his eyes, not sure how to respond. They walked together toward the overhang and the two bouncers at the double metal doors, and the intensity of this new experience increased with every step closer.

Vicky whispered, "I went out with him." He pointed to one of the behemoths guarding the door. "Oh. There's Alyssa and Tyler." Vicky shouted toward them. "Hi."

Two people on the porch, leaning against the wood railing, turned and waved. "Hi."

Stephie knew them. They were two of the people Vicky had recruited to help with the Stephanie project and were noticeably excited to see how she looked tonight.

Vicky walked toward them and extended his arms. "It's great to see you."

"You too." They hugged and kissed, then Alyssa turned to Stephanie. "Oh. You look adorable. Oh, I'm pleased." She turned to her friend. "We need to go into business."

They both hugged and kissed Stephie and then Vicky offered, "And this is Jake. He's our next project."

Jake greeted them with a 'hi' and a friendly smile but his face changed as Vicky's statement registered. They turned and headed to the door and the two gargantuan men guarding it.

"Hi Desmond."

A deep resonating voice replied, "Hi Vick. How are you?"

Vicky smiled as Desmond's voice reverberated through the group. "Good. You?"

"Excellent today."

He checked their ID's and when he reached Jake, glanced up and Vicky affirmed, "They're with me."

He took their cover charge, and stamped the back of their hands.

Jake entered the building and as he walked out of Desmond's earshot, turned to the group. "He's huge!"

Vicky responded to him loud enough for the entertainment of the entire group. "Let me tell you sweetie. He's more huge than you can imagine. …Scared the shit out of me."

Tyler and Alyssa laughed. Jake kind of smiled. Stephanie didn't quite understand.

Vicky turned to Tyler. "Where's Mike and Lisa?"

"They went in ahead of us to get us a table."

"Oh good. Text them. I'll go to the bar and get us drinks."

He turned to Steph and Jake and screamed over the beginning of a new song. "Follow them. I'll go get us drinks."

"Hi everyone." Alyssa and Tyler introduced Stephie and Jake to Mike and Lisa and after the greetings, Lisa and Mike went right to the dance floor. The place was dark, crowded and loud and Jake had Stephie's hand and was bouncing to the beat. He caught her eye and Stephie stared in bewilderment at him.

"What? I kinda like it."

She leaned next to his ear. "Who *are* you?"

"Hey, look at all these people. Who the hell is going to notice us two?"

He leaned toward her and gave her a kiss. It was the first time he kissed her with so many people around, and her heart fluttered.

The crowd was young and far more mixed than the community the club was in and everyone seemed to be having a great time. Vicky came back with three beers and two white wines at the same time Lisa and Mike came off the dance floor. Everyone at the table shared introductions again, then Vicky told everyone Jake and Stephanie have never danced and the table went crazy telling them they were going to get one intense lesson tonight.

By the end of drink one, Stephie was feeling more relaxed and started edging Jake onto the dance floor, when Alyssa grabbed Jake's hand and Vicky grabbed Stephie's and the whole group rose and headed toward it. Jake started out more willing, but to everyone's surprise, Stephie was a natural and started moving incredibly well, and incredibly feminine. After a few moments, she noticed the entire group watching her and felt herself slowly turn red, with a big grin on her face.

Tyler leaned toward Jake and yelled over the music, "Watch."

Tyler went up to Stephie and started slowly moving with her and inching closer until they were touching front to front, and Stephie immediately let Tyler lead and matched his rhythms. Alyssa went over to Jake and grabbed his arm, "Your turn." and started copying Tyler and Stephie. Stephie turned to watch Jake and Tyler grabbed her hips and continued the dance with her now facing away from him. He sensually pressed against her from behind; intermittently running his hands down her sides and then slowly raising them until they were over his head. Vicky went up to the front of her and made her the middle of a playful sandwich, while Alyssa danced against Jake, facing away from him. The third song ended and everyone sat down. Jake and Stephie linked as soon as everyone else let go of them; each the other's lifeline.

Lisa leaned toward them. "So what do you think?"

"Stephie volunteered quickly, "Fun!"

Alyssa pointed her finger between both of them. "Oh Yeah. Wait till the two of you get a rhythm together. You'll be hooked."

Mike leaned in. "Damn Steph. You can move. Where'd you learn that?"

"No clue!" But to her surprise, she felt unexpectedly sexy and free for her first time in a crowd. A crowd. People. No one judging. No one caring. Everyone just having fun. Hell, no one even noticing anyone else. She looked around and smiled. "I could get used to this."

Lisa placed both hands on the table, "Well, we didn't come here to sit." and everyone heeded her prompt and headed back to the dance floor. The group danced every combination possible, including Jake and Vicky. Both teased the other as much as possible and everyone thoroughly enjoyed their playful clowning.

When they returned to the table for a breather, Jake leaned toward Vicky. "Is it time for your monthly hug?" and Stephie jokingly smacked him on his shoulder. He grabbed her around her waist and pulled her in for a soft kiss and she immediately melted.

After a few minutes of recuperation, Vicky secretly caught Alyssa's attention, raised an eyebrow and gave the softest nod. She grabbed Stephie's hand, and a moment later Alyssa grabbed Jake's and the four of them rose. When they walked around the table, Vicky put Stephie's hand in Jake's and grabbed Alyssa's, and let Jake and Stephie walk in front of them toward the dance floor. Jake's nerves formed his uncontrollable grin and Stephie's mind overwhelmed her with different feelings, but when they turned to each other, her mind instantly cleared, and she started moving in front of Jake like a young seductress.

His eyes gleamed and the smile lighting his face told her he was more than pleased with what he was looking at, and the feeling coursed through her being. At that moment, she was female. Every part of her outside and inside had for the first time become the same and the conversion registered in the deepest recesses of her soul.

She moved closer to him and softly brushed against him, teasing him… teasing her. She wanted to feel him as much as she knew he wanted to feel her, and she moved closer until they were softly front to front, and though he was slightly stiff, her movements against him were perfectly fluid and natural. She could feel his breathing deepen, just like her breathing had deepened and when she felt his hands caress her waist, she swayed her head back and let his electricity flow through her. Their legs teasingly intertwined and their slow matched rhythm made her feel like she had never felt before. She was in a place she had never experienced and it was nothing short of electrifying.

They danced until her thighs couldn't hold her any more. She stopped and grabbed Jake's hand, and without a word, led him off the dance floor. They fell into their chairs next to each other, breathing heavily and grinning in complete satisfaction.

Tyler motioned toward the dance floor looking at Jake. "You getting used to it yet?"

Jake leaned forward. "It might take me a few visits, but I like its potential."

Tyler smiled and nodded in agreement.

~~~

Chris and Morgan knocked on the side door and opened it yelling, "Hi!" They were expected and they were well past the point in their relationship, where they would wait to be let in.

They heard a faint "hi" come from the family room and walked toward it, and as they walked past the dining room, Chris playfully bellowed, "Oh! …A *dining* room dinner." Genna loved when he acknowledged the connection he had with her. She was just proper enough for him to have his definition of 'ammunition' to tease her, and she fully enjoyed the game that accompanied their friendship. "If I had known, I wouldn't have brought this domestic beer."

Genna fired back. "Yes, you would. Who you kidding?"

She loved playing up to him in his little teases. Her outfit for the evening was an excellent example. She had on a simple casual dress. Chris and Morgan both wore jeans for an occasion like this and Morgan wouldn't think of wearing a dress unless someone was getting married or had died. Connor rarely wore jeans either. He was always in casual pants, but rarely jeans. Their outer differences were always celebrated, but their inner qualities and standards were the only things which truly mattered to any of them.

Chris walked in with the six-pack in his left hand and shook Connor's hand. Morgan stopped at the family room wall, caught Genna's attention, "I'll get us a glass of wine." and returned to the kitchen.

Chris held up the beer to Connor. "Want one?"

"Yeah, but not one of those. Want one of mine?"

"No, I'm good."

Connor stood up and headed toward the basement fridge. Morgan finally came back, handed Genna her wine glass, and sat on the loveseat in the spot she had come to claim over the years. They enjoyed each other's company in the family room until dinner was ready and then ate, drank and laughed at the dining room table. Finally the conversation got around to the kids.

"Can you believe they're coming to the end of their second year?"

Morgan glanced up from her plate. "No, I am *not* that old." They laughed.

Morgan reached for her glass. "I understand they're both doing excellent."

Genna sipped her wine. "And we have twenty first birthday parties to plan on their break."

"Did they pick their four year school yet? Oh my god, I just said that like it was a done deal." Morgan waited for Genna to look up. "Sorry. I don't know that. Whatever they decide. I don't care."

Connor joined. "I'd be surprised if they don't choose to go the rest of the way together."

Genna placed her glass down. "So would I. Can you believe they've been together since kindergarten?"

Morgan smiled. "I know. It's so cute, isn't it? Do you remember them standing at the bus stop together? They were so small. What happened?"

Genna's reaction reflected her recall of the memory. "It's been fantastic watching them grow up together." Her voice mirrored her sentiment. "I know how much you both love Steven."

Chris glanced up quickly. "I love that kid."

Genna smiled, "No qualifications?" glancing at Connor without explanation.

Chris confirmed his construction-worker mentality and accompanying commitment. But she pushed further, "What if Steven was suddenly...different?"

Chris laughed. "I don't care if the kid turns purple or grows another head."

Morgan studied Genna. "Why would you ask that? You know we adore him."

Genna met Morgan's eyes and the look let Morgan know it was only her patented preface. Genna was only leading into something she didn't feel like just blurting out.

Morgan put her fork down. "Is he alright?"

Genna gazed softly at her. "He's fine. But Connor and I think he's going through some changes and we wanted to see if you two are okay with what we think we see."

"What? Did he ask you to co-sign for a gun permit?" Chris sat up and smiled at Morgan's scowl. "What?" Morgan stared at him, then turned back to Genna.

Genna sighed. "We've noticed he's adjusted certain things about himself and his clothing which leads us to believe he may have come to certain realizations about who he is, and though he hasn't said anything to either of us, he came from me and I read him like he's from me."

Genna and Connor shared the things they had observed.

Chris placed his fork next to his plate. "Oh, Christ! I thought the kid had joined a frigging cult or something." And in Chris's fashion, blurted out, "Who gives a shit. If he's happy, I'm happy. I don't care what he is."

Morgan added, "So...is he alright?"

"I think so. He seems to be, though he's keeping things secret right now. But seriously, he's my baby."

Morgan murmured her agreement.

Chris reached for his beer. "Does Jake know?"

Morgan turned to him. "Jake *must* know." Then faced Genna, "Do you know if Jake knows?"

Genna tilted her head. "They're together almost every day. Jake must know and it doesn't seem like it matters at all to him. Your son is…I love your son." Genna's eyes grew glassy.

Morgan tilted her head and offered. "I love your son too. There's no difference and there hasn't been for a long long time."

Genna inhaled. "Can you love him unconditionally?"

Morgan's straightened in her chair. "Oh, absolutely. I'm a woman and a mother. It's the *only* way I can love one of my children. How do we make him understand we don't care who or what he is?"

Genna stared at the tabletop. "I don't know yet. It's the wonderful thing about being a mother, isn't it?" She looked up. "Sometimes you don't quite know how to handle something you want to fix yesterday for your child."

Morgan poured her more wine and Genna thanked her with a soft smile.

"Well, I think this is fantastic." Chris reached for his beer and sat back. "I mean, if the child has found himself, then hooray for him. Life's too short and he has all the life-lines he could need." He met Genna's soft stare. "…and whatever *you* need, you let us know. You're like a sister to me."

Genna felt his words once again confirm a commitment she had learned to count on. He was her brother and had been for years. She smiled at Chris to let him know nothing meant more to her than words like the ones he had just spoken. She knew his words were gold.

He leaned forward and shook his head. "I love your Italian food." He took another mouthful of pasta.

Connor finally spoke. "Hey, the kids' birthdays are coming up. Man, they're both twenty-one this year. Can you believe it?"

He didn't say much, but his statement set a better tone for the rest of the evening as they drank and planned birthdays for both their kids.

~ ~ ~

Stephie and Jake had more fun dancing than they ever thought possible, which made the night go by faster than they expected. After the long evening ended, the group decided to head out, and walked together slowly to the front doors; certain people tired, others a little achy. They hugged and shivered their goodbyes on the outside porch, in the cool damp night, and Vicky Steph and Jake headed back to Vicky's apartment.

Vicky turned the car onto the road. "So, what do you think?"

Stephie beamed. "That may have been the best thing I ever did. Well..."

Vicky glanced in his rear view mirror at Jake. "Well, I guess it's time to raise your game." Then he laughed.

Jake had his head back. "That was fun, wasn't it? And where the hell did you learn to move like that? Wow!"

Stephie smiled ear to ear. "I have no clue." She hopped in her seat and turned to Vicky, "How often do you go dancing?"

"Why? You want to do it again already?"

"Yeah." Her immediate response brought another grin to Vicky's face.

Vicky pulled up to his apartment and the three of them got out and met at the front of his car to hug goodbye, then all three realized; Stephie couldn't go home like that. They laughed and went in. Stephie quickly changed to Steven, and they were once again ready to leave.

"So, are you two alright?"

"Oh Vick. I had the best time and you're a doll." Steven and Vicky hugged like sisters.

Jake smiled and hugged Vicky. "You're awesome."

"Thanks. Talk to you soon. Be careful going home."

Jake and Steven got into the cold car and Steven waited until they were moving, to whisper half to Jake, half to the passenger door, "Oh, I wish I could stay Stephanie." He folded his arms and covered himself like he was cold even though he wasn't. "I would've loved to stay Stephanie tonight." He sighed. "I had a blast."

"Could you dance like that as Steven?"

Steven snapped his head toward Jake. "I don't think so."

Jake laughed. "Steph, you were incredible. Seriously. In heels? I didn't think you could walk in them, let alone dance."

Steven perked up. "Well, believe me, Vicky and the others have been giving me serious girl lessons, so it wasn't all natural. But wow, I had a great time."

"You looked phenomenal. I mean, wear that dress more often."

Steven's mouth twisted. "Do you mind Stephie not being here to go home with?"

Jake sighed then smiled. "Not as much as you think."

When Jake parked, he leaned over and kissed Steven softly. It caught Steven off guard and his heart jumped. He didn't know what to say. He smirked and pointed toward his lap. "Sheer black lace." …opened the door quickly and ran toward his kitchen door.

Jake rolled down the window. "That's mean!"

~ ~ ~

The short distance between the two houses was always appreciated but never as much as when the four of them spent an evening eating and drinking together. Morgan broke the silence as she stood behind Chris, patiently waiting for him to unlock their kitchen door. "Do you think Jake knows?"

He struggled to find the keyhole on the dark porch. "Of course Jake knows. They're best friends."

She broke the next momentary pause. "You don't think Jake and Steven…"

Chris turned toward her with one eyebrow raised. "You have a problem with that?"

His response surprised her. "You don't?

He shook his head and smiled. "No."

"Well…" She hesitated. "I'm not sure."

He stopped for a moment but didn't turn toward her. "Sweetheart, I couldn't care less what they're doing when they're alone. I want them each to find happiness. And either you're okay with them finding happiness or you have a problem with them not meeting some contrived social standard in your mind." He finally found the keyhole.

She whispered to his back. "No…I'm fine."

He looked at her over his shoulder. "Are you sure?" He hesitated, and waited for her response. When she didn't offer one, he continued, "The fact that you brought it up makes me think you're not sure." He pushed the door open and as it swung away, reached for the handle to re-shut it and turned to her on the outer concrete landing. "Do you need to think about whether you're fine or not?"

She didn't know what to think. "I'm sure it's not even worth thinking about."

He responded instantly. "But this isn't something you can easily pass off. This is what life's about." He took a deep breath of night air. "People are spending way too much time and effort trying to make other people meet their contrived level of social conduct, and I think it's bullshit. Don't you think it's time we stop putting our social bullshit on others?"

A silent pause accompanied the cool night air, and she watched his upper body expand in the dark and then heard him release his breath. "They're two twenty-one year olds. Aren't twenty-one year olds allowed to fool around, like twenty-one year olds have been doing since the beginning of time? Like you and I did, when we were twenty-one?"

"Well, of course. Yes." She crossed her arms as she began feeling the chill in the night air, but Jake was probably inside and this conversation needed to be done outside his awareness.

"We have a saying in construction; *what's it matter to you if I'm doing chickens?* Would you have a problem if they were genetic boy and girl?"

"Of course not. That's a stupid question."

"Ah, not really." He opened his arms and motioned to her. She stepped into his arms and he rubbed her back as he hugged and kissed her. "And I hope you can get past any delineation so you can see them for what they are; just two people who care for each other. The level doesn't matter."

She shivered in his arms, but not from the cold. The level did matter to her, and the thought disturbed her. She decided to let the conversation pass without feeding it though, and waited for him to finish.

"Even temporarily, it's special, and we all need to stop the bullshit which makes it anything but special. Because when two people caring for each other is worse than other completely socially accepted activities like war, corporate greed and religious hate, then inner beliefs need to be re-questioned and re-evaluated."

He continued to rub her back. "Now let's go take the chicken out of the closet and the three of us fool around."

She smacked him on the back of his head as he kissed her again, and he moaned "oww" in her open mouth.

~~~

Steven and Jake didn't really talk before their first class. They never made it with much time to spare, though they always made it. They were both twenty and in certain ways, their age showed. The bike didn't offer much of a chance to talk either, so when they met after their initial class, they were truly greeting each other for the first time each day. One of their better schedule ideas was to leave the second class period open, in case any homework or an upcoming test needed last minute attention. They met at the same lunch table every school day and they always set up their books for a study lunch, but today, Steven was quieter than normal.

Finally he shared. "I can't stop thinking about dancing the other night."

Jake perked up. "Me either. I had a blast."

"No. I'm talking about how it ended."

Jake studied him with slightly narrowed eyes. "I thought it ended great."

Steven stared at him without saying anything and Jake felt an immediate apprehension. His eyes narrowed. "Is everything okay?"

"I just wanted..." Steven stopped for a second and looked around. He had Jake's full attention. "I just can't wait for the time when we can end an incredible night as boyfriend and girlfriend."

Jake's voice softened. "It's alright."

Steven countered dejectedly. "No, it isn't. I wanted to be your girl all the way to the end."

Jake leaned forward and whispered, "Steph." He looked around. "You *are* my girl. I thought you understood."

Steven took a small breath. "Well...."

"Well what?"

Steven breathed deeper. "Well, it's…hard."

"What's hard? Tell me what you're thinking." Jake's breathing quickened.

Steven scanned the room again. "I…I just really like when I can be female. And I wish I could look the part more…more often, I mean…or when we go out, I could stay a girl the whole time. Does that make sense?"

Jake closed his book on his index finger. "Yeah. But I'm trying to show you I'm okay with you doing what you have to do. Us doing what we have to do."

"No. It's not you." Steven lowered his stare. "The whole back and forth thing is starting to get to me."

Jake eyed Steven quietly, trying hard not to show an opinion one way or the other. "You thinking you don't want to do it anymore?"

Steven's head shifted back. "No. Oh god no. Just the opposite."

Jake grinned. He had decided he was there for Steven and he was there to show it, and though he really did like Stephanie a lot, he cared enough for Steven, to understand it wouldn't be fair to influence such an important decision.

Steven watched him and his eyes widened. "You want me to be Stephanie too." He looked around; sure he had said it too loud. Steven leaned forward and spoke softer. "Well, I want to be Stephanie more than you want me to be Stephanie. And I had such a terrific time as Stephanie the other night, I was mad I had to change back to…this…before we were done with the night. I wanted to…" He glanced down.

Jake reached for him and then drew his hand back, but the movement made Steven look up.

"I didn't get to end the night like I wanted."

Jake shrugged his shoulders. "Well, we don't have a choice right now."

Steven sighed and stared at him. "Just because I know that, doesn't mean I'm okay with it. I need to do something to make me alright with how the night ended."

"Okay. What?"

Steven whispered. "Can we have a date Friday during the day…you and me…alone?"

Jake leaned forward, rubbed his hands together, and whispered like a giddy six year old. "Me and Stephanie …alone?"

Steven smiled. "Yes. You and Stephanie…alone."

"Oh, goody goody goody."

Steven couldn't hide his change in demeanor. "You're an idiot."

Jake reopened his book. "What's your point?"

Steven stared down into his textbook. The softest satisfied smile on his face.

Jake broke the next extended silence. "I have a paper I have to write by then, but it's no problem." Then shook his head slightly and confessed. "God, I love when you ask me out on a date. It's so frigging sexy."

Steven lit up a little more.

"But relax, will you? We'll get there. I promise. You looked gorgeous by the way. I mean, seriously. Frigging gorgeous. I caught guys checking you out."

Steven quickly looked up. "No way."

"I swear. Guys were checking your ass out."

"Well…" He smirked. "Right now, it's covered with little pink hearts on a light purple background."

Jake shook his head. "That's still mean."

They both grinned and buried their faces in their textbooks.

～～～

The morning was Genna's definition of gorgeous. She loved the rain and loved driving in it, but the soft pounding on the car roof and the lack of anything interesting on the road were putting her to sleep. She woke much earlier than normal, due to the sales appointment in the remote town, and now figured she had better do something to stay awake. She picked up her phone and dialed her mother. "Hey, Mom."

Her mother offered her normal response in a wonderfully soothing tone. "Cara."

Genna's tone lightened. "Want to have lunch together tomorrow?"

Genna visited her mother nearly every other week, but they tried to make a lunch date as often as possible. They had developed a simple understanding;

Lorraine let Genna schedule lunches around work. Lorraine didn't mind even the most instant of requests as long as she had enough time to prepare, but she caught the subtle difference. "Does this count as a lunch date?"

"I wish it didn't mom, but yes, it does. I'm sorry."

"Oh no cara. I'm just teasing you. I don't care where I see you, only how often I see you."

Lorraine was witty, kind and more intelligent than was good for her, since there was a time when her intelligence was a little threatening to the men she interacted with. It didn't hurt she was exceptionally well built with light green eyes and light brown hair. When she finally met her equal, she and Robert fell in love almost instantly and after a short engagement and quick marriage, set off to conquer the world together…and they pretty much succeeded. She had a beautiful house and car and a bank account which allowed her not to have to worry financially another day in her life, but they had offered their share of risk and worry as compensation.

Everything about Lorraine was noticeable though, and she still carried herself with enormous confidence and grace. She was elegant, but she also loved with soft humility and made no one feel less than her. And Genna had learned well from her mom; grace, humility, loyalty, confidence…and how to feed anyone. And she inherited a few remarkable traits also; a soft heart and a highly intelligent mind. Genna also had a keen business sense, but didn't quite have the taste for business her mother and father had. She watched them work and worry too much to want to sacrifice other things she found more fulfilling.

"I'll be in your area tomorrow. I thought I'd pick up something nice and bring it over. Okay?" It was a lie that would be safe. She was making a special trip on Steven's behalf.

"I'll cook cara."

"Mom, you're awesome but no. It'll take nothing for me to pick up something someone else cooks, I just want to sit and talk. Okay? Please?"

Lorraine responded with love, grace, and only the slightest hint of a cook's disappointment.

"You're right. It's a better idea."

Genna smiled at her mother's graciousness, but she wasn't giving in. She had decided it was time to start mothering Lorraine every once in a while. "What do you want? Anything special?"

Lorraine perked up. "Yeah. I could go some nice sushi."

"Great choice! I'll see you around one? Okay?"

"See you then my beloved."

~ ~ ~

Jake was still sound asleep next door when his mother looked in on him. He'd been up late the night before completing a school project and hadn't gotten to bed until after midnight. Morgan quietly opened his bedroom door wider to take a better peek at him, as she readied for work. Chris turned the hallway corner as she shut Jake's door, and whispered, "What you doin?"

She whispered back as she finished closing the door as quietly as possible. "Looking at my son. I haven't seen him in a while. We haven't seen Steven lately either."

He grabbed his coffee and leaned toward her to kiss her goodbye. "So tell them dinner's over here tonight. You're their mother. They won't have a problem with it. Gotto go. Love you."

He headed out the kitchen door, as she poured herself a cup of coffee.

Forty minutes later, she gave one last peek down the hall in the hopes of saying goodbye to Jake before she left for work. No such luck.

~ ~ ~

Steven had set the alarm for eight but popped awake well before it went off with a big grin on his face, and a moment later realized it wasn't the only thing he woke up with. He laid there feeling unbelievably excited about the day. He had worked on his schoolwork fairly late last night and was ready for a day of just him and Jake. Well, Stephanie and Jake. *I wonder if Jake has to lift today. I should encourage him to lift every day.* On a normal day those thoughts and the state he awoke would have led to another activity, but there was a chance that would take care of itself later as well. He waited until he calmed down before leaving his room and met his father in the hallway on his way to the bathroom.

"Good morning son." Connor grabbed him around his neck and kissed him on the side of his head. "How are ya?"

"Good, Dad. You?"

"Your hair's getting long."

He loved his father's subtlety. Chris would have told him; *get a haircut*. Not Connor. But the words meant nearly the same thing. He felt his dad's choice though, had the hint of *it's your decision* in it, and at twenty, appreciated the subtle difference. Steven smiled and continued toward the bathroom.

He passed his mother on his way back to his room a few minutes later. "Mornin, Mom."

"Good morning sweetheart."

He noted her ever-present cheerful morning demeanor and wondered if it was a symptom of some mental illness. He grinned. If it was, he was catching it. He'd been waking up in too pleasant a mood for a while and he was in an even better mood than normal this morning. If he knew Jake, and he did, Jake finished his project last night and today was going to be one long day as girlfriend and boyfriend.

He moped around making mental plans until Genna also left for her office then went in to take a bath. He started the hot water then went back to the bedroom for the bath oil, and his eyes opened wide. It wasn't there. He instantly panicked. He searched in a few other places, then ran into the bathroom, and as he did, stared at the bottle in the far corner of the tub. "Shit! Shit!" He breathed deep. Maybe no one noticed. …No way. There's no way mom didn't see it. *Well, it's too late to worry about it now.*

He finally calmed down and stepped into the steamy water. He breathed in its fragrance as he lowered himself slowly and settled there, thinking what to wear and how to do his hair.

After she finished her make-up and hair, and checked every corner of the bathroom with a slight paranoia, she went to the attic and the suitcases hiding her growing wardrobe and picked out an outfit. She brought the things back to her room and dialed Jake before getting dressed.

"Jake?"

"Hi."

Stephie heard what sounded like a textbook landing on a table. "Are you up?"

He gathered himself. "Yeah. Been up."

"Did you finish your paper?"

He smiled. "Yep. All done. Nothing to do for the rest of the day."

She instantly smiled. "Awww, poor baby. Want some company?"

He hesitated. "I guess. Nothing else to do."

"Well, if you'd rather not, I'll understand."

He was immediately done calling her bluff. "No! It's alright. You can come over."

She teased. "Are you sure? I wouldn't want to bother you or be in your way or anything."

"No, Please come over."

This game tickled her and she teased back. "Are you sure?"

The volume of Jake's voice playfully increased. "Do you want me to beg!? Because I will. I'll beg if you want, but it won't be pretty."

She laughed. "You're an idiot."

"So when do you think you'll be ready to visit your idiot.

"Ten minutes?"

"That soon?"

"Are you starting again?"

He yelped. "No, ten minutes is good!"

"You sure?"

"Yes!" He lowered his voice. "When did I lose control?"

Steven laughed. "August."

He sighed playfully. "Oh, yeah."

"Bye."

"See you in ten, sweetheart."

Steven loved when Jake pretended to let him have control, but she knew all too well that Jake was just being her best friend. She grinned as she put the phone down and finished getting dressed, anticipating being with him as soon as she was ready. She studied the mirror, and her smile grew. She turned every angle possible, making sure she looked as feminine as possible, slid on a pair of white slipper shoes and headed out her kitchen door. She knocked and then entered his door. She knew he would be waiting for her and her anticipation increased with every step. She finally stepped into the family room and smiled. He stood as she expected and his soft smile matched hers.

"Hi!"

She could feel her legs weaken as soon as she heard him speak, and she couldn't take another step. She stood there waiting for him. "I missed this."

He walked to her and slipped his arms gently around her. "I missed this too."

He lowered his lips to hers and their mouths opened fully on each other. Finally, she was in the place she had yearned for, since leaving Vicky's after dancing. She whispered in his ear. "I needed this so much, you have no idea. I wanted to attack you while we were walking to the bike after we left the library yesterday."

He leaned away enough to jokingly stare at her. "You know, it isn't an attack if I don't resist."

She giggled as he kissed her repeatedly down the side of her neck and then their mouths opened and sealed together. He softly broke their kiss before she wanted and led her to the sofa. She cuddled against his chest, and burrowed herself snugly in his arms. Her need to be surrounded by him seemed to increase with every intimate encounter. Inside his arms had become her definition of the best place in the world.

Their mouths came together again as her hands ran over his back, his shoulders, back to his neck, and through his hair. She touched his lips, his eyes, his cheeks, his neck. She unlocked her mouth from his and started kissing his neck and tasting the amazing scent coming from him. He was intoxicating, but he cut her activity short. He took her lead and began kissing her soft neck and tasting her sweet fragrance, then surrounded her earlobe with his warm mouth and she gasped with pleasure. His attention to her was taking her breath away.

He kissed her forehead and her eyes, then her nose and cheeks as they both lay there in each other's arms, enjoying the next level of their connection.

He kissed every inch of her face, then worked his way down to her neck. He kissed, tasted, and breathed deep warm breaths on her neck and ear, hoping to raise goosebumps, and he found them more than a few times. He loved her involuntary reactions to his attention. He could think of no better way to judge the true pleasure he was giving her.

His hands started wandering, and she started melting. He paid particular attention to every reaction she had to his caresses. He could sense her complete trust and surrender and the intimacy gave him pure pleasure.

His hands went from feeling her to worshipping her. He softly embraced her ribcage, registering how feminine she felt. This adorable princess he was holding was his. She leaned into him, as her head fell into the crook of his neck. Every move, every sound indicating she was all too willing to offer him her entire being.

She was stirring feelings in him, he never imagined he could feel and he needed to claim every inch of her. He slid his hands over her, and as their mouths opened wide and sealed together, he slid his hand down to the hem of her skirt and gently moved his fingers under it. She breathed in the air in his lungs and stiffened. He tenderly slid the tips of his fingers to the edge of her delicate panties, and she gasped again in his mouth. "Jake?"

His reply was tender. "Yeah?"

She rested her head on his shoulder. "I've spent the last few days and weeks hoping you'd want me, but because of that, can I ask a favor?"

He slid his hand over the back of her hair. "Sure. What?"

"I've imagined, our first true complete night together. Believe me, I've imagined it..." She exhaled, "...over and over and over..." She looked up and gazed into his eyes and the corners of her mouth rose, "I even bought an outfit for that night... But I want it to be a night, a whole night, you and me, behind a locked door, somewhere alone. Not any place elaborate or fancy. No champagne. But a night where I get to hold your hand and walk into a room with you, as your girl and we make love like I want to make love to you. Is that okay? Do you understand?"

A small huff of air left his lungs and his eyes narrowed as he whispered. "You're perfect."

He thought to himself. *When did she become so amazingly perfect?* "That sounds fantastic."

His right hand slid up her back and spread fingers slipped through the back of her hair as he lovingly pressed her mouth to his, taking all voluntary choice from her, and her submission instantly matched his gentle force.

After their kiss, she lowered her head down to his shoulder. "Let's take a little nap…okay?"

He smiled. "Sure."

He reached for a sofa blanket and a floor pillow. She helped him spread the blanket over them and they cuddled together under it. He watched her close her eyes as she rested her head on his shoulder, smiled, and closed his eyes.

When he awoke some time later, she was still in his arms, and he carefully lifted her and carried her to the sofa. They sat together and cuddled, making small talk ranging from shallow to deep; their bond continuing to strengthen by the complete comfort they felt with each other.

He lightly kissed her neck. "So who's house should we have dinner at tonight?"

She turned slightly and leaned against his chest as he wrapped his arms around her. "Let's go over to my house. I feel like, if anyone's going to read into the differences they might see, I'd rather it be my mom first."

"That's okay with me. But you do understand I'll take on any human who has a problem with anything about you, don't you?"

She leaned her head back and looked at him. "Yeah. but we can hope."

"But you don't have to fear anything."

She reached up and caressed his cheek. "You're great. Oh, speaking of changes." Her voice rose. "I always need your honest opinion on everything. No one should tell me something is less than what it should be, more than you and I'm not going to count on anyone to make sure I'm not embarrassing myself, more than you. I promise not to get mad at you, because I realize it would shut the honesty down. I know you love me, so don't think I don't realize you wouldn't hurt me or say something just to be mean."

He smiled softly. "You have my promise I have your back on every level. We're going through this together." He half grinned. "I do love the way you just told me you know I love you." He made eye contact with her and grinned. "You know I love you."

Her breath left her and her eyes widened. She didn't mean it the way he meant, so when he said it, she interpreted his affirmation in a way her heart was afraid to even consider. She knew he loved her like a best friend, but she didn't know he was in love with her, and her heart had such a reaction to his words, she started hyperventilating. She inhaled and looked deeply into his eyes. "I love you too."

The hug that followed comforted her down to her soul and she kissed him like only a life-long best friend and new lover could.

For all outside appearances, the rest of the evening was typical. Jake told his mom he was eating at Steven's and Steven told his mom Jake was eating there.

Morgan didn't hide her disappointment. "Ok, but the two of you need to have dinner here tomorrow"

"Deal, Mom."

"I was going to ask you both to have dinner here tonight."

"Tomorrow, Mom. Okay?"

"Okay."

All six of them felt every part of Jake's and Steven's lives included two families and two homes. There was no longer any delineation in any of their minds.

~ ~ ~

Genna was a few minutes early but she had learned her mother was always ready when it came to company, especially her family. She had also arrived bearing gifts; a beautiful covered tray of sushi, a bottle of sake and a six-pack of Japanese beer, along with edamame and two glistening seaweed salads. There was enough for four, but both could eat their share of this meal. Sushi was Genna's favorite though she dare not say it out loud in present company, or she'd be lovingly admonished.

"Cara mia."

She didn't see her mother come out of the house, and she continued to gather the things in the back seat. "Hi. Here you go Mom." She handed her mother the sake, then the beer. "I'll get the rest."

Lorraine asked the question she always asked. "How are you?"

"Good. You?"

"I'm fine."

Genna followed her mother into her kitchen, and watched Lorraine drop the bottle of sake in the already heated pot of water on the stove, then turn to her. "How long can you stay today?"

"I have time today. We can have a nice long visit."

Lorraine smiled happily. "Good, good."

Lorraine transferred the food to a beautiful ceramic serving platter while Genna poured the sake and beer. She set the hot tokkuri flask on the tray next to the cold beer, then with tray in hand, followed her mother out to the living room and the make-shift setting on the coffee table. After a pleasant "*kanpai*" and accompanying sip of sake, they both served each other.

Lorraine made small talk asking about everyone, intermixed with anecdotes from the reunion, and waited patiently to find out why Genna wanted to bring her lunch today. She was a model of graciousness and always genuinely pleased when Genna came to visit. Besides, she had everything she could want at the moment and was settling comfortably with her warm sake and cold Japanese beer.

"Oh, I love the way sake feels going down. Is there any better compliment to a nice beer?"

"Oh, Mom. I'm so my mother's daughter." They laughed. A few more sakes and they would both be laughing at things not necessarily funny, but just the happiness of being in each other's company.

Finally Lorraine asked, "So what's new?"

She had asked the question once before when Genna first came inside, but she received this inquiry as it was meant; and smiled at her mother's insight. She sighed. Her mother reached for her hand and smiled. There was nothing Genna could say that Lorraine couldn't handle, short of illness or death, and this meal obviously wasn't for either.

She turned toward her mother. "I qualified what I'm about to share when I talked to Connor, and though I'm searching for a way to softly lead into our discussion, the only way I can think to answer your question is to start a little stronger than with an easing introduction. Please forgive me..."

Lorraine looked up and offered a soft soothing smile.

She folded her hands on her lap and inhaled. "Connor and I have noticed a few changes in Steven and I'm here to make sure he's protected. I realize that sounds somewhat hurtful considering the love you've shown us always, but you're of a different generation which is why I'm his liaison today."

Lorraine reached for her hand. "What have you seen cara? Does he have a problem?"

"No. You mean like drugs or something? No, not at all. Connor and I think Steven is adjusting to a somewhat different lifestyle, and I want to make sure you're not personally hurt or confused by it. He loves you dearly and I believe he'd be devastated if you were hurt by who he's discovering he is. I need to make sure his path is lined with love, where possible."

Lorraine smiled. "That's one of the most beautiful things you've ever said to me. You've never confronted me our whole lives and the first time you show a need to consider it, it is not for you but for your child. I've been blessed."

Genna sat up straight and smiled as the compliment registered. She loved when her mother saw herself in her.

"You're right to pave his way. He's your most prized possession. What could you be that would make you less than my most prized possession?"

Genna hesitated.

"Nothing cara. Nothing. And I see you've taken that lesson into your soul as well. Well done."

Genna smiled.

"I would expect your greatest love to be Steven. Subsequently, he is the jewel of my jewel. He can do nothing to lose any of our love. He can do nothing to gain more love. Our love for him is complete. We love him because we made him. We love him because he exists and only because he exists."

"But the definition of love, cara mia, is not in words; only actions." Her mother's words triggered a wonderful fleeting memory of her father also saying those same words many times as she grew up. She smiled perceptively, and listened intently as her mother continued. "So, let's plot to be his greatest allies in this new undertaking of his. Tell me what you see and what you think you will see. Then tell me what you want to do to help him, whether he knows of our help or not." Lorraine lifted the small sake glass and sipped the warm liquid, then smiled. "I feel like an adventure and I'm pleased he'll give me something to focus on with my idle time."

Genna paused for a moment, and absorbed her mother's words.

"You don't have an appointment out here today, do you?"

She could feel the playful guilt appear on her face. "No."

"I can read you like you came from me." Her mother raised an eyebrow and tilted her head, to make her point. They clinked glasses and drank, and discussed Steven in tremendous detail.

Chapter Eight
Connection

Steven and Jake worked hard over the next few weeks, finding a school open to Steven's concerns. They were conducting informal interviews with admissions departments, and actually getting good at it. They kept a chart and had a fairly extensive list of all aspects of their ideal next step and methodically weighed everything in its order of importance, from philosophy to logistics, and after a good amount of work, were pleasantly surprised to find the university one town over fit their needs and desires rather impressively.

The school was close enough to everything they didn't want to leave, yet far enough away to allow them as much privacy as they could want. It had an impressive and state of the art computer school and an equally impressive business school and finance and accounting departments and the university was large enough; all aspects of their academic and personal life could be nurtured and enjoyed. The institution's progressive attitude and philosophy also permeated past its many buildings and through the town itself.

"I think this is it. I think we're spending the rest of our education right here." Stephie pointed to the name on the home-made chart on the bed between them. "How lucky are we?"

Jake rolled over on his back. "We still have to settle a lot of things. We're not quite done."

She looked at him, hoping for additional signs of agreement. "I know, but this is a biggie."

"I agree."

She bounced on the bed. "I can't wait to share this with my grandmother. I think she's going to be thrilled." Steven adored his grandmother and she was doing well enough financially to show her love for him, in ways many can't. Well enough to have made her only grandchild an offer when he was young, like the offer she had made years ago to his mother. It was one of the reasons she was so pleasantly surprised by Steven's decision to start at a community college and he eagerly looked forward to her next acknowledgement of his continued decision to help Jake.

Lorraine constantly modeled deeds over idle words and he was eager to show her his continued ability to offer actions like she had so often shown. She knew Steven's initial college choice was in Jake's best interest. She had come to be an extended part of the Harrison household, for the times when family functions were shared with them, and he knew his selflessness was well recorded in the mind of this wise business woman.

In her original offer, she would not only pay for everything regarding college, but with a certain level of grades, would throw in additional perks, and Steven was meeting her highest expectations. His accumulated grade point average for his first two full years of college was only thirty five one-thousandths of a point below perfect. He couldn't do much better.

Steph couldn't stop smiling. She grinned ear to ear as she folded the chart, and looked at Jake. "Let's take a break."

"Sure."

They both cleaned up the books and papers spread out on the bed and floor nearby and while they straightened up, Jake stole kisses on whatever part of her head, neck, or face he could reach with his lips. As they were finishing putting things away, she waited for him to look away and hit him waist high with the softest attempted shoulder tackle possible and he immediately started laughing. "Are you starting something?"

She grunted but he didn't budge. "What if I am?"

He spun in her grip, lifted her up and flopped on the bed with her snugly in his arms. "If you are, I may torture you."

"You're not so tough."

Their mouths came together in a wonderful playful kiss as they lay face to face; Steph on her left arm and Jake with his right arm tucked under the pillow under his head.

"I feel really good about making this decision. It's a big load off my mind." He rested his left arm on her waist.

She inched closer to him. "I feel good about it too." Her grin turned devious.

"…What are you up to?" Her expression raising a matching smile.

She motioned to climb on top of him, so he rolled on his back and let her straddle him and pin his hands by his head. She leaned forward and tenderly placed her open mouth on his as he moved their interlocked hands under his head. When their kiss broke, he looked into her eyes. "Wrestling with you is way more fun now."

She breathed deep and smiled seductively. "…and it's only going to get better."

Her statement raised his breathing and a deeper smile. He reached behind her head and tenderly brought her mouth down to his.

~~~

The sun was slower to rise as each week passed and the change of seasons brought with it the normal bite to the morning air. Jake stood next to the started bike, bouncing to keep warm when Steven walked over. "Kinda miss my old clunker now." Guilt prevented him from asking for a replacement when it died, but now he felt guilty for not having asked.

Jake handed Steven his helmet. "I'm sorry I ever badmouthed that old piece of shit. This is crazy."

Steven loosened the chin strap. "Yeah. And it isn't even freezing out yet. Sure does wake you up…except when I fall asleep on the way."

Jake spun like he'd been hit with something. "You fall asleep?"

"Just once or twice. I lost my lunch once. We got to school and I didn't have it."

"That's awful. Are you crazy?"

She responded meekly. "I tuck myself in the best I can."

His voice reflected true exasperation. "It's a frigging motorcycle. There's no place to tuck yourself in. That's it. We're asking the four of them if we can buy a car. It can be another P O S, but at least I won't have to scrape you off the road because you were tired. Besides, I'm frigging cold."

Steven slipped the helmet on, then raised his voice to answer Jake. "I'm all for it. I hate this ride, especially in the morning. Do you want your own or do you want to split one?"

Jake slipped his helmet on and pulled the chinstrap tight. "It wouldn't be bad to split one, you know. We could buy a P O S twice as nice."

"I know. We'll ask together and I'll ask if I can match your amount. They can't say no."

Jake climbed on the bike. "You don't have to."

Steven climbed behind him and slipped his hands in Jake's jacket pockets. "Yeah, I do. Besides, it's the deal Nana made with me and Mom. She said she didn't want me getting a job while I was in school, and I've been holding up my end, grade wise. I have to be the only student who reads the next semester's textbooks before the semester even starts."

Jake revved the bike. "You are strange."

He play punched Jake from the pocket his hand was tucked in and held on.

Jake turned his head. "You know you're going to pay for that."

Steven hugged him differently than if he was just a best friend. "You don't scare me."

They only had specific courses to take to finish their two year degrees, but they continued the routine of scheduling the same starts and the same breaks during the day and met between classes always. When Steven walked up to their regular lunchroom table after their first class, Jake was already seated with his books open, and Steven spoke before Jake noticed he was there. "I flipped the coin after class and I lost."

Jake looked up from his textbook. "Oh, the family meeting?"

Steven opened his backpack and removed two books. "Yeah."

"Isn't it amazing how whoever flips that damn coin, loses?"

Steven sat and opened his book. "It really is. We have to find a new imaginary coin."

Morning breaks were always spent in the noisy lunchroom, where they could eat if they wanted, but they preferred the quiet of the library for afternoon free periods. It was definitely a better work environment, but they weren't allowed to eat in there. It was also where they met at the end of the day.

Steven was waiting by the library door when Jake turned the corner. "Hey. Want to go home and study in my room? If we finish, I'd be glad to kick your ass in whatever videogame you choose."

Jake smirked. "Oh, my dear friend, haven't you caught on yet? I've been letting you win for years."

Steven leaned into Jake as they walked toward the bike. "Let's eat at our own houses tonight."

They bumped together every few steps as they walked, both wanting to touch the other more than socially acceptable. "Okay." Jake thought for a second. "It's funny how they both get pissed when we choose the other house, isn't it?"

"They're strange. Gotta love 'em."

Jake brought the bike to a stop in front of his side steps and Steven hopped off. His phone rang as he removed his helmet, and he read the caller ID while Jake propped the bike up behind the steps. "It's Vicky." He hit the accept button, "Hey, Vick, what's up?"

"I'm having a Halloween party next Friday. Can you and Jake make it?"

"Let me ask him. He's right here."

Steven lowered the phone and got Jake's attention. "He's having a Halloween party next Friday night."

Jake nodded. "Sounds like fun. Tell him I said hi. See you after dinner." Jake headed up his side steps.

"Okay." Steven walked away still on the phone.

His house was silent when he entered a few moments later and he walked to his bedroom, still on the phone with Vicky. "So, do you need help with anything?"

Vicky laughed. "I need help with everything."

"Count me in." He opened his books on the desk as he talked. "Are you decorating?"

Steven and Vicky were getting closer each time they talked and quickly becoming close friends. "A little. Believe me, for this crowd, the booze is the only decoration they care about."

"I can help you Friday morning if you want or maybe Wednesday or Thursday night." Steven straightened up as an idea registered. "And you can help me figure out what to be."

Vicky sounded playfully exasperated. "Help you figure out what to be! Girl! Your costume is the easiest. It's the only week of the year you can go out dressed as a girl, no matter how bad you look, not that *you* have that problem. But your costume is whatever dress and heels you pick."

"Oh, wow!" A big smile broke on Steven's face. "Perfect!"

"I'll text you when I'm decorating. If everything works out, maybe we can make a day of it."

"Okay."

"Okay sweetie. Talk to you soon."

"Bye." Steven finished setting up his desk and stared at the textbook, but all he could think about was this new opportunity for Stephie to have a normal date with Jake. He loved the thought of being socially allowed to be with Jake as Stephanie. Alone was great, but the idea he could be Stephanie in a normal, people filled place, with Jake, was fantastic. It was a degree of normal that had to be denied before it could be fully appreciated, even under a false pretext. True allowance wasn't a paradigm worthy of a thought.

He sat there staring at the open book, but his mind wandered to thoughts of Jake. He would have lost a bet only a short time ago, thinking he and Jake couldn't be any closer. The semester had been crazy so far. School was becoming almost routine; a lot of work, but definitely routine. But the rest of his life, and him and Jake, were not anything like he imagined they would be only a few months ago, and he was scared to think how close it came to not happening. He ran his hand over his chest. He was amazed at how much he wanted to be with Jake, and how much Jake meant to him. When he was with him, no matter where they were, he felt...right. Like he didn't care who else was around or what else was going on. But when they weren't together, he always felt a little lost. Like he didn't belong where he was, no matter where he was. He half grinned as he remembered the times he was Stephanie with Jake. He couldn't believe how amazing it felt just being with him.

He let out a soft sigh, then shook his head. *Get to work. He's coming over later and if I finish my work, we'll be able to play.* He adjusted the book and tried to concentrate. Not a minute later he jumped up and ran to the attic for an outfit to hide in his room.

Jake went into a silent house. His parents were still at work and he had the house all to himself. He went straight to his room, dropped his backpack on the bed, and changed into his work-out sweats and a t-shirt. He stopped in the kitchen, grabbed a bottle of water out of the fridge, and headed down to the basement

He set the dumbbells on the weight bench, far enough apart to sit between. He loved when he was in the mood to exercise. It freed his mind and let him think. Problem was, he couldn't think of anything at the moment but Stephanie and playing with her. He smiled as an innocent kiss came back to him, the smell of her clothes and hair.

He sat on the plastic bench and bent over with his forearms on his thighs; looking forward but not registering anything, then straightened up and grabbed at the weights without lifting them. It wasn't so much a pre-workout ritual as it was a delay in a level of intensity he knew all too well required more energy to start, than he was in the mood to exert.

But today, he had specific reasons why he didn't feel like starting immediately. The thoughts in his mind were too soothing to dismiss. He was enjoying peaceful thoughts of his girl. He smiled. *My girl. How funny.* His mind purposefully pendulated between the male and female identifiers that described her. He saw how they all fit and he saw how none fit. His *girl* was just the person he pictured and the accompanying thoughts were always so peaceful and without complexity.

His thought then turned to how fast the relationship developed; so fast he couldn't remember how it had progressed to this point. And in an instant, remembered the crazed workout a short time ago, when he thought things were hopeless. He pictured that workout in his head and his stomach instantly tensed. And that fast, his current lack of fear or worry about their future made him take a deep satisfying breath. Steven's love seemed so deep…so absolute…so feminine. Jake shook his head as his breath left him. *How funny; he's the girl of my dreams.*

He wrapped his hands around each dumbbell, breathed deep, lifted the weights and pressed them overhead. He raised them repeatedly until his shoulder muscles wouldn't allow another rep, and dropped the weights on the bench at his sides. He remembered her asking him when shoulders day was, and grinned. After a short break he lifted the weights again and continually pressed them up until his shoulder muscles throbbed, and then dropped them on the bench. He stared at the wall in front of him, until the pain subsided and after a few more moments, repeated the process, and when he dropped them, he blindly reached for the towel on the bench bar, and grabbed nothing but air. He turned and looked before grabbing again, but it wasn't there. He narrowed his eyes and scanned the immediate area. "Shit. Where did I put it?" He quickly searched the exercise area. "…Mom must have washed it."

After the quick search, he ran upstairs and grabbed another out of the hallway closet and ran back down, wiped his face, threw the towel over the bench bar, and lifted the weights again.

He heard his father's truck, and then the kitchen door open. "Hey, Dad."

Back came the deep and resonating reply, "Jacob" and he half grinned and lifted the weights again until the burn came back. He sat there for a moment with the new towel in both hands, wiping his face out of habit more than need; picturing Stephanie's long smooth legs, and the first time he saw her in a skirt.

He exchanged the dumbbells on the bench for lighter ones and sat back down. *God, Steven looked so amazingly hot in that gold dress.* His heart sped beyond the level the weights caused. He lifted the weights to failure again, and as soon as he dropped them, instantly thought about how he wanted to slide his hand under Steven's skirt and make him squirm. He lifted the weights again and when he finished the set, realized how hard he was breathing. *Damn, he could kill me…*

He heard the shower go off and his father leave the bathroom, as he sat with the towel over his head trying to calm down. *Short and sweet. Good workout.*

By the time he finished his shower, his mother was home. She knocked on the bathroom door. "Are you home for dinner?"

"Yeah, Mom, unless it's a bother."

"No problem. Is Steven eating over here?"

"No. He's eating at his house."

"What, did the two of you have a fight?"

"Very funny. I'm going over there to study later."

Steven took a break from his studies and dialed his phone, "Mom. I'm home. Do you want me to do anything for dinner?"

"I was only going to cook peas and garlic in chicken broth. Could you start the pasta water for me?"

"Sure."

"I'll be home in twenty minutes. Dad should beat me. I just talked to him. Love you."

Steven had the table set, the pasta pot boiling and the garlic and onions sautéed when Genna walked in, and she breathed deep when she opened the kitchen door. "Oh, you're a doll."

Steven smiled. "No problem, Mom."

Dinner was on the table thirty minutes later.

"Is Jake working tonight?"

"No. He's coming over after dinner. We're going to work and if we get a few things done, I'm going to whip him in whatever video game he picks."

Jake opened the kitchen door as Steven loaded the last dishes in the dishwasher. "Hey."

"Hi."

He raised his voice. "Hi, Mom Dad B!"

A chorus came from the family room. "Hi Jake."

Jake stepped toward the family room. "I'm going to go in and sit with them real quick, till you're done."

"Okay. I'll be another five minutes. Oh! Vicky called me. He's having a Halloween party next Friday. I told him we'd go."

"You told me already." Jake hesitated. "Do we have to dress up?"

He turned from the sink and glanced at Jake. "Yeah, we have to dress up."

Jake stepped back into the kitchen. "Well, what are you going to be?"

Steven waved him closer and whispered, "I'm going to be Stephanie."

Jake straightened up. "Definitely. That's exactly who you should be. Absolutely. But what am I going to be?"

"I was thinking. Dad has a silk robe and a pipe."

"Excellent. And I like the cost and the prep work."

Steven glanced at him again. "Go visit. I'll be in in a minute."

A few minutes later, Steven turned the corner to the family room and Jake immediately grabbed his school backpack, and glanced at Genna and Connor, "Bye."

"Have a good night studying."

Jake flopped on the bed as Steven shut and locked the door behind them. "When I told my mom we were having dinner at our own houses, she asked if we had a fight. How frigging funny is that?"

"Pretty funny." Steven flopped on the bed next to him. "You have any studying you need to do?"

"Not really."

Steven smiled. "Want to play a video game?"

Jake leaned on his forearm. "Not really."

Steven moved closer. "What do you want to do?"

Jake shrugged. "Want to just relax together?"

"Sure." Steven sat up. "Can I put something on?"

"Sure." Jake rolled on his back, and propped his head up with the folded pillow. "Are you going to change in front of me?"

"No." Steven grinned. "You're going to go to the bathroom."

Jake grinned back. "Do I have to go bad, or can I hold it a few minutes?"

Steven tilted his head. "The sooner you go. The sooner Stephanie gets here."

Jake immediately jumped up, and scared him. "Man, do I have to go!" He hurried out of the room. He could hear Steven's faint laugh behind him.

When he opened the door on his return, Stephanie was laying stomach down on the bed, propped up on her elbows, wearing a short pastel yellow skirt and a plain but very feminine white cotton top.

Jake locked the door immediately behind him and Stephanie rolled a little on her side, propped her head up on her hand and smiled. Jake slid contentedly beside her onto the bed, turned on his back and gazed up at her. He pulled her face down to his and she immediately opened her mouth as they kissed. She never failed to project an immediate enthusiasm when he kissed her and that enthusiasm connected directly to his heart. The feeling was instant. He thought, *the speed of electricity,* and sighed.

He could feel her grin as they kissed. He pulled slightly away and eyed her. She didn't explain. She just leaned back down and opened her mouth on his.

After kissing a while, Jake twisted on Steven's pillow, folded it and propped up his head. He motioned for Stephie to join him in his arms and she lay against his chest with her arm around him. He pushed his head back. "This is nice."

"Very." She slid her arm down around his lower waist causing a surprisingly pleasant reaction inside him. She hadn't had her face that close to his lap before and the thought of doing something had his heartbeat steadily increasing, but the thought of her parents in the other room gave him hesitation. He whispered. "Do you want to fool around?"

Instantly, she responded, "Yeah. A lot." She turned her head and rested her chin on his chest. "But not with my parents in the other room."

He fidgeted to get comfortable. "I know. I was thinking the same thing."

She beat him to the next question. "Want to have a date as soon as we can?"

"Oh, yeah."

She scooted up and placed her mouth on his.

After their kiss, he whispered, "But you know what you're doing to me, don't you?"

She whispered back. "You're doing the same thing to me."

They both snickered and she lowered her head back down to his chest. Jake laid there with his arms around her for another few moments, unconsciously rubbing her back. His face contorted as he tried to form the words for the thought that had entered his head, when Stephie whispered, "I wish we could do this without hiding and without the secrets."

Jake's stomach stiffened as her statement registered, and he propped himself on his elbow. "I was trying to figure out how to say the same thing."

Stephanie looked up at him. "Really?"

He gave a soft chuckle. "Yeah. But I was worried you'd take it the wrong way."

She responded quickly and eagerly. "I wouldn't."

"No. It's hard for someone not to. I can see what you're going through. How hard it must be to feel one way and have to pretend and act another. But if I say something, you might think I'm pressuring you and I can't do that. I can't do that to you."

"Yeah, but all this secrecy and hiding isn't fair to you. You deserve better."

He stroked her hair. "Sweetheart, nothing's fair and I believe no one deserves anything. And I've been working on adjusting to those concepts for a while now, so don't worry about those things with me. I choose you, with all the unfairness and undeserved nonsense that'll come with choosing you. And when you're ready to take the next step, I'll take it with you."

She looked at him like his words were magic, and then immediately saddened. "I wish I had your guts. This would've been taken care of from the first week and I would've let things fall where they fell."

"But that's not you. That's not even me. I'd like to pretend I'm that sure of myself, but I can't actually say I'd have had enough guts to just blurt this all out. Besides, I'm pretty sure that isn't a good idea anyway. We've handled things like they needed to be handled as they came up. Let's not regret where we are. Besides, where we are isn't so bad."

"Yeah, but I want to finally come out and be myself. When I'm with you or we're together or I'm studying…in the back of my head I'm constantly getting up and walking out to the middle of the living room and getting this over with. Saying, Here I am. This is me."

He stroked the top of her head. "Please don't do that without me standing next to you. Please let me be with you. Promise me. Please promise me you won't do that unless we're close enough to hold hands."

She looked up at him. "You're too funny. You want to take the brunt of anything coming my way, don't you?"

He smirked and nodded. "Yeah. If either of us is going to get their ass handed to them, my choice is it's me."

Her voice softened. "Damn coin. We need a new one."

His reply was quick and softly adamant. "No, we don't."

He kissed her on the top of her head. "It's getting late. We have school tomorrow." He tried to get up and she held him tighter, but he sat up against her efforts and brought her into him with less effort than she exerted on him. He kissed her and their mouths instinctively opened. The kiss was different than earlier kisses. This kiss was a kiss of love and departure.

He smiled at her. "I'm going to turn my back. Put on your boy clothes so you can walk me out."

She sighed and grabbed Steven's jeans and sweat shirt and Jake turned his back as she changed in the corner next to her bed. And when he shut the closet door after hiding his girl things, Jake turned. "Ready?"

Steven dropped his head and displayed complete disappointment. "Yeah."

Jake lifted Steven's chin. "Relax. We'll get there." He leaned forward and gave Steven a soft kiss then turned toward the closed bedroom door. He glanced back. "Everything good?"

Steven looked around again and Jake unlocked the door. "Tomorrow morning at the bike?"

Steven lowered his head again, "Yeah" and walked behind him to the kitchen door.

~~~

Steven followed the other students out of the room after his last class the next day, and decided to give his grandmother a call on his way to the library, and Jake. He cut out the closest door and walked along the outside walkway as he dialed.

"Hi Nana."

"Cipolline! How are you my sweet?"

"I'm great, and I just wanted you to know; Jake and I picked a school for our four year college."

"Wonderful. Where?"

"Mom's alma mater."

"Really! She must have been thrilled to hear."

"I didn't tell her yet. I'm calling you first."

"Me? Oh sweetheart, why me?"

"Because, you're a big part of my college, and as soon as we decided, I wanted to call and tell you."

Her soft voice reflected her sentiment. "I love that you feel that way. I love being a part of your life. You're what I live for now. Are you happy?"

"Very, Nana."

She sighed. "That's all I want to hear."

"Jake and I want to come visit you. I haven't seen you in a while and Jake wants to pig out on some pasta. Can we visit?"

"Can you visit? I live for your visits. When do you want to come? I'll make a feast for the three of us."

"Don't go crazy, but is it okay if I ask Jake what he wants you to make?"

"The two of you decide what you want and call me. I love cooking for him. He flatters me with his love of my food."

Her connection with Jake fed his love for her and he sighed at her ability to exude love. "He loves you too."

"I know he does cipolline. I know he does."

He walked up the steps leading to the front of the library. "Okay Nana, I'll let you know. Love you."

"I love you too."

He put his phone in his pocket as he approached Jake. "I just told my grandmother about picking a school." He paused and waited for Jake to walk toward the bike with him. "And I told her we'd visit her soon. She asked me to ask you what you want her to make."

"I love that woman."

"You love her food more."

Jake glanced at him. "What's your point?"

They bumped continuously as they walked toward the parking lot. He wanted so badly to reach for Jake's hand. Instead, he sighed and pursed his lips. Two of the most important people in his life had just declared their love, but he wasn't allowed to show even an innocent hint of his feelings, for where they were, and the thought didn't escape him.

He held on a little tighter for the ride home, and secretly cuddled against him. No one could tell he was doing anything but holding on.

Jake walked in his side door, after saying goodbye to Steven, and went right for the fridge, foraging for a snack.

Morgan heard him come in and was greeted by the open refrigerator door as she attempted to turn the corner into the kitchen. She maneuvered around it and slid her hand over his back.

"Hi love."

He answered without lifting his head. "Hi Mom." He shuffled a few containers around.

She smiled and shook her head in amazement. His shoulders filled the open door space. "How are you?"

"Good." He continued his search. "You?"

"Good." She didn't want anything special, just a little interaction. The mother in her missed bonding with him every so often, for no reason, and this was one of those times she took her secret fill. "I can't believe you're nearly done another semester of college. How are you making out this semester?"

He straightened and examined a closed plastic container, filled with left-over chicken. "Good Mom."

"And Steven?"

He turned toward her. "He's a brainiac. I swear." He removed a bottle of water and the container of chicken from the fridge and brought it to the table. "He's so smart and organized; it's even fun to watch. We were studying together the other day…" He opened the lid and paused for a brief examination. "…and he couldn't remember this one thing, but he knew where it was on the page of his notes. He's scary." Jake grinned as he twisted the cap off the water bottle. He lit up when he talked about his best friend and she treasured the idea that for all these years, their friendship remained as strong as ever.

She leaned against the sink and discreetly enjoyed his attack on the left-over chicken. "How are you making out searching for your new school?" She shook her head at him but he wasn't watching. "Can you use a fork?"

He looked at her. "Can you hand me one? Good. Really good. We think we have it nailed." She waited for more, but he stopped before she thought he was done.

She folded her arms, "And…?" amazed at how she still had to draw every small bit of information from him. "…where is it?" Her voice reflecting playful annoyance.

"I'm not telling you. I think Ste…" His whole body jumped slightly but noticeably and the movement briefly caught her attention, but he continued. "…Steven and I are going to tell the four of you together. Can you wait a few days?"

After watching him stand there and take a few bites, she shook her head again, pulled a napkin from the holder on the counter and handed it to him. "Are you both going to the same place?"

He looked at her and smiled. "You had doubts?"

"Well, I don't know until you tell me. You're a typical guy. No more words than absolutely necessary." She walked up to him and stroked the side of his face, then lightly smacked it. "Keep me in the loop, will you? I'm not going to interfere. I just live for you. I need to hear what's going on in your life."

She hugged him and playfully pushed him away. "And I can wait a few days. But I'm dying to know. And if I die before you tell me, you'll be guilty for the rest of your life."

He grabbed at her waist to tickle her and she jumped and smacked his hands away. "Don't do that to your mother."

He wrapped his arms around her and kissed her. He was a head taller than her and nearly twice as wide at the shoulders, "I love you mom."

"I love you too. You make me proud. You're a good boy…man." They hugged for an extended moment. "Want anything special for your birthday or Christmas this year?"

He turned back to the chicken. "Yeah. Prepaid gas and fast food cards."

She shook her head. "Only you. Only you would ask for prepaid gas cards for Christmas."

He never broke his concentration on the inside of the chicken container. "I don't need underwear."

She smacked him on the back of his head as he shoved a piece in his mouth. "I love you, but you're such a guy."

A wide smile appeared as he raised his head, and the chicken in his mouth muffled his words. "I love you too Mom."

She walked out of the kitchen, secretly filled with another interaction, and slightly amazed at how she still needed more.

CHAPTER NINE
PROCESSION

Steven pushed the reference book away and surveyed the library as he waited for Jake to stop writing, then leaned toward him. "Want to have the family get-together tomorrow night and tell our parents about school?"

Jake glanced up from his notepad. "Sure. Mom's bugging me to tell her what we decided. We can talk about a car too."

"Good idea. I forgot about that. I'm going to do it, okay?" Steven took out his phone and sent a text to all four parents. *Can we get together to share some things tomorrow nite? Is tomorrow nite okay?*

He placed his phone on the light blue table top and continued his homework. Minutes later the third reply vibrated and he picked it up.

"Everyone's good so far." The fourth and last response broke Steven's concentration one last time and he grabbed it. "Mom H is good. Family dinner tomorrow night." Jake didn't acknowledge. He was concentrating on writing. Steven looked at him and half smiled. *He won't remember.*

Steven hit phone keys with both thumbs and sent the same message to both his mothers. *What's for dinner? love u.*

He looked at Jake, "Good to go." Jake glanced at him, then back down at his book.

He looked back down to his textbook and tried to concentrate, but instead, quietly envisioned the event he had just set up. He loved when he had an excuse to gather everyone. He thought about past family gatherings and equated them to the most comforting times he could remember. Never any real agenda to any of them. Just gathering to be with each other.

He pictured his two mothers texting back and forth figuring out dinner and his two fathers taking charge of the drinks, and daydreamed about their unique family unit. He really did have two mothers and two fathers, and he had come to love and respect all four. He glanced up at Jake, trying to remember if he ever looked at him as a brother, and though they were always family, he couldn't see it. His breathing responded to the thought, but he really never looked at Jake like a brother. Jake was different. He was more than that from as far back as he could remember. He noticed his breathing slow and become deeper.

Now he's everything. He felt the twinge that accompanied the thought. He had this feeling before…more than a few times. The extent of their relationship overwhelmed him, and he wished during moments like these, he could sit against him. The contact would make him feel more connected and content. Sometimes he noticed its absence, and his craving for it. He knew he had this *touching* need. The family joked about how physical affection was part of their culture, but it was true. He liked the touching, and was always confused when he saw other families refrain from physical contact. He would touch Jake more if he was allowed. He would lean against him or hold his hand. He wondered if there were any places where that was allowed.

He looked at Jake across the table and caught his attention. "What?"

"No, I was just thinking about something I just read."

Jake offered a soft smile and he tried to look back down in his book, but he needed to stare at Jake for just a moment longer. He inhaled silently. *I wonder if he has any clue how much he means to me.* He wished they were home studying. If they were, he would have attacked him. One of these days, he was going to attack him, but he thought how much nicer, being attacked by him…taken by him…made love to by him would be. He looked down and saw the black letters filling the pages, but they weren't registering as thoughts or words even remotely as satisfying as his inner thoughts, so for the moment, he chose to concentrate on those.

His phone began vibrating and he picked it up. "Chinese."

Jake looked up, made a favorable face and reburied himself in his book.

He watched his everything for a moment longer and enjoyed the accompanying blissful feeling.

~~~

Steven went immediately back to his bedroom desk and his schoolwork after dinner and was concentrating on an open textbook when his phone rang. "Hi Vick. What's new?"

"Steph, Steph." He sounded out of breath.

Steven straightened in his chair. "You okay?"

"Am I okay? I'm great!"

Vicky's response tickled him and he started laughing. "What's going on?"

"You're never going to believe what happened to me today. I'm doing this woman's eyes and we're talking and minding our own business and this guy comes up to me and asks if he can interrupt me for a quick second. His eyes were dark and his hair was dark and he had this short dark beard. He was gorgeous. I asked him how I could help him and he handed me a note and walked away..." He breathed deep and started again, "and the note said hi I'm Jonathan and I think you're really cute and I hope you got a good look at me because I would like if you called me. And he gave me his phone number on the note. He's really cute and... oh my god I can't breathe." He huffed like he just ran a mile.

Stephie quietly giggled, both from the news and the delivery. "Vicky, that's fantastic!"

"I know! He's really cute."

"Did you call him?"

"No. ...I can't. I don't know what to say."

Steven laughed out loud. "You! Stuck for *words*? Now *that's* funny."

"Stop!"

Vicky was trying hard to solicit sympathy but Steven had never been on this side of their playful parrying and decided to enjoy the position for a few moments more. "Does the teacher need lessons from the student?"

Vicky gasped audibly. "Oh! They giggled. "Nice...real nice."

But Steven couldn't let his friend down for even a moment. "Is he that cute you can't think?"

Vicky's voice turned matter-of-fact. "He is really cute." He paused and playfully scolded. "So are you going to help me or not?" ...which turned to pleading. "Stephanie, I don't know what to do...I need encouragement!"

Steven calmly replied. "Why don't you text him first?"

"That's a great idea! I can text him. Should I tell him to call me?"

Steven smiled; thrilled she could offer something more to their relationship. "Yes. It's not easy starting a relationship without talking."

"But what if I can't think of anything to say?"

Steven sat up. "First, that's funny. And second, you don't know anything about the guy. You can ask any question you want and I can think of a hundred off the top of my head."

Vicky perked up. "So can I."

"Are you good?"

"I guess I am."

Stephie laughed. "You are too funny. Call me later. I want details."

"Thanks girlfriend!"

Stephie gleamed. "My pleasure. Love you."

"You too."

By the time Jake returned home from work, he knew Steph would probably be asleep but he was wired. It had been a long night, and an even longer time since they were alone together, and he could feel the tension. He knew he probably shouldn't call her but he needed some release of energy or he was never going to sleep. He jumped into bed and dialed.

Steven stretched for his phone on the end table next to his bed, "Hi."

Jake's greeting had an unnatural intensity. "Hi. I just got home."

He could tell by Steven's response that his tone had its desired effect. "You doing okay? ...Need anything?"

"Yes, actually."

Jake's answer woke Steven completely. "What?"

"Meet me between the cars."

Steven's voice tensed. "Okay. Do you want me to bring anything?"

"No."

"See you in three?"

"Okay."

Jake hurried to his kitchen door, as much to see Steven's concern, as his need to be with him. He enjoyed seeing Steven's heart and wasn't past manipulating his best friend for even the slightest exposure. They both quietly opened their kitchen door, but Steven was moving a little faster than Jake, concerned he actually needed something. He knew Steven took his words for face value more than he should. He even knew he was being playfully selfish, but what he didn't realize was how much Steven's response affected his heart. The concern on Steven face tickled him to his core.

Steven whispered as he walked toward him. "What do you need?" Jake motioned Steven to the back of his mother's car, and Steven went over with an anxious look on his face and whispered a little louder, "What is it?"

Jake grabbed him and pulled him into his arms and gave him a long kiss. After a minute and a half they separated. "I needed a kiss."

Steven's eyes widened. "You drug me out of my nice warm bed so you could have a kiss?"

A devious grin rose on Jake's face. "But I needed one."

Steven tried desperately to continue his adamant tone. "Well I'm out here, so why are you talking?" He wrapped his arms around Jake's neck and kissed him again. Their mouths softly pressed against each other as they kissed in the dark behind the cars.

The aftermath of the kiss could be heard in Steven's voice. "I don't think we've ever kissed anywhere but behind a locked bedroom door while our parents were home."

Jake grinned in the dark. "I like it. I feel like we're being daring or something."

"This is fun. But if we don't stop…we're both going to be uncomfortably in trouble."

Jake's grin increased. "Too late. I'm already in trouble."

Steven's voice turned softer. "So am I."

They kissed again. Each kiss taking them further away from being able to stop. They broke their kiss and he went right for Steven's soft neck.

Steven whispered. "Jake. ...Jake!" He wasn't listening. Steven whispered louder, "Jacob!"

Jake stopped and stood a little straighter.

"Jake." She tried to compose herself. "I have dreamed and rehearsed how I would tell our parents about me and us, but not once in any of those dreams were we caught kissing between our cars."

Jake chuckled, "Oh, how I could do you right now."

Steven shared her last remaining adamancy. "Knock it off!"

Jake's words were raising the femininity inside him, like lava in a volcano. "Ok, I have an idea. Let's both go back to bed. Give me five minutes and then call me."

"Really?"

"Yes." Steven gave him a quick kiss and ran away from him. This was the only bluff she had in her and if he grabbed her again, they were doing something right there between the cars.

He watched her but didn't make another grab for her. She was right and he knew it. And he wasn't going to sacrifice good sense for momentary stupidity. But he liked the idea of being in bed talking to her. He went inside, climbed back into bed, and dialed her.

He whispered. "Hi."

She whispered back. "Aw honey. Are you all worked up?"

"God Steph, I want you right now."

"You do?" Jake could hear Steven's heart yearn in his breathy response.

Jake softly sighed. "You have no idea."

"Let's make plans then, because I need you too. Can we make plans?"

He breathed deeper as his love's words registered. "I definitely want to make plans."

They lay in their beds in the houses next door and flirted and whispered; both feeling an intense yearning. Steven rolled on her side. "I think about being under the covers with you, in your arms."

"I think about it too."

"We need to make love Jake. Please?"

"Do you want to come over here or should I come over there?"

She smiled. "Not tonight, idiot."

He smiled. "I know." After a slight pause he whispered, "I really do love you."

His words registered deep inside her and she responded, "I can't believe how much I love you."

They whispered back and forth about nothing until both their minds wound down and were ready for sleep. Jake whispered the last message; not sure if Steven was awake to hear it. "Good night sweetheart. Sleep tight."

He smiled, inhaled deeply, and shut his eyes.

~ ~ ~

"You ready to head home soon?" Steven could see the autumn sun starting its decent from the big library window. "I don't feel like being on the bike after dark. I can't see."

"Alright. Five more minutes." Jake sped up his writing.

"Besides, we called for the meeting. We'll get our asses handed to us if we aren't there when everyone else gets there."

Jake never looked up. "Yeah. They have a problem sitting together drinking. Besides, like they'd ever holler at us for studying late."

Steven smirked and nodded playfully. "It is a great excuse. If I had known what it would've gotten me out of when I was younger, I would've studied more."

"You *did* study more when you were younger...nerd."

"Hey! Look who wants to go home and who's working."

Jake shut his books and looked up. "Since I can't seem to have my last five minutes..."

Steven began putting his books away. "You don't need another five minutes."

"If I had *your* brains, I wouldn't need to work this much." He playfully glared at Steven, "C'mon." and grinned, and Steven grinned back.

The ride was fast but they were both numb getting off the bike. Jake flipped his helmet off, "Yep. We're buying a car. Radio and heater. That's all I want. A radio and a heater, and I'm testing the heater before the radio."

Steven's smile turned into a shiver. "Meet at your house in a bit?"

"Come over when you're ready. Don't wait for mom and dad."

Steven answered as he ran to his kitchen door. "Okay. See you in a bit."

Thirty minutes later Steven walked out of his room and headed next door. He knocked, then opened the Harrison side door. Jake was sitting at the kitchen table with his books spread out.

"Wow. Have you been working since we came home?"

"Yeah. This semester's a lot of memorizing and stuff. But I think I'm going to use all of this."

"Cool."

Chris turned the corner into the kitchen. "Hey."

"Hi."

Chris slid his hand over the back of his hair. "What's new?"

Steven looked at Chris and immediately perked up. He loved Chris like a second father and Chris showed a genuine love for him that blood uncles didn't express. "And ruin the news we have planned for tonight?"

Chris joked. "Nah. Can't have that... Did you bring popcorn? The show's going to be popcorn worthy, ain't it?"

Steven made a face. "Popcorn and beer?"

"Anything and beer, son. Anything and beer. And I think I will."

He grabbed a beer from the fridge and headed back into the family room. That fast, the kitchen door opened and Morgan walked in. "Hi kids."

"Hey, Mom."

"Hi, Mom H"

"How're you two doing?"

They responded in unison. "Good."

She dropped her purse on a kitchen seat. "I can't wait to hear what's going on tonight."

"Mom, do we have popcorn?"

"We have some in the cabinet there, why?"

Steven responded for him. "Dad H wants some after dinner."

Steven pulled out a seat, sat across from Jake at the kitchen table, and watched him work for two minutes. "You're boring. I'm going to go get a book." And as he said it, he heard car doors shut. His mother and father had pulled up.

Jake straightened up. "Better idea…food." He shut his books, piled them quickly and headed out the door to help mom B. She looked up at them as they appeared on the landing. "Perfect. You boys have this?"

"Hi, Mom."

"Yeah."

"Good. I'm going to go change. We'll be right over."

"Hi Dad."

"Hi Dad B."

"Hey boys." He headed to the side door. "See you in a few."

Jake and Steven carried everything to Jake's and put it on the kitchen table. "Mom. Food's here."

Morgan turned the corner and breathed in. "Smells good."

Jake laughed. "I love that smell too. Grease!"

Chris yelled from the other room, "I smell popcorn." Ten seconds later, he turned the corner into the kitchen. "So where are the Blairs?"

Steven offered playful sarcasm. "Fashionably late, of course. Only losers show up on time."

Chris didn't hesitate. "Haven't you been here an hour already?"

Steven tried to control his growing grin, but he couldn't. Like his mother, he never seemed to get the better of Chris.

Chris reached up and cradled the back of Steven's head then opened the fridge for another beer. "Hey, if you boys want, you can have a beer or two tonight." He turned and reached for a dumpling and Morgan nailed the back of his hand with a spoon. "Ow!" He backed up against the kitchen cabinets sipping his beer, still eyeing the food.

Connor opened the kitchen door. "Hey everyone."

Chris turned. "Come on in. The party's about to start. Genna, you're fashionably late." Chris looked at Steven and grinned.

Steven blushed as Genna met his eyes and playfully scowled "Okay. What'd I do?" Steven watched his mother fight the same grin he had earlier.

"Nothin' Mom. Chris is being Chris."

Genna played along. "Irritating, isn't it?"

"Hey! If I was sensitive, that woulda hurt."

They all laughed at the idea. Chris…sensitive.

Chris grabbed Connor a beer. "You boys want one?"

"I'll have one Dad."

"I kinda want to try the wine."

Morgan answered Steven. "Sure sweetie" and reached up for a glass out of the cabinet. "Here you go. But be careful. Wine can kick you."

Chris added, "Especially the good box stuff. The vintage on this box was February, and I believe February was a very good year."

Genna quipped. "Thanks for digging through all the boxes to pick it out for us."

"You're very welcome Genna my dear, but it was no trouble at all. It was right in front."

Morgan shook her head. "Shall we eat?"

Jake chimed. "Always."

They ended up in the family room, joking, laughing and having another impromptu party. Finally Connor turned to the boys who were both sitting on the floor next to each other. "So, you going to tell us what's going on, or what?"

Steven turned to Jake. "Go ahead."

"No, you."

Steven held his eyes on Jake for another pause before turning to everyone. "Mom, we chose your old school."

"Really! That's fantastic!

Morgan hesitated. "Oh, ok! Both of you?"

Jake answered. "Of course, both of us. We're not splitting up now."

The moms stood and hugged and kissed the boys, and the boys shook their fathers' hands.

Jake continued. "But guys. It's an hour away and we don't want to use the motorcycle."

Genna calmly replied, "No. You're not using the motorcycle. It's already been worked out."

Steven's voice rose. "What do you mean?"

She turned and faced them. "Have you two ever been in nana's garage?"

Steven and Jake stared at each other, then back at Genna. Jake shook his head no as Steven replied "No. Why? …What's in nana's garage?"

"Your grandfather's car."

Steven's eyes narrowed. "I don't understand."

"She's been saving it for you."

"For us?"

"Yeah."

"But it's nicer than your car."

She wrinkled her nose. "But it's terrible on gas and I drive to sales calls every other day. No thanks."

"Dad?"

"Mine's newer. No thanks."

Jake looked at Steven. "It isn't the black one he used to drive, is it?"

Steven turned his head toward Jake, "Yeah," Then turned to his mom, "So, we can have it? You trust us with something besides a big old POS clunker?"

Morgan interjected. "But it wouldn't be Jake's. It would just be yours."

The tone he responded with was reserved only for when he stuck up for Jake. "Oh, no. It's either both of ours or we're buying our own."

Connor looked at Genna then grinned at Chris. "These two are too strange." He turned to Steven. "Okay. You strike a hard deal. It's both of yours. But we don't want to hear anything when you both want to use it for a date on the same night."

Steven raised an eyebrow. "That's not as much of an issue as you think."

Jake choked on his beer, but no one questioned the statement any further, so it went unexplained.

Genna looked at each of them. "Your grandmother has been planning this for a while. It's your twenty-first birthday present. Happy birthday present to both of you. Just be careful. It's an expensive car to fix."

Even though the sale was completed, Steven continued to sell. "Great! Jake's twenty one before me."

Jake sat up. "I have to give something toward this. I was planning on spending the two thousand I saved. Can I give it toward my share?"

Genna met his eyes and lowered her chin. "No. Use your money for school."

"But..."

"Sweetheart, my mother has it, don't worry. And this is what she lives for at her age."

Steven's voice softened. "When can we go get it?"

"Can you wait for a birthday?"

"Mom B, we can't. The bike... It's so cold to ride in the winter."

Jake glimpsed at Steven for support and Steven received the signal. "Mom, it's dangerous and it's really cold, especially early in the morning. If it's just sitting there, can we please use it? Besides, the bike is not the safest thing to drive."

Jake smiled at Steven. "Yeah, it's more dangerous than you think."

Morgan stood and reached for Genna's glass. "I wouldn't mind them in a car instead of on that thing."

Jake and Steven made eye contact again and Steven continued. "And it's even more dangerous being a passenger, Mom."

Genna glanced at Connor, then turned back to the two of them. "Oh, okay. You're right. What's a few weeks anyway. I'll call her tomorrow."

Steven jumped up and hugged her. "Thanks Mom."

"Don't thank me. This is entirely your grandmother. I'll give her a call tomorrow."

"So will we."

Jake turned to Genna. "I have work tomorrow but I'll call her when I'm done. Or should I? I don't want to sound like I own part of it before she's okay with the idea. I mean. I don't even have to."

Steven's voice turned softly adamant. "Yeah, you do. I want us both to own it just like we were going to split a P O S. I'll explain it to her. She isn't going to have a problem. She loves you. Besides, she's the coolest seventyish person ever. I'm telling you. Not a problem. But if there is, I'll text you."

Genna looked at Connor. "What's a P O S?"

He squinted, "A piece of shit." and chuckled at his words. "Never had one?"

They sat and laughed the night away. After a while, Steven went in the kitchen and made popcorn.

~~~

Genna turned from the kitchen sink when she heard Steven's feet shuffling toward her the next morning. "I talked to your grandmother earlier."

Steven perked up as he gave her a quick morning kiss, but didn't offer a reply.

"She's completely fine with Jake owning half."

The words stopped Steven in mid-reach for a coffee mug, and he turned and embraced her again. "Thanks mom."

"She thinks it's great how you care for each other."

He sighed. *If she only knew.* He glanced at her, hoping he could read her permission; thought about it for another moment, then paused to let his senses recover.

"She said you could come get the car any time, and then asked if you wanted to come for dinner." Though her voice made the idea seem like an option, her eyes told him they had no choice, but he already knew. Besides, he actually loved sitting and spending time with her; asking her about all the things she and his grandfather did when they were scheming to make their mark in the world.

He spent the day coordinating their visit and finalizing the menu, in-between his schoolwork tasks, and by late afternoon, sat anxiously waiting for Jake. When his phone finally beeped, he never glanced at it. He hurried out his kitchen door and across the drives to Morgan's car, as Jake came out the side door.

"Hi."

"Hi."

Jake reached for the driver door as Steven opened the passenger side. Whenever Jake and Steven had a long drive, no matter whose car they used, Jake drove, and Steven's grandmother lived nearly an hour away. After getting situated, Jake rubbed his hands together and gazed at Steven with big eyes. "I can't wait to eat. I'm starving. Nobody makes this food like her and I plan on gorging myself."

"I swear you go to visit the food."

"That's only partly true."

They laughed. They enjoyed these trips alone together. They both felt they didn't have enough alone time and there was a mutual feeling of added bonus for trips like this.

They weren't driving long when Steven yawned. "This is so relaxing, I could fall asleep."

"Me too."

Steven spun his head immediately, then playfully grinned. "You're an idiot."

Jake reached across the console and poked him in his side.

They were quietly enjoying the ride when Jake broke another momentary silence. "Can I ask a crazy question?"

"Sure."

"Would it be okay, when we're alone like this, if I held your hand once in a while?"

Steven's heart fluttered and he looked at Jake. "Really?"

"Yeah." Jake glanced at him. "Why not?"

Steven's breathing instantaneously elevated as he held his hand out over the middle console, and Jake softly placed it in his.

Steven's breathing never slowed as he constantly glanced at his hand in Jake's and when he looked away, his tactile sense took over immediately. He couldn't think of anything but his hand in Jake's. The rest of the ride was too short.

The feast would have easily fed eight but Jake did his best to put a dent in it. He sat back and patted his stomach. "That was great!" He held to his word and had stuffed himself.

Lorraine smiled lightly. "I'm pleased you liked it."

Jake helped them clear the table, but there wasn't much to clean up, and after the table was cleared, Lorraine motioned to Jake. "Go sit in the living room. We'll be right in."

Steven waited for him to leave and turned to his grandmother. "Can you believe what he ate?"

She smiled. "There's a special joy, watching someone you love enjoy your cooking."

As they were finishing the last dishes, Steven and Lorraine casually turned face to face at the kitchen sink. She wiped her hand on the side of her apron, cupped her hand, and gently caressed his face. She peered deeply into his eyes and smiled warmly as she slowly ran her thumb over one of his eyebrows. Then she gently pulled his head toward her and kissed him on his forehead. She didn't say a word and neither did he. They stood there for another second. Lorraine smiled softly and turned toward the sink. Steven needed a moment to re-focus, but he gathered himself and continued to help her clean up.

When they were done in the kitchen, they went into the living room and joined Jake, who had found a game on TV and sat watching with the sound muted. They sat and relaxed the night away until Lorraine finally said, "You boys ready to see your car?"

They glanced at each other. "Sure!"

When they opened the door to the garage, they both had ear to ear grins, Jake was first to comment. "This is crazy! I was expecting to own something without all its paint."

Lorraine laughed. "Sorry to disappoint you."

Jake stared at her with his mouth slightly open as Steven opened the door and climbed into the driver's seat. "We spent a week trying to figure out where to get something with heat and a radio."

With a big smile, she playfully responded, "This has heat and a radio."

They made quick eye contact and replied in unison. "We know."

She laughed. "You're pleased?"

"Nana, are you kidding? I don't know what to say."

Steven got out of the car and they hugged and kissed, then they both pulled Jake in and hugged standing there in the garage. She reached in her pocket and pulled out two sets of keys. "Here you go."

They each reached for a set and beamed at each other.

"The tank is full and the paperwork is in the glove compartment. Pull it out of the garage and come back in this way, so we can say goodbye at the front door."

They kissed, said their goodbyes, thanked her again, and Steven followed Jake home.

~ ~ ~

Monday morning, Steven walked toward Jake as he stood by the back of the car. "I flipped the coin in the kitchen. You're driving."

Jake looked up. "Are you sure?"

Steven walked around to the passenger door. "Yeah. You always drive."

Jake hesitated moving to the driver side and followed him with his eyes as he watched his friend pass him. "Because it was my bike."

Steven raised his chin without looking at Jake, and replied pompously. "Too bad. Now open my door and take me to school."

Jake pointed the fob at Steven's head and the car unlocked. Steven hit the seat warming buttons and casually watched Jake set the radio stations while they let it warm up. Jake glanced at him. "This is screwy. We went from freezing our asses off on a bike to driving to school in this? How the hell did we pull that off?"

Steven smiled. "I have no idea, but it's pretty terrific, isn't it?"

Jake's focus moved from the radio to Steven's eyes. "Oh! Nice line about them not having to worry about us both needing the car for a date. That wasn't funny."

Steven sat back and beamed. "Oh yes it was."

They pulled into the school lot twenty minutes later and Jake parked in a remote back corner. Steven couldn't hold his curiosity, and softly sung his words. "What are you doing?"

"Your mom made me paranoid. I'm afraid to get a ding on it."

"That's fine" Steven pointed to the building. "…but what do we use to drive the rest of the way?"

Jake turned and made a face. "Your legs." Then reached over the console and slid his hand onto Steven's closest thigh.

"Don't do that or you're going to make us late for class!"

Jake leaned closer and Steven immediately opened his mouth in anticipation of his kiss.

Their eyes stayed locked as the kiss ended and Jake's smile grew as he sat back in the driver's seat and grabbed the steering wheel with both hands. "Yep, I like the car."

He glanced at Steven and smiled at the reaction his kiss caused. "You alright?"

"Yeah…I guess."

Jake motioned sideways with his head. "Come on. Let's go get smarter."

He walked in silence next to Jake, every so often glancing discreetly at Jake's closest hand.

"See you after."

He offered no response but his eyes followed Jake as they both headed in separate directions to their classes.

Steven was already studying when Jake finally walked up to their table and sat down after his first class. "Hi."

"Hi. Why are you late?"

"Stayed to ask the professor a question after class." He removed two books from his backpack and plopped them on the table. Steven went back to studying, and without looking up, offered. "We have Vicky's party tomorrow night."

Jake dug out another book from his backpack. "Yeah. Cool. What're you wearing?"

"I'm not telling you." They both grinned.

Jake leaned forward and whispered. "Will it make me want to drag you into the bathroom and attack you?"

Steven looked up. "It better! Or I'm going to attack *you* and not in a good way."

Jake laughed. "Haven't you given up on the idea you can attack me yet?"

Steven raised his brows. "Do you want me to stop attacking you?"

Jake's facial expression and playfully contrite tone tickled him. "No."

"Okay, but your answer really didn't matter. I'm going to attack you forever."

Steven stared at Jake, looking for his reaction, and was pleased with the ever so slight smile he produced. He inhaled softly and buried his eyes back in his book.

After a short silence, Jake whispered without looking up. "I need the robe for my costume."

"It's hanging on the inside of your closet door."

Jake looked up. "When did you do that?"

"When you were at work." He glanced up. "When I brought it in, your mother asked me what I was going to be and I froze. I need to have more lies prepared."

Jake closed his textbook on his hand. "What did you say?"

"I told her I didn't know."

Jake grinned. "Smooth."

Steven softly threw his pen at him.

Chapter Ten
Orientation

Steven took a break from his morning schoolwork, stood up from his bedroom desk and dialed Vicky. "Hi."

"Hi."

"Am I coming over early to help you set up for the party tonight?"

Vicky replied meekly. "Would you?"

"Will I be able to get ready for the party there?"

"Of course hon. I'll do your make-up."

Steven's voice filled with enthusiasm. "Deal!"

"Don't forget your costume."

Steven nodded and half grinned. "I won't. What time?"

"Any time after two?"

"Okay. See you then"

Steven had spent more than an hour in the attic after school the day before deciding what to wear. Stephie's wardrobe was growing slowly, but it was growing. He had three short dresses spread out on the clothes rod that hung between two roof braces, and her intimates as evenly spread on the open suitcase as he could make them. *I should wear something tight to go with Jake's costume, but I don't feel like. I want to be more…feminine.* He removed one and carefully tucked it away.

He finally removed the second dress from the rod and put it away, then found the intimates that matched the dress he chose. He dug through another suitcase pocket and found black lace top thigh highs, then carefully folded the remaining things and packed them away. He then opened his modest shoe collection and removed the black patent leather high heels, packed everything carefully in his video game bag and buried it in the back of his bedroom closet. The bag seemed to get heavier and heavier each week, with *essentials* being added regularly. He smiled. He loved every aspect of being a girl.

He texted Jake, *Vicky asked me to go over early to help her set up for tonite. I'm dressing there. Your costume is hanging on the inside of your bedroom closet door and the pipe is in my …with me. No. I don't trust you to remember it. See you there. Confirm then erase this message.*

His phone vibrated a second later. *Got it.*

He finished the thought. *B early. The earlier you are the more time you get to spend with Stephie.*

…erase that too.

When Steven's pre-set two-fifteen phone alarm went off, he closed his books, grabbed his video game bag and headed for the hall, but instead of making a left to the kitchen, he turned right to his parents' room. He went in his mother's top left dresser drawer and borrowed one of her silver bangle bracelets, then slipped it over his hand, shook his arm to make sure it was on for the night, and continued toward the kitchen. He grabbed a light jacket on the way out and headed to Vicky's.

Vicky met him at the door. "Hey sister."

"Hi Vick. How are you?" They hugged.

"Stressed." Vicky stepped aside and let Steven in.

"We'll get through." Steven felt a wonderful inner joy, for the opportunity to help Vicky. "Let me go hang up my dress and we'll knock everything out." He came back and surveyed the living room, "Ok, What do you need me to do?"

They decorated and made a liquor and snacks run and were sitting relaxing by quarter to six. Vicky sat on the loveseat, sprawled out with his arms on the back and his legs spread with feet flat on the floor. "Thanks for helping me today. I can't believe we're ready."

Steven smiled. "We make a good team. Can I jump in the shower and get ready? I told Jake to come early. I want to be with him for as long as I can."

"I understand sister. You can even have some private time if you want before the party." Vicky shared an exaggerated wink and they both laughed.

"What kind of girl do you think I am?" They giggled. Steven turned toward the hallway and bathroom beyond then asked, "Oh, is Jonathan coming?"

"Oh! I forgot to tell you. He texted me last night." He waved his hand in another exaggerated motion. "He is!" They both started laughing again.

"Oh good, I can't wait to meet him," Steven walked away shaking his head and laughing.

Stephie came out of Vicky's bedroom a little while later, dressed in a cute floral dress, black lace-top thigh highs and matching black heels, looking absolutely adorable and absolutely feminine, "Ready when you are for my make-up."

Vicky looked up as he rummaged through his make-up box next to the chair in front of his little kitchen nook. "You're so pretty."

Stephie sighed. "I wish."

"Why do some girls have such a hard time believing they're pretty and the ugly ones all think they're the bomb?" They laughed.

"You know, we're in trouble tonight if we already have the giggles."

"I can't help it. I love hanging with you. You're like my little sister."

"Stephie smiled. "You're definitely my older sister…brother?"

Vicky raised Stephie's chin with two soft fingers. "Somewhere safely right there in between."

Stephie smiled. "It really doesn't matter, does it?"

Vicky's voice had that patented softness. "Not really."

Vicky became immersed in his work, as he seemed to do most times he made someone up, and Stephanie enjoyed watching him in his element. She could not only see how he loved his work, she could feel how calm and relaxed he became when he worked his trade, and his tender application added to the joy of the experience.

"Who's coming? How many?"

"I invited fifteen to twenty and most of them will bring a friend, so we should have a nice crowd. Mike and Lisa and Alyssa and Tyler will be here. So will Leelah. And Desmond. He goes around collecting the booze money for me. If people had any idea how soft and gentle he was, they'd be blown away. Who else? Four friends from work. Oh! And Jonathan. One of the bartenders from the club. You two.

Two neighbors; it's always good to invite the people who'd complain about the noise…and another old boyfriend I've stayed friends with. How's that?"

Stephie smiled. "Do you dance?"

Vicky stopped and gazed at her. "Do we dance? Do you want to dance tonight?

Stephie could feel her face blush. "Yeah, kind of."

Vicky gave a big grin. "Oh yeah we dance. We kinda get crazy. You'll see." They both had big smiles, each looking forward to the night. The doorbell rang and Vicky looked up from the last touches of Stephie's make-up. "Come in."

Jake opened the door and stepped in wearing a long black silk robe over dark blue silk pajamas. He had dyed the sides of his hair gray. "Hi."

Stephie stretched to look around Vicky. "Hi."

Vicky did a double-take. "Oh, you look great." He hugged and kissed Jake. "Thanks."

He eyed Stephie sitting on the bar stool. "Hi sweetheart. You look gorgeous." His growing smile confirmed his words.

"Thanks." She leaned toward him and gave him a kiss. "Vicky isn't done yet."

"You're still gorgeous."

Stephie blushed again. She didn't see what Jake or Vicky saw, but she was attractive and feminine. It was only a lifetime of feeling disconnected from her true being, blurring her vision.

Vicky interrupted their mutual focus. "Let me finish you up so I can jump in the shower." He softly pushed Jake aside and wedged himself between them, "Help yourself to a beer after you tap it."

Jake glanced at him.

"Can you tap it for me sweetie?"

He stood straighter and spun his head. "Sure, where is it?"

Vicky pointed over the counter behind Stephie. "Right behind here."

Jake stepped into the kitchen and finished the beer keg.

Vicky stood up straight. "There! Done! You're officially a Vicky masterpiece." They both laughed.

Jake looked up from the keg, "Don't go away. I'm about to ruin her lipstick."

Stephie's heart flittered and she perked up, quietly eager for him to fulfill his statement.

"She can redo her own lips. I have to go get gorgeous!" He glimpsed at Stephie, grinned and rolled his eyes.

Vicky headed toward his room as Stephie stood and faced Jake. He studied her. "I still can't believe you're mine."

He inhaled slowly, as if he had this sudden empty feeling, and she was about to fill it. "Hi."

She never responded. His mouth was on hers before she could. Her arms slipped around his neck and they softly hugged and kissed. She sighed as the moment built.

She whispered as their kiss broke. "Oh god I missed you." She knew he knew what she meant. Stephie missed him, and for as much as he loved Steven, all his greetings indicated he missed Stephie just as much.

They held each other as the kiss ended. "Oh, I like how the pajamas feel. Where'd you get them?"

"Today at the mall. I had the robe, but nothing for under it."

She slid her fingers lightly through his gray hair. "Nice. Sexy."

He studied her face as she touched his hair. His eyes narrowed slightly and he smiled. "You're gorgeous. Seriously."

She lowered her eyes to his. "So are you."

He held her hand and stepped away from her, then took a deep breath, "Holy shit, Steph."

She lowered her chin and softly looked up. "Do you like?"

He breathed deeper and squinted, "You're really mine?"

Her heart filled with an instant yearning and she exhaled, "More than you know."

The first guests started arriving around eight but most didn't get there till almost nine and everyone was dressed to the nines. Vicky wore a pirate's outfit with a shiny dark purple silk shirt, a big hoop earring, a sword which couldn't have been any smaller or cornier, and a see-through eye patch that came with an explanation for everyone he welcomed. "So I don't break my neck."

Jonathan walked in around nine thirty dressed as a fifty's milkman in a very strange white uniform which was perfect according to Vicky. He whispered to

Stephie and Jake, "He isn't trying too hard to impress. It shows he has confidence."
He laughed. "Plus, he has to know he looks terrible."

A few of the females were showing as much flesh as they could. There was a genie, a schoolgirl, and a cheerleader who came as dates. Desmond was a male genie and impressive to the point of bewilderment. The female genie kept staring at him and they both found it highly entertaining. Stephie couldn't figure out if she was terrified of him or wanted to go home with him.

Vicky turned up the music around ten, and the party reached another level. When the increased volume caught Stephie's attention, she took a break from helping Vicky, grabbed Jake's hand, walked him out to the middle of the crowded living room, and instantly picked up where she left off at the club. Jake started moving opposite her but he couldn't help but stare at her, and watching her dance in front of him was ruining his rhythm. He sighed noticeably as she moved closer, barely touching him and teasing him the best she could. She intermittently brushed against his silk outfit, purposefully making it all but impossible for him to keep his composure.

He leaned forward and slowly inhaled her perfume and his noticeable approval fed her female soul. He placed his hands lightly on her hips as she teasingly slipped her silk-covered leg between his when the opportunity arose, only to remove it just as quickly. She gazed into his eyes and smiled mischievously, playfully letting him know she knew exactly what she was trying to do to him. He responded by pulling her into him and giving her a passionate kiss, and as soon as his tongue entered her mouth, her weight increased in his arms. When the kiss ended, she gathered her composure the best she could, but she didn't quite recover and finished the song rather awkwardly.

When the next song ended, he took her hand and walked her over to a quiet corner near the front door and stood almost blocking her from the rest of the crowd. She glanced up a little confused, until he bent toward her and kissed her passionately. He startled her for a moment, but she quickly gave in to him. He broke their kiss and went right for her ear, mumbling "god, Steph" before putting it between his lips and tasting it.

His warm hard breath was affecting her ability to stand. She dropped slightly, and he instinctively reached down and caressed her skirt covered bottom to hold her up, and when she registered where his hand was she straightened up. She gasped in his ear, but didn't stop him. In fact, she was pretty sure she wouldn't be able to stop him ever again.

Her heart raced as she turned slightly; doing her best to make sure her derriere was at an angle she considered least visible. She buried herself further in the corner, and though her move was subtle, he smiled as he recorded her willingness to accommodate him, and buried his mouth between her neck and shoulder. She shut her eyes and concentrated on him fondling her.

With her last thought before falling into complete bliss, she pulled down on the hem of her dress with the hand between them. She then reached up with her other hand to caress his head and without opening her eyes, found his mouth with hers, and as they kissed, he pulled her gently up by her bottom, and she gasped again in his open mouth. The gasp made them both subconscious, and they seemed to come back to the present at the same time, and though he let up on the upward force, he left his hand exactly where it was in the middle of their kiss. She turned her back a little more to the wall and leaned against him, still holding the front hem of her short dress.

Vicky spotted them and walked over. "You two having a good time?"

Jake slid his hand from Stephie's panties, to her waist. "Yeah!"

"Need anything?"

"No, we're good." Jake glanced at Stephie. "Want a water or a drink or anything?"

She breathed, "Water please?"

He walked to the kitchen and Vicky turned to Steph. "You having fun?"

"Yeah!"

He pointed to his right. "I haven't seen you out there dancing."

"Yeah we were. We just came over here for a quick break."

"Okay." His head tilted slightly and his brows lowered. "You alright?"

"Oh, yeah."

"Okay." Vicky turned and headed to another corner of the room, playing host. Jake came back with two waters and handed Stephie one, then opened his and drank it completely down. When he lowered it she asked, "Want to dance again?"

He smiled. "Sure."

They found an open spot at the far end of the living room and started dancing, but he didn't let go of her. He held her as they danced and his hands slid softly over her hips and back, down to her rear and up to the back of her head. He was restricting her, but she didn't mind. His hands always carried enough electricity to far outweigh any restrictions.

When the song ended, she leaned to his ear. "Bathroom. Be right back."

He found a seat as she disappeared to the other side of the apartment. She stood in line against the wall behind the cheerleader, turned her head toward the kitchen and noticed a guy dressed as an airline pilot, watching her and smiling. She smiled back innocently and he immediately stood and walked toward her, checking her out from her head to her heels then back up again. His actions didn't quite register. She thought he was admiring her costume.

"Hi, I'm Pat."

"Hi. Stephanie."

He admired her cute black dress with the pink and red flowers again. "What are you supposed to be, Stephanie?"

She never thought what her costume was and she didn't feel like explaining *girl*. She blurted out, "A flower girl." and grinned at her answer.

Though she didn't quite understand, he wasn't going to question any answer she gave. "Are you here alone, Stephanie?"

She smiled as things registered. "No, sorry."

He reached into his jacket pocket. "Well, just in case you're ever alone and don't feel like being." He handed her a card.

The cheerleader passed in front of her and caught her attention. She didn't say a word, but turned and went into the bathroom, not knowing whether to laugh or what to think. *Oh my god. A guy hit on me. A guy hit on me.*

She walked back to Jake when she was done, grabbed him and pulled him up to dance and though she became immediately immersed in the music, she couldn't help but look around to see if anyone was watching her. She made eye contact with Pat and nonchalantly turned her back to him.

The rest of the night was full of energy and laughs. The party went strong until one in the morning, but started thinning out when Vicky went around with a gigantic trash bag combining drinks and throwing empty cups away. Stephie saw him and started helping. Then Alyssa joined in and everyone got the idea and started saying their good byes.

Jake went up behind Stephie while she was combining half-filled cups. "Do you want to drive home together and we'll come back tomorrow for the other car?"

She softly glanced into his eyes. "I'd rather end the night with you as Stephie. Would that be okay?"

"Sure. Is it okay if I head out?"

She smiled, "Sure." …suddenly thrilled with the idea she was going to walk him out and give him a proper goodnight kiss. "Let me go empty these."

She came out of the kitchen and held his hand. "Vick, I'll be right back."

"Okay hon."

The night air was damp but the temperature was mild for autumn, and Jake's car wasn't parked far. Suddenly she wished they were out for a nighttime stroll. "This is nice, isn't it?"

He glanced up at the night sky. "Yeah. Good party."

She breathed deep. "I had fun. Did you?"

"Yeah. I had a great time."

When they reached the side of Morgan's car, he leaned against it and she gently fell into his arms. He reached up and caressed the back of her hair as they kissed, but as the kiss intensified, his hands fell to her bottom. He left his hands there as their kiss broke, and it took her entire concentration to think of anything else.

He held her against him. "You look so sexy and beautiful tonight."

"Thanks. We need to have another private date…soon."

He grinned at the idea. "I agree."

She stared into his eyes for a long pause, as she slid her fingers through the gray of his hair. "I'm going to get back and help him clean up."

"Okay. Do you want me to drop you off?"

She took a breath of clean night air. "It's a half a block. I feel like walking."

"Okay. I'll let the car warm up so I can see you're back."

She smiled at his chivalry. "Fair enough."

Their mouths opened and sealed together. He took a deep breath through his nose as they kissed and her heart melted. She would have ended up in bed with him if he requested, but instead their kiss finally ended and they each said goodbye. She started walking back and imagined him watching her, and the thought made her stride instantly awkward. She did her best to walk the last twenty steps as femininely as she could, but the thought of his eyes on her affected every fiber of her being. She sighed. *If he only knew what he means to me...if he only knew.*

It wasn't early but Stephie's phone woke her the next morning.

"Hi."

"Hi Vick. Great party!" She thought back as two different instances popped into her mind and left just as quickly. "Did you have a good time?"

"Yeah! It's always so much work though, which is why I only do it like twice a year...maybe three."

"What's new?"

Vicky's voice turned serious. "I just wanted to tell you something."

Steven hesitated. "Okay."

"One of my neighbors thought you were hot and asked who you were."

She sat against the headboard. "Really?"

"Yeah. You walked past when I was talking to him and Kayla and he turned to me and asked, 'Who's that?' I told him to be careful; you were already taken. And he said he'd gladly get in line."

She gasped. "No way!"

"Uh huh."

Steven shared her own surprising news. "The airline pilot gave me his card."

"Who was the airline... Oh, Patrick! Pat?" Vicky laughed. "That's too funny. Told you you were hot."

"Did you and Jonathan have a good night?"

"The best we could I guess."

"Did you get a chance to be alone at all?"

"No, but he asked me out before he left. We're going to catch a movie tonight."

She sat up a little more. "That's great. Text me how it goes."

"Okay. Oh, and thanks for all the help, especially cleaning up. You're a doll."

"Oh no problem. You're great too."

Steven hit the end button with a big smile on her face. Vicky always made her feel great.

~ ~ ~

"And I have a special surprise for you today."

Professor Jenkins walked out from behind his fake wood podium, clumsily twirling the marker in his hand. "Remember when I told you we would wait until the semester was under way before I shared the details of your final? Well, today is that fateful day."

He grasped the wrist of his opposite arm behind his back as he strolled across the front of the room. "I've decided your final will be an oral report with a partner. You can pick any topic appropriate to the class, but you'll need to submit it for approval by the end of class next Thursday."

"The rubric will be as follows." He waited for everyone to be ready to write. "Sixty-five percent of the grade will be based on the information you will be sharing. Good precise appropriate information should always be your primary concern when you're in the workforce. Twenty percent of the grade will be how you interact with your partner. How you feed off each other, how you support each other and how good you make your partner look during their part of the presentation. And the last fifteen percent will be how comfortable and aware you are during *your* part of the presentation."

Steven's heart sank. He hated these types of projects. He always put more work and effort into them than the other person, and was always more nervous about the final grade accordingly. He knew how to get A's by himself, but he never quite knew how to get other people A's. He also sat front and center in his classes, which was a definite disadvantage when it came to knowing which students were the good choices for a project partner. He stood there lost, until a shy girl tapped him on his shoulder. "Need a partner?"

A feeling of relief came over him and he turned and smiled. "Yes. You?"

She inhaled. "Hi, I'm Vanessa. Friends call me Ness or Nessa."

"Hi. Steven. Nice to meet you."

"Want to be partners?"

"Sure." He breathed a silent sigh of relief and spent the rest of the class sitting alone with his new partner, working out the details of their proposed presentation.

Steven met Jake on the way into the lunchroom after his class. He plopped his backpack on their table. "Want anything?"

"Yeah. A soda and an apple."

"Okay. Be right back."

Jake set up his books and started reading.

Steven slid the tray onto the table and cracked the lid on his soda. "Jenkins gave us a partner project for our final."

"I hate that shit. Let me get my own grade."

Steven stared straight ahead in a daze, digesting Jake's words and gauging his complete agreement. Finally he sat up, then focused like he woke from a trance, "So..." He smiled. "What do you want for your birthday?"

Jake stretched, raising both arms straight up and yawned his reply. "I dunno. What'da you want?"

"I asked you first."

Jake moved his head sideways and mimicked, "I asked you first. ...Well, I was thinking it."

With a big grin, Steven flipped his pencil at him and taunted, "Will you answer me?"

"You."

"Seriously...you."

Jake calmly replied, "No. That's my answer."

Steven's eyes widened. "What?"

Jake shut his book, and stared at him with the quirkiest grin. "You heard me. ...You."

Steven's heart jumped in his chest, his mouth opened, and he swallowed noticeably. He was suddenly confused but he didn't know why. He wanted to make love to Jake. He wanted it more than anything, but he was scared. Not scared of the act, but scared he wasn't enough, and Jake would want more than him. The thought of them making love had built up so large in his mind that the whole idea now overwhelmed him. He tried to compose himself as quickly as he could, but his brain wasn't close to functioning properly.

Jake leaned forward and rested both forearms on the table. "Can I have my birthday present?"

Steven's heart beat a mile a minute. "Yes."

"You alright?"

Steven inhaled. "You just caught me off guard."

Jake looked confused. "Why? Don't you want to?"

Steven's eyes widened. "Are you kidding? I want you more than you could ever know. But you really want me?"

Jake lowered his chin and smiled ever so slightly. "You know I do."

"You'd think...but you'd be wrong."

Jake's eyes narrowed. "Still not convinced?"

"Not totally."

"Why? What do I have to do to convince you?"

Steven just shrugged and made a face.

"You still can't tell yet?"

"Yeah, I can. I just can't figure out why."

Jake leaned closer and whispered, "Because you're fantastic." He sat back and grinned, as if proud for naming such an excellent twenty-first birthday present. "So. When do I get to unwrap my birthday present?"

"Well, not until your birthday." Steven was happy he had a legitimate excuse for his reprieve, and immediately thought of Vicky.

Jake leaned forward even further and playfully beamed. "I'm going to kiss every inch of my birthday present...over and over."

Steven's heart fluttered and he could feel himself turning red; knowing he was giving Jake way too much ammunition for future teasing.

Jake continued flirting. "What do you want for *your* birthday?"

Steven's heart pounded again, as his brain registered the unexpected reprieve, and he sat up straight as he felt his answer appear on his face before it came out of his mouth. "A front row seat to ten...no...twenty weight lifting workouts."

"You're an idiot."

Steven energized instantly. "Hey! You asked and I answered. When do I get the first installment of my birthday present?"

Jake tilted his head. "Seriously?"

Steven smirked. "Dead serious."

He felt the weight of his words increase his heartbeat, and wondered if Jake was having the same reaction. He discreetly glanced at him then quickly looked back down at his open book; trying desperately to control his immediate need for more oxygen, and hoping to once again begin registering the words he was staring at. He paused and secretly smiled at his inability to do either.

As soon as he was sure he could speak calmly again, and without looking up, Steven muttered, "Gold."

He glimpsed up without raising his chin, quick enough to see Jake raise his head in confusion and repeated, "Gold." then looked up with a devious grin and pointed down between the edge of the table and his stomach, "Shiny gold silk."

Jake smiled, looked down and shook his head.

~ ~ ~

Vicky was sitting on the sofa having a cup of coffee when his phone rang. He picked it up and answered all in one motion. "Hi Sweetie! What's new?"

"Not much. How are you?"

"Good. What's up?"

"Did I tell you Jake was turning twenty-one next month?"

Vicky perked up. "That's great! You throwing him a party?"

Steven never registered the question, for the message he needed to share. "I asked him what he wanted for his birthday yesterday…"

Vicky replied calmly, "Yeah."

"…and he said *you.*"

Vicky's startled voice startled Steven. "He said me?"

Steven's voice increased. "No, he said *you*…as in me!"

Vicky gasped. "Oh, dearie. Don't scare me like that."

"Sorry!"

Vicky sounded hesitant. "But that's great! Right?"

"Well…"

"Well?" Vicky hesitated long enough to emphasize his next sentence. "Have you two fooled around?"

Steven tried desperately to sound convincing. "Of course!"

"How come when someone answers that question that way, it's always a sign they don't have a clue what *fooling around* means." He started laughing.

"Vicky."

"What?"

Steven pleaded, "Can you help me?"

"Of course I can help you. Have I not helped you with everything so far?"

"Yes."

"You were worried?"

Steven lied. "No."

"Professor Vicky will get you through this too!" He laughed again.

"Where's your beau?"

Steven answered meekly. "At work.

"You have the day off?"

Steven smiled. "Yeah."

"So do I. And it's teaching time. Class trip."

"With me?"

"Yeah, with you honey! How am I going to take care of my little sister better than teaching her everything I know." Vicky laughed at his statement.

"So…what are you going to teach me?"

"Let's see… First the doctor has to make a diagnosis. That means you have to answer a few medical questions."

Steph shot back. "I thought you were the professor?"

"The professor has his doctorate, woman! And I can prescribe medicine. What're you going to be difficult now?"

"No!"

"Remember, I'll flunk your girly ass!"

They both laughed and Stephanie started feeling better. "Now, are you ready to behave, or what?"

Steph meekly replied, "Yes. Yes, I promise."

Vicky snickered. "That's better. Now don't be scared. Vicky's got medicine for what ails you."

Steph silently gulped, then breathed deep. "Okay. I trust you. I think."

"You better! I am your girly lifeline."

She laughed. "You're too funny."

"So, the ten thousand dollar question. Are you ready?"

"You're driving me nuts! What?"

"Have you ever…have you ever made love to him?"

Stephie's heart jumped! And with a pause she anxiously replied "No, and I'm kind of scared. I mean, I want to. I want to a whole lot. But I don't know what to do."

"Then we need to go shopping!"

"When? For what?"

"Oh honey, wait till you see. How fast can you get over here?"

"Pretty fast. What's good for you?"

"Pick me up in an hour. We'll spend the afternoon together and go to lunch. Okay?"

Steph perked up. "Sounds like fun!"

Vicky and Stephie continued getting closer and closer and the relationship fed Stephie. She felt so at ease with him. After all, he knew more about her at that moment, than anyone beside Jake. Vicky was her friend, older sister, part-time mother and most of all, a window into things Stephie had never realized existed, and both loved and needed all his roles.

"Oh! And as for what? No, not for what, for who. And the answer to that question is Jake. This trip is all about Jake." Vicky giggled.

Stephie looked at her phone and laughed. "You're absolutely a kook and I love you." Stephie had no idea where they were going, but for Jake, she was willing to go places she wouldn't go for herself. Besides, she trusted Vicky more than any friend she had.

Stephie knew if she was going out with Vicky, she had better wear something girly and in full make-up. She did herself up and headed to Vicky's. She parked and knocked. Vicky was ready to go and walked out after kissing her hello. "Come on girl. Let's go play."

Vicky walked over to his car. "We're taking my car sweetie."

Stephie couldn't contain her curiosity. "Where we headed?"

"Relax girl. I ain't kidnapping you."

Stephie followed Vicky's lead; taking the seat next to him and moments later they were headed toward the highway. "So how's Jake? Everything good at school?"

The road reminded her of her new school. "Did I tell you Jake and I are registered at the university?"

"No. You got all your classes and everything?"

"Not yet. We're going to do all that next week when we're off. It's where my mom went. She was telling us about it and we've been checking it out online. The school's gigantic and the buildings are really cool! You ought to see the pics of the caf. It's huge."

"Oh girl! Be careful! You do not want to trade Jake in for fruit loops and tater tots." They made eye contact and giggled.

They reached the school town and without a hint, Vicky pulled into a small outside shopping mall right off the main road and glanced at Steph, and she met his eyes as her mouth dropped open.

"Here?"

Vicky snickered. "Oh god girl! How could you be so innocent? You are so adorable."

Steph turned red. "I'm not innocent."

Vicky turned his whole body toward her, "Do you really want to play that game?"

Steph's eyes wandered up to the sign on the front of the store. "What is this?"

Her response tickled Vicky. "Wait till you see honey. Wait till you see."

The store looked nothing like she expected and Stephie's first reactions were pleasant surprise and wonderful relief. It was a brightly lit and tastefully decorated upscale store. "It's a regular store. Well, almost regular."

Her eyes moved from the cute lingerie on the left, to a big shelved white wall filled with cosmetics bottles, then to the right; three walls in a large alcove covered in different packages, on hooks from the ground to the ceiling. And in the middle were stylishly decorated displays with other gadgets and things.

They enjoyed a quick tour together; both exploring all the different erotic things available for people to use in private. There were fancy shoes and cute high heel slippers, different types of stockings, and clothing that ran from bridal baby-doll nighties to all different costumes. A schoolgirl skirt costume caught Stephie's eye and she held it up, examining it closer. Vicky whispered to her. "Get the real thing sweetie. The realer, the better!"

They were having a blast examining every display. They came to a wall display of men's intimate garments and Stephie gasped. "Oh, look at these!" She held up a box to Vicky, with a picture of a guy in nothing but a little pouch covering his private area. "Oh my, this is sexy!"

"So buy him one. It won't be the only thing you buy with him in mind today." Stephie blushed.

Next was the cosmetics wall. Stephie picked up a bottle and read. It was lubricant. Her mind registered the information on the back. "Oh. Oh!"

Vicky watched with a distanced satisfaction. "*That's* going to become your best friend."

She felt herself blushing. "It'll never replace *you*."

"Aww." Vicky scurried the three feet between them and hugged her dearly. "You are going to make me cry." They both laughed.

They started examining different tubes and jars, whispering and giggling.

"Can I help you?"

Steph stiffened like she had been caught doing something wrong. The sales lady stood behind them smiling. "This stuff is fun, isn't it!?"

Instantly Steph knew the lady was there for more than just ringing up purchases. She turned to the woman, "Hi. This place is great."

The lady smiled. "You haven't even gotten around to the good stuff yet. But if I can help you with anything, anything at all, please let me know. I'm Cathy. ... May I ask, do you know what you're looking for or do you need help?"

The lady's soft attentive manner made Stephie feel immediately comfortable, and her shoulders dropped slightly. "I need help. I'm trying to prepare to have sex with my boyfriend. I haven't ever, with anyone. And I could use all the help you could share?"

"Sure! I know a lot about nearly everything in here. Is money an issue, because there are different price-ranges on these, but I can recommend one for you either way."

Vicky heard the last sentence and chimed in. "No. Please give her your best. No worry about price."

Stephie faced Vicky while he spoke, silently trusting her dear friend.

"Then I recommend this one." She handed Stephie a small thin bottle. "It's the best we carry."

Stephie sighed softly. *One step closer.*

The door opened with a chime and a middle aged man wearing nurses' scrubs walked in and went over to a wall that they hadn't explored yet, and the clerk turned, "Welcome. Can I help you?" and walked over to him.

The two of them turned the corner and came face to face with more gadgets and toys, and they eagerly examined and constantly giggled, though nobody seemed to mind.

The two continued around the outside walls and just as they passed the storage room door on the back wall--

"Here we are! The good stuff!"

Stephie glanced up to see what Vicky was referring to, and gasped. Her mouth opened as she tried to comprehend the quantity of different size and color private part replicas and things in plastic packaging hanging on the wall in front of her. Two floor displays to their right, had things which appeared to be made of glass.

Vicky softly whispered, "Pick one that reminds you of him."

Steph stared at all the things on the wall hooks and became overwhelmed. She couldn't see one item for the overload of visual input she was receiving from *all* the items. That fast, Vicky had changed his concentration from Stephie to the same wall, and was now shopping for himself.

Finally, Stephie spotted a box and lifted it off its hook. Vicky glanced at her, then continued his own search. Steph opened the box and removed the plastic bag covered item. She held it softly in her hand and her breathing unconsciously quickened. She started caressing it, holding the replica like she was holding Jake, and her breathing deepened.

"That's it girl. Study it."

Stephie came out of her focused concentration and turned her head toward Vicky and they both started giggling again. She raised her hand to her mouth. "I think this is him." She instantly looked at it differently, thinking how she wanted to do things to its twin more than ever, her heart pounding inside her thin frame.

"Okay!" Vicky watched her place it back in the box. "Take a look at these."

Vicky held up a glass object which was as much a work of art as it was a useful aid, but at that point, Stephie was overwhelmed and eager to get home to familiarize herself with Jake's secret twin in the box in her left hand.

The cash register counter was next along the last wall, and Cathy stood there waiting for them. "Need anything else?"

They turned to each other. "No. We're good."

She rung up their purchases and put them in pretty purple bags. "Thank you. I hope you'll come back with your boyfriend."

Stephanie blushed slightly, wondering if Jake would ever come here with her. She clutched her bag. "Thanks!"

On the way out they browsed a bridal shower section with different types of party favors, party games and even chocolate private parts lollypops. The door chime rang as they left.

Stephie bounced, heading toward the car. "That was fun!"

Vicky grinned. "It was, wasn't it?"

"Where should we go for lunch?"

He pleaded. "Anywhere but a mall."

They returned to the car after a wonderful lunch and after they were on their way, Vicky offered, "We have one more store to stop in."

Stephie answered without a thought. "Okay."

Vicky smiled and her voice softened as if she was now speaking to herself. "We're not done shopping yet."

They were almost home when Vicky turned down a different street and into a drug store parking lot. He parked without a word, and looked at Stephie. "Come on sweetie. One more thing to buy for you and Jake."

Stephie followed him like a little sister following her older sibling, until Vicky found what he was searching for and lifted the item off the shelf. Stephie knew what it was but seemed a little confused, then inhaled deeply as things registered. Vicky smiled as he watched Stephie piece everything together.

"Oh, so that's how I make everything…"

"Very good."

"Wow, Vick. I… You're great."

"Not great, honey. Just love. Read the instructions and whatever you do… find a good clean hiding place for this. No one has to be aware of the steps you take to be everything you want to be for Jake."

Stephie answered timidly. "Understood."

"So. Did you have a good learning day?"

She brightened up. "I owe you so much it isn't even funny! You're a wonderful sister…brother."

"But I like doing these things with you. It's fun having someone to care about." They hugged in the aisle.

"Okay. Come on. It's been a long day and I'm tired."

Stephie qualified their time together. "It was fun though."

Vicky smiled, "Yeah it was, but you have studying to do when you get home."

The statement took a moment to register, but she turned red when she realized Vicky was well aware of what her night entailed.

~~~

He wasn't sure he had the energy to cover the last few steps. At best, there were seven, but he needed conscious effort to make those final seven. Jake worked the double shift as a favor to his manager and the long day was now taking its toll. He undressed slowly, climbed into bed, and slid his hands under his head as he stared at the black nothingness above him, trying to let his body and mind unwind.

He was exhausted but he knew this was one of those nights where a decompression was needed as a precursor to sleep. He loved the fact he had a full and productive day. It was so busy in fact, he hadn't thought about anything but the tasks the day brought, but those tasks were done and what little time was left before sleep was his, and he wanted to spend it thinking about life…and his future.

A soft snort accompanied his next thought. He could not see a life or a future where Stephanie was not present. He breathed deep, thinking about the possibilities before him; trying hard to temper his thoughts with the understanding he had very little control over tomorrow. He twisted to relieve a dull ache that had caught his attention and when the ache subsided, a mental picture of Stephie led him back to his daydream. The day had been intense and the semester even more intense, but what he learned outside school over the last three or so months was far greater than he ever imagined it could teach, and these outside lessons seemed to reduce the significance of everything else he was currently learning.

He didn't know why so many revelations had happened over such a short period, nor did he understand why so many had revealed themselves at this particular time, but were these revelations really new? A quick flashback came to him; Steven sitting in the top right corner of the aluminum bleachers on the first base side of the high school baseball field, alone, facing him at third; watching. How he used to think even back then that Steven was his, but in a different way. Players' girlfriends would come and go during the season, but Steven was always there; his. More than a few times, he compared Steven to the other girlfriends, and more than a few times he wished he could show some form of greater connection when the game was over and they were all leaving.

He could feel his muscles struggling against their newfound inactivity and he inhaled and carefully stretched, trying to convince his body he was done abusing it for the day. His mind wondered back to the present. *Stephanie's everything I want.* The thought made him smile as he realized how comfortable he now was, with the idea that Stephanie was as beautiful on the outside as she was on the inside. He felt his breathing increase with his next inner question; *how fantastic would it be to spend the rest of our lives together? What would it be like to lie next to her in the dark and feel her warmth…to cuddle next to her for the rest of my life?*

He pictured them making love. He needed to make love to her, and he felt his heart instantly increase as soon as the thought developed. *My birthday present! How could I forget my birthday present?* He made a mental note to remind Steven about his birthday present, then inhaled quickly as his heart yearned with the thought, and sapped some of his remaining energy. He sighed and breathed deep. There wasn't a part of Steven that wasn't his definition of a perfect complement to his life. Not a part of him.

His mind wandered to a mental picture of sitting across from Steven in the school library, reading his psychology text; thinking how psychological revelations had begun to erode the social assumptions that once flooded his mind. It's why he loved philosophy and psychology. He pressed his palms against his eyes, then slid his arms under the comforter. *Shame you can't make a living with the subjects.* He thought it one of the funny things about how his world had evolved, and gently shook his head at the philosophical implications that certain subjects which could teach a bigger picture, were now being marginalized into obsolescence.

He breathed deep again and smiled, realizing how pleased he was with the recent turn of events. He now found it impossible to remove Steven from any part of his life, and no thought pleased him more. Even holding Steven's hand... *Amazing how I didn't recognize how much this was what I hoped for...who I am.* Another smile unconsciously appeared as his mind slowly decompressed to a point where exhaustion impaired coherent thought. Moments later he was done making conscious thoughts till morning.

CHAPTER ELEVEN
DISTINCTION

Jake shut off the car and rubbed his hands together. "I'm excited about today."

Steph half-heartedly replied. "So am I."

They had decided to spend one of their days during Thanksgiving break, at their new university, and they chose this specific day because it was one of the few invitation only orientation and enrollment days during the week. They figured it wouldn't be nearly as crowded as a weekend enrollment and decided to get their next semester's logistics out of the way. After, they planned a stroll down Main Street, window shopping and a nice lunch. Stephie also wanted to ease herself into the idea of attending the last two years of her education as Stephanie.

He turned to her and tilted his head. "You don't sound it."

She imitated him and made a face. "You don't sound it."

He laughed. "You're a frigging riot. Will you please lighten up? I bet we have a blast. Besides, you look awesome."

She wore a cute beige chiffon dress, imprinted with faint pink and red flowers, with a hem that fell to mid-thigh and lay perfectly on her frame. Her make-up was impeccable, her hair looked adorable, and she had the cutest matching flats finishing her outfit.

She ran her free hand over the front of her dress as they walked toward the large brick building. "I feel self-conscious."

He glanced at her. "Do I have to throw you on the ground and attack you to make you realize you're hot?"

She looked away and whispered, "Maybe."

The inside of the main building buzzed with activity; pleasantly different than the first time they visited, and the buzz made the atmosphere much friendlier. What started out as self-consciousness, ended up being so much mental activity, Stephie finally relaxed and started enjoying the experience. There was an orientation in the huge inside amphitheater, and then a scramble to get in line to head to the computer rooms to register for classes.

A thin woman in a denim dress held up a sign near one of the double door exits. "All the sciences, arts and humanities, and education majors follow me."

A shorter woman followed with different instructions, in front of different doors. "All business studies, finance, and economics majors here please."

A younger man in light green scrubs lifted the third sign above his head at the next set of exit doors, and spoke last. "All nursing and medical related fields here please."

Stephie's stomach quivered when she realized her and Jake had to separate due to their different majors. She stared at him and he shrugged and mouthed, "text me" as he disappeared with his group. She followed the lady holding the business studies sign, along with roughly sixty other students.

The lady lowered the sign as she spoke. "You will be using the computers in rooms one twenty one through one twenty five. After you pick your classes on the computer, please write them down on the form we gave you. Don't forget to put your student number on all papers and programs, for your records. And don't forget to include the course numbers."

She sat at one of the computers and started searching for the classes her counselor had recommended, and while she searched, a male student spotted her and sat at the computer next to her. "Hi."

She glanced up. "Hi."

"I'm Dawson. Are you new to the school too?"

"Hi. Yes. I'm Ste… Stephanie."

He faced her, with no pretense of looking for classes. "Are you a freshman?"

She answered as she worked. "No. I went two years to a local community college."

"Cool. So did I. What're you taking?"

She tried to be polite, but desperately wanted to finish the task at hand. "Finance and Accounting."

"I'm in Hospitality Management , but I'm thinking I'd like to learn more about finance."

Her heart jumped! *Oh my god…he's flirting with me.* She tried not to turn red, faced the computer screen and concentrated on finding classes that fit her and Jake's schedule. Minutes later, she logged out of the computer program, quickly finished filling out her paper forms and gathered her things.

Dawson watched. "I hope we see each other in the halls at least."

"Me too," she lied. *Oh my god!* She grabbed her phone while she walked and started texting. *Jake!*

Hi! How u doing?

A guy just flirted with me.

He texted back. *Do u need me to break his legs?*

U R an idiot, Jake! I think he thought I m cute.

U r cute! U R strange. But u r cute. …give u a $ if he asks for your #

Thats not funy!

She followed everyone else as they rushed to the bursar's office to pay, and with the turmoil of the morning, became so concerned with her mission, she forgot about any and all anxiety. Though she stayed in touch with Jake the entire time, her determination to succeed in school offered enough of a drive to not only make her forget any lingering self-consciousness, but actually helped her enjoy the day's experience. She was having fun and so was Jake. She continued the text conversation.

Im kicking A! …got every class I wanted.

U r too funny.

She replied. *How u doin?*

Good

She typed as she walked. *Im headin to bursar to pay*

He was more methodical and a little behind her. *Meet in main aud & txt me when there?*

Sure

She didn't stand there long before they made eye contact. She could spot him in a crowd as easily as he could spot her, and as soon as she spotted him she lit up and rushed over to him.

"Oh my god Jake! That was fun."

He hugged and kissed her in the middle of the crowded auditorium. No one noticed. Everyone was too busy living their own life.

"Did you finish? Are you enrolled and paid for?"

He held up his paperwork. "Yep. Good to go."

She scanned the auditorium. "Wow! I can't wait to come here. I love this place. I don't want to leave yet. Let's walk the halls."

"Okay." He held her hand as they wandered slowly through all the hallways they could find, enjoying the newness in every way their senses would allow. And as they explored, she continually glanced up at him walking next to her, and every so often caught him looking at her; watching her reaction to every new turn. He made the joy of the experience even more special by the way he held her hand and stole kisses whenever he could.

They visited the library, the computer building, the business studies building, the student activity center and the cafeteria and though they were enjoying their secret tour, they were getting tired and hungry.

He offered the first thought on the rest of their day. "You ready to head down Main Street?"

She bounced with her reply. "Yeah! Let's go window shopping."

"Okay, and keep an eye out for any apartment for rent signs."

Her heart jumped. "Oh yeah. How great would it be to get an apartment somewhere around here and really enjoy the last two years of college?"

"Tell me about it."

Main Street was only a block and a half from the Student Activity Center so they cut through the campus and were both surprised where they came out. "Look where we are."

Jake grinned, "I know."

Their speed changed when they turned onto Main. Their work for the day was done, and they had accomplished all they had set out to accomplish. She held his hand and they slowly started strolling past the small shops, businesses, and restaurants.

~ ~ ~

Genna slid the last sales binder into her briefcase as Maureen stood and extended her hand over her desk. "Thank you for coming to see me today. It's always a pleasure doing business with you and your company."

Genna stood a moment later, shook her hand and softly smiled. "My pleasure. Call me if you need anything else."

Genna walked out the front door of the brick townhouse office and into a beautiful fall afternoon. She paused at the top of the steps in front of the building, and casually surveyed the street, beautifully decorated in what was left of the autumn colors, and spotted Jake holding hands and walking with an attractive brunette in a cute skirt. She smiled. She was close enough to yell to him but didn't want to embarrass him in front of the girl.

She watched them walk away for a few moments. *I didn't know Jake had a girl.* She peered more closely and her heart jumped. She took out her phone and dialed Steven.

"Hi sweetheart."

"Hey, Mom. What's up?"

"It's a gorgeous day. I was wondering what you're doing on your day off."

"Jake and I are at the university walking around."

"That's great. Love you. Can I say hi to Jake real quick?"

"Sure."

Genna stood on the elevated brick landing and watched the young girl pass the phone to Jake, and sighed. "Hi Jake. It's Genna. I just wanted to say hi."

"Hi, Mrs. Blair. How are you?"

"I'm doing good sweetheart. Are you two having fun?"

"Yeah. Just walking around window shopping."

"Good. I'm glad you're out having a nice day. I love you."

"I love you too, Mrs. Blair."

"Pass the phone back to Steven?" She watched the exchange again and immediately felt empty. She crossed the side street and stopped at the corner, still watching them walk away.

"I love you."

"I love you too, Mom."

"Do you understand I love you?" Steph heard her mother's voice change. "Do you understand how much I love you?"

She hesitated, trying to read her mother's voice. "Yes, I know you love me very much."

"No sweetheart. I love you a lot more than just very much. I love you more than you could ever understand. Because human words cannot begin to describe how my being and your being are forever connected. You came from me. Do you understand what that means to me? Can you understand how much I love you?"

Steph stopped walking as she listened to the words, and turned toward Jake. Jake looked at her, confused. "Are you okay? Is something wrong?"

"Please answer me sweetheart. I need to hear it."

Stephanie looked behind her; almost staring in her mother's direction. "Yes, I know how much you love me." She could hear her mother crying and she started to cry. "You love me."

"Oh my precious child, I love you beyond your ability to understand. I love you because I made you. I love you because you exist. Do you understand?"

Tears began flowing down Stephie's face and Jake's voice quickened in panic. "Does she need us? What's wrong? What can I do?"

Stephie knew. "If you were here, I would hold you and tell you I love you."

"I'm so sorry I need that. Please forgive me, but I really need that. Is that okay?"

"Mom! I need you to hold me." Her voice reflecting her broken heart as tears flowed down her cheeks.

"Would it be okay?"

Stephie frantically searched her surroundings. "Where are you?"

"A block behind you."

Stephie turned and started running. Jake instantly started running behind her and immediately caught up. "Steph! What's happening? What can I do?"

"You'll understand in three seconds."

And within a second and a half, Stephie saw a woman step from behind the building at the cross street in front of them; her face covered by both hands and with each step closer, more things became clearer. Mrs. Blair stood there wiping both eyes with the tissues in both hands, clutching her phone in one.

Stephie ran up to her and damn near tackled her. They embraced in a love embrace like they hadn't done in years, and Genna began kissing her everywhere she could. And between each kiss came a loving word or sound. Stephie tried to turn her head toward Jake as her mother smothered her with kisses, wanting to make sure he understood completely, and sighed as she caught a glimpse of his satisfied smile.

"Oh god! Oh god! I love you. Do you understand? I love you. I love you more than I love anything, love you."

"I love you too, Mom. I love you so much."

Genna opened one arm and beckoned Jacob in. He went immediately. "Do you know I love you with all my heart too?"

He hugged them. "Yes, Mrs. Blair, I do."

Genna squeezed them both. "No, you don't understand. I don't love you like you're the absolutely special next door neighbor kid who is my precious child's best friend. I adopted you in my heart from the first day I met you and you've interwoven your existence into mine for what seems like your entire life, love you. You are my other precious child, love you. Do you understand?" She sighed, "... Oh, if only you could understand."

He sighed, and hugged them. "I love you. You've always been my other mom. I can't believe I'm lucky enough to have two moms. I love you a lot." They were all now huddled together on the corner feeding each other's souls through the embrace.

Genna slid her hand over the top of Steven's hair and looked into his eyes. "Sweetheart. I'm so sorry my love for you was never conveyed well enough for you to understand there's nothing you could want to do or need to become, that you couldn't count on me as the first person you could confide in. I apologize."

"Oh no mom! That isn't why. It's...it's complicated. But no. I know you love me. I really do! Please don't think that."

"You do know that's the only reason I'm crying, right?" Genna pulled out a few tissues from her pocket and handed him one. "I mean...I need to make sure you know the slightest separation of our souls is all that upset me, don't you?"

Stephie dried her cheeks. "Yes Mom, I do. I honestly understand."

"Okay then! Our souls sewn tight again?" She smiled reflectively. "Let me look at my baby."

With tear swollen eyes and a small but growing smile, she let go of them, but kept Stephie's hand in hers.

"Oh sweetheart, you look so...feminine."

Stephie blushed and lowered her head like she was five again.

Genna studied her, raising her chin with a few soft fingers. "Oh, by the way. I've seen this gradual change for nearly two months now and I've been doing some major reconnaissance for you. Oh my god are we going to have fun shopping and getting our nails and hair done."

Stephie smiled ear to ear, and watched Genna reach for Jake's hand and bring him closer.

"And you Jake. You who've been by her side forever, is still by her side?" She shook her head in amazement. "Oh my god you're wonderful."

Jake reached for Stephie's hand and eyed his second mother. "Do you understand how much I'm by her side?"

"Sweetheart, your love for my baby has been well recorded, and her love for you equally documented. If you think for a second, the greater your love for each other, the less it is in my eyes, then again I've failed in my job to show you what love is."

"I love her."

"How perfect!"

"And, Mom, I love him."

"How fantastic! You two are part of the lucky few who get to love their best friend and be best friends with their lover. It's actually rare. Hollywood's made us believe it doesn't work. Actually, if you're not best friends with your lover, *that's* when it doesn't work. Oh god Steven..." Stephie watched her eyes narrow as his name faded in her voice.

"I've chosen Stephanie, Mom. Actually, Jake chose it for me."

"Really! She softly stared at Jake, and then caressed his cheek. "You're amazing."

Stephie looked into her mother's eyes. "I think I have a *lot* to tell you."

"Well, I'm done my business call. Let's go to lunch!"

Jake and Stephie's eyes met and they both turned to Genna. "Sure!"

"Terrific!" She grabbed both her children by a hand and walked a few steps, stopped and moved Jake to Stephanie's other side, so each could hold one of Stephanie's hands.

"Mom, I feel so lucky right now I can't believe it."

"Sweetheart, you might be too close to this to understand, but I'll make it a point to explain it from now on. My love for you is unconditional. I really do love you because you exist, and there's no additional requisite on your part that will add to or take away from that. I love you both because you exist. I can even separate my love for both of you from the actions you do. My love for both of you is complete." A single tear dropped from each eye and she quickly brushed them away, then lightheartedly offered a new idea. "Now …there's a cute little Cajun restaurant up here on the left. Let's go there."

They were seated at a small round table against a side wall with Stephanie between both of them. "Can I have a glass of unsweetened ice tea?"

"Yes, Ma'am."

Stephie and Jake both watched the server. "Ice tea."

"Me too."

Genna reached for each of their closest hands. "Okay people. You have to come home. Don't get mad at me but your father and I have already discussed this and your grandmother and I have talked…" She faced Jake, "…and dad and I had dinner with your parents." She turned back to Stephie, "and guess what? Everyone supports you and loves you for who you are."

Jake raised his eyebrows. "Do they know we're a couple?"

"No. That, they don't know." Genna grinned. "But I'll tell you; anyone who has a problem with that is going to have a problem with *me*! But I can't wait to see everyone's face when they find out." She laughed out loud. "Because I think it's the greatest thing in the world."

Stephanie searched for confirmation. "Why?"

"Because my two children have made the best choice either of them could have ever made. Oh, and your grandmother is not only completely fine with it, but wants to actively be part of helping you any way she can."

"Nana?"

"Dearie, let me tell you something. Your grandmother's one of the sharpest human-beings you'll ever meet and though she sometimes appears to be no more than a gentle older woman, she has an intelligence and a self-actuated drive like very few people you'll ever meet. The woman is all action. Always has been. Don't be surprised if she amazes you. So seriously, when are you coming home?"

Stephie took a deep unsteady breath, slightly overwhelmed and somewhat confused, and Genna responded with heartfelt understanding. "When is Stephanie coming home?"

Jake answered for her. "When should we come home? How should we come home?"

Genna reached for her water glass. "Let's figure this out. You have the choice of sooner or later. Since everyone not only knows but also supports you, my choice is sooner. How about you?"

Stephie looked at Jake, "My choice is sooner too, if everyone's alright with it." She hid her anxiety.

Genna smiled. "Then if the choice is sooner, can I text everybody for a casual pizza dinner tonight?"

Stephie eyed Jake and he reached for her hand. "Are you okay?"

She inhaled quickly. "A little nervous."

Genna looked from Jake to Stephie, "The only way to get past where you are is to go through the next door, let me text and see if we can all get together tonight and get you past this point."

Stephanie studied her mother's eyes. "You are nana."

Genna laughed at the comment. "Thank you. I take that as a high compliment. Jake, I hate to do this to you, but I'm cutting your date with Stephanie short. Stephanie, we're going to go get you new glasses..." she reached up and moved Stephie's hair back and away from her face, "...and your ears pierced, and your fingernails and toenails done. And girl-talk about all the other things I want to do with you." She could see in her mother's eyes; all she wanted was to be reconnected completely.

"Jake sweetheart, can I steal your girlfriend for the rest of the afternoon? I promise you'll like what I bring back."

Jake lit up like he was getting a present in a few hours. "Sure!"

They finished an enjoyable lunch and Genna's now continual smile became the reassurance both her children secretly sought.

~~~

They said their goodbyes to Jake, then Genna and Stephie sat in Genna's car. "First things first." Genna grabbed her phone and started texting Connor, Morgan and Chris, then held out the phone to her. "Does this sound good, sweetheart?"

She glanced at the text on the screen. *Can we all get together for dinner 2nite? Quick pizza and beer@ our house. My treat. Nothing special. Want to share some things. Let me know.*

"Looks good mom. Should I hit send?"

"Yep." Genna started the car. "Okay…invitations done."

The statement increased her anxiety, but she did her best to hide it. *No turning back now.* Stephie's stomach grumbled. She wanted to blame lunch, but knew better. She breathed deep and Genna heard, and reached for her hand. "Everything'll be fine. I promise."

Stephie offered a faint smile, as she offered Genna her phone.

"No, you read their replies while I drive."

She cradled both phones on her lap.

Genna's phone beeped twice and Steph read the texts. "Chris and Morgan both said they can come."

"Fantastic…You look beautiful in that dress. Do you have clothes?"

"Not a lot but some."

Genna's eyes lit up. "I know what to get you for your birthday."

Stephie smiled a little deeper.

"You really are feminine. What did you change to make yourself so feminine?"

Stephanie tilted her head and raised her shoulders. "I stopped hiding it?"

The answer surprised both of them. Stephie wanted to add *I stopped fighting it* but decided she couldn't share that much at the moment. She was afraid the additional disclosure would lead to a discussion she wasn't quite ready for.

Genna's phone beeped again and Steph read Connor's response. *NP. I'll buy the beer.* "Dad said he'll take care of the beer for tonight." Genna acknowledged the statement but didn't offer a reply.

They drove in silence for a short time, until Stephie shared another secret. "I wore one of your bracelets to the Halloween party Jake and I went to."

Genna smiled softly. "You can. They're yours if you think about it."

Genna glanced at her, with a curious look. "So whose party did you go to?"

"Vicky's. He's been like an older sister to me." She smiled. "That probably didn't make much sense. He's a guy who I went to at the department store. He works in the perfume and make-up department. He did my make-up for the first time and we became friends." She bounced as she turned slightly toward Genna. "He's awesome, he really is! His name is Victor but he likes to be called Vicky." She perked up further. "Can we see if he's working? I'd love you to meet him."

Genna smiled. "Well, the mall's the perfect place to start, so that sounds great! We can get your glasses and your ears pierced there and pick up a few sets of earrings for you. But we have to get our nails done and we need to stop at a few of my favorite clothing stores if we have time. Do you have many shoes?" She glanced at her and laughed, "Like you can ever have *many* shoes!"

Stephanie began feeling better. At least there were consolations to the psychological rollercoaster she was about to ride. She lifted her phone. "Let me see if Vicky's working."

She started texting, *Vick. …U @ work?*

She wrapped her hands around her phone and cradled it on her lap.

Her phone went off a few seconds later and startled her. *I start in a half hour. U coming to visit?*

Yeah. And I'm bringing my mom.

What??

Stephie grinned and typed, *U heard me.*

She knows?

Yeah she knows.

Way 2 go sister! Come visit!

She turned to her mom. "Vicky can't wait to meet you."

"Genna smiled. "I can't wait to meet her …him."

Stephie nodded slightly. "Somewhere safely in between, Mom. Somewhere safely in between."

~~~

Vicky kept glancing down the long isle he knew Stephie would use and when he saw her, he turned to the young girl sitting in his make-up chair, "Would it be okay if I go greet a dear dear friend I need to say hi to?"

The young girl shook her head yes and softly replied, "Sure."

Vicky patted her shoulder. "I'll be right back."

He hurried to Stephie and hugged her tight. "I'm so proud of you!"

He could feel his emotions well as he heard her muffle something that sounded like, "I didn't really do anything." but her mouth was covered by his shoulder and the words didn't come out completely audible. But the reply didn't matter. This was too exciting to let words interfere.

He opened his eyes as their embrace continued and realized the woman standing so close was her mom. He quickly released Stephie; suddenly fighting back unexpected tears as he extended his hand. He tried to talk but nothing came out, so he turned and pointed to his make-up chair.

"He has a client, mom." Stephie scooted him with the back of her hand. "Go. We're coming."

Vicky scurried back and a moment later, both were standing next to him.

He glimpsed at Stephie, put his hand over his heart, and whispered. "So how did you tell your mom?"

Genna extended her hand. "Hi. I'm Genna."

Vicky's mouth opened. "Sorry!" He took her hand with one hand and fanned his face with his other. "Hi Genna. It's so great to meet you. So very very great."

Genna smiled at Vicky's reaction, "Thanks. You too."

"Vick. Mom spotted me and Jake at the new school. She saw us walking, holding hands."

He gasped as he kept working on the young girl in his chair but continually glanced at Stephie. "How funny!" He looked at Genna, "Are you okay?"

Genna nodded. "Completely."

He stared at her eyes a moment longer to verify, then breathed deep and faced Stephie. "You're so lucky."

He finished the last touches on the young girl in front of him. "There you go sugar. You're very pretty."

The young girl stood and headed directly across the aisle to the closest mirror she could see, then turned back, "Thanks!"

"Oh, you're welcome honey." Vicky turned to Steph. "Sit."

"Oh Vick, I can't. We don't have time."

He tilted his head. "You know I'll get in trouble if you don't sit." He quietly pleaded. "Sit for two minutes?"

Steph sat while Vicky quickly touched up her eyes. "So what's going on?"

"Mom and I are going to get my ears pierced and our nails done. Oh, and get me glasses."

Vicky turned to Genna. "I love you." His breathing quickened as he turned to Stephie, "Is that alright to say?"

Stephie started laughing. "Yeah, it's completely okay. But we have to get going. I'm going home as Stephanie tonight!"

He playfully scolded her. "Well, what are you doing sitting here? Get going."

Steph was no sooner out of the chair and Vicky had her in his arms hugging her. He leaned close to her ear. "Love you little sister. Call me after if you can."

Stephie squeezed him. "Love you too big sister. I will."

Vicky's eyes welled as he watched his friend walk away, breathed deep and scanned the area for his next customer.

~ ~ ~

Stephie quickly glanced back at Vicky as they headed out to the mall and then eyed Genna with an almost apologetic look. Thanks for meeting him.

Genna smiled deeply. "My pleasure. He's as cute as can be."

"Mom, he really is. He has the biggest heart, and he and Jake are a riot together. She thought about trying to explain all Vicky had done for her and taught her, but decided that conversation would be too deep for their first girl time together. Enough trauma had already taken place today and she saw more before the day would end. She also envisioned countless future opportunities for heartfelt conversations that would visit the depths of her needs and their love.

But for the rest of this initial girl time, she wanted to do her best to let her mom know she was enjoying their time together and that meant bringing a lighter hearted appearance to the rest of their shopping trip. "So, where we headed?"

Genna replied, "Ears."

They studied the directory and found the store they needed. A half hour later, Stephie's ears were pierced, with a small gold post earring in each and in her hand, a small bag with four other sets inside. She kept gently touching her ears.

Genna's eyes gleamed. "You like?"

Stephanie beamed with an inner joy Genna noticeably savored, "Yeah mom! A lot!"

She could see her mother's satisfaction grow deeper with every experience they shared. They headed toward one of Genna's favorite clothing stores in the mall. "So what clothes do you have?"

"Mainly a few skirts and tops. Oh, and a few dresses."

"Do you have any jeans?"

"Girl jeans?" Her heart skipped a beat. "Yeah. Two pair."

Every secret the child shared felt like a small failure to Genna. How could she have let her child go through this alone? She had to try to retroactively rectify for her own well-being. "Let's go see what we can find, shall we?"

The underlying motive behind their excursion gave Stephanie an emotional warmth she didn't realize was missing. She met her mother's eyes with a guilty look as she hesitated putting a cute casual dress back on its rack.

"You can have it, sweetheart."

"No. I have enough already." She separated the other dresses and hung it back on the rack.

Her mother reached beside her and removed the dress again. "Maybe so sweetheart, but maybe I need to buy it for you."

Her face showed a curious confusion which Genna noticed. "You'll understand when you have a child."

Genna bought her a few tops, jeans and skirts, and the cute casual dress. "Okay, I'm not sure we have enough time to get you new glasses, so let's save that for another day, okay?"

Stephie raised the bags in her hands. "I'm following you."

Genna smiled. "Then follow me to the nail place."

Steph's heart jumped. The idea she was going to get her nails done thrilled her. They headed to the car, and ended up at a small strip mall near their house.

"I have to order pizza before we leave here. Remind me. Where should we get them from?"

"How about Five Points? Can we get a thick one too?"

"Sure. And I'll get one white."

The bell above the door chimed as they entered the salon. "Hi. Welcome Mrs B. Who is the pretty girl?"

"My daughter Stephanie!"

The woman turned and gazed at Stephie with a welcoming smile. "Oh. Okay."

Genna pointed to the shelves filled with little bottles. "Go pick one. You can have a different color on your toes, but not today. I want to see you all matched. Okay?"

Stephie's heart jumped each time she heard she was going to do something feminine. "Sure!"

She stood there with her mouth slightly open, scanning the entire salon, then walked toward the shelves. Just thinking about being able to color her nails excited her. The dozens of tiny bottles overwhelmed her though, and she couldn't pick a color. She had five different bottles in her hand.

Genna whispered behind her. "You having fun?"

She turned slightly, "Oh, yeah!"

"Did you pick a color?"

She could feel the newness of the experience threatening to overpower her. "I can't decide!"

Genna laughed. "You're such a *new* girl."

"Mom!"

"Oh, relax. This is a safe haven dear."

Genna eyed the bottles in Stephie's hands. "Four of them are a shade of pink. I'd pick a pink one."

Stephie gave a soft chuckle as she examined the colors, then held them up. "Which one?"

Genna looked and pointed, "This one."

"Okay." She turned to the girl. "This one please."

"And you Mrs B?"

"French please."

"White and clear?"

"Yes."

They both sat and two girls started working on their nails. Stephie stared in amazement and studied each finished nail. *Oh, I can't wait to show Jake.* She came out of her trance and sat up, "Pizza."

Genna smiled and gripped her phone. "How many?"

"Extra. Jake can eat a whole one and so can Chris."

"It's amazing, isn't it?"

They smiled at each other and Stephie's heart raced when she realized she was going home with painted nails. She examined her left hand and grinned. "I can't wait to show Jake!"

"I bought four." Genna grinned at Stephie's remark. "Two regular, one white, and one thick. Does that sound like enough?"

"Yeah, I think so."

"So how long have you and Jake been more than best friends?"

"For a while now. Pretty much since August." Stephie's heart jumped, remembering how their deeper relationship started.

Genna asked softly. "Is that what made you decide this?"

The question hit Stephanie in the middle of her chest, and she immediately felt an emptiness. "No….No… Not at all. This isn't a decision, Mom. This is who I am." The question seemed simple; even innocent, but it trigged nondescript flashbacks of years of confusion and heartache, and Stephie immediately wondered if her answer seemed too quick or mean.

The question unintentionally opened a wellspring of thought that threatened to take Steven down a path far more overwhelming than anyone would understand. The present, though wonderful and positive, was equally traumatic, and Steven already had enough accumulated trauma for a lifetime. Years of confusion, tied to emotional turmoil lay piled within his memory and though he knew his mother would never hurt him, the confusion was closer to the surface than anyone could understand. Typical twenty year olds enjoy twenty years of experience being who they are by the time they turn twenty, but it was very clear to Steven that she had roughly four months of broken experiences being who she really is, and they were preceded by countless years of fighting and fearing the realization.

But she also knew Genna loved him, and she knew in her heart she meant no harm by the question, so she chose that as her focus. It was the only way he could re-lock the mountain of confusion inside him. It was the only way he could salvage the rest of the broken chain of normality he hoped for the rest of Stephie's life.

Her heart beat faster, waiting for the next question, but her mother didn't ask another. She refocused on the young lady painting her toenails as her mother's voice softly entered her awareness. "So what do you think?"

Stephie gazed up with her mouth slightly open. "I love it. I really love it."

Genna's face displayed her pleasure. "Good."

~~~

Jake heard a car pull into the driveway between the houses and opened his kitchen door. He stepped out onto the landing and watched with nervous anticipation as Genna and Stephie stepped out of the car.

"Jake, can you get the pizzas for us?" Genna popped the trunk.

His eyes remained fixed on Stephie. "Sure Mrs. B."

Steph met him at the back of the car and held out her hands. "What do you think?"

"I can't believe you're standing here ...Steph's standing here...with me."

She hugged him and spoke in his ear. "This is the day we were waiting for."

"I know."

"I hope my legs hold out."

"I'll hold you up."

She leaned closer and playfully whispered. "Just don't do it the way you did at the party, okay?"

"I promise." He laughed, then turned to Genna. Who's house, Mrs. B.?"

She walked up the side steps, "Where was the last party?" and looked down from the concrete landing. "Your house... Bring them over here."

He followed them into the house and laid the boxes on the kitchen table. "I have to go put my books away. I'll be right back."

Stephie immediately sought to keep her reconnection with him. "I'll come with you."

"What if my dad comes home?"

"Mom said he already knows, didn't she? Besides, if he sees me, I'll feel less on display tonight."

"Good point." Jake felt completely nervous for her. He really didn't know what he could do for her, and his helplessness made him feel lost, but he was going to support her the best he could.

"I'm going next door with him for a few minutes." She walked over to him and turned to her mom. "We'll be right back."

Genna leaned against the counter. "Okay, sweetheart."

They went next door and Stephie shut the door behind them. She walked over to him, stood in front of him and dropped her forehead onto his chest. He took her cue and wrapped his arms around her. She sighed. "Ugh! What a day."

He held her softly. "I think it's crazy but I think it's terrific. Hey, it'll be over soon and I bet it ends up not so bad."

"I know. It's just... I have so many different thoughts. It's weird." She sighed. "What am I supposed to do if my dad is upset or disappointed with me wanting to live my life as a female?" She looked up at him. "I don't want to hurt him, but how can I not be who I am?"

He slowly rubbed her back. "I don't think your dad will have a problem."

She rested her face against his chest. "I hope not. I've been fighting this way too long and I don't have any more fight in me, to fight anyone else."

"You don't have to fight anyone else."

She breathed deeply. "I hope not."

Jake stood there holding her and he was going to stand there holding her for as long as she wanted. He whispered, "You alright?"

"Yeah."

"Any second thoughts?"

"No."

"Just the day?"

She sighed. "Yeah."

He hugged her tighter. "You really are gorgeous."

"Thanks."

"Do you want my dad to see you?"

"Kinda. I just think he'll be accepting. I don't know why."

"Because he loves you?"

She sighed again. "Yeah. I'm counting on it."

He reached down and patted her bottom. "Let me put my books away."

"Okay." She held on long enough for him to wonder if she was going to let go, but she finally did. He started piling his books.

"I think your parents are going to be more shocked about us being a couple, than the way I'm dressed."

He glanced at her. "You may be right. I guess we're going to find out in a little while."

"So, you're okay with what they'll think of the two of us?"

He slid his hands under his books and stood up, made a face and tilted his head. "Yeah." He nodded. "Yeah, I am."

"What if any of them don't like it?"

He stood there with the pile of books. "Then they'll soon learn they have a choice. Accept us or don't. I can't live my life worrying about what other people want. I really can't. I'd love to! It'd be nice to meet everyone's expectations. But I'm pretty sure that only happens on another planet. Not this one. Don't get me wrong. I'm hoping not a single one of them has a problem. But since I have no control over whether they do or not, me caring isn't going to matter. There's one thing I can tell you though; their level of acceptance isn't going to change my plans for you and me."

She shook her head. "You're amazing."

He looked back at her as he headed down the hallway to his room. "No, I'm really not. But no one's going to tell me I can't love you. Not even my mom and dad."

She shook her head again. "You're amazing."

They heard the kitchen door open as he dropped his books on the floor next to his dresser. "Dad?"

The normal resonating reply came back. "Jacob."

He stood straight. "Okay! Here we are! How do you want to handle it?"

Her eyes opened wide and she took a deep breath. "Let's walk by him nonchalantly and head over to my house."

He couldn't control the grin on his face but the expression wasn't all happiness. His nerves had taken control of his smiling muscles.

"What're you grinning about?"

"I can't help it!"

He tenderly grasped her hand and they headed out of the bedroom and into the hall toward the kitchen. Chris was placing his work boots on the top basement step as they approached the side door.

"Hey, Dad."

"Hi, Mr. H."

"Hey Jake."

He gave Stephie a quick glance. "Hi sweetheart." Then he stopped and his head jerked around again. "HI SWEETHEART!!"

He stood up, went over to her and hugged her. "Hi! How are you? Is this the pizza news?" He couldn't stop smiling.

"Kinda."

"Kinda?"

"See you at pizza!" They both were through the kitchen door that fast.

He opened the outside kitchen door as they crossed the drives. "Did your father buy beer?"

She yelled without turning around. "Yeah."

They hurried up the other steps and inside their other house. "Mom, Chris just saw me! And he was completely okay."

"I told you!" She ran her fingers through her hair. "Why don't you both go in the family room and relax. You have to be exhausted. I know I am."

Jake glanced at Genna as she said the words, and noticed the stress of the day quickly catching up with her. He motioned to her. "Let's all go relax and wait for everyone." He held out his arm and waited for her to walk in front of him.

Genna fell into her usual spot on the family room sofa and they sat on the loveseat together. He wrapped his arms around Stephie and whispered in her ear. "I could get used to this." Then looked up. "Is this alright, Mrs. B?"

Genna lifted her head off the back of the sofa and opened her eyes for a quick glance. "Oh god yes."

All three were dozing off when Connor walked in. They heard him plop the case of beer onto the kitchen table and Stephie's heart jumped. She looked at Jake for support and watched his uncontrollable grin appear instantly. "Here goes another one."

Connor called out from the kitchen. "Hello?"

Jake raised his voice. "We're in here."

Connor walked into the family room, first noticing Genna. "Hi." He started walking over to her to give her a kiss and casually turned his head. "Hi." His double-take was far less exaggerated than Chris's but obvious none the less. He breathed in, dropped his briefcase, turned to Stephie and held out his arms. She rose and walked into his open arms, and they just stood there in each other's embrace. No words spoken. He held her and she held him. His hand moved to the back of her head and he gave her forehead a kiss then went back to hugging her. They stood, tenderly embracing, neither moving.

Jake and Genna made eye contact, subtly acknowledging each other's approval.

Connor placed his hand on the back of her head again, and kissed the side of her hair. "Pizza smells good."

Genna's voice echoed her approval. "We bought four."

"Sounds right. Did you buy a thick one?"

Stephie answered as she cuddled against him and rested her head on his shoulder. "Yeah, Dad. For me and you."

She could feel his breathing. "Perfect." He leaned toward her ear and whispered, "I love you."

She said I love you too in a slightly deeper way. "Are you okay?" She was afraid to add *with this*, but he seemed to know what she meant.

"Sweetheart, if this means you're happy, I'm very okay. If it means I can have hugs again like this, like when you were younger, then I'm thrilled."

He kissed her a half dozen times on her forehead, then leaned and kissed her on her lips and her heart melted. He hadn't kissed her like that in a while. She didn't want to let go. "I need you, Dad."

He squeezed her a little tighter. "Do you think for a second I need you less?" He kissed her forehead again. "Can I look at you?"

They broke their embrace and she stepped back, but not enough for him to view her completely. She couldn't step back more, even if there was room. Each inch seemed to make her more uncomfortable. He kept hold of her hand and studied her face. "I love you."

She stared at him and her eyes welled up. "I love you too Dad."

Jake finally spoke. "This is great!"

Genna responded, completely out of character. "He's going to get so lucky tonight."

The three of them laughed.

"I'm serious. If we didn't have company coming over….he'd be getting lucky right now."

The mood in the room instantly turned festive and Jake and Genna both stood. "When's your parents coming over…any idea?"

"None. Want me to call them?"

"Yeah! Tell them to get over here. Doesn't your father know there's free pizza and beer over here, waiting for him?"

Connor eyed everyone. "So how did this come about?"

Genna responded. "You'll hear in a bit, but let's wait till Chris and Morgan get here?"

"Okay, I guess." He met Jake's eyes and Jake reached out and rubbed his shoulder. "That's what the pizza party's for."

His eyes moved to each of them once again, but no one volunteered any further information.

"Alright." He picked up his briefcase and walked toward his bedroom.

Genna headed to the kitchen. "Jake. Can you take the rest of this beer downstairs and put it in the fridge please?"

"Sure."

She opened the refrigerator and fit as many as she could. He carried the remainder down. Stephie stood there and watched for a moment. "I'll get paper plates and napkins."

She filled the napkin holder, thinking about tonight's gathering. They were for information sharing, but she knew they all appreciated these get-togethers for their main underlying reason; coming together as one family, and over time, she and Jake learned to treasure the times their entire immediate family gathered together. It always turned into a small party and often, a cherished memory.

She caught herself and paused for a moment. She had just spent the last few minutes, living life as Stephie without a conscious thought about the change. *This feels so…natural.* She looked down as she slid her hands down the front of her dress. *Look at me. I'm feminine. Can anybody not see it now? I'm feminine. …But I'm still a person. I'm still human. I can love. I am smart. I'm kind. I'm thoughtful. …And I'm feminine. Is it so much different than being loving, kind, thoughtful, smart, and a boy?* She sighed. *Isn't the kind, thoughtful, loving part supposed to matter more than the girl or boy part, anyway?* She scanned the room, measuring whether the world looked different, and noted how everything looked exactly the same. Nothing exploded. Nothing came to an end. No one was hurt during the change.

She pictured someone telling Steven, this was a choice and he should grow up or seek help. She thought sarcastically. *A choice…a choice, to feel I was born the wrong gender…like being born without a hand is a choice. Yeah, we must have thought or done something wrong in the womb. I'm not pretending to be a girl. I pretended trying to be a boy. But who could really understand? I'm living it and it's hard to understand.*

But am I finally allowed to be who I am? Am I really allowed to be who I know I am inside? Does it really offend some people that I'm feminine? Is it really offensive? I think I look feminine whether I'm dressed as a boy or a girl, and when I'm dressed as a girl, nobody even questions my femininity. I've even proven I'm feminine for the few times I've gone out as Stephie. But one way or the other, I'm still the same person I've always been.

~ ~ ~

Chris heard his kitchen door open and yelled from the bathroom as he shaved. "Hi!"

Morgan dropped her purse on the closest kitchen chair and glanced up. "Hi."

"How you doin'?"

She walked toward him. "Beat. Long day."

"Well, come and get ready. I think everyone's waitin' on us."

She reached the bathroom door. "Why? What's the rush? What's going on?"

He grinned. "The child picked today for his reveal."

"Really!"

The news seemed to energize her instantly. She disappeared into their bedroom. Not ten minutes later, she turned the corner of the family room and Chris smiled. "Ready?"

"Yep." She grabbed her purse from the chair and they headed next door. A few seconds later, she opened the Blair kitchen door. "Hi."

"Come on in. We're in here. Grab yourselves a beer."

"Already on it!" Chris opened the fridge door. "Anyone need one?"

Genna yelled. "Yes please. There's frozen glasses in there. Get me one?"

They walked in, beers in hand, and Morgan greeted everyone. "Hi."

Four *hi*'s came back as Morgan looked around and found Stephie sitting in Jake's arms. "Hi."

"Hi, Mrs. H."

A tight lipped smile broke on Morgan's face. "Let me see."

She stood up. Chris gave Genna her beer and glass, then moved behind Morgan and watched. Morgan inhaled as she eyed Steph. "You look so cute. Wow. Oh my, your nails are done. Let me see." She held out her hands and Morgan examined them. Chris sipped his beer, then reached in front of Morgan, for Stephie's closest hand and gave her a quarter spin as he pulled her toward him. "You're beautiful!"

She handled the move completely and never lost eye contact with him.

"Do you have a new name?"

She beamed. "Stephanie."

"Beautiful!" He pulled her into him and kissed her on her forehead. "As beautiful as you are."

He opened her like a flower, "Jake named me!" She looked at her mother. "Changed it anyway."

"Now *that's* funny." Chris let her go, almost leading her back to the seat next to Jake. "How'd it happen?"

She peeked at Jake and he took over. "Oh, there's a lot to share tonight." He slid onto the floor and sat on the other side of the coffee table facing Genna and Connor and reached for Stephie's hand and she sat on the floor next to him, leaving the loveseat for his parents.

Chris noticed the slight tension from Morgan and softly offered, "Before we start gabbing, can we start eating? I'm starving."

Connor slapped his thigh and leaped to his feet. "So am I!"

Chris made the kitchen first and started opening boxes while Connor handed out plates. "You two can have beer with your dinner if you want."

They made eye contact and turned in unison, "No thanks." Jake followed it, "Not right now."

Genna pointed to the fridge. "There's soda in there."

After filling plates, everyone headed back into the family room, food and drink in hand and sat in the same spots.

When all were situated, Connor led, "So who's starting?"

Genna smiled and spoke, "I was leaving my appointment today and when I walked out of the building, I saw Jake walking with a girl. So I called Steven to see where he was and the girl next to Jake answered his phone."

The right side of Jake's mouth curled up slightly at Genna's choice of words. He knew she could have said *holding a girl's hand* but he also knew her grace. She wouldn't share things that weren't hers to share. But the time had come. He inhaled. "Yeah. We were holding hands, walking along Main Street." He started the sentence eyeing no one specifically, but finished facing the only adult in the room he thought hadn't given her complete consent and as he expected, Morgan stopped chewing when she heard the sentence. They made eye contact and Jake held his longer than Morgan held hers.

"Today's her coming out party, but it's also our coming out party. We're boyfriend and girlfriend. Or boyfriend and boyfriend…"

Chris chimed in, "Or Ralph." which was his way of saying, "Who cares what you call it." Jake and Genna laughed. Both had heard Chris explain *Ralph* all too many times in the past.

Connor decided to join in, "So you two are Ralph."

"Yeah, Dad. We are."

Jake reached for her hand without turning his head anywhere toward his mother. He made a mental note; *I'll be as polite as she is tonight and we will talk as soon as possible.*

Chris's enthusiasm increased. "So when did the two of you start dating?"

Stephanie sat up, answering with the same enthusiasm, "Officially August, but I think we've liked each other for a long time."

Jake listened to Stephanie's voice and how she meekly yearned for acceptance. Then confirmed, "A long time." and glanced at his mother. She displayed no emotions.

"I think it's great! I'm serious." Genna looked at both of them. "I'm sorry. Neither of you could have picked a better boyfriend, girlfriend. I'm very pleased." She eyed Stephie. "…I had a clue though something was going on with you. You left a bottle of bath beads on the side of the tub."

Steph sat straighter. "I knew it! You didn't find my clothes though, did you?"

"No, where are they?"

"In the attic."

Genna scrunched her nose. "Ugh! We have to get them out of there tonight. They'll get that attic smell."

"Chris stood up. "Anyone want another beer?"

Three *me*'s came immediately back.

"Can I have one too, Dad?"

Chris glanced at Jake and smiled. "Sure son. Anything for you sweetheart?"

"No, Mr. H. I'm fine."

Connor showed his natural ability to normalize a conversation. "So, is school set?"

"Yeah. We're both registered and we have our classes. We were going to look for a cheap apartment too, and that's when mom spotted us."

Genna joined. "Did you manage to get the same schedules?"

"Yep! We did good. Mom, the school is gorgeous. I love it. We had so much fun. We wandered every hallway we could find."

Connor smiled. "The two of you better stay on top of the apartment idea if you're going to get something decent."

"We will, Mr. B. It doesn't have to be anything special. Just something so we can enjoy the last two years as part of the college, and not just commuters."

"I agree." Genna offered nothing further, but her confirmation seemed to have a hint of something more attached to it. Jake discreetly studied her a few moments longer. Certain statements from her always felt like more than just idle words.

Everyone started loosening up and the evening turned into a genuine party. Everyone happy to be part of Stephanie's coming out party. Nearly everyone just as happy with Stephanie and Jake's coming out also party.

The impromptu party didn't end till early morning and by the time it ended, more than two of them weren't feeing any pain. Chris and Morgan kissed everyone goodbye and Chris led her toward the kitchen door. Jake discreetly held Stephie's hand as they followed Genna and Connor out to the side landing. He hesitated. The energy of the entire day left him less than sure how to say goodbye to his girl. He wanted to pull her into him and kiss her goodbye, like any normal couple, but he felt completely awkward in front of everyone. He was amazed at how loving and understanding her parents had been during the entire ordeal, but millennia of social prejudice cautioned him regarding this next simple step. He decided he would be the last to say goodbye. He wasn't leaving before properly saying goodnight to her and hearing privately that she was alright.

The four of them watched Morgan shut her side door and headed back to the family room.

Stephie excitedly shared her next thought. "I can't wait to text Vicky. He wanted to know what happened tonight."

Her father blurted. "Who's Vicky?"

"One of my new friends. Mom met him today. He's a sweetheart!"

Connor glanced at Genna. She met his eyes and held his hand. After twenty-some odd years of marriage, they could now communicate with very little effort.

Connor turned to his child, "Did you have a good night?"

She met his eyes, "Scary, but yeah. But we both knew it was going to be scary. It's probably the main reason we put it off as long as we did." Jake knew it was mainly her, but he had no problem with how she responded. She had shared enough today.

Genna reached for her hand. "How about the day? Did you have fun with me?"

"Hell yeah!" He watched Genna's loving reaction to Stephie's words and smile, and the resolidified connection fed his soul. Genna smiled, wrapped her in her arms and kissed her. "Good."

Steph turned to her father and he extended his arms. He kissed her on her lips as they hugged, and she melted in his arms. She breathed deep and hugged him tenderly. " 'night mom. 'night dad."

"Goodnight."

Jake waited to hear their bedroom door shut, then sat on the loveseat and pulled her closer as she sat next to him. He kissed her softly. "You doing alright?"

She looked into his eyes. "Yes. …I guess. I may crash after you leave, but I'm okay."

He stared into her eyes and momentarily lost his focus. She had amazing eyes. "We did it. We made it."

She rested her head under his chin. "I wouldn't have made it without you."

"Oh, I think you would have, but I'm glad we did this together."

"Can I text Vicky real quick?"

He smiled. "Of course."

She cuddled in his arms and started texting. *Hi U up? The nite went great! nerves but great!*

Vicky responded moments later. *I'm up. Waiting. Great! U need to talk or just txt?*

its late Txt now talk tomorrow?

NP so it went great?

yeah! Jake came rite out and told them about us! my dad kissed me…on the lips!

Vicky confirmed, *that's great right?*

hell yeah!

I'm so happy for you girl! …so happy! Luv u!

luv u 2!

She placed her phone on the coffee table, then burrowed deeper inside his arms. "I love you too Jacob Harrison."

He felt his entire body absorb her words. "I love you too, Stephanie Blair. …I love you too."

They sat and held each other, and he used her embrace to secretly decompress. He felt like every little battle they went through solidified their relationship, and their bond was already greater than any bond he had ever felt.

He offered a thought for their next connection. "I don't have work until five tomorrow night. Can we hang a little bit tomorrow before I have to leave?"

Her face lit as she studied his eyes. "Sure. What time?"

"I'll call you …around nine?"

"Okay." She leaned up and kissed him.

He reluctantly stood, reached for her hand, and walked her to the kitchen door. He kissed her again, and registered his depth of connection with her, then caressed her bottom as their kiss ended. "Sleep tight."

"You too."

He ran across the drives, then turned and watched her disappear inside her kitchen door as he stepped behind his.

CHAPTER TWELVE
VARIATION

Stephie's phone rang at nine on the dot. She glanced at the screen and hit the send button. "Damn, you're good!"

"Why? What'd I do?"

"It's exactly nine."

"I didn't do it on purpose."

She smiled. She knew he didn't. "What's up?"

"My mom and dad went out shopping for new curtains or something and I'm sittin' here alone. And I was thinking… I have to lift. Do you feel like your first installment of your birthday present?"

Her heart jumped. "Really?"

His tone lowered. "You are too weird. How soon can you come over?"

She hopped. "I'm almost ready. Ten minutes?"

"Sure. Hurry."

His instruction went straight to her heart and her speed increased. She had set her alarm earlier than normal for a Saturday morning, just in case he said come right over, and the corners of her mouth curled up thinking how well she knew him. He was a constant in an otherwise confusing world, which was one of the many things she loved about him.

She already had her definition of the perfect outfit for the day; a short purple chiffon dress, and a pair of black slippers. Her hair was finally getting long enough to style and she curled the almost shoulder length ends slightly toward her neck. She was hoping she could wow him this morning and she thought her chances were panning out rather nicely. She spritzed herself with a little perfume and hopped across the drives.

She knocked and Jake immediately opened the door. He was noticeably as anxious as she was to see him. She stepped in and he swooped her into his arms and gave her a long, deep kiss. She slowly raised her arms and curled them around his neck and his desire for her reaffirmed her new female mindset. When their kiss softly broke, she tapped her toes on the hardwood floor as she regained her balance. "Hi!"

"Hi. How you doing this morning?"

She casually looked around to confirm they were alone. "Good. You?"

"Good." Though his tone backed his answer, he wasn't completely fine. This concern he had with his mother was a continual thought in the back of his mind, but nothing he wanted her to worry about.

She looked into his eyes. "I saw your birthday invitation on our kitchen counter. You're having an autumn barbeque?"

"Yeah! Sounds like fun, doesn't it? Everyone's invited." He wrapped his arms around her again and spun her. "I can't believe we're turning twenty-one."

She hugged his neck tighter. "I know. It's crazy. I don't feel like an adult."

"Shh. Don't tell them that. They couldn't handle it."

He tickled her waist and as she fought off his hands. He reached around and grabbed two handfuls of her rear and she slapped him on his shoulder. "Are you going to give me a show or not?"

"Is that what I am… a show?"

She asked demurely, "Are you doing your shoulders?"

"No. Lats."

Her eyes narrowed. "What are lats?"

He reached around to his back with the opposite hand. "These."

"Oh. Okay." She hopped. "Will you be getting all sweaty?"

The right side of his mouth rose. "Probably."

"Oh, that's a shame." Her blatant dishonesty noticeably tickled him and she found herself craving every additional reaction.

He grabbed her bottom again and made her jump. She playfully scowled. "Will you wait till you're done exercising before you reach for your reward."

"Oh! Is that what you are now? My reward?"

She playfully countered, "Aren't I?"

He turned toward the basement door. "Watch your head coming down the steps. It may not fit."

He led her into the basement and she plopped down on the old living room chair which filled one corner of the exercise area. She bounced again, anticipating the show.

Jake rolled a small dumbbell away from the bench with the top of his foot. "So, did you have fun last night?"

She felt a comfort envelop her and a reflective smile appear. "I had a blast. I love your father."

Jake glanced at her as he straightened the rest of the metal weights. "He amazes me sometimes. It's great how he's completely okay with the new you, isn't it?"

She smiled and slid to the edge of the chair. "Yeah! He always lets me know there's a special place in his heart for me."

"I loved the way your dad hugged and kissed you."

She sighed. "He made me feel fantastic. I needed that. He isn't as open as your dad, and it meant a lot to me."

"Me too. Your mother and father are aces."

He went around the back of the lifting bench, unhooked the pulley on the weights, and added two large metal disks and then three smaller ones onto the three that were on the machine. She walked over to the bench, grabbed the towel laying over the horizontal bar without looking at him, and sat back down, ready for her show.

He gripped the ends of the long bar which hung on the other end of the pulley, sat and wedged his knees under the diagonal braces at the back of the machine and pulled down as hard as he could. Her jaw dropped as she watched the stack of metal disks rise on the other end of the cable. The effort went directly to her chest and her mouth unconsciously opened.

The last rise of the bar in his hands seemed to pull him off the floor and he stood. He focused on her eyes and smiled, "One." She sat straight backed at the edge of the chair but offered no response. Sixty seconds later, he grabbed the wide bar again and repeated the first exercise almost exactly.

~ ~ ~

Chris rubbed his protruding belly and grabbed Morgan's hand as they walked across the diner parking lot to the car. "That was excellent."

Morgan was sure he would bring up last night during breakfast, but not a word. She didn't want to talk about it. Not because she had a problem with having a problem. She just knew him. *Any discussion will turn ugly if I don't see it his way.* She loved how strong willed and opinionated he was, up to when they disagreed anyway. "It was, but are you too full to go to the stores you promised to take me to?"

He glared at her playfully. "You know I'm going to bitch in store three whether I'm full or not, but I promised, so I'll do my best to at least keep the bitching short and low."

She grabbed further up his arm and they walked arm in arm for the last thirty feet. He hit the door locks, went to her side and opened her door. She looked up in shock. "Are you sick?"

"Can't a guy open the car door for his bride?"

"He can. I just didn't think you could. Do you want to go home that bad?"

"Hey!" He kissed her as she got in.

He hesitated shutting her door. "Where we headed?"

She answered softly. "The mall."

She sighed deeply for the moment before he joined her from the other side. She badly wanted to be alone. She needed to be alone, but any change to these previously set plans would raise conversations and offer less chance of getting her head around the events of the night before.

She thought, *my world just turned upside down*, and she could feel the thought drain her. She knew Steven was different. She had actually prepared herself for Steven's eventual revelation. *But Jake? Her son? No. Steven was doing this. This wasn't who Jake was. There were no signs of this …anywhere …ever. Why would Steven do this to him?*

The car shutting off in the next parking lot interrupted her introspection, and she came back to the moment; aware that her movements needed to remain purposefully natural, to avoid an adverse reaction from Chris.

Moments later, she found herself sitting once again in the passenger seat, not having registered a thing she had looked at inside the store, but she was exactly where she needed to be. She needed these short car rides to think…to figure this out.

How am I supposed to be alright with this? How could everyone else be alright with this? Yes, they're our children, but this isn't right. They love each other, I get it. They've always loved each other and they should love each other, but not like this. This is wrong. For so many reasons…this is wrong.

~ ~ ~

By the time Jake grabbed the bar for the ninth time, he was glistening with sweat and noticeably feeling drained but he stared at her the entire set and even gave her a soft grin as he pulled down the last time.

She looked at him, confused. "What are you smiling about?"

"You're helping me. I'm trying to show off for you and you're helping me do more."

She walked to him as he sat on the bench and slowly started wiping the sweat off his shoulders and arms. She wanted to put the towel down and slide her hand over him instead, but refrained. She didn't want to interrupt his workout, but she wouldn't mind it being over. She felt her breathing deepen. Was this amazing man really hers? She traced over his shoulder. It was so different than hers. His skin felt harder. She moved behind him and stared at him, then realized she had lost focus and began wiping his back and neck again.

She silently sighed as she finished and returned to the chair. His smile indicating her actions and her breathing, tickled him. She felt herself blush.

~ ~ ~

Chris parked the car in front of the next store, and continued discreetly watching Morgan. He knew last night was weighing heavily on her mind and he knew she wasn't okay. But he pretended nothing was wrong; giving her space as she went through the motions of shopping. He could see her preoccupation. He could see she didn't notice his awareness, but they had been connected too long for even the subtlest deviations not to be completely recognized.

He made up his mind to go easy on her today. He could have tried to hammer his opinion into her, but he knew it wouldn't be as true or as permanent as her own change of heart, even if that took time. The day was bright and sunny and last night was thoroughly enjoyable. He thought he'd ride that feeling a while longer. Besides, he knew he could bring up a conversation about the kids whenever he wanted. Maybe he could even soften her up a little first. But then he thought, *I'm not trying to win her over. Hell, I'm not sure it's even my place to try to teach her something.*

His patience continued until he reached for Morgan's hand as they walked out of store five and his mouth kicked in without warning. "So, are you going to play a power-play with the boy?"

His words startled her. "What do you mean?"

Chris gave her a soft glance as he unlocked the car. "Morgan, how long we been married?"

Her heart jumped and her mind instantly sped. "Do you think anyone else noticed I had a problem with them?"

He wasn't concerned with Genna or Connor noticing. He was only concerned with the children noticing. He lifted an eyebrow at her. "Do you think Jake noticed?"

She dropped her head. "I know Jake noticed. Shit. I couldn't help it. It's not what I was taught was acceptable. I mean, I wish them everything I would wish anyone, but I can't get past some of the things I was taught. Especially since it's so right here."

He emitted a single snort. "That's funny. Those are the things I've worked my whole life getting past."

Her voice mirrored her self-doubt. "I know. I know. How'd you do it?"

"Work dear. I literally worked through it. I started with questions, when I saw the discrepancy between the supposed offense and the injustice it was receiving. I weighed the implications. I measured my own answers. I questioned all of it. And it took me a long time to realize the injustice and hatred is contrived and based on the opinions of a few anonymous authors who lived thousands of years ago, sprinkled with the influence of cults as old as the book they swear they represent. How backward and immature some beliefs are; how sad some of our societal mores go happily unquestioned. Humans letting humans from two thousand years ago dictate beliefs without so much as a humble inquiry questioning those opinions, and if you do, you're declared a heretic or worse." He shook his head. "It has stopped my entire species from moving forward." He breathed deep and narrowed his eyes as he studied her. "Has Steven or Stephanie ever been anything but an amazingly beautiful loving child? Ever?"

She looked down. "No."

"Do you think Stephanie noticed?"

She breathed deep as she looked up. "God, I hope not. Shit. You know I don't have a problem with her, don't you? I just wasn't ready to see her snuggled next to Jake when we walked in."

He felt his smile grow as he pictured them in his mind. "That's funny because it tickled me." He started the car. "Do you think you'd have handled it better if they broke that news a little softer?"

"Probably…I think so." Her face contorted. He could tell she wasn't sure, but at least she was working the paradox. And as long as she was working it, the next step had to be done by her. He eased the tension. "Want to have a late lunch at Logan's?"

His suggestion was like a reprieve. "Hell yeah."

He reached across the middle console for her hand, and she interlocked her fingers in his.

~~~

He unhooked the cable from the weights and removed three metal disks. "Three more sets."

Everything he was doing was making her want him. Every sound, every smell, making her think of nothing but being buried under his strong sweaty body and him taking her any way he wanted.

She silently decided she wanted the show to be over. She had better things for them to be doing. She watched him finish the last set and she stood as he walked around the bench and sat on its red plastic seat. He bent over and rested his forearms on his thighs, and she silently walked around to his back and started toweling him off. He lifted his sweat-soaked shirt over his head and she stared in amazement as she quietly wiped his back. He sat there enjoying the attention, and didn't move. When she was done drying his back, she moved around to face him and he sat up. She softly wiped his neck and shoulders, her stomach not inches from his face. She knelt in front of him and dried his chest, then down his stomach; memorizing every contour. He was exquisite.

She rose and he patted her behind. "Time for a shower."

She felt her heart respond. She wished he had other things in mind before his shower. She silently placed the towel over the bar and followed him up the stairs.

She followed him into his room and he grabbed a shirt and sweats from a drawer. He turned and gave her a quick kiss. "Use my phone and text my parents and see where they are. I'll be back in five minutes." He ran out of the room stripping as he headed to the bathroom.

He wasn't lying. He was gone five minutes and re-entered the room.

"They're headed to one more store and then they're going to have lunch at Logan's. They asked if you wanted to meet them there. I told them you had work at five and would probably be gone by the time they got home."

She stared at his upper body, then let her eyes wonder down to his muscular thighs and smiled. "Thanks for the show."

He shook his head. "You're welcome. You're strange, but you're welcome."

They spent the next few hours secretly alone, kissing, cuddling and talking, and finally fell asleep in each other's arms.

What seemed like no more than an instant later, his phone alarm went off and she felt him jump in response. He grabbed the phone and shut it off. "Stephanie."

She had no idea of the elapsed time and made no move to awake fully from her current bliss. "Stephanie." He waited a moment. "Sweetheart, we have to get up."

She reached her arms around his neck without opening her eyes. "But I was having the best dream." She still hadn't opened her eyes.

He kissed her. "Come on. Wake up. Please?"

She slowly came out of her daze, but only opened one eye.

He separated from her embrace, rose from the bed, then opened his closet and started changing into his work uniform.

She squinted in his direction. "Where you think you're going?"

"Work."

"You suck." She curled up and fell back asleep.

He was fully dressed now. "Are you getting up or am I leaving you here?" She peered at him with a squinted eye.

"I know. I suck."

She sat up. "What time is it?"

"Four fifteen. I have to leave in ten minutes. Are you okay?"

"Yeah."

"I should've gotten my shift covered."

"Yeah. ...You suck."

He picked her up and kissed her. "You're gorgeous."

Her head popped up. "Where's my shoes?"

She spotted them as soon as she said it, slipped them on and glanced at him with wide eyes. "Can we kiss goodbye at my door?"

He took her hand as they walked to her side door. "That was a fantastic date."

"I agree."

Her still sleepy voice echoed her love. "You do suck though."

He glanced at her, "Why?"

"For leaving me."

He swallowed her in his arms and her back arched like a ragdoll. Then he placed his open hand on the back of her head and kissed her until she went limp. When their kiss broke, her voice echoed the result of his forcefulness. "god, Jake."

He grinned at her tone. "What."

She lowered her head to his shoulder. "You really don't suck." She hugged him and sighed. "Be careful at work."

"Okay sweetheart. Have a good night."

"You too."

Stephie watched him get in their car, before heading inside and down the hall toward her room. "Hi, Mom. Hi, Dad."

Her mother's voice followed her down the hall. "Hi. Does Jake have work tonight?"

"Yeah."

Then her father's voice went straight to her heart. "Come visit for a while."

"Will in a sec. Be right back." She went in her room and changed into a new top and a pair of girl jeans, then headed out to the family room. "Hi."

They both replied, "Hi."

Genna lowered her book. "Were you over Jake's?"

She inhaled and smiled. "Yeah."

Genna smiled. "Did you have a good day?"

"The best."

Connor muted the TV and turned to her. "What's your plans for the rest of the evening?"

"I have a school project I have to finish. The end of the semester..." She frowned, "Everything's due at once. And I have to call Vicky. I promised I'd call him and I haven't."

"Mom and I are going out to dinner. Want to join us?"

Her shoulders drooped. "I wish I could, but I really have to finish the school project." She thought for a moment. "I wish I could. I want to hang out with you guys more. You were both super yesterday. ...That's not the reason why. You were always great. But I'd really like to see you more."

"We understand you're busy sweetheart. No worries." The genuineness of his smile reassured her. "Semester's almost over. We'll have a good holiday season this year."

"Thanks, Dad. I love you."

"I love you too sweetheart."

He eyed Genna. "It's just you and me. A date! Maybe you'll get lucky tonight."

Stephie smiled, shook her head, and walked contentedly back to her room. She laid back on her bed and dialed Vicky.

"Hey girl!"

"Hi Vick! How've you been?"

"Great! I had a date with Jonathan last night and it was awesome. He's the nicest guy. We went out to a bar and had drinks and dinner. We had a great time just sitting and talking. I feel so relaxed with him and he's a fabulous cuddler."

Vicky's good fortune satisfied Stephie to her soul. "Too great. I'm so happy for you."

Vicky perked up, "Thanks! Now tell me about you."

Stephie arched her back on the bed, put her head back and exhaled. "My mom and dad are the best, and Jake's father is incredible. The night was scary but as it happened, it wasn't bad. Jake was funny though. He didn't know what to do for me. But when it came time for him to tell everyone we were a couple, he just said it. He's so brave. He's so great."

The news tickled Vicky. "I couldn't be happier for you. We need to double date."

"Sure." Stephie sat up. "We need to go dancing!"

"Oh! So you like dancing now?"

Vicky's words made Stephie grin. "You know I do. Besides I bought a shiny silver dress I want to wear to see if I can make Jake's eyes pop out."

"I like it. Okay!"

"Jake's birthday is next Saturday. Did you get off?"

Vicky's voice changed. "Is it normal to have a barbeque this time of year?"

Steph went immediately into sales mode. "No, but they're calling for nice weather."

"Yeah. I can get off. I'm owed so many days off I lost count."

"Okay. Around two I think. Promise?"

"Can I bring Jonathan?"

"You better. See you then. Love you."

"Love you too little sister."

~ ~ ~

Genna spent Sunday relaxing around the house, mostly thinking about Friday's events. She was anxious to share those events with her mother, but whenever possible and unless time sensitive, saved news and any need for outside communication, for other days. She and Connor had come to enjoy their *alone time* and had adopted Sundays as their favorite day to have *alone time.*

She also thought the phone was an intrusion on her personal and her family's together time, so she saved even the biggest news for during the week. She had to be on the phone enough for work, and it absolutely affected her personal use. She grew to dislike the thing conversely to its growing convenience, but when Monday rolled around, she felt the strong urge to share the events of Friday with her lifelong source of wisdom, and dialed her phone. "Mom. Hi."

"Hi cara. How are you?"

The love in her mother's voice, reflected in hers. "Good. Great in fact. I was wondering if you felt like a Monday lunch together."

"I always feel like a lunch together. Doesn't matter the day."

"Excellent. See you between one-thirty and two?"

"I'll be waiting"

Her scheduled Monday was only for light office work and appointment coordination, and as long as no emergencies arose, the day would be easy. She finally finished all the tasks not previously crossed off the legal pad she kept on her desk, and left on time to pick up her mother. She pulled up at quarter to two and Lorraine was there waiting. She watched her mother lock her front door and they were on their way without Genna getting out of her car.

"Hi mom."

Lorraine softly touched her cheek, "Hi cara."

They drove a few minutes before her mother broke the silence. "So what's the occasion?"

Genna glanced at her. "Steven. Or shall I say Stephanie."

Lorraine's smile grew. "Has the child shared some things?"

Genna matched her smile. "Yeah. I spotted him holding Jake's hand, walking down Main Street near the university."

Lorraine's eyes widened. "How did you spot that?"

"I was coming out of an appointment, and but for another minute, would have run right into them. Oh, Steven was wearing the most adorable flower print chiffon dress. At first, I didn't think it was Steven. I thought Jake met a girl. But I had thought Steven told me he was spending the day with Jake, so I dialed him, and it was Steven holding Jake's hand. We went to lunch, and I convinced them to come out that night."

"And did they?"

"Yeah." The thought brought a soft smile to Genna's face. "And we had a great rest of the day and night. I stole her from Jake and we spent part of the day as mother and daughter. We pierced her ears and had our nails done, and then we went home together."

"How did Connor's react?"

"Perfectly! He took her in his arms and stood there hugging and kissing her." She thought about her declaration to him regarding getting lucky and smiled at the early Sunday morning result, though her smile seemed like a remembrance of the hug the night before. "I bought pizza and beer and the Harrisons came over. They were as understanding as they said they would be. Chris was too funny. Seems he has a soft spot for a daughter. His reaction to Stephie lit her up. It was fantastic."

The softest smile appeared on Lorraine's face. "I can't wait to meet Stephanie. I've been doing research and reading since we last talked. There's a good bit of evidence regarding the natural occurrence of different types of males and females, I had never given thought to. None of it, surprising though. After reading some of the information I realized we see the differences every day."

Genna eagerly replied, "What do you mean?"

Lorraine offered. "You know Mr. Landon?"

"Of course."

"Did you know he's an administrator at the university?"

Genna voiced surprise. "No. Is he really? I had no idea what his profession is, to be honest."

"Yes. Has been for years. I went and talked to him and shared some of our last conversation. It's not his subject of expertise, but he's friends with an associate in the psychology department. He introduced us and I met with her. She graciously gave me access to the library system and the psychology databases. It's been a long time since I was in college. Every Peer Review Journal Article is online and accessible, and I've spent a few of my afternoons at the school library. It's very interesting." Lorraine smiled deeply. "Some of the students are assuming I'm a student. It's really cute, the greetings I'm getting." She refocused. "With the guidance of this professor, Dr. Laurian, I've found some extraordinary information. I read articles dealing with variations in sexual development, and gender identity, and I'm amazed so much information exists." She turned in her seat toward Genna. "The variations are completely natural, yet the stereotyping of any variation is almost completely inaccurate. Did you know there are many in the Biological Psychology field who believe there are up to roughly eighteen distinct and separate categories of male and female? Isn't that staggering?"

Genna glanced at her with narrowed eyes. "I don't understand."

Lorraine smiled. "I'm sure you've never formally recognized it, but you do understand. You live it."

Genna glanced at her again, confused.

"You have absolutely met masculine females and you have a son who is feminine in many of his characteristics, a feminine male, and there are different levels of every combination; even physical proof. Our society benevolently *catches* those of extreme physical ambiguity at birth and *fixes* them, so they resemble one gender or the other, and even though our own culture doesn't fully recognize the natural ambiguity that can occur, it seems, the Creator made more variations of humans than both our myopic ancestors and our understanding modern society give Him credit for. Some sixteen more, as far as some in Biopsychology feel."

"The health psychology sub-field backs these assertions with their own perspective; they believe we are all five part beings…physical, mental, emotional, spiritual, and social. And when a person is only one part gender A, and four parts gender B, even if that single part is the projected physical aspect, then that being is not the gender they project."

Genna smiled at her mother. "You're having a ball with this, aren't you?"

Lorraine's eyes lit up. "You have no idea. I have something to learn. I was searching for something lately, and you gave it to me, and I'm very happy. I have so much information; it's almost too much to share. Stephanie is just one of the versions of human the Creator made. It's only humans who aren't bright enough to recognize or mature enough to accept what they see every day when they leave their own houses."

Genna petitioned for more information. "So give me your best opening statement, so I can try to put all this in perspective."

Lorraine gladly obliged. "There are masculine males. There are masculine females. There are feminine males, and there are feminine females, and there are variations in each group that range from the mild to the extreme, but the scale is not stepped, it's inclined, and runs together so smoothly, most humans can't differentiate one from another, until the difference becomes too distinct to deny. We would like to think we're two distinct and separate genders, but in actuality, since both male and female hormones flow through all of us, there are more gender variances than anyone would guess. Are you ready for how common this is?"

Genna looked at her in amazement. "Sure."

Lorraine smiled. "Modern medical technology has developed measuring techniques that preliminarily estimate the incidence of intersexual development at one in every hundredth person, with one in every two thousandth having enough ambiguity to make its male or female status uncertain. Seems nothing in the universe is only black or white." Lorraine inhaled. "The physical universe has operating laws and everything in it only fits those laws. No exceptions. Not even for humans. How's that?"

Genna chuckled. "Mom. You scare me."

Lorraine's voice increased. "Cara, I scare me when I think I'm old enough, I don't have to learn anything more, and then I discover there's so much to *always* learn. Shame on me for thinking I was done."

Genna glanced at her, "I know you. You've never taken in information without using it, so what do you see?"

Lorraine's eyes glistened like she was twenty. "The first thing we do is make sure he understands the definition of normal. The best thing you can do for children is make them understand they're normal. Many of them are uncomfortable thinking their idiosyncrasies are theirs alone. What they don't realize is; their idiosyncrasies are never uncommon. Where we go from there is open, but not our first concern."

The rest of their lunch date was as happy and energetic as the car ride. Lorraine shared her new knowledge and Genna shared details from the moment she and Stephie first met to the end of that night. By the end of their date, Lorraine only referred to her grandchild in the feminine.

Lorraine held Genna's hand before she departed. "I have to call her and tell her I love her. I need to make sure she knows I'm alright with everything."

"I'd expect nothing less." They kissed goodbye. "I do have to ask one more thing though…"

Lorraine let go of the door handle and turned back to Genna. "Sure carina."

"Does any of this explain Jake? He's…he's so masculine."

Lorraine nodded. "Yes, it does! The problem is, almost none of his situation is explained in a physical sense that would help most understand and as many as fifty percent of humans cannot think in formal operational terms, so if they can't comprehend the explanation physically, they declare it unfounded. But there are complicated underlying factors that pertain to hormones, pheromones, the brain and its complicated reaction to electro-chemical stimulation, even before-birth factors go into the final complicated make-up that ends up being the person. None of them obvious. None of them necessarily physically measurable. One of the more interesting preliminary measuring factors I found, is subconscious scent responses. We seem to use our sense of smell to smell things we're not even aware we record, and the brain subconsciously registers and reacts to those smells in ways we're just discovering."

Lorraine softly chuckled. "But Jake's situation has another twist. People are attracted to secondary sex characteristics, not primary. People don't display their genitals before deciding to date. People are attracted to the masculine and feminine secondary sexual characteristics as their primary drive toward a physical relationship and they are boyfriend and girlfriend. I understand the next level of relationship as well as anyone, so I understand where a relationship has to go, but what if a masculine male is attracted to a masculine female who has more male characteristics and is more masculine than a feminine male? Who is what?" Lorraine paused as if she were waiting for an answer. "It wouldn't matter though if people didn't have a need to categorize. Without categories, do you understand how everyone is just a person? What's funny is; the problem with categorizing only exists when humans aren't smart enough to make enough categories, or declare certain completely natural categories, unacceptable."

Genna's brow twisted and her eyes narrowed. "How much have you read?"

Her mother breathed deep. "I've just scratched the surface."

"Yikes?"

Lorraine shook her head almost unnoticeably. "The only thing I've concluded so far is; only those without a depth of knowledge on the subject, have an opinion. If you learn anything about the subject, all it does is wipe away all previous conclusions. We have definitively proven we are still developing a definitive understanding and with that conclusion, it is necessary to maturely understand we must have no opinion on what the beliefs should be." She patted Genna's hand. "What has existed from the beginning of time, is indeed natural. And what is natural cannot be forcefully suppressed. Did you know the incidence of same sex intimate physical contact almost triples in places where women are covered completely?"

They both softly snickered and kissed goodbye in the front seat before Lorraine left.

Genna left her mother in a great mood and decided to drive through some old neighborhood streets she hadn't been down in years, before heading home. Things had changed just enough to make her realize how many years had passed since she left the area. She finally turned onto the highway and a thought came back to her. "Damn." She picked up her phone and dialed. "Mom!"

"Cara."

"I forgot to tell you. They want to look for an apartment near the university and I was wondering if you have any connections which could help them."

"Let me see what I can do."

"You're great."

"Thanks. Love you."

"Love you too."

~~~

Jake reached for his suddenly noisy phone on the end table without looking, and pressed the call accept button as he raised it to his ear. "Yes?"

"Jake."

Stephanie's voice coming through the cell produced an immediate wakening, and an accompanying smile. "What."

"Want to look for an apartment today?"

His best friend asking to do something together, had been producing the same reaction for his entire life. The idea his best friend was now his girlfriend, and she wanted to look for their first apartment together, produced an even greater feeling. He popped up from his pillow and leaned against his headboard. "Sure. Sounds like fun."

"Then can we come home and have dinner together?"

"Sure." She quietly tickled him when she shared her need to be with him. "I can be ready in thirty five minutes. Eat before we leave or get breakfast on the way?"

He could be ready in twenty, but he knew she couldn't. Her prep time had noticeably increased with her ongoing change.

"Let's eat here so we have more time to look, okay?"

Even her voice seemed to be changing. He clearly heard his girl on the other end of the call. "Sure."

Thirty minutes later both kitchen doors opened and they walked to their car. He discreetly watched her enter the passenger side, and caught himself smiling. She was feminine and her feminine idiosyncrasies seemed to grow more natural with every passing day. Or was his growing love for her seeing only what he wanted to see? He felt his smile increase as he realized how little it mattered. She, in her current state, was everything he ever wanted or could want. He took a discreet breath before getting in the driver's side.

He leaned toward her and kissed her over the middle console. "I called Vicky last night. He's coming Saturday."

He started the car and held out his hand for hers. "How's he doing?"

"Great. He and Jonathan are hitting it off."

The news pleased him. "Too great."

"He wants the four of us to double date."

"Sounds good to me." Jake grabbed the top of the steering wheel with both hands. "We got the wheels. The four of us can go parking after." He glanced at her. "Do people go parking anymore? Can you even find a submarine, let alone two racing?"

She grinned. "You're an idiot." Then sat up. "Oh, I got a call yesterday. A counselor from the school. They want me to come in and talk to them."

Jake's right eyebrow rose as he looked behind them and pulled out. "The university?"

"Yeah."

His voice changed slightly. "About what?"

Stephie shrugged. "They didn't say."

He glanced at her quickly, and offered a thought after a slight pause. "Mind if I tag along?"

Her eyes narrowed. "No…but why would you want to?"

He reached for her hand again. "I just want to. I promise I won't say anything."

Her voice turned playfully adamant. "Promise me you won't punch anyone."

He glanced at her and grinned. "Now what makes you think I'd punch someone?"

She glared at him and shook her head. "Promise."

"Okay, I promise. I'll behave better than everyone else. How's that?"

"Jake, don't make us have to find another school."

"Will you relax? I promise."

She rubbed his hand as it held hers and he examined hers in his. He softly exhaled. She had delicate hands.

"Okay. Our job today is to find a place we can afford, where the rats don't outnumber us."

She stared at him, then playfully rebuked him. "Where do you come from?"

He smirked. "Sorry."

They drove in ever widening circles around the university, exploring every local street, and after realizing the task was more challenging than originally anticipated, they went back into the school and searched on community bulletin boards. Pickings were scarce and the cost of the ones that were available had them both depressed by the time they headed back to the car.

He hit the key fob and the car's lights blinked. "Okay. It's the first day. Let's go home and re-evaluate our search criteria. We'll find something."

She nodded in agreement. "I'm not worried. Not yet anyway."

The day was sunny and the sun was warm. Jake opened the sunroof then held out his hand for hers and they both sat back and enjoyed the ride home. She broke the silence. "You're still coming over tonight, right?"

"Of course."

His smile caught her attention and she sung the next question. "Whatcha smilin' for?"

"I get to cuddle with you on the loveseat later, and watch TV and just be with you."

Stephie smiled.

He glanced at her. "What are you smiling for?"

Her smile widened. "The fact that makes you smile."

CHAPTER THIRTEEN
ASSIMILATION

Thanksgiving break was long enough to ruin the rhythm they were in and short enough to make it seem like it flew by, but Stephanie's alarm went off like it was supposed to and as soon as her eyes opened, she realized she had to be Steven again. She sighed and slowly rose out of bed, put on his robe and walked to the bathroom. It almost seemed like someone else was getting ready for school.

It wasn't a comforting shower. Even the water hitting him felt irritating. *How could I not have remembered I had to be Steven again?* He went through the motions of getting ready, but for the first time in a long time, wished he could skip school and crawl back into bed.

He wondered back to his room, purposely less than fully cognizant. He knew his mood would deteriorate further, as soon as he woke fully. He also knew why he felt like this. He was mad at himself. He even knew the reason was ridiculous, but at the moment, his emotional being controlled his intellectual being, and his emotional being was mad he had to be Steven.

Instinctively, he opened his closet and was immediately confronted by Stephanie's clothes, and realized he had forgotten where Steven's clothes were. He diverted his eyes down and quickly shut his closet door. It hurt to look at her clothes, and it hurt more to put on Steven's clothes.

He noticed his unpainted nails as he pulled on Steven's pants. His brain was fighting even the simplest of tasks. He felt like skipping school, and locking himself in his room and the thought produced a deep sigh. This was the first time skipping school was more than a passing thought. A fleeting pleasant thought countered the feeling; Jake would be there. And that fast, its counter thought; but he has to see Steven.

He hesitated at the inside of the kitchen door. He felt the force telling him not to go, but he knew the only energy greater than the resisting force of stepping outside, was the attraction of being with Jake. He needed Jake when his world was out of kilter. Jake was his leveling mechanism. He breathed deep and opened the kitchen door. No repelling influence had a potency equal to the attracting dynamic Jake possessed.

His heart jumped as he spotted Jake leaning against the back of the car and as Steven approached, his best friend studied him and asked, "You alright?"

Steven lied. "Sure."

"What's wrong?"

He exhaled. "Stephie isn't here."

Jake quipped. "Yes she is. She's just crossdressed."

Steven's face lit. "You're an idiot."

Jake laughed.

The school day was long and tedious and Steven remained uncomfortably conspicuous the entire day. He reached the library first, for their afternoon break and picked the table most hidden from the expansive study area. Jake finally found him and they began working silently.

Finally, Steven broke the silence. "Aren't you upset by seeing me like this?"

Jake never hesitated. "No, you idiot. I love you."

Steven responded just as quickly. "You love Stephanie."

Jake never glanced up. "You *are* Stephanie."

"No I'm not. She's not allowed to be here right now. People wouldn't understand."

Steven waited for Jake to offer a counter argument but none came, and they spent the rest of their afternoon break working in silence.

The ride home was quiet and they were almost home when Jake finally spoke. "Do you want to study together tonight?"

The offer felt like an instant added weight on his heart. "Mind if I just study alone in my room tonight, then crash early?" He could tell Jake saw the wear the day had caused.

"No. I don't mind." Jake hesitated. "You gonna be alright?"

He sighed. "I'll be fine. Just tired."

Jake reached over the console and softly squeezed Steven's hand before they exited the car and went to their side kitchen doors.

He heard Genna's voice from the family room as he entered, "Hi sweetheart." and walked toward it.

"Hi, Mom. You're home early."

Genna's looked up from the papers and envelopes spread out on the coffee table. "Slow day. Thought I'd come home and take care of the bills."

Steven sat down on the loveseat facing her and patiently waited for her to stop writing. "Can we talk about my birthday?"

She met his eyes. "I know! What do you want to do? It's a biggie. Twenty-one."

He wondered why he felt so much younger. "I kinda would like to just go out to dinner like with the six of us or so."

"We can't forget your grandmother. She'd be devastated."

"Sorry. Of course she's included."

"Good."

"But I'd like to go to a nice quiet dinner place. Nothing fancy but nothing that would be rowdy either."

"What? No twenty-one shots?" Genna smiled.

Steven gave her a scornful smirk.

"Sure sweetheart. That sounds nice."

He continued his thought. "Is it okay if that's all we do?"

"Sweetheart, it's your birthday and what you're requesting is actually easier on both your mothers. On your *three* mothers. Just let me know where you want to go."

He straightened his back. "I thought about that too."

Genna grinned. "You're taking all the work out of this for me. Let me guess. Can I guess?"

His eyes narrowed and he smiled. "How do you know? I know you know."

Genna opened her eyes wide and in unison, they shouted. "Sakana!"

Steven snickered. "How do you do that?"

Genna laughed. "I'll save the answer for that night during dinner. Remind me, okay? There aren't many big tables there. You better call and reserve one immediately."

The house was empty when Jake walked in and he methodically set up the kitchen table for study. He became so immersed in his schoolwork; the door suddenly opening startled him.

"Hi, Mom."

Between his school and work requirements and Morgan's work, they hadn't had time for more than a casual exchange since the pizza party, but neither had plans tonight, other than spending the evening at home.

"Hi love. How was your day?" She walked behind him and gave him a kiss.

"Good. Yours?"

"Boring. Things are slow there. It's a little scary." She dropped her purse and a white grocery bag on the counter. "Want to have dinner together?"

"Sure. Where's dad?"

"Working late. They're finishing up a job and he's working on the punch-list. It's just you and me."

His heart skipped a beat. He had rehearsed what he wanted to say to her since last Friday, but he wasn't prepared for a no-notice meeting. "What do you feel like eating?"

"Are sandwiches alright? I'm beat. I don't feel like cooking."

She didn't look tired but he could tell she was as uncomfortable as he felt, and her quick glance away from his stare confirmed it. She opened the bag she had placed on the counter and reached inside. "I stopped and bought some fresh rolls and lunchmeat on the way home. We won't see your father until late for the next week or so."

He did his best to lighten the mood. "Sandwich week. Every job ends the same. No problem with me!"

She shook her head. "God, you're just like your father."

Jake piled his school books on an empty seat and they both set the table.

She did her best to avert silence. "You have more homework to do after?"

"Yeah. Semester's getting to the end."

The tension between them was very noticeable. They had things to discuss but nothing he felt they couldn't work out. He pulled two glasses from the cabinet. "Want ice?"

"Yeah."

They continued to cross paths as they helped each other set up for dinner. He took the ice tea pitcher from the fridge and sat down. Finally, she sat across from him and broke the uneasy silence. "First, I want to say I'm sorry."

He immediately felt sorry for her. He had rehearsed a confrontation with her more than he ever had, but her apology made it the opposite of what he now felt. "For what, being human?"

"No." She met his eyes for the first time since she walked in. "For being less okay than everyone else in the room Friday night."

He reached for her hand across the table. "It's okay. I love you."

She squeezed his hand tight. "No, it's not okay. I just wasn't ready for him in your arms.

"I understand." He looked at her and exhaled softly. "But we have to talk."

"I know. Your father never yelled at me either the whole next day. It drove me nuts. He made me think about it and never said a derogatory word to me. Bastard."

They both laughed and she picked up her napkin and blotted her eye.

Jake glanced up occasionally as they each fixed a sandwich, then finally broke the momentary silence. "So, you want to start or do you want me to?"

She looked at him. "You can, but just know I love you."

He smiled. "I know, Mom. I love you too. And I know there's a lot of stuff that goes into being human too. I was really upset with you Friday and the weekend. I lost that edge somewhere around Monday."

"I'm also a little better than I was over the weekend." She lowered her chin. "You pretty much rocked my world." She lifted her head, and he noticed her breathing. "I dreamed of being a grandmother…having a daughter-in-law. I really wanted, and looked forward to those things, and I was upset about losing them."

"But mom, I want all that too, for you and me."

"But you…and Steven." Her eyes narrowed.

"Yeah mom." He nodded. "We're a couple. …But I still see all my hopes and dreams for both of us being alive just the same." He inhaled deeply. "It doesn't mean I don't want the same things I've always wanted. I want everything you and dad have. I always have, and that won't change, just because Steven and I love each other."

His words seemed to hit her in the chest and she took a deep and very noticeable breath.

He paused a moment to let her rejection lose its sting, then continued with full composure, "And I'm less concerned with the difference between Steven and Stephanie than she is. I love him…her. I'll call her *her*, since she wishes to be seen as a she." His heartbeat increased, from his own admission. The words were the truth, but reactions like Morgan's made them equally difficult, and the realization made him slowly shake his head.

"I love her. She's the most beautiful thing I've ever met. Inside and out. Nobody's close. And she loves me enough to make me feel like she worships me sometimes. *And* she's my best friend and has been since before I knew I was alive." He paused as his heart and mind verified the confirmation. "…With that said, there are some things I've learned over the last couple of years I want to—No… need to share with you, which are unbelievably important to me."

He watched her swallow hard, then bite her sandwich; never taking her eyes off his.

He sipped his drink and continued, "Computers aren't my first love."

Her head tilted. "What do you mean?"

"I'm learning computers so I can pay my bills someday. But my first loves are psychology and philosophy. It's like the window into humans. It gives a formal name and face to everything I've ever seen. It's fantastic and it not only helps me understand things, but it has taught me so many things. It's why, every time I have an elective I take a psych or philosophy class. You just can't find a job later if either is your major." He paused, knowing he had just shared more about his education, than he had ever shared, and noticed her increased breathing again.

"Okay. With that explained, I know why you were set back Friday night, or, with the help of a few psychology classes, I'm at least pretty sure I have a real good guess." Their eyes met. "It's been beaten into you that a relationship like mine and Stephie's is somehow wrong." She exhaled and he matched her exhale then breathed deep. "Am I right?"

She nodded. "Yes, but it's not just me. A whole lot of people have a problem with it."

He nodded, "I know." and continued. "And you were pushing yourself, just accepting his…her change?"

She nodded again and picked up a chip without looking down at her plate. "Yeah."

"Her in my arms was too much. I understand." He sat a little straighter, paused again, and with a softer voice added, "But can I try to help you put things in perspective, using what I've learned in philosophy and psychology?"

"These classes taught you that this is alright?"

"No Mom. These classes taught me how to verify that this is alright."

"Well I don't see how that's possible. It's been believed, for thousands of years, that some things aren't acceptable."

He shook his head unnoticeably and inhaled. "Yeah Mom…but not necessarily correctly. Want to walk through the philosophy and psychology of the issue?"

Her breathing was still noticeably elevated. "Yes. Am I allowed to disagree if I don't believe something?"

"Only with a sound argument."

"Good. I want to share what I believe too."

He chuckled. "Of course, Mom."

He bit his sandwich. "Do you want to start at the top or the bottom."

Her head shifted slightly. "What do you mean?"

He tilted his head softly. "We can start at a perspective from God or we can start at the relationship level of the two of us. Your call."

She immediately straightened up. "You think God is okay with this? But God not being okay with this is the reason I'm not okay with this. …So please …God first."

He welcomed her choice. "I agree. He is first. He's perfect, don't you agree?"

"Yes." Her eyes narrowed.

He smiled, and continued. "What's your definition of perfect?"

She held her sandwich as she rested her hand on her plate. "I don't know. We were taught He's perfect."

He also lowered his sandwich to just above his plate. "Can He get angry?"

She smiled. "Hell yeah."

"Does He ever hate? Does He ever take sides?"

Her breathing increased again, and she smiled. "Some of the stories seem like it, sure."

"Some of the stories do seem like it, don't they?" He thought about those words for a second, and inhaled. "May I expand on the popular dogmatic version of perfect?" She nodded and he continued. "Perfect, the typical two thousand year old dogmatic view taught in some of our finer institutions is; the perfect God has some interesting human qualities, including jealousy, anger, frustration, impatience, even though they acknowledge his perfection. Certain well accepted mainline stories have God creating us and almost immediately being disappointed in us and telling us we can't be in heaven with Him without outside intervention. He is more often than not, dissatisfied with us, and very few get to be on His good side, especially if you're human."

He stared at her for a moment before continuing. "Is it okay if that's not my definition of perfect? Is it okay if I share *my* definition of what I perceive is the definition of a perfect God?"

She looked at him curiously. "Sure."

He tilted his head and offered a half smirk. "My definition of perfect is without flaw in every and any action. He loves perfectly; by definition…unconditionally. That means He's never angry or dissatisfied with us. He made us human, which means He has no problem with us being human. Seems silly to think otherwise, doesn't it? Dad loves me even though I'm human. Dad doesn't have a problem I'm human. Do you mean to tell me God could take a lesson from dad? Or is God perfect at it?" He paused and eyed her for a reaction to anything so far. She offered none, so he continued. "He forgives perfectly. Dad forgives me for being an idiot and dad isn't perfect. How could dad be better at it than God?" He paused and they both took a bite of their sandwiches. "Do you and dad have intentions of someday leaving me this house?"

She sat up, pleasantly surprised by the change in topic. "Of course. Do you think you'd ever live here?"

He breathed in. "Do you think God would make a house for us and not have us live in it? Do you think He wants us to, but doesn't always get His way? How about not make enough room for us when a universe of rooms take nothing more than a fleeting thought, the room He has to work with is the entire spiritual universe and no one takes up any room? Not my definition of perfect. Yours?"

Her reply was emotionless. "No."

"I know this is going to sound weird, but I thought of something God can't do."

She smiled at his sudden vigor and waited with a look of curiosity.

"He can't do anything not perfectly. And you know what that eliminates?" He paused and smiled at her. "Every childish human emotion. Hate, anger, jealousy, pettiness...all of them. It seems the dogmatic and human definition of perfect has the flaws humans have. How funny is that?"

She quietly looked at his face and shoulders and sighed. Her non-reply caused him to wonder if she was hearing him, but he had to continue. He straightened out the chips on his plate, then picked one up. Her stare caught him off guard. "Is it okay to go on?"

She nodded, "Yes."

He paused and looked at her to confirm her reply, then continued. "Do you think anything so perfect would ever create something He wasn't aware He was creating? How about something He disliked? He can create anything, any way He wants. Could He really be bothered creating something that offended Him? Or is He flawed? Or are we too stupid to realize He's not flawed?"

She stared at him through narrowed eyes. "I'm confused by the way you're wording things. I want to explain to you how I learned things growing up, but the way you're wording things is making it hard for me"

"I understand and I'm sorry. But you don't have to supply an argument right now. What I'm telling you is a lot, and I love you. I'll always be open to your argument. I promise."

He paused and offered a contrite smile. "May I continue?"

She nodded softly.

"My definition of perfect means He chose to create everything He created, and that includes the different kinds of humans He made. Can there be any doubt about that?"

Her head tilted. "There's just men and women."

He sighed. "That's one of the problems, Mom. There aren't just men and women. People two thousand years ago thought there were only just men and women, but our far more advanced society has proven otherwise. You see Steven. Is he like other men? Is he like dad? Has he ever been like dad?"

Her eyes grew narrower and she inhaled but didn't answer.

He slowly finished his bite, then met her eyes once again. "Ready for the next part?"

She pursed her lips. "Sure."

"His rules." He raised an eyebrow again. "We know what is and what isn't acceptable by His rules."

She sat up. "Correct. I know His rules. I studied them all my life."

"Excellent! God specifically wrote ten rules, correct?"

She squinted. "Yeah, but that's not fair. There are way more than ten rules."

"Yep. That's one of my problems. The clout the rest of the rules have been given. If He had a rule that was as important as one of his other ten, do you think He would have written it?"

She tilted her head slightly. "Yes."

"If He wanted us to have thirty rules, the movie shown every spring would be called the thirty commandments, don't you think?"

"Where do you come up with thoughts like that?"

"I'll explain that to you in detail someday, but not today. But I will tell you, it comes from trying to understand the discrepancies between what I've learned and what others would like me to believe, how's that?"

He continued, "The ten rules. I've read them a hundred times. I still can't find anything remotely directed at two people loving each other. He has a couple against hating. None against loving. But it isn't the ten that are an issue. It's the other five...hundred? Where did those extra rules come from?" He sipped his drink. "I can understand blindly believing the ten. They're impressive enough to believe they came from an other than human source. They are also inarguable, but blindly believing the other five-hundred?"

She gladly defended years of belief. "Yes. They're all the same."

He looked directly into her eyes. "But they're not all the same. And I can't figure out why all the ones after the first ten are given the same credibility."

"Because we're told to." She caught her own words and her eyes narrowed.

His tone changed to a slight plea. "But if they weren't written by God, humans wrote them. Isn't that a drop in the divine integrity of those rules?"

She defended her religious paradigms. "They were special humans."

He lowered his brows. "Who said?"

She raised hers. "It's just what's believed."

He shook his head and breathed deep. "So, right now we have a bunch of people, including you, freaking out about an eleventh rule that seems to have been developed in a completely different time and place, by a special but anonymous human author?" He bit his sandwich.

She nodded, "Yes." and bit hers.

He picked up a chip. "Are you ready for a neat perspective on that rule?"

She placed her sandwich down and folded her hands on the far side of her plate. "Sure." Her breathing indicated she wanted nothing less. She took a single deeper breath and met his eyes.

"What if the fire and brimstone that supposedly hit those cities was nothing more than the normal and now well recorded balls of primordial rock flying around the cosmos, that every so often land on this planet, like they have pocked the entire moon, but the well intentioned tribesman that wrote about it had no clue of the cosmos and our place in it or what was flying around in it? What if all he saw was the devastation and concluded, using his limited knowledge of the cosmos, the only thing his non-modern brain would allow him to conclude; God must have been mad at something. After all, there was, at the time, no understanding of anything flying around in the sky that could *accidentally* hit us. The destruction had to be on purpose and a direct result of anger. And then he concluded, since in his mind, God is the only Being capable of raining fire and brimstone, that God must have been angry at something, and then went about making a reason to fit his wonderfully limited intellectual capacity." He sighed and shook his head. "Yet no one had the same conclusion when three quarters of Chicago was lit on fire. Why? Was God mad at the trees in Siberia when either of those two fireballs came through?" He continued to shake his head. "Amazing? Arguable?"

Her breathing quickened. "But we aren't allowed to question things like that."

His eyes widened, "Mom! Who said?" He smiled. "I believe we *are* allowed to question things like that, and I not only questioned them, but after learning so much more about our place in the universe, I think my argument is a pretty good one, don't you?"

She fidgeted in her chair. "It could be a possibility, I guess."

His enthusiasm increased. "I'll settle for that. It could be a possibility. Isn't that enough to stop this *unquestioning* habit we got into? Isn't that enough to question finite opinions based on obscure and tentative information?"

"I don't know. I was told not to question things like this."

He looked at her, sighed, and continued, "If you had an ant farm, would you have a problem with two ants in it fooling around?"

She sipped her ice tea as she studied him.

His voice calmed. "God is further above us than we are above ants. He's perfect and we're flawed. Yet we could care less whether two ants in our ant farm are doing *things*, whether they're two guys, two girls, two whatevers. I believe God also doesn't care who's making love to who. Know why I believe that?"

She exhaled, "Why?"

"He didn't write a rule against it. I believe He has a problem when one of us murders someone. In fact, it's one of His rules. Making love? Loving somebody? Seriously?"

She reached her hand out to him. "But I'm only worried about you. What if it is against God? I don't want you to be doomed. I love you."

"Mom, that brings us back to the definition of perfect. The real God made me and Stephie, and he loves us too. Perfectly. I believe He loves everyone. Perfectly. And I truly believe He has better things to do than throw some of us away, for no greater crime than being how we were made. I also truly believe we can love whoever we want to love. I believe He has better things to do than be angry or destroy. I don't believe a God who would make something just so He could destroy it, can fit my understanding of the definition of perfect…and I *know* He is."

"But how can you know?"

He smiled. "Either there's an imperfect God ruling over this place, or the current human interpretation of prefect is more antiquated and myopic than we ever gave it credit for. My guess; it's a human interpretation problem, due to *our* small imperfect minds. Because my definition of perfect is just that…perfect. No flaws. Flawless. No human qualities. Way above us in every perceivable aspect of existence. Perfect."

"I also believe God sees everyone as equal, like we see ants. Everyone. Completely equal. No exceptions. I believe I can absolutely love Stephanie. I'm also smart enough to believe loving her could and probably will cause issues that loving a natural girl would not, but I've watched some guy-girl relationships end in complete disaster. There's a human quotient there which supersedes all other factors."

He breathed in and looked at her, and shook his head gently, almost mad at himself for being this fervent about these topics. "I'm sorry this is so much. I'm passionate about these things. I'm passionate about God. He's perfect! I'm passionate about Stephanie. She's damn near perfect in my heart."

He sipped his drink. "And I understand the difficulty you're having. The dogma you've had to swallow growing up is caught in your psyche."

She eyed him and finished her bite. "But what if it isn't dogma? What if everything we've been taught is true?"

"And God is the exclusionary, sometimes unforgiving, sometimes vengeful Being depicted? And literally all but a handful of us are doomed? If I gave you something else to think about, would you?"

She hesitated. "Of course."

He silently registered every breath that preceded her permission, as an indication she was only showing her love for him. "I've read an alternate explanation for the tree of knowledge. Ready?"

"I guess." They both laughed at the tone of her reply.

He picked up another chip. "We are taught we have free will, correct?"

"Yes."

"The ability to choose between right and wrong, correct?"

She nodded affirmatively.

"How were we supposed to know good from bad, right from wrong without knowing what the bad and the wrong were? How were we supposed to make a decision without that knowledge? Second idea; what perfect father puts a tree with the best fruit in the middle of a front lawn and then tells his kids not to ever eat from it? Would dad do that? Would dad plant a tree with the best fruit and tell you and me we can't have any? Does that compute to the actions of a perfect loving father, in any stretch of the imagination?

What if He put the tree there *so* we would eat the fruit and learn? What if that's when we moved from wild animal to sentient being? What if that's when we became His children? What if that coincided with an interpretation of us feeling like we were thrown out of a garden we weren't able to see as anything past how a rabbit or zebra sees it? The alternate perspective still fits the definition of all of a sudden knowing we were naked. All of a sudden, we were aware. Think about it."

He looked apologetically into her eyes. He knew he was making her question a significant part of her being, and the thought made him uncomfortable. He didn't know why he was so willing to question and she all but refused. He didn't know why his questions didn't resound in her mind. His heart deflated as he realized how hard it is for people to question.

He smiled oddly and continued. "The events probably happened. But as we become more aware of our existence and the existence of billions of planets, most likely with billions of life forms, circling billions of stars, some of the existing interpretation sure stretches the imagination, doesn't it?"

He begged with his eyes for her agreement, but she offered none.

His voice turned softer and somewhat defeated. "Yet very few question it. And I have a two-thousand five hundred year old request from the only gentleman ever to be declared enlightened. *Question Everything.*"

He breathed deep and his voice changed to a plea. "Given the fact we have irrefutable evidence this place wasn't created in six days, can we at least start to question the interpretation of some points that are incongruent with logic? Has dogma bound us so strongly, we are still literally forbidden to question? …still bound us so completely, we're afraid to question even basic concepts we know to be all but well outdated? Are certain organizations *still* stopping us from declaring things like the earth is not the center of the universe? Is that the way sentient beings mature and grow in wisdom? Is that how children of perfection grow to understand and appreciate all the potential a perfect Creator gave us?"

She stared at him and softly shook her head.

His eyes narrowed. "What?"

"My god, you're a man…and incredibly intelligent. Where did you get your intelligence? You didn't get it from me."

"Yes I did. But I've been working on the wisdom part, Mom. It's completely different than intelligence and seems to take a lot of completely different work. I even asked God if I could have some. He said we could ask for some if we wanted." He smirked. "Thing is, we're so pathetic we can't be sure we received any."

After a bite of his sandwich, he lowered his head and continued with a softer tone. "Now, can I ask a big favor of you?"

She widened her eyes in anticipation. "Sure, love."

"Can I request you re-evaluate in your heart, the definition of perfect, especially how it pertains to a perfect perfect God, and your understanding of who is allowed to love who? If God is love, then doesn't it only make sense that it is better to love completely wrong than it is to hate completely right? God is so far above hate. There isn't a hate fiber in His being. Love doesn't offend Him. Hate does. Even the most well intentioned hate. And if in your re-evaluation you sincerely decide someone isn't allowed to love or be loved, would you try again? All it means is you missed the lesson again." He stared into her eyes for an extended moment. "But… whatever you do…" He inhaled slowly "…whatever you do …please don't make me choose between you and Stephie."

She breathed in with a force that startled him, and broke the stare. He stood up, went around the table, and motioned her to stand, then softly wrapped his arms around her, and held her.

He would always be her child, but he was no longer her baby.

~ ~ ~

Jake dropped the stack of plastic lawn chairs by the chiminea now sitting in the middle of the yard and looked at his father, "Hey dad! Can we talk?" Chris looked up from the temporary wood pile he was building. "Always son. Always."

He pulled the top chair off the stack. "Stephie's really nervous about today. Not for herself, but for us. She has her mother's heart."

Chris continued stacking the firewood. "It's beautiful. But why for us?"

Jake yanked the next chair off his stack. "She's worried we're going to lose family because of her, and she's pretty sick over the thought."

"My friend, my son," Chris stood straight and slowly shook his head, "Did you explain to her, you and she are our immediate family and the rest are distant family at best?"

Jake straightened up. "She knows." Then his shoulders hunched forward. "Do you think she needs to hear it though?" His eyes narrowed. "She needs to hear it."

Chris picked up another log. "As soon as we're done, go make her understand where she stands in the pecking order of our family. Nothing will put things in perspective better."

"Thanks, Dad. I count on your perspective."

"My pleasure."

He lowered the chair in his hands. "Dad? Can I share another thought about today?"

Chris smiled and turned away from the wood pile again. "Sure."

"You do realize I'm going to literally kick the living shit out of anyone who raises an unsolicited voice or hand to her, don't you? I mean …anyone."

"Son, if you don't immediately, I'll walk over to *you* and punch *you* in *your* mouth. Then I'll go over to whoever raised their hand to her and literally kick the shit out of them, in your place." Chris playfully smirked. "There's a time for peace and a time for war. Where there's peace, make no war. If war starts, treat it as such." He squinted at Jake. "Somebody said that. I can't remember who said that."

People started coming in every door and gate, all carrying food and drink. Half of it requested, half of it out of the goodness of their hearts, and the unexpected abundance caused chaos as it did every family party at every family house, for as long as anyone could remember …and everyone enjoyed the commotion! The men seemed to always make it outside first and always seemed to take the beverages with them, but the women didn't mind. This was the way these family functions had been handled for longer than anyone there could remember.

After making sure his set-up chores were complete, Jake went straight to Steven's room and knocked on the closed door. "Sweetheart?"

She let him in, then resumed her position, rocking back and forth on her bed. He shut the door behind him and turned to her. She was dressed in a unisex shirt and baggy boy jeans but had no make-up on, with her hair pulled back. He sat on the edge of her bed, reading his best friend. He always knew when she wasn't okay. He had been reading her emotions for quite some time now, and like a guy, felt obligated to offer solutions. He reached for her hand. "You don't have to *come out* today, if you're not ready."

She muttered. "Yeah, I know. I just wish…"

He raised his focus from her hands to her eyes. "What? What do you wish?"

She glanced at him as she rocked against her headboard, rolled up in a ball with her chin resting on her knees. "Everyone gets to be who they are. And I know this wouldn't sound like a big deal to most people, but I wish I could be who I am, in front of them…with them…without feeling like I'm going on trial or display or something. They're my…family."

He moved closer to her and held both her hands with both of his. "I…I didn't…I still don't know…" He inhaled. "…what could that feel like?"

The words weren't quite there for him, but the way she looked at him changed. She studied his eyes and the lingering hurt he saw made him yearn for the words that would heal her. He stared deeply into her confused eyes, and they pierced his soul. "I'm here. I'm next to you. I am where you are. Now. In an hour from now. A day from now. Until further notice. Whether in our back yard. Or in your bedroom. Or in this neighborhood. Or not. I'll be beside you, whatever you choose to do today, and I don't care what you choose today. And I will hold your hand, or not. Or sit with you, or not…as you need. When you whisper your needs in my ear, understand you are whispering to your best friend."

She gazed at him with glassy eyes and breathed deep. "How brave can I be today?"

He raised an eyebrow, but didn't say a word.

She looked at him with one eye raised and a twisted mouth. "Will you wait here while I get ready?"

"Yeah." A faint smile appeared. "That falls under the time and place speech I just gave."

She laughed softly.

"I'll be sitting in the hallway. Okay?"

She whispered. "Okay."

He turned to her at the door. "No pressures. No rules. No right. No wrong! Whatever you need to do…"

The door shut behind him, but she didn't move. She stared at it and her eyes welled up. When he declared his devotion like this, all he did was reinforce his claim on his best friend's soul. She wanted only two things. She wanted to be who she was…and she wanted to be his. And when he opened up to her, she was never sure which one mattered more.

The more he told her she didn't have to do or prove anything, the more she wanted to do it for him. She slowly searched her closet. Her mother had bought her more things than she could track. She owned four pair of jeans and the same amount of sweats when she was a boy, and now her closet was full and it seemed like her mother brought her home a new shopping bag every week. She made a mental note to tell her to stop.

She picked out a fairly conservative jean skirt and flats, then put on a very conservative long sleeve dark blue top. She quickly made-up her eyes, put on a light coat of lip gloss and re-did her hair. She seemed to be relaxing more with each step. She also kept thinking about Jake in the hallway. No words accompanied the thoughts. She pictured him sitting there, like her body guard. He was so assuring. She slowly turned, scrutinizing her outfit in the mirror, and nervously opened the door.

He looked up at her with no judgment and no opinion, just a soft smile, stood and took her hand. They walked out together but not holding hands, though he couldn't help but place his hand on her back more than twice as she made her way to the back yard.

CJ, her four year old cousin, immediately ran up to her. "Stevie?"

She bent over toward him. "Hi CJ! Now I'm Stephanie, sweetheart. Is that alright?" They were in earshot of a few of the allies and they were watching intently.

His little face looked up at her. "You're prettier."

A few adults behind her chuckled.

"Thank you sweetheart! Can I have a kiss?"

"Yep." And he pursed his lips for her. She kissed him and that fast he ran away to continue playing.

Chris was close enough to take two steps to her and without a word, kissed her on the side of her head, then went back to the grill. She scanned the small patio and spotted her grandmother; walked to her and kissed her. Lorraine reached up and softly slid her hands on each of Stephie's cheeks, whispered, "Cipolline" and smiled.

Stephie timidly surveyed the rest of the party, and noticed Vicky and Jon watching her and hurried to her newest lifeline, hugging and kissing him deeper than usual.

Stephie had wandered out as far as she dared at the moment. She pulled a chair next to her new dear friend and tried to relax. Vicky lovingly held her hand.

Jake paced around the grill. He was trying to relax but having no success. He had nervous energy he didn't know what to do with, and the grill was close. "Need a hand Dad?"

His father jokingly scowled at him, "Who are you and what have you done with my son?! Go get two beers, will ya?"

As the day progressed, more and more people spotted Stephie and everyone seemed fine. Some came up to her with the best intentions and some casually said hi as they passed, but all seemed accepting, for the most part. After her nervousness passed, she stood to go inside and walked by Uncle Dave who turned and looked her up and down, "So, do you still have your little thingy?" and laughed.

Jake saw the chance meeting in advance and was closer to Dave than Stephie, but from his other side.

"You tired Uncle Dave?" He said the words loud, for the hearing pleasure of certain others. Vicky stood, and his reaction caught Chris by surprise. He smiled deeply.

Dave's voice lightened immediately, "No."

Jake's next words were a little louder and a little angrier, "Then take a few steps away from the nap you're about to take. Back up quickly."

Dave turned toward Jake with his arms raised, palms out and his back slightly arched away. His father casually happened to also be close, by the time the sentence was over, and added, "Make sure his head hits the grass. You don't want to kill him. You just want to put him to sleep."

Dave's eyes moved from Jake to Chris, with palms still showing, "Oh no, I didn't mean anything by it."

Chris took over with short separated words. "Dave. Time to leave."

Dave stepped back. "I just got here."

Chris continued calmly, "Why yes you did…and it's already time to leave. You can walk if you want. But do choose quickly before my son gives you a well-deserved lobotomy. I have no problem washing the blood off the grass, but I'm not driving you to the hospital." Chris raised his voice again. "Goodbye Uncle Dave. Forget where I live. Have a good life Uncle Dave."

Stephie wanted to cry and quickly looked around for a place to hide. Jake grabbed her by the hand and pulled her toward the closest unoccupied chair. He sat and pulled her on top of his lap as Dave reached the side gate, then wrapped both arms around her, held her and kissed the back of her head. He wasn't letting her hide or Uncle Dave win. He whispered to the back of her head. "It's more okay than you understand. I promise."

Jake held her with both arms wrapped around her. After a few minutes, he leaned close to her ear, "Did you need to go inside?"

She whispered. "Can we just sit here? I don't think my legs will carry me right now."

He held her and felt her warmth, and every once in a while leaned toward her and smelled her neck and hair. She was his. He wasn't nobility but his oath of devotion was no less noble. He didn't need to swear it though. His actions would be measure enough. Jake discreetly watched for any sign of Uncle Dave from the direction he had left. Peace continued. Dave left as told. Everyone else was as family should be.

Genna and Morgan walked next to each other carrying three glasses of white wine. Morgan gave one to Stephie. "Welcome to adulthood sweetheart." They toasted in unison.

Chris flipped Jake a beer, held his up and grinned. Jake searched for Connor. He was tossing a small metal washer at the wood target twenty feet away, with a beer in his other hand. They played music and washers and horseshoes and the younger kids ran around playing nothing, like little ones do. Connor and Chris tag-teamed on the grill all day and Morgan and Genna ran the rest of the show. And throughout the remainder of the day, Vicky noticeably watched out for Stephie, along with Jake.

There was always too much to eat at these parties. And after the food was all in and left-overs divided and claimed, the remaining people congregated around the fire. Vicky told Jake and Stephie that he was going to leave but since he had confided in Stephie when he was invited, that he had never been to a family barbeque, Stephie wouldn't let him. "Nope, you're staying till it's over. You teach me things. I teach you things."

The sky turned dark almost without notice and the party steadily thinned out until there were only eight of them left and all eight were circled around the glowing wood fire.

Chris turned to Vicky. "Vicky, it's a pleasure meeting you. How did you meet Stephie and Jake?"

Vicky sat up. "Stephie came to me not long ago and asked me to teach her how to do her make-up, and during those forty minutes we became friends. And I'm thrilled that over the last few weeks, we've become close friends. I adopted her. She's my baby sister now."

Chris eyed him. "You know…that makes you family. We're her parents. And that makes you our adopted child."

Vicky's jaw dropped and he stared at Chris. Connor picked up on Chris's statement and the reaction it was having on Vicky, "Would you like more family?"

Vicky covered his mouth with his left hand. "I don't know what that is." He paused. "My family disowned me." And as the last words came out, he started to silently cry. Jonathan rubbed his back as Stephanie stood, went over to him, and made him stand so she could hug him.

Genna and Morgan both wiped their eyes and so did Chris. Chris, in a deeper, more official sounding voice asked, "Will you accept our formal invitation to be our third child?"

And everyone laughed including Vicky who was laughing and crying.

"You guys are the best. I never even went to a family barbeque before and here I am…and this." He glanced at Jonathan. "Wow."

Connor peered around from the other side of the fire, "Your family did that to you?"

Vicky wiped his eyes. "Well, I am different."

Jake sat forward, "No, you're not." And he surveyed everyone else. "He may sound a little different, but I've gotten to know him and see how he treats Stephie and everyone else, and he's not different at all. He has a gigantic heart, a beautiful soul and a whole lot of love. He's not different in any way, if you're paying attention."

All four parents smiled at the maturity his words revealed.

Jake looked at Vicky. "We're not. We're exactly the same as everyone else. We want the exact same things. We have the exact same morals and standards. In fact, I'd like to put your standards up against any of the people who are abusing others in the name of corporate profit, religious dogma, or partisan politics, to name a few."

Connor eyed Vicky. "You're not. You've been told you are by a noisy corner of society but you're not. And the people telling you, you are, are the people who are different. It's a maturity thing."

"And a wisdom thing."

Genna looked at Morgan. "You're right. People seem to be preaching the parts about hate and exclusion, but not the parts about love and inclusion."

Chris lifted his beer and twisted his head slightly, "But that doesn't mean we don't get it."

They all seemed to take his lead and sipped their drink. The fire glowed and softly flickered on everyone in the circle, and the crackling wood sounded sweeter than music. Everyone sat back and enjoyed the rest of the beautiful night.

CHAPTER FOURTEEN
MODIFICATION

Steven raised his head from the reference book he had open on the library table, leaned back and stretched his arms out. "I'm going to miss this place."

Jake looked up from his book and squinted. "Why?"

"I don't know." Steven looked around. "I got used to the place and everyone was nice. Kinda feels like an extension of high school, doesn't it?"

Jake grinned and leaned forward with both arms on the table. "But Steph gets to go to the next school."

Steven dropped his hand to the table. "I'm so tired of this place. I can't wait to get the hell out. This place is like a high school."

Jake lowered his eyes back down to his book. "You're an idiot."

"I'm almost done with the reference books. Then we can head home. I'd rather finish this at home anyway. This way I can pass out when I'm done working."

Jake turned his page. "Alright. I can study either place."

Steven finally finished and shut the reference book louder than he intended. Jake looked up and noticed five quick stares from around the room as Steven whispered, "Sorry." He then turned to Jake. "Okay. Let's get outa here."

Their workload intensified as the semester's end neared. Finals started in a week and they were both mentally at the brink from the inner pressures they had placed on themselves. They were studying and reading, whether together or alone and both agreed they were an absolute distraction to each other. They decided they were better off finishing some final assignments and studying for finals, separately.

Sleepy and tired of working alone in his room, Jake took a quick break and dialed his phone, "Hi."

"Hi. You doin' okay?"

Jake chuckled, "Same as I was two hours ago. You still working?"

"I just finished my term paper for Griffin's class. I think it came out good."

Jake yawned. "Cool."

Steven continued, "I'm done. I'm crashing…right after I put on this cute little pink nightie to sleep in."

Jake's voice raised. "Damn, don't do that to me!"

Steven feigned innocence. "Do what?"

Jake's voice increased. "I'll come over there. Damn, you woke me up! I was ready to pass out."

Steven teased. "Bet you can't guess what color panties I have on underneath!"

Jake shook his head with playful exasperation. "Why you doing this to me?"

"None! I'm not wearing panties."

Jake tried to threaten, "I swear I'll come over there."

Steven continued his tease. "The nightie barely covers my hiney. You should feel how smooth it is."

"Damn!" Jake's voice changed to a resigned whisper. "I'm not going to get to sleep for an hour. I may attack you tomorrow when I see you."

Steven responded passively, "I'm so okay with that."

Jake could feel his heart beating and smiled. "See you tomorrow morning. Warning. If you tell me what color panties you have on tomorrow, you will be in trouble."

Steven laughed off the threat. "That's all it'll take? What color would you like?"

"Seriously. You're driving me crazy! Goodnight Stephanie."

Steven sung his response, "Goodnight Jacob."

Jake hurried getting ready for school the next morning and as soon as he was ready, he swung his back pack over his left shoulder, went across the drives and knocked on the opposing kitchen door. Steven opened it moments later, as he pulled his shirt down. "Hey. What's up?"

Jake stepped inside and pulled Steven into him. "Do you know what you did to me last night? I was up for two hours."

Jake caressed the back of Steven's head and brought Steven's face to his. Their mouths immediately opened and seconds later, Steven went limp. Jake held him up to finish the kiss. As the kiss broke, Steven offered with more breath than voice. "What was that for?"

Jake's breathing confirmed an equal reaction. "For torturing me last night. If we had time I'd be stripping your pants off and playing with that smooth round bottom you told me about last night."

Steven tried to catch his breath. "I like the delayed response."

"Come on. Let's go to school before we decide to go into the bedroom instead."

Steven whispered. "Are you sure?"

The only sound in the car was the radio. Jake reached for Steven's hand over the middle console, still thinking about the morning kiss. He could still hear Steven's breathing.

They walked in silence toward the buildings, bumping softly into each other along the way. "See you after class."

Jake smiled at him as they went down separate hallways.

~ ~ ~

Steven had his head buried in his open laptop when Jake walked up, stood across from him and lifted the back pack off his left shoulder. He glanced up. "I have the counselor's meeting tomorrow. I'll go myself if you don't feel like going."

Jake softly dropped his back pack on the table. "I'd rather go with you."

"I'll be fine."

He removed a textbook and it made a thump on the table as he dropped it. "I know. But I feel I increase the okay factor. Do you mind?"

"He's a professional. I'm sure everything will be fine." Steven wasn't comfortable with meetings like this but he didn't want Jake to have to suffer through it too. He did secretly dread it though. *Why does he want to see me? Is something wrong because I'm different? Does the school now have a problem? Does he have a problem? Can he make a problem for me? I hate when people can't just let other people live their lives. I'm not harming anyone.* He spoke after the slight pause. "But I've been thinking..."

Jake paged through his book. "Yeah?

Steven leaned forward. "I want to go in and talk to him alone. I mean, you can come with me for the drive so we can do something after if you want, but I want to do this alone."

"Why?"

"Because I have to do things like this. I've been avoiding things like this and that was alright when I was younger and confused, but it's not alright any more. This is a great chance for me to grow. I'm not incapable, I'm just different. If I can't handle it...you ...Mom...I have loved ones who will help me. But I want to try to help myself first."

Jake folded both arms over the open book in front of him. "But I know you don't like doing stuff like this, and I'll do it with you."

Steven reached for Jake hand across the table, then caught himself and looked around. "I know, and I know you mean well, but I want to be able to take care of us too. We're a team. You remember calling us a team of idiots, once? Well, I want to hold up my end of the team too. I don't want to go through life as some kind of helpless soul. I need to learn to be strong too. Besides, I'm more confident as Stephanie because I never felt more like the same person inside and out, than I do when I'm her. Steven would have been more intimidated because he was already confused, but Stephanie wants to get stronger." He looked around to make sure no one was listening. "Don't I seem more normal to you when I'm Stephanie?"

Jake smiled. "You never seemed not normal to me."

"Well, I didn't always feel normal, but I feel more normal now than I ever did." He looked into Jake's eyes. "I'm sorry I was born with a confusion that confuses everyone else too, but I feel less confused right now than I ever did. I tested it out dancing and at the Halloween party and it worked out good, don't you think?"

Jake smiled. "Real good. Especially standing in the corner at the Halloween party."

The reply sent a soft flutter through his heart and he shook his head. "Well I want to test it out a little more."

Jake laid his arm on the table in Steven's direction. "Can I at least come along for moral support?"

"You don't have to but you can always come along as my boyfriend, for anything, anytime you want. But I want to go into the meeting alone." Steven kept his focus on Jake's eyes. "Okay?"

Jake breathed in. "Okay, but I'm going."

Steven smiled softly. "Meet at the car at eight thirty?"

Jake pulled out his phone and set the alarm, looked up and smiled. They worked silently for the next two hours; discreetly glancing at each other every so often.

Stephie woke early the next morning. She tried but couldn't get back to sleep when she remembered what she had to do. She crawled out of bed and went looking for a comforting face, and smiled as she turned the corner into the kitchen. "Mornin' Mom."

"Morning sweetheart." Genna finished stirring her coffee. "What are you doing up so early?"

Stephie grabbed a mug from an upper cabinet. "Jake and I have to go to the university today."

"What for?"

"A counselor wants to meet with me."

Genna sipped her coffee. "What for?"

Stephie poured a cup. "I have no idea, but Jake's going with me. He wants to know too."

After a moment, Genna volunteered, "Let me know if there's anything I can do."

"I will, but I'm sure it's nothing."

~ ~ ~

Jake turned the car into the student parking lot after a fairly quiet ride. "They really didn't tell you why they wanted to see you?"

"Nope. Only that I'm supposed to see a Mr. Matthews in the academic counselors' office."

"Why a guy? Every psych class I've ever taken is eighty percent female. Tell me they don't have a female counselor you can talk to." He paused and exhaled slowly, moving his head side to side almost unnoticeably. "So glad I came."

They found the building and then the hallway and finally the counselors' offices. Stephie turned to the small metal desk just inside and to the left of the big gray metal door. "Hi. I'm Stephanie Blair and I have a ten fifteen appointment with Mr. Matthews?"

The young gentleman sitting behind the desk lifted the phone receiver. "I'll let him know you're here." He pointed with his free hand. "You can sit over there if you want."

They sat and waited. Stephie couldn't stop squirming. "I hate this. Why do these kinds of things make you uncomfortable? Do they make you uncomfortable?"

Jake seemed more twisted than Stephanie. "Yeah. I hate 'em. It's like you're being evaluated or measured or something. All of a sudden some of us are being evaluated in ways the evaluators wouldn't want to be evaluated."

"Mr. Matthews opened his office door. "Stephanie Blair?"

Jake whispered. "I'm here if you need me."

She whispered back. "I know. That's why I'm doing this alone. I want to be able to say that to you if you ever need me."

She stood up. "I'm Stephanie."

"Nice to meet you." He held out his hand as she approached. "I'm Brian Matthews. Please come in."

He stepped back and pointed to the two cushioned chairs to the left of the door. "Make yourself comfortable."

She politely sat with her back as straight as possible. His eyes traced over her as he sat behind his desk and the visual evaluation caused an immediate discomfort, raising her breathing slightly. "You make a very attractive girl."

Stephanie turned her head slightly and narrowed her eyes, but refrained from a reply. She continued to sit straight, with her hands on her lap, noticeably uncomfortable and now feeling completely uneasy.

He broke the silence again. "Please relax." He leaned forward and folded his hands on the desktop. "Is there anything I can do to help you relax?"

She continued to stare at him and though she swallowed hard, tried her best to show composure. "No." Her reply was soft but impossible to shorten. She wanted desperately to know what he wanted, but decided it was best to remain quiet.

"I brought you in today to get to know you. I see you're one of our more unique students." He smiled awkwardly.

She continued her silence as she tried to make sense of his statements.

"Do you have anything to add?"

She softly replied, "No." She focused on remaining composed, though she had questions to ask. She wanted to know why he requested the meeting and why he gave no explanation for the request. She wanted to know if her enrollment was in jeopardy, and what authority he had over it, but she wasn't sure she was allowed to ask, so she kept focused and silent, neither smiling nor relaxing her posture.

He glanced down at her legs. "May I ask how long you've been living as a girl?"

Her eyes narrowed again. "No."

He inhaled at her terse reply, frowned, then paused uncomfortably. "Do you know the school has a Wellness Center, available to all students?"

"Yes. It's explained during orientation." She dropped her brow even further. "You know it's explained during orientation, don't you?"

"Yes. I'm aware." His eyes wandered down the front of her outfit again. "Do you have any issues you'd like to discuss?"

"No."

He met her eyes and tried to offer a softer smile. "You're not very talkative."

Her mind and heart raced and the more it did, the more she resolved to keep her composure. *Does he want me to sing and dance?* She smiled politely.

His voice hardened. "Well, the wellness center addresses all aspects of wellness, and I believe it is a place where certain types of people can benefit greatly from its services."

Her confusion drew a response from her, she couldn't control. "I'm sorry?"

"The Wellness staff is highly trained in all aspects of wellness management." He waited for a response, but she offered none. "Does your silence indicate the possible need for these services?"

She voluntarily ended her self-imposed restraint. "Is my enrollment contingent on me using these services?"

The reply caught him slightly off guard, and he answered quickly and professionally, "No. Not at all."

And she decided to use the power his answer gave. "Do you feel I need to talk to these people?"

He sighed and continued his alternate tactic. "I think you would be wise to consider it."

She hesitated a moment to digest his reply. "And why is that?" She was surprised by her own response; though she was sure her breathing showed him signs of weakness. "Do you know me well enough to feel I'm not well adjusted in any way?"

His noncompliant response caught her off guard. "Your unique circumstance could indicate a better than normal chance of such a condition."

She narrowed her eyes. "But you have no specific information on me, other than my transcripts?"

"Other than your transcripts, no I don't, which is why I wanted to talk to you." It was a lie she would never discover.

She tried to convey indifference, "So am I here today so you can evaluate me?"

"I think it would be to your benefit, yes."

His answers were striking her deeper than she expected and each reply produced a moment of hesitation. "And why do you think I would benefit?"

"Because I can evaluate whether I …we …can help you in any way." He stared into her eyes for a longer than comfortable pause, then purposely glanced toward his computer.

She clung uneasily to the little equality she felt remained. "And what if I told you I'm as normal as any other person, including you?"

His eyes met hers again for a brief pause, then he inhaled and sat straight. "Well, just from your unique circumstance, I would say you're obviously not as... typical as most other people, and thus, not as inclined to be as issue free." He nodded once to confirm his opinion.

She tilted her head slightly. "Those not typical are more inclined to have issues?"

He sighed all but unnoticeably, realizing there was no connection between her unique circumstance and any reach for help, whether traditional or ... unorthodox. "There are degrees of issues that I believe can be measured by certain other indicators, which is why I wanted to meet with you."

"But if I felt I needed help, don't you think I would ask for it?"

He adjusted in his seat and continued to hold fast to his alternate agenda. "I don't know that and I thought I would talk to you in person, to see whether you needed it or not."

His answer revealed just enough audacity to build her resolve. "But you could have offered that over the phone. You could have even offered this meeting under that premise. But you didn't. Instead you told me I needed to meet with you, without explanation. Why?"

He breathed deep, noticeably annoyed by the short but uncomfortable effect the meeting had produced. "In retrospect, I guess I should have been more upfront regarding why I thought we should meet. I am sorry."

She was now miffed by his admission and though she shouldn't have felt the need to once again prove her level of normality, she pointed to the desk and calmly inquired, "May I ask, do you have a copy of my transcripts in your pile of papers there?"

Mr. Matthews suddenly appeared noticeably tired. "They're on my computer." He continued without turning toward it. "You're an impressive student."

She folded her hands on her lap again. "It hints at an absence of certain other...issues, don't you think?" Her heart continued to pound and she tried desperately to control her immediate need for oxygen.

He smiled indifferently. "It would appear so...on the surface, yes."

She inhaled as she registered his refusal to once again acknowledge her claim and pointed to his papers. "Please note, Mr. Matthews, that I'm a well-adjusted, highly intelligent, highly motivated member of our society, and when I learn more about my specific place in it, I'll consider stopping by to share things I feel you would benefit from knowing. How's that?"

He stood, obviously anxious to end the very awkward meeting. "Very good Ms. Blair. It was a pleasure meeting you." He extended his hand.

She stood as ladylike as Vicky and his contingent taught her, moved her focus from his face to his hand, and hesitated for more than a moment before accepting it; then gave a quick but emotionless feminine smile, turned and left his office. Her eyes immediately connected with Jake as soon as she passed the private office door, and without acknowledgement, watched his eyes follow her as she headed through the reception area and out to the hallway beyond. Her legs were less than steady as she walked past Jake, but she felt like celebrating. She stood up for herself! She could feel the exhilaration growing inside her, but gave no outward sign.

He caught up with her and grabbed her hand as they walked toward the far double doors leading out to the main corridor. "So?"

She walked another five steps, stopped, and turned to him.

"You alright?" He stood straight with raised eyebrows and wide eyes.

"Ugh!" She inhaled deeply and met his stare. "Yes. Yes, I'm alright." She gave an involuntary shudder. "But that was creepy." She looked into his eyes, and her smile slowly grew. "But Jake, I handled it. I handled it like you would have, I did good!"

He laughed. "I had no doubts."

"The hell you didn't." They both laughed. "Jake."

"What?"

"I'm Stephanie."

"Good. I kinda like her."

She did a double take at the way he said it. "But *he* was creepy."

He took her hand and turned toward the main corridor. "I'm growing a definite dislike for adults in authority. They demand an end to bullying but I've met very few who don't, when they know there are no ramifications."

She eyed him. "I can't figure out why he wanted to meet with me, though."

He slowed up, making her turn toward him. "Do yourself a favor…better yet, will you do me a favor right now?"

Stephie stopped and looked at him. "Sure."

"Go back in there and request a change in counselors."

She straightened up, thought for a second, and then walked back toward the large metal door.

Jake's voice followed. "I'll wait out here. Leave the door open. I suggest you request a female, but that's your call." Jake slid to the floor and propped himself against the corridor wall as she went back in.

A minute later his head turned as she came back through the opening. "Done. Megan Tanner."

She reached for his hand as he stood, and they walked twenty feet before she spoke again. "That was creepy." She looked up at him. "You don't think he wanted something else from me, do you?"

His voice turned deep. "Guys are assholes."

She pulled his arm and he met her eyes. "No generalizations."

"Okay. He's an asshole." He wrapped his arm around her shoulders and smiled at her before continuing toward the far double doors.

~ ~ ~

Finals week finally arrived and Jake looked exhausted walking toward their lunchroom table for their second period break. Steven lowered his notebook. "How'd you do?"

"Good. But damn that was intense. This shit wears me out," He plopped his back pack on the table.

Steven's mouth twisted as he felt his best friend's frustration. "It'll be over soon."

Jake looked overwhelmed. "Why does every class have to have a final? I'm not taking one more class after I get my four year degree."

"Hate to break it to you, but your company may make you."

Jake stared at him. "You don't like me, do you?"

Steven went back to reading his notes. "No, not much."

They each had a final in their next class and the hour break flew by. Jakes phone alarm went off and the sound appeared to have shot them both. They wrapped up in silence and headed to the door. "Good luck."

Steven looked back as he walked away. "You too. Library in an hour…pass or fail."

Jake's voice lowered. "Very funny."

Jake was early and sitting back relaxing when Steven finally walked through the library doors. "Where you been?"

Steven leaned against the table as he removed his computer from his back pack. "The professor said we could stay a little longer if we needed to, so I checked my paper before I handed it in." He studied Jake. "How'd you make out?"

Jake inhaled slowly, then nodded. "Good."

Steven smirked, "You always do better than you think." then pointed to the library doors. "Did you see the notice on the bulletin board between the doors?"

Jake looked past Steven at the double glass entry doors. "What notice?"

"The school's sponsoring a trip for the end of the semester."

Jake's eyes grew. "No way."

Steven tried to make his grin give the lie away. "No."

Jake stared at him, confused. "I don't get it."

Steven glanced up from his open computer screen and spoke slower, "Jake, the school is sponsoring an end of semester overnight get-away, in honor of your twenty-first birthday." lowered his chin and raised both eyebrows.

Jake energized immediately. "For me?"

Steven glared at him, "Idiot. I was thinking!"

"Really?"

Steven moved his computer slightly to the side and leaned forward so he could whisper. "Are you kidding? Jake. Do you have any idea how bad I want to be alone with you? The school is sponsoring a trip next week, and we have to go," Steven twisted his head slightly to make sure Jake understood.

"You're brilliant. …They aren't, right?"

Steven grinned. "Well, they are now. Even if we're the only two who know about it and are going. Two day, two night trip. Leave Tuesday. Back home Thursday?"

Jake ran his hand over his chin. "We'll need to tell them to where."

Steven's smile softened. "Details to follow. Want to go?"

He squinted. "I'm not sure yet. Depends on where."

Steven glared at him, "Don't make me get up and kick your ass in front of all these people." then stood to move next to him.

Jake smiled and raised his hands. "No, please don't kick my ass."

Steven scowled. "Don't make me call you *idiot* three times in an hour." Steven sat down and pulled his chair closer to Jake's and Jake grabbed him around the waist and started tickling him.

Steven mock scolded him. "Will you knock it off!" He smiled at Jake, spun his laptop around between them and started surfing. They leaned together until their shoulders touched, then Jake wrapped his arm around the back of Steven chair and they discreetly sat against each other.

"Whatcha searchin' for?"

"To find out where the school trip's going."

He made sure Jake could see while he searched the local resorts. He clicked on one. "Tall Pines Resort and Campground. What do you think?"

Jake nodded his approval. "I like it. Camping. Hiking. Sun. Fresh air…and we ain't going to do any of it."

Steven whispered. "Nope. In fact, we need to bring food and vitamins to wherever we go, cause you ain't leavin' the room. Oh. Water. You're going to need your fluids."

Jake rested his elbow on the table and his head in his hand. "But why am I going to need fluids?"

"Cause I don't want you cramping up on me."

Jake shook his head. "You're an idiot." He thought for a few seconds, and then lowered his hand to the table. "Actually, this is a good plan. A very good plan."

"Okay. But you'll have to lift every day to build your stamina and since I need to make sure I'll be supervising daily, but it doesn't count against my birthday." Steven's grin confirming the satisfaction of his declaration.

Jake leaned his head closer and whispered as softly as possible. "I could so fondle you right now."

Steven spoke softer and slower. "We would get arrested, 'cause I wouldn't stop you."

"Think they'd give us a cell together? Think of the money we could save on the trip."

~ ~ ~

Steven paced impatiently in front of the library. He had finished his last final for the semester, and waited anxiously to see Jake walking from his last class and toward their designated meeting place for the final time. When Steven saw him, he couldn't help but hurry to his best friend, and when they were close enough, Jake dropped his shoulders and playfully sighed. "Done! Last one."

Steven momentarily quelled his desire to celebrate. "How did you do?"

Jake took a deep breath. "Good, I think. This was the toughest semester yet."

Steven's enthusiasm accompanied his consolation. "Because a two year degree in your major can get you a job."

"I know. I'm not complaining."

He waited for Jake to lead them toward the path to the parking lot, then softly asked, "So, how do you think you did for the whole semester?"

Jake nodded, but answered unconvincingly. "I think I did good."

Steven bumped against him; glancing frequently in his direction as they walked. "I'm sure you did good. You work harder than me."

Jake replied instantly. "You're smarter than I am."

He hopped. "Oh bullshit."

Jake laughed. "I never heard you say that! Man, my father's wearing off on you."

Steven smirked as he glanced at him. "But seriously, how long do you have to match my grades before you convince yourself you're as smart as me? I'm tired of hearing it. You *are* smart. An absolute pain in my butt, but smart."

Jake immediately reached behind Steven and grabbed his ass, and Steven let out a girl shriek in the middle of the path.

Jake playfully smirked. "Not yet, but it's in my plans."

Steven's heart sped up and his breathing immediately increased. Jake smiled at him, and raised his right eyebrow.

The car's lights blinked as Jake pressed his fob, but before he got in, he leaned on the roof and pointed back to the library and the buildings behind it. "Say goodbye."

Steven half turned in the direction of the empty center courtyard. "I know. This is it, isn't it?"

Jake leaned on the roof and scanned the quiet campus. "Yep. One more hurdle done."

The ride home was more festive than any ride home from school in months, and as far as Steven was concerned, they were alone and Stephie could come out. He pulled off the rubber band holding his growing hair, ran his hands through, and shook it.

Jake glanced at her and his entire face brightened. "Hi Steph!"

She gave him a gigantic smile. "Hi!" Opened the sunroof, turned up the music, raised her arms through the opening, and let out a shriek. She hopped in her seat as she spun toward him. "We should celebrate."

His shoulders dropped. "You know I have to work."

She playfully whined. "Do you really?"

He frowned as he glanced at her. "Yeah. I haven't worked a shift in a week. Besides, I don't think I could get it covered. I switched for tonight so we could have tomorrow off."

"I know." Stephie made a sad face, then just as fast turned completely excited. "Then let's celebrate tomorrow."

Jake smiled. "Sure. In the meantime, why don't you call Vicky and see what he's doing? And I'll see you first thing tomorrow morning."

They pulled in front of his house and stared at each other. She broke the quick pause. "I don't want to say goodbye yet though."

Jake grinned. "Why don't you come in real quick?"

"Can I go change first? I'll be fast."

"Okay. But I only have thirty minutes before I have to leave."

She ran to her door as soon as the car stopped.

Jake started dialing his phone as soon as he shut the kitchen door. For as much as he tried, he couldn't get her counselor meeting out of his mind. He set his back pack down next to his dresser as he walked into his room. The idea the school would be open and accepting to people like Stephanie was the reason they chose the school. The counter idea that, after they registered, a counselor would need to meet with her over those same issues, twisted him and he needed a second measurement on where the school stood, with regard to people like her.

"Hi, I'm a new transfer student starting this coming semester and I was wondering if I could come in and talk to a counselor."

"Sure. May I have your name?"

"Jacob Harrison. I'd like to meet with Ms. Tanner."

"Sure. Would you like her to be your counselor during your undergrad studies here?"

"Yes."

"When would you like to come in?"

"When is her first available appointment?"

"Monday at nine."

"Perfect. See you then."

Stephie opened the Harrison's side door. "Jake?"

"Back here!"

He could hear her running to his room as if every second counted in her mind. She turned into the room and attacked him, but he was ready for her and caught her in his arms, laughing. "I love your seduction method."

He moved her with little force and they fell sideways onto his bed, his arms around her waist, hers around his neck. "Hi!"

"Hi!" Their mouths found each other and they kissed deeply. Instantly he had a yearning for her and instantly his craving was being satisfied. Her tongue was so soft and delicious. It struck him, just how feminine she was. She was every bit a female; from her smell to her shape to the softness of her skin.

She caressed the back of his head as she lay against him, quietly inhaling his incredible masculine scent. "We need to finish our school trip plans."

He took a breath between soft kisses. "Tell me about it. I can't take it anymore. I need you." He kissed all over her face and neck. "It's all I can do to not take you, when we're alone like this."

She ran her fingers through his hair. "I want to just…" Her sentence faded as she became lost in his attention, and her voice changed to a sensual whisper. "I want you more than I've ever wanted anything."

His phone alarm went off twenty seconds later. "No!" She peered into his eyes and exhaled. He gently caressed the side of her face and kissed her as tenderly as he could, then started getting up. She gave him a look of complete disheartenment and it made him smile. He stood next to the bed and stared at her. "I love you."

She curled up and answered back with an almost inconsolable whisper. "I love you too."

Then she shrieked as he jumped on top of her, pinning her hands slightly above her head. He watched her for a moment, then leaned down and tickled her neck with his mouth. She laughed as she struggled to free herself and sighed at the fantastic feeling of not being able to move him at all. He broke their embrace and jumped off her in what seemed like one move and she just laid there.

He eagerly offered. "I promise I'll abuse you tomorrow."

She half-heartedly mumbled, "Yeah…"

He opened his closet and reached for his work uniform. "No really!" He turned and put his hand over his heart. "I promise!" She jumped off the bed as he pulled his work pants up, and lunged at him. "Come on! I have to change for work." He started laughing. "Stephanie!"

She ignored him completely but was getting nowhere. Finally she glared at him. "You need to start putting out mister."

His laugh made her laugh. "Oh Jeez! I'd be putting out now if it wasn't for work."

"Well, I'm tired of that lame excuse."

He finished pulling his work pants up while she hung on them. "I am a second away from giving in. Are we doing this now or tomorrow?"

She looked up with big sad eyes and hesitated before answering. "Tomorrow, I guess."

He picked her up off her knees and surrounded her in his arms. "I love you more than you know. Everything about you is all I could ever want." His hands slid over her rear as their mouths came together and they kissed passionately goodbye.

"You can drive me if you want the car tonight."

"Nah. I'll use my mom's if I go out."

They walked out his side door together. "Call me when you get up tomorrow."

"Okay."

"Love you."

"I love you too."

~ ~ ~

The thinnest sunbeam pierced between the edge of the curtain and the shade behind it, but it was enough to open Stephanie's eyes, and a wonderful thought immediately entered her head. *Finally! A morning with no work to worry about.* The semester was over except for the crying, but they had both found, the more work applied during, the less crying after.

She grabbed her phone from the end table and dialed. "Hi, you up?"

"Hey! Wow…is school really over?" She could tell she woke him. "Did we survive another semester?"

"Yep. Isn't it great?"

"Hell yeah! His voice lightened. "Watcha wanna do?"

She semi-sung her response. "I dunno, but let's do something. I need to be out."

"I agree. How about breakfast then search for an apartment again?"

"Absolutely. I really want to find an apartment as soon as we can. If we have time after, we can do some of our Christmas shopping."

"Ah, a plan. Don't you love a plan?"

She softly smiled. "Yes, I love a plan."

"How long?"

"Depends." Her voice rose. "Do you have to lift?"

His tone lowered "We won't ever leave the house."

She smiled. "You're right."

"See you in an hour? My side steps or your side steps, whichever you choose."

She shook her head. "Side steps it is."

"One hour…side steps."

She bounced all the way to the bathroom feeling a level of peace and contentment that matched the quiet around her. The heat and steam of the hot shower warmed her through, and the warm feeling freed her mind. It had been a while since she and Jake were alone together for any length of time, and yesterday's tease only confirmed her desire to finalize their secret vacation plans. Just the thought of him brought a deep satisfying smile to her face. She turned the water hotter and daydreamed spending the entire day with him. The thought was warmer than the water cascading over her.

Still warmed by the shower, she searched her closet for something that would make Jake's heart race. She found a dark gray cotton knit dress her mother bought her, and felt an inner peace as she slipped it over her effeminate frame. She straightened it and then ran her hands through her hair as she spun to face the mirror. She was pleased at how she looked in it, and semi-skipped to the bathroom to do her make-up and hair. Her hair was finally getting to the length she longed for back in August, and it made her feel extraordinarily feminine to throw it around like a girl. When she finished getting ready, she grabbed her purse and an oversized knit sweater and faced the mirror one last time. A last little tug at her hip and she was ready to spend the day with Jake. She opened the kitchen door and looked down. He was sitting there on her steps and she felt a different kind of warmth envelop her. "Morning!"

He stood and greeted her with a tender kiss "Nice outfit. Good morning." He leaned forward and gave her another kiss. "You look hot! Want a quickie?"

Her heart jumped but she reached for his hand and pulled him toward the car. "No, you had your chance yesterday." He playfully grabbed her bottom and she jumped and shrieked as usual. She pressed his seat warmer button as soon as the car started, buckled herself in and immediately turned to him, filled with excitement. "I made another decision last night."

"What?" He glanced at her and reached for her hand.

"I realized last night that I can get rid of all my boy clothes...I'm getting rid of all Steven's clothes. I'm Stephanie from here on out. Full time. Always."

"Wow. Are you sure you won't have to be Steven anymore?" He paused. "I mean, I don't mind."

She squinted slightly, and hesitated. "I want to only be Stephanie."

"Okay, but all I mean is I'm okay with whatever you have to do." He waited a moment. "You're not upset I said that, are you?"

"No. I don't mind..." Her voice hinted the slightest dejection, then changed to a soft plea, "but ever since I accepted who I am, I couldn't wait for this day. I'm Stephanie. And the more I'm Stephanie, the more I'm sure I'm Stephanie."

"Okay, but I've been trying hard to let you know I'm in love with the person you are, and I want you to know that I love you past any distinction."

"I love that you love me like that, I really do. But I'm even Stephanie in my mind when I was dressed as Steven. I really am Stephanie. I feel feminine in my heart and mind and I want to be the person I feel I am."

"Well, hopefully you get the idea I love you inside and out no matter who you are."

"I think it's phenomenal actually, but I want to be your girl." She thought for a moment. "Does me wanting to get rid of my boy clothes help you better understand who I need to be?"

"I guess the last three months...I was just trying to tell you I'm okay with you, no matter."

Her voice was as soft as her words. "I understand, but I'm a girl inside."

"And you're my girl inside and out."

One side of Jake's mouth edged upward, "Did you tell your parents about the school trip?"

She smiled. "Yeah. You?"

"Of course."

They drove for a while holding hands. "I can help you pack up your boy stuff if you want. Can I help you pack up your boy stuff?"

She turned her head and sighed. She didn't know why, but his offer made her slightly emotional, and her voice softened. "Of course you can. We can say goodbye to Steven together."

Jake turned off the highway near the university, and they wandered in an out of five apartment complexes; none close enough to enjoy campus life, but all still offering a start to their adult lives together.

They locked the door of the last one and decided to time their ride back to the student parking lot. Stephie set her phone stopwatch after pressing Jake's seat warmer button. Twenty seven minutes later, they were pulling into the lot.

She looked at him. "Not terrible."

"Nope. It's definitely in the running."

They headed back out again in a different direction, but their concentration had reached its limit for the day. He slapped himself on his cheek and it snapped her out of her trance. "Okay. I'm daydreaming about us sitting on the love seat together and don't have a clue what we've passed in the last ten minutes."

She eyed him. "Me either."

"You too?"

"Yeah. We either have to go walk around somewhere or go back to the house or something, but I'm falling asleep."

"Want to stop somewhere and get something to eat? I want to take you out."

His declaration surprised her. "Aw! You've never said that to me before! … No."

They started talking at the same time.

"Oh my god, I haven't!"

"I kinda know why we haven't gone on a real date."

"But believe it or not, I have a reason why I haven't. Wadda ya mean no!?"

"Because I don't want you spending your hard earned money taking me out." She reached for his hand and it slowed the conversation. "I don't care what we do. I just love being with you. I love sitting and doing nothing with you. And it's okay."

"It's because I was worried you weren't comfortable going out as Stephie, in public. That's the only reason. I swear!"

"Would you relax?!"

They eyed each other and chimed, "Idiot!" and laughed!

Jake glanced at her. "So what are we doing?"

"I kinda like your daydream." She turned in her seat. "Let's go to your house. We haven't had dinner with your parents in a while."

He held his hand out for hers, without looking. "Perfect. Call my mom and tell her we're hanging out with them tonight."

Stephie took out her phone and dialed Morgan. "Hi."

"Hi! What's new?"

"Jake and I want to come over tonight and visit with you. Okay?"

"Sure. Dinner?"

"Is it okay?" Steph looked to Jake.

Morgan answered, "Of course it's okay. It's always okay."

"Okay, see you in a bit." Stephie hung up her phone and stared at Jake. "Boy, we sure can celebrate up a storm, can't we?"

They went home, had a quiet dinner and sat and visited with Chris and Morgan for the night.

CHAPTER FIFTEEN
DEDICATION

"Mr. Harrison?"

Jake rose from the seat in the waiting area and gave Ms. Tanner a friendly smile. "Hi, I'm Jake Harrison."

The counselor extended her hand. "I'm Megan Tanner. It's nice to meet you."

She sat facing him behind her desk and waited for him to get comfortable. "What can I do for you today Jacob?"

"Please call me Jake."

"Okay, Jake."

He took a full breath. "I want to talk to you about something that's very important to me, and I have a reason for asking the way I wish to ask. If it seems kind of odd, please forgive me."

She rested her arms on the top of the desk. "Is it something you'd like to discuss with a life counselor in our healthcare facility instead?"

"No actually. I need to talk to you about my main concern."

She sat forward slightly. "I promise to answer the best I can. My instincts are to try to help you, and you have my promise I will not judge how you state your concern."

He breathed deep and slowly exhaled. "Thanks. I'm transferring here with my best friend, Steven Blair. Your records have him listed, I believe, as Stephanie Blair. She...she's been my best friend since we were five. She lives next to me and our families are now related. I look out for her, always. We chose to go to college together and we researched, looking for a college which was open to her wishing to live as a female. We chose this college because the admissions department assured us the school is very progressive in its view of the diversity of people, and I need to confirm the school's forward thinking concerning people like her, through you as a representative of this specific office."

She motioned to speak, but he continued. "Is the school okay with Steven wishing to live her life as Stephanie? Do you and this office have the ability to not only believe a person can be different and still completely normal; but also honor that person's dignity by treating them as if they have no issues, at least until they reveal an issue they'd like to share with you? Is the school as progressive as we were told?"

She smiled. "Wow, your concern has a depth that makes me appreciate your preface."

Her reply produced a broad smile. "I didn't know that was in me."

She folded her hands on the top of the desk and smiled. "To answer what I believe is your main question, yes; the school is very progressive in those regards. We have an impressive psychology department, and my colleagues and I are always asking them for the latest information on the people we might come in contact with. And I've learned, and take great pride in understanding people are far more diverse and far more complicated than any conservative or uneducated opinion would ever have us believe."

Jake sat up, suddenly aware of his own increased breathing.

"I can also tell you, yes, I believe Stephanie is normal. I will even go as far as telling you I'll still think she's normal even if she comes to me and tells me she has an issue she needs or wants help with. I can advise her academically and I can lead her to other parts of the school if she expresses a need that's not academic. How's that?"

He took a deep breath. "I hope I meet more people who think like you, here."

She smiled. "I think you will."

Her answer gave him a feeling of comfort and a connection he wanted to develop further. "Can I share something about Stephanie?"

She smiled softly. "Sure."

"There was a time when I was a little worried about Steven. He kind of tried to withdraw from all of us when we were in high school. I always thought it was just the transition to high school, but I learned it was more than that."

She digested his words. "As his best friend, how'd you handle it?"

"I wouldn't let him. He was living as a male at the time. He was my best friend and I wasn't letting him walk away from me for no reason."

"How'd his parents deal with it?"

"I think his mother did the same thing. He just became quieter than normal and wasn't as willing to do things. But he came back around after a while. I thought it was school, like I said, but his grades never went down."

She gently probed further. "So how is she now?"

"Completely fine. We laugh. We joke. We challenge each other with school. She's an A student. She's unbelievably smart, unbelievably motivated, unbelievably loving and unbelievably normal. I don't think she has a problem being who she is now. She's just feminine. But there's nothing wrong with her. Nothing."

She smiled. "Am I Stephanie's academic advisor too?"

He sat up. "Yeah, it's why I asked for you."

She turned to her computer. "I can share yours, but I can't share any of her information with you, but would you mind if I pulled up the academic information on both of you?"

He motioned gently toward her computer. "Please."

She turned and typed, then stared at the screen. "Impressive."

"Stephanie?"

She maneuvered the computer mouse. "Yes."

He watched her study the screen. "Could be an indication of normal, don't you think?"

She answered him without taking her eyes off the screen. "Very strong possibility it's an indicator of a well-adjusted person."

"Thanks. She's my definition."

She quickly typed again and concentrated for a moment. "You're not far behind her academically."

"You have no idea how much she helps me."

Ms. Tanner joked. "I hope you mean with motivation."

He laughed. "She's been a great influence on me as far as school's concerned. I try to out-study her, but she's a genius, so she does less and still does better than me."

"You think very highly of her."

He leaned back slightly and smiled. "Yeah, she's pretty great as far as I'm concerned."

Ms. Tanner probed further. "So in your mind, she's special, but completely normal?"

"Definitely."

"And is it okay to quickly judge you as completely normal?"

His eyes widened. He had never questioned it. "I think I am." He squinted and his voice suddenly reflected astonishment. "I just realized I fall outside the definition. I never realized that before."

She turned toward him. "Well, for whatever reason you feel is behind your revelation, my belief in the professional definition makes your disclosure inaccurate as far as I'm concerned, but for argument's sake, if you do, so does your family structure. Is your family anything but normal?"

His voice echoed a slightly different bemusement. "My god, they're my definition of normal."

She smiled and continued. "Not many people are aware that *normal* includes either a far greater percentage of people, or a far smaller percentage of people, than the average person recognizes. It depends on whether you wish to use the provincial conservative ideal as your guideline, or you're open to recognizing that normal is not driven by the hope for a higher standard of individual, but subjugated to the actual. Did you know almost eighty percent of all households fall outside the societal definition of normal?"

He sat straight. "Yeah, I do. I'm a computer major but my first love is psychology, for facts just like that. I take psych classes for all my electives."

She leaned toward him. "Really! It's an amazing subject, isn't it?"

He energized. "I love it." Then his eyes narrowed, "But how could I have not realized I wasn't considered normal, before now?"

"Because you *are* normal. The definition has the problem. Not you." She turned to her computer and quickly studied the screen again. "I see you're all set for the next semester. Are you in need of any academic counseling at the moment?"

His voice echoed a new satisfaction. "Nope. I'm good."

She faced him and rested both arms on her desk. "It was an absolute pleasure meeting you." She stood and extended her hand. "I hope you stop in occasionally to tell me how you and Stephanie are doing, and don't hesitate to stop in if there's anything I can do for you."

He stood and offered her a wonderful smile along with an eager hand. "Thanks Ms. Tanner. I appreciate the offer."

Jake felt amazingly peaceful on the drive home. He relived the meeting. *Now that's what a counselor's supposed to be; just an ally. There to help. No bullshit.* The thought made him far more comfortable about the next few years. The radio was loud but he wasn't listening to it. He smiled as his thoughts turned to Stephanie.

He wasn't paying full attention to the road, when the large cream colored building off the right side of the highway caught his eye and it triggered a completely different thought; school trip. His heart raced as he impatiently anticipated the next highway exit. *It's perfect!* He made a right at the end of the off-ramp and headed down the parallel side road. He grinned and turned down the radio as he pulled up to the parking lot surrounding the gigantic building. Twenty minutes later, he dialed Steph as he exited the hotel's automatic glass doors.

"Hi."

"Hi." He could feel the uncontrollable grin on his face. "I got us a room for two nights."

She screamed, "No way! Really?"

He held the phone away from his ear and laughed. "Yeah."

"Oh my god Jake! For when?"

He brought the phone back. "For Tuesday and Wednesday night."

"Where?"

He responded casually. "The Tall Pines Resort Country Club and Campground or something."

She pleaded. "Jake!"

He laughed, "I'm not telling you. It's a surprise."

Her voice rose. "That's so romantic! I have to get my nails done. I have to get Vicky to do my make-up. I have to go buy you water and bananas." Her voice grew even louder. "I have to go. What time do we have to be there?"

"Any time we feel like. After one."

"Well, I don't want to give away an hour we're paying for."

Her reply tickled him to his core. "I have no idea what to say to that. Wait. Let me think what my father would say to my mother." He thought for a second. "Got it!" He paused. "Okay."

"Are you making fun of me?" She didn't give him a chance to answer. "I have so much to do. I don't have enough time. Ugh!"

He looked at his phone. "You are truly a kook. I thought you told me to get something this week."

"I did. But now I have things to do."

"Like what?"

"Things! I have to go. I need to go. Talk to you later."

"Are you okay?" Jake heard silence. "Are you there?" No answer. He stared at his phone. *She's nuts! But god, I love her!*

~ ~ ~

Stephie felt like a schoolgirl as her heart pounded in her chest. *Oh my god! So much to do! I can't believe it!* The thought of being in his arms for a whole night made her involuntarily shudder. She couldn't think of anything more wonderful.

She dialed her phone. "Vicky, are you working tomorrow?"

"Hey girlfriend! What's new?"

"Jake made reservations for us to go away tomorrow, for two nights and I was wondering if you were working tomorrow."

"Yeah. I start at ten."

"Fantastic! Can I come by and you do my make-up?"

"Of course hon! You know I'm always here for you."

"Oh! My mom wants to know if you want to come over Christmas."

"We're going to Jonathan's family's house, but maybe we can stop?"

"Of course you can stop. How is he?"

"He's great. He's a really nice guy. I like him a lot."

"I'm so happy for you. You're great. All you had to do was show him. See you tomorrow?"

"See you tomorrow little sister."

Stephanie softly smiled as she hung up. *I love him.*

She dropped her phone on the end table, ran to the attic, and grabbed a suitcase; ran back, threw it on her bed and opened it. *Oh my god, what am I going to bring? What am I not going to bring?* She smelled the suitcase then found her perfume, sprayed the inside and leaned over and sniffed. *Better...Oh shit! Mom's going to know, when I pack all my girl stuff.* She sighed. "Oh well."

She opened her closet and moved her clothes away from the few items hanging in the corner, hidden under a white plastic bag. She removed the hanger from the bar and gently lifted the plastic, and her heart raced at the sight of the little white nightie underneath. She bought it with the hope of wearing it someday for him, but now she knew the date of someday and looked at it differently. It was even cuter and more feminine than she remembered, but would she really look like a girl in it? Her eyes unfocused as an overwhelming flow of emotion came over her.

She sighed. She knew her current activity was the precursor to her happiest fantasy, but the thought triggered an awareness that once again showed her the separation between who she was and who she could only hope to be. Her eyes blurred further as they began filling with moisture. Was she allowed to enjoy this without reproach? If only she were born a girl and allowed to appreciate this without hesitation, the way most people are allowed. Each additional thought carried her further from the unrestricted joy she wished she could feel. She squeezed her eyes shut and turned her focus toward Jake. She loved him with an intensity befitting any girl. Any person. She loved him more than she loved anyone or anything, including herself. Yet she never wished more than at that moment, she was born different; too emotionally confused to understand the importance of her love for him, and too self-doubting to understand his desire for her to be exactly who she was.

She sighed deep, and reached toward the nightie. The delicate feel of the silky material gave her a deep inner resolve. She may not be all she wanted to be, but she would offer him everything she is, and this is who she is. She could put his wishes before anyone else and she was sure he wanted this as much as she. There was more strength inside her for him, than for herself and she wanted him to have his desires more than she needed to be alive.

She lifted the nightie off the hangar and laid it on the bed, and its removal revealed the light pink nightie behind it. She sighed and smiled. *This works for night two.* She laid it on the white one.

She draped the plastic back over the hangar and hung it back in the corner of her closet, then slid her lingerie drawer open and her heart jumped again. She took out every pair of panties she owned. There really wasn't much to them and she made a small pile next to the two nighties. *Should I bring a dress?* She scanned the suitcase. *There's plenty of room. Why not?* She spread each hangar; quickly flipping through each dress and skirt. *Oh my god, I have to wear something to the hotel! I have to take a long bath. I have to bring my bath stuff. Oh! I have to bring my other stuff. Okay, I got this.*

She realized she had no idea what she just looked at, breathed deep and moved back to the first dress, then slowly and consciously examined every hangar. She moved a short black dress with see-through sleeves against the one before it and her heart jumped for what it revealed; a delicate white chiffon bell mini dress, with gold tone embroidery around the neckline. It felt so soft and light. She slipped her hand between the two layers, and examined how the silky material gathered slightly under the bust line. She ran the back of her hand over it again, sensing how delicate and sensual it felt, then lifted the hangar off the clothes rod and held the dress against her as she turned to the mirror on the back of her bedroom door. She breathed slowly then hooked the hangar over the outer doorknob and went back to her closet.

The next dress was also something she had bought with Jake in mind; a simple tan pleated dress with a stand collar and asymmetrical hemline. She moved it from the closet bar to the other side of her closet door. Her eyes narrowed and refocused on the closet floor…shoes. She reached for her white high heels and the clear high heel slippers. *I definitely need more shoes.* She half smiled, knowing she meant more high heels. *Why do women complain about wearing them? They're so feminine.* The pile on her bed had grown, but she wasn't done. She reached down to the other corner of her closet, grabbed her video game bag and laid it next to the suitcase. She unzipped it and peeked inside. Would it be wrong to bring two bags for two nights? It isn't like they won't fit in the car. *What am I doing? I should be wearing very little most of the time.* A soft exhale exited her nose. "I don't know *what* I'm doing!"

She heard Jake pull up and park, and ten seconds later, her phone rang.

"I'm home. Are you alright for tomorrow?"

His question confused her. "Of course I am. Why?"

"I thought you lost it when I told you about the room."

She replied meekly. "I know. I got a little excited. Sorry."

"I don't mind, as long as you're alright. Do you need me to go to the store for us for tomorrow? I will."

"Nope. I can stop on the way home from the mall tomorrow." Then she excitedly announced, "Vicky's doing my make-up at ten."

"That's great. Want to have dinner together tonight?"

She inhaled, "Yeah, where?"

His pitch rose. "Your house?"

"Sure. Then let's sit in the family room with my mom and dad, okay?"

"Okay. What time?"

She stared at the dress hanging on her closet doorknob. "Around five thirty, six? Maybe I'll start dinner."

"See you then. I'm going to go pack. Bring something you can wear to dinner."

She straightened up. "Okay, but we may not leave the room."

His voice lowered. "I know."

~ ~ ~

Stephie took the lead when dinner was done. "Go relax. I'll clean up."

Genna and Connor both replied, "Thanks" and disappeared into the family room.

Jake waited for her, before rising from his seat, and she met his reluctance with a second offer. "You can go too. I got this."

"No, I'll help you."

"Why?"

He shrugged his shoulders. "I just want to."

She made eye contact with him and smiled, but as he turned away to retrieve a drying towel, she quietly stared at him. She would be his tomorrow, and the thought filled her with so many emotions. All she could think was how he seemed to always be next to her, no matter how far back she remembered, or what she was going through, and it seemed almost inconceivable. He met her eyes again and she casually smiled and rinsed the pan she was holding, but her hands were going through motions disconnected from her thoughts.

She glanced at him again and caught him staring at her. "What?"

His strange grin appeared. "You really are beautiful."

She turned back to the pot in her hand. "So are you."

When they were done cleaning up, they joined Genna and Connor in the family room for the evening. She waited for him to get situated on the loveseat, and then sat nestled in his arms. The evening took on a gentle calmness with neither paying attention to anything outside the awareness of the other. But she did exchange glances with her parents and the soft grin on her father's face secretly delighted her.

Connor softly broke the quiet. "So where are you two going tomorrow?"

"Tall Pines Resort and Campground."

Jake added. "The cabins sleep four, so we're bunking with two others. We don't know who, but it'll be fun."

Stephie sat calmly as Jake made up the story. *I can lie as good as him!* "Jake's in charge of buying the beer."

"So your cabin will be the party cabin?"

Stephie looked at her father. "We hope so." They both kept straight faces, but this would be enjoyed together later.

"Oh, Mom! We may have found an apartment."

"Really? You didn't sign anything, did you?"

"No." She sat up slightly. "I figured you and Dad would want to make sure everything was alright before we did. And I'm sure Nana will have to be okay with it too."

Genna smiled. "It really is best, sweetheart. Give me the details when you get home and we'll work on it."

Stephie had no idea of the time that had passed. She wasn't paying attention to anything in particular; just how comfortable Jake's arms felt, but his whisper in her ear brought her out of her cozy daze.

"What time are we meeting tomorrow?"

She whispered back. "I should be done with Vicky around eleven. I guess noon?"

"Okay. I'm going to call it a night." He couldn't suppress the grin and it made her grin, and her grin was starting to make her turn red. She discreetly hit him on the arm. He glanced at her and whispered. "I can't help it."

She reached for his hand as he stood and said "Good night." and they walked to the kitchen.

She turned to him at the door. "You're bad."

He pulled her in. "You know I can't always control my screwy grin."

She scrunched her face at him. "There's something wrong with you."

He looked down apologetically, but his voice echoed only playful impudence. "You can give me a thorough exam tomorrow and try to figure it out."

She shuddered and he chuckled. "What was that?"

"You."

He shook his head. "This is better than Christmas when we were six."

"Tell me about it." She paused, then whispered, "I love you" and then rested her head on his chest.

"God, Stephie. I love you." He surrounded her in his arms. "See you tomorrow around noon. Make sure you pack your phone charger."

She hugged tighter. "I want to shut our phones off when we're in *the cabin.*"

"You're bad." He kissed her softly. "I can't stop thinking about…"

"Stop. I'm not going to sleep as it is."

He took a breath. "Okay. I need to get outa here."

She leaned up and kissed him. "Love you."

He patted her bottom. "Love you too"

She stood on the landing and watched him cross the drives, and she felt the cold go through her just as he started running. The temperature had dropped the last few days and the chill was piercing. He stopped and looked at her from the top of his landing, then hurried inside.

She walked straight to her room. "Night Mom. Night Dad."

They answered in unison. "Night sweetheart."

She plugged her phone in and placed it on the end table before climbing under the covers. Her alarm was set, but she doubted she would need it.

~ ~ ~

Stephie woke just early enough to walk out of her room and say goodbye to her mother. "See you Thursday night, Mom." They hugged and kissed.

"Okay sweetheart. Be careful. Have fun. Call me if you need me."

"I will." She walked back toward her room. *The hotel could burn down and I'm not calling her. How would I explain it?*

As soon as Stephie heard Genna's car leave, her stomach quivered. *Oh, what a day.* She walked to the bathroom, coffee mug in hand, and turned on the bathtub faucet. She did everything Vicky taught her and when she was done, put on the white dress and her coat and headed to Vicky. She was early but Vicky was already there waiting for her.

"Hi sister!" They hugged and kissed.

Stephie sat in his make-up chair and exhaled. "I'm so glad to see you. I'm so nervous."

Vicky studied her eyes. "Why are you nervous?" His stare made Steph blush.

"...Oh ...my ...god!" He lowered his chin and his voice. "Are you still a virgin?"

Stephie felt her heart flutter and her face turn a deeper crimson. "You know I am."

Vicky raised his hand to his mouth and giggled. "Oh this is fantastic! I never made someone up for their virgin sacrifice." He jumped slightly. "This is too great!" He turned to his make-up cart, picked up a jar and applicator, and then turned back to her. "Is he?"

Stephie fidgeted as her heart fluttered again. "I think so."

Vicky shook his head with joy. "Could you two be any frigging cuter? I swear! You two are too cute for words! But I have to ask. How have you not jumped him before now?"

She sighed and spoke barely above a whisper, "Believe me, it hasn't been easy. But I wanted our first time to be special and I kind of told him that, like, from the beginning. Besides, we both live at home. It's not easy having a special night when your dad is one room away."

"I guess you're right. But here it is! The big V!" Vicky giggled again. "Sorry, I can't help it." He stared at her, then bent over, made a funny noise, and began laughing. "I never knowingly made someone up for their deflowering!"

Stephie sat up and looked around. "Vicky!"

"I'm sorry. I'm sorry." He stood straight and breathed deep. "So you're giving him his Christmas present early?" An uncontrollable snort finished the question and made them both laugh.

Steph playfully scorned him. "Don't screw up my make-up! No. This is his twenty first birthday present."

"Oh my god Steph! He'll never forget it." Vicky wiped tears from his eyes. "But you won't be able to tell anyone what you gave him for his twenty first birthday…ever!" They both giggled and Vicky wiped the corner of his eye.

"I'm sorry. I'm sorry." He couldn't hold it and another funny noise came out of his nose. "Sorry." He covered his heart with his hand, shut his eyes and took a slow deep breath, then opened his eyes and stared directly into hers. "Girl, you had better call me Friday."

Stephie tried to change the subject. "Want to double date this weekend?"

Vicky reached for a different applicator. "It's Christmas weekend. I have to work through Christmas. But let's hook up sometime next week, just the four of us."

"Are you stopping Christmas day?"

He casually concentrated on his task. "Yeah. Around two, for a little. Then we're heading to his family's house for dinner. I had a good year. I went from no families to two."

Stephie beamed, "And I went from no sisters to one. It's great if you can stop, but it's okay if you can't."

"Okay! You're done!" Vicky stepped back. "Your eyes are gorgeous." He sighed. "You're so beautiful."

Stephie played off the compliment. "Ah, you're in love."

Vicky smiled. "I am. It's true."

Stephie stood and they hugged and kissed like sisters and Stephie whispered in his ear. "I don't know what I would've done without you."

He hugged her a little tighter. "Love you little sister."

"Love you big sister."

"Have fun!"

Stephie's heart jumped again.

She pulled up in front of Jake's house at quarter to twelve, and texted. *U home?*

Her phone beeped four seconds later. *I heard you pull up.*

He came out the side door, walked to the car and kissed her. "You look amazing! Here, let me move it to the drive. Did you buy us snacks?"

She hopped with excitement. "Yep! All I have to do is get my overnight bags."

He turned his head as he sat in the car. "Bags?"

She felt her heart jump as she met his eyes with a playfully guilty grin. "Yes."

His smile spread ear to ear, but he didn't say a word. She followed as he backed the car into her drive. "I'll get your bags, madam."

She sarcastically replied, "Thank you sir!"

He grabbed her ass as he walked past her and she jumped like normal.

He loaded their things in the trunk, then went to the passenger door and opened it for her, and her heart melted. She sat in the already warmed passenger seat and made sure his was on. A moment later, he got in and stared at her. What he saw made him take a noticeable breath.

"You're gorgeous."

She stared into his eyes. "You're in love."

He shook his head up and down as he softly exhaled, "Yeah, I am." smiled and put the car in drive.

He held her hand the entire drive but discreetly eyed her as he turned the car into the hotel parking lot and saw her mouth drop.

"Jake! This is perfect."

She looked at the top of the building, like she had never seen a nine story hotel, and his face lit up with approval. "Welcome to Tall Pines Resort and

Campground. We have streams and lakes and bike paths and foot trails along with campfires and more, for your enjoyment. Oh yeah, and beer…because I can."

"You didn't, did you?"

"Hell no. I'm sober for every minute of the next two days."

She bounced in her seat. "Oh Jacob, we have to hurry."

He stopped the car just past the front doors. "Wait inside with the bags and I'll park."

She frowned. "I don't want to leave you."

"I'll run without the bags. Besides, you're in a dress. It's cold. I promise I'll only be a minute."

Her frown morphed into a smirk. "It's okay if you get a little sweaty running."

He grinned. "You're an idiot. Gorgeous, but an idiot." He dropped their bags and cooler in the lobby and kissed her, "Be right back." then disappeared out the door as she sat on the beige leather bench next to the bags. A gentleman approached her and lightly pointed to them. "May I get them, Miss?"

"Sure. We're just registering though. I'm waiting for my…husband …to park." Her heart jumped when she said it and the feeling delighted her more than she expected.

"I'll put them on the cart and leave them right here for you. I'll take them to your room when you're ready."

She smiled softly. "Thank you."

A moment later, Jake came through the doors, walked up to her and reached for her hand. She leaned close to him and whispered, "Should we say we're married?"

"Sure. Why not?" He smiled as they walked hand in hand to the counter. They registered and the gentleman in the black suit accompanied them to their room. He unloaded their bags. Jake gave him his tip and locked the door behind him, and as soon as the door locked, she jumped him from behind, and shrieked. "Yay!"

His smile grew. "Hey, will you get off me for a second so I can attack you?"

She softly screamed. "Jacob! We're alone! I mean, alone alone!"

Jake leaned his head back, looked up and took a deep breath. Every word she uttered went right to his heart. He couldn't believe how she continually tickled him to his core.

She let him turn and surround her in his arms, as she wrapped hers around his neck, and their mouths met in a long passionate hungry embrace. He removed her coat and his jacket without breaking their kiss, and once again wrapped his arms around her, and his heart felt overwhelming warmth as he caressed her in her delicate outfit. His hands slowly slid over her until they found her silk covered bottom and when his hand found her rear, she let out a soft sigh directly into his mouth.

Their kiss continued, but now he wanted to see what he was feeling. He knew she was beautiful, but he wanted to enjoy the visual pleasure in his arms. He softly broke their kiss and held her hand as he stepped away from her, but she didn't understand and moved instantly into him. "No. Let me look at you." He stepped back and this time she stood there, slightly embarrassed at his request. He softly and slowly eyed her, from her hair to her soft short dress, to her high heels, and then slowly back up again.

"Jacob." Her head tilted as she fought her need to be in his arms.

He inhaled. "You're gorgeous. You are absolutely gorgeous."

She lowered her eyes. "You're embarrassing me."

He stared at her. "You're eye candy. Do you realize how feminine and beautiful you are? Your dress is absolutely stunning! And you're mine? You're here with me? I almost can't believe you would be here with me." He inhaled again, "You're gorgeous."

His words produced a soft red hue on her face. "Jacob, you're embarrassing me. Do you really think I'm pretty?"

He peered into her eyes, enjoying the flush of her skin. "God, Stephanie. Seriously. You're my dream. If I could draw my secret ultimate girlfriend, I would draw you. Everything about you. Your eyes, your lips, your face…your heart." He reached up and gently traced her cheek with the back of his hand. "Every time I look at you I can't believe you're as beautiful as you are. I mean, I know you're pretty, but every time I see you I think, god! She's more beautiful than I thought."

She playfully teased. "You do know you were already going to get lucky, right?"

His heart jumped. "Even you saying that has more of an effect on me than I ever thought possible." He looked down at her body in what he thought was one of the sexiest outfits he ever saw. "I can't tell you how you're making me feel right now. It's amazing."

She walked up to him, slipped her arms around him and moved her head so he would kiss her, and he wrapped his arms gently around her and met her mouth with tender eagerness. Their kiss was slow and gentle; both happily aware they had all the time they could possibly want, to enjoy every moment to its fullest.

He gently picked her up, and with her arms tight around his neck, sat her on his lap on the edge of the bed and immediately, their mouths sealed together again. His hands glided slowly over her delicate dress, from her back to her soft concealed chest, and then he slid his hand under the silky material on the second pass. He finally broke their kiss and moved directly to her neck; his hand still fondling her beneath her soft outfit.

"Jake?"

"Yes?"

"Can I change into what I want to wear for you?"

"Sure." But he made no motion to let her go. He continued uninterrupted, kissing and fondling her.

"Jacob?"

"Yes?"

Her voice hinted playful exasperation. "You're not letting me go."

"Okay."

Then changed to a mild plea. "I want to put something on for you."

He continued to kiss and fondle her. "I'm not stopping you."

Her words were now more breath than voice. "Yes. You are."

"No. You can go." He never paused, kissing and caressing her.

"No, I can't you pain in the…"

He lifted his lips off her neck for a moment. "But I'm having fun. Why do you want me to stop having fun?"

She pulled his mouth into her neck and lifted her head as much as she could. "I don't want you to stop having fun, but can we at least get comfortable?"

"I am comfortable."

She softly sighed as every kiss seemed to melt her a little more. "No. What you are is a pain."

"I hope you brought some stuff for that."

She gently smacked him on the back of his head. "Yes, I took care of it. Will you let me go so I can get changed for you?"

He breathed deep, "Okay." and finally released her.

She walked over to her things and looked back at him playfully. "I think you'll like it."

His heart jumped at her words, and he smiled as he watched her unzip her suitcase and remove two small inner bags and a hangar, then disappear into the bathroom.

He glanced at her other bag. "Did you bring our video games?"

She sung her response from behind the door. "You're an idiot."

He sung his response. "What?" He looked around the room. "I plan on being done in three minutes, taking a nap and then playing video games. What do *you* want to do?" He changed into his navy blue silk pajama bottoms and pulled the covers down.

He heard her muffled voice from behind the bathroom door. "I'll show you in a minute what we're going to do for the next two days." His heart jumped.

Chapter Sixteen
Consecration

On the other side of the bathroom door, Stephanie focused completely. She slipped out of her dress and carefully hung it on the hanger, and gingerly slipped into the white babydoll nightie outfit, bought months ago just for this occasion, and what she saw made her heart suddenly pound with anticipation.

She felt wonderfully feminine, and wanted nothing more at that moment than to be Jake's deepest fantasy. She gathered herself, lifted a thin jar out of the second bag, removed a small hand towel off the chrome shelf next to the sink, breathed deep, hesitated a moment, and opened the door.

Jake jumped slightly when he heard her reenter the room and his mouth dropped when he saw her. He was speechless. He had never seen anything so stunning and his heart filled with expectation.

He immediately stood and she instantly smiled. "Do you like?"

He breathed long and deep. "Steph, you have made me speechless before, but oh…my…god."

He took another deep breath as she snuggled against him and his heart pounded as he wrapped his arms around her. She felt as soft and feminine as she looked, and he kissed her as delicately as she appeared. His lips tenderly touched hers as if she would break with any force whatsoever.

"Oh Jacob, this is what I've dreamed of for the last five months. Thank you for being such a fantastic best friend and allowing me this fantasy."

"Oh Steph, this is *my* fantasy. I love everything about where we are right now. Everything."

She wrapped her arms around him and gently squeezed him. "I love you Jacob." Her mind recalling in a fleeting moment, a love for him that extended as far back as she could remember.

He smiled. "I love you Stephanie." He didn't know why but he yearned to also say *I love you Steven*. He thought for a second about saying the words but decided they might hurt or confuse her, so he just thought it. *I love you Steven*. He held his best friend as tenderly as he could. *I love you Steven*.

"I love your PJ's!"

He smiled. "Good. I'm glad."

She spoke after a moment. "Are we just going to stand here?"

His heart skipped once. "I'm sorry. I've never seen anything as beautiful as you. All of a sudden I'm stuck for what to do next."

She gazed into his eyes and smiled contentedly, "Anything you want."

They both moved to the bed and lay next to each other and when he thought she was comfortable, moved until he was softly lying against her. Their eyes met. Her eyes were glistening and so perfectly feminine. "You're gorgeous. ...you're exquisite." Their connection registered in his soul.

They lovingly explored each other and slowly and tenderly made love, and when they finished, he noticed her eyes were gleaming and he shared his elation. "*That*...was amazing!"

"Oh Jacob! It was *everything* I knew it would be. I love you. I love you so much. We're *lovers*!"

Her words gave him goosebumps and his strange grin. "Yes we are! And *you're* everything I imagined. You are ...uhhh! ...I don't have a word for how phenomenal you are." He caressed the back of her head and pulled her to him, meeting her open mouth with his. As the kiss broke, giddy joy erupted from her voice. "Jacob!"

"What?"

"We just became for real lovers!"

His heart filled as he witnessed her joy. "We were always lovers."

"Yeah! But now we're *lovers*."

"You are too funny. Yes, we're lovers!"

She looked into his eyes, with eyes that mesmerized him. "Do you love me!?"

"Oh sweetheart, yes, I love you. You *know* I love you. I love you more than I've ever loved anyone."

She lowered her chin and stared through his eyes and into his soul. "You know I love *you* that much, don't you?"

"Of course I do." Both their smiles were as wide and genuine as could be.

She turned her head and rested on his shoulder. "Oh Jacob, this is the best present you ever gave me."

His eyes narrowed "What."

"The room. Tonight. The two nights. Waiting. Everything."

"Well thank you for my birthday present."

She looked up. "You're welcome, but that was only part one."

"Oh!" He couldn't control his grin. They both held each other; enjoying the afterglow of their union. After quiet loving small talk, soft caressing, and a short blissful nap, she stirred and he slowly opened his eyes and moved his neck, causing her to wake a little more. He smiled at her. "Hi."

"Hi." She felt the cover on her. "How'd the blanket get here?"

"It wasn't easy, but I grabbed it with my toes while you were sleeping."

"Wow. Nice. We're really in bed now." And snuggled tight against him. He grinned at how she marked every little change in the depth of the event, and tenderly caressed her. They made love a second time and cuddled and enjoyed tender conversation, until he shut his eyes again.

Stephanie opened her eyes first and softly hugged him, squeezing lightly and breathing in his masculine scent. She began exploring him in secret while he slept and carefully slid her hand to his chest and then higher to his shoulder. She couldn't believe how remarkable he felt. She traced down his bicep and her heart beat faster, but differently than its speed when she was about to make love to him. This was solely an emotional exercise. She was feeling an unbelievable emotional connection to him which grew deeper by the moment. Deeper for each euphoric response to every caring caress. She didn't realize this secret rendezvous would cause deeper feelings. She didn't think deeper feelings were possible, expecting this to just be the physical act to their already complete emotional connection. She sighed softly as she realized there were even deeper connections to enjoy.

She laid against him in complete contentment as her fingers lightly traced over his upper body; her mind in a soft bliss as she registered the intimacy they were sharing. *We've been connected since before I can remember. What would it be like if we're together as long as our parents?* The possibility delighted her.

She didn't see Jake wake. She didn't know he was watching her. The tender traces of her hand over his arm had gently brought him from his sleep, in a way that allowed him to let her continue undisturbed. He watched her touch him. He watched her trace his upper body. He wanted to tenderly caress her but restrained and quietly enjoyed her secret attention. He strained to control his breathing as he tried hard not to disturb her, but she glanced up and realized he was awake. "Hi."

He cooed. "Hi. That feels nice."

"What."

"What you're doing."

She rested her chin on his chest. "I thought you were asleep."

"I was."

He scooted down until they were face to face, mouth to mouth, and softly whispered, "Hi, sweetheart."

"Hi! I love when you call me that."

He kissed her tenderly. "How you feeling?"

"Oh Jacob! This is heaven. This is perfect."

He kissed her again, and when he stopped, she kissed him. They traded kisses. Each getting a little longer. Each…a little deeper. She wrapped her arms around his neck and the kiss that followed was as emotionally passionate as their kiss could be.

She softly whispered as it ended. "I can't believe you were the one who took my virginity."

He responded immediately. "You took mine."

And his confession sent a jolt of happiness through her. "Did I?"

"Of course you did. Who do you think I've been with?"

"You nerd!"

His eyes lit up and he grinned ear to ear. "Yeah, like you're not?"

She straightened indignantly in his arms. "Not like you. You turned twenty one, still a virgin." She relaxed. "I, on the other hand, lost my virginity *before* my twenty first birthday."

"Days?"

"So you agree!"

He poked her waist. "I agree you are the most wonderful beautiful sexy *idiot* I know."

She jumped but didn't acknowledge the reaction. "You're just jealous you're a nerd and I'm not!"

"Are you trying to start something?"

He opened his hands on her waist and started tickling her, then grabbed her rear and she jumped again. She tried to control his hands, but it was useless. "You know, you're supposed to let me win these fights now. I'm your girlfriend."

"Oh yeah? Are those the rules?"

"Yes! And you need to start learning them."

Every change in her voice was a conscious heartfelt joy to his heart. "I love you."

"I love you too."

"You're beautiful."

She turned slightly and met his eyes. "So are you."

"God Steph. Seriously. Can you see us doing this in our own place?"

The thought brought a smile to her face. "That's what I want for my birthday."

"What do you want for Christmas?"

"Our own place, so I can attack you whenever I feel like, in the middle of the day or the middle of the night when you're asleep."

"No, seriously. I don't have the slightest idea what to get you, do you want anything?"

"Seriously? I don't want a gift from you. You're all I want."

"Steph, I want to get you something. Something nice."

"I want an unsmelly sofa for our apartment."

"That's not a gift."

"It is a gift because it means you and I have an apartment together. It's a gift because it means you want to live with me. It's a gift because it means we have what I want to have with you; the start of our lives together. You asked me what I want. I want that more than *anything*."

"You have all that, Steph."

She affirmed. "Then I already got what I want."

His eyes pleaded. "Do you want anything else?"

She declared, "Peace on Earth."

He playfully groaned. "You're an idiot."

She jumped on top of him. "Nuh uh."

"Yeah, you are!"

He tenderly kissed and caressed every inch of her neck and chest, then continued his kissing journey back to her loving mouth.

She squirmed and cooed as each new kiss in each new place sent pleasure through her, she never thought possible. When he finally returned to her side, face to face, her eyes narrowed and stared deeply into his. "You love me that much?"

The statement triggered a myriad of thoughts. His first reaction, "Of course I do." His second and almost simultaneous reaction, "You weren't sure?"

She moved tight to him and offered him her mouth, then sighed as the kiss broke. "Oh Jacob." She softly shook her head.

He tried to read her. He wanted to read her, but he had no experience what her soft head shake meant. "What sweetheart?"

"Do you really love me this much?"

She wasn't soliciting an additional response, but he didn't fully understand. His face softly scrunched as he thought for a moment. "I wish I could tell you with words. But there aren't any. I've heard my father say, *nothing shows I love you as much as time*. So I won't be able to show you for years."

She reached her arms around his neck, squeezed him tight and didn't move. She held him so tight, it was uncomfortable, but he softly wrapped his arms around her and gladly let her.

He rubbed her back. "You alright?"

"Oh yeah."

"Is it official? You know I love you and I know you love me?"

"Yeah. But you still may have to tell me regularly. I sometimes don't believe it."

He sighed. "I will."

She pulled the covers up to their necks and snuggled beside him. "Did you ever imagine making love would be this much fun?"

He inhaled and smiled softly. "I knew it would be fun, but this is pretty damn great."

"This is the best thing we ever did." She leaned away and met his eyes. "This is way better than all the holidays of the year wrapped up in one."

"Think so?"

Her eyes glistened. "Yeah! When we get our own place, can we have days where we stay in bed all day?"

"Hell yeah! I say we do this whenever we can."

"Do you think we'll ever get tired of it?"

He kissed her forehead. "Let's do it till we get sick and tired of it, then we'll take a week off and start all over."

She rested her head against him. "Okay."

~~~

Genna picked up her phone and looked at the text message from Morgan. *kids away. Want to go out the 4 of us 2nite?*

Genna responded immediately. *Sure. How about Logan's?*

You're brilliant. 7…7:30?

Sure but let's drive together so we only take 1 car

ok

Genna turned the outside kitchen light on and opened her side door at seven. Connor saw Chris open his side door ten minutes later and grabbed his coat off the kitchen chair. "Sweetheart, they're ready."

She stood up from the sofa, slipped her coat on and grabbed her hand bag. "Right behind you. You want to drive?"

"Chris started Morgan's car."

"Good enough."

Logan's was a typical neighborhood bar; nothing special, but friendly and with good food. It was Chris's first choice for a night out and every once in a while, Genna suggested it for just that reason, though she always had a good time there. Logan's was certainly relaxing; sports always on the TV's and the beer always ice cold. Sometimes the four of them would sit at the bar, when they could get seats around a corner, but they chose a table tonight. They decided on beer and ordered a couple of pitchers to start.

Connor poured everyone a glass and saluted. "To no kids tonight."

Genna smacked him on his hand.

"What? I thought that's why we were out together tonight."

Morgan sipped her drink. "I'm glad the kids decided to go on the school trip. They deserve a reward for all their hard work."

Chris eyed Morgan and grinned. "Remember when we used an excuse like that to go away once?"

Morgan's eyes widened. "We did not."

He tilted his head. "We did too."

She gasped. "Oh my god! We rented that cabin from your partner when you were an apprentice and we went away for the weekend with my girlfriend and her boyfriend. I forgot all about that. That was fun."

Chris turned to Connor. "Her father tried with all his might to keep us from sleeping together and we were in bed three weeks after we met."

She hit him on his forearm. "You're awful!"

"What awful? You were hot and I was easy!" He rubbed his forearm. "Well, I hope they're lying through their teeth and they're alone in a nice room somewhere."

Genna lifted her beer toward Chris. "So do I." They both snickered.

Chris leaned toward Genna. "But we can't ask them till they're like thirty."

Genna's voice burst out. "I know. Sucks."

Connor showed complete confusion and made eye contact with the three of them. "No! They were over our house last night and they told us all about it. There's no way they were lying." He glanced at Chris and then Genna. "Really? You think?"

Connor's cluelessness struck Genna funny and Genna laughing struck Chris funny. "Let's hope."

Morgan lifted her glass, "To our two children!"

Chris eyed her and raised each brow separately, "Hooray!" clinked her glass and drank. His left hand reached for her right as he put his glass down and they held hands for a bit; her approval of his acknowledgement, very noticeable in her smile.

Connor's face changed from somewhat confused to rather pleased as he began considering the idea. "Isn't it awful we can't convince our kids, we're just older kids ourselves? Ah, if only they knew."

"Amen brother! I haven't aged a day since I turned nineteen."

Morgan raised her glass again. "I'll vouch for that!"

Genna looked at Chris and leaned forward, "You know, there's a way we could find out."

"How?" Chris playfully smirked as he lifted his beer.

Morgan eyed Connor. "Is this wrong? We shouldn't be more immature than our kids, should we?"

Connor shrugged. "I don't know. I kinda want to find out they're somewhere alone having a frigging ball together."

Genna turned to him. "You know, lately you've been saying and doing things that are just going to get you lucky, way more often."

Chris leaned sideways toward Morgan and whispered, "Maybe they'd want to borrow our chicken."

"Well, tell me what they are and I'll memorize them."

Chris pointed to Genna. "Hey, no getting off the subject. Tell us how you could find out."

Morgan filled everyone's glass.

Genna hopped in her chair like she was seventeen and leaned toward Chris, but her head swiveled to all three of them, "All I would have to do is go home and look in her closet. It's so wrong. Shame on me." She paused and offered a scheming smile. "I could look to see what she brought with her. If she brought boy stuff, you and I have to give them young-people lessons. But if she took her girl things…" She straightened up. "Why am I so excited to know?"

Chris sat straight. "Because you want your kids to have a happy full life and them making love somewhere beats the shit out of some dopey school camping trip?"

Genna stared at Chris for an elongated moment. "Yeah!"

Morgan glanced at Connor, and then Genna. "Does that mean you're looking when we get home?" Genna lowered her head, then lifted her eyes to meet Morgan's and Morgan responded, "Three Hail Mary's and three Our Father's."

"Yes, Father." They all laughed.

Genna straightened up. "Hey, I've been keeping a secret for roughly a week now and it's driving me crazy." She pointed her finger at the three of them. "Can you all keep a secret?"

Three *sure*'s came immediately back and the three leaned forward.

"I told my mother they couldn't find an apartment near school that they could afford, so she's been searching for them and she found one she likes…and she rented it for two years for them. She's giving it to them for Christmas!"

Chris and Morgan both chimed, "What?"

Connor blurted, "No way!"

Genna leaned forward. "She figured she saved that much on tuition alone with Steph going to community college and all, and she said she hasn't ever given Jake anything special. …So that's what she's decided to give them."

Morgan covered her mouth. "Oh my god. That's crazy. I don't know what to say."

"Say thank you on Christmas." Genna reached for her glass. "Believe me, she loves doing things like this, and it isn't like Jake costs anything more." She lowered her voice to a whisper. "It appears they'll be sharing a room."

"First the car, now an apartment. I'm dumbfounded."

Chris turned to Morgan. "So let's buy them some furniture for Christmas."

Morgan tilted her head as she turned toward Chris. "Are you okay with them picking it out? They have to pick out their own furniture. That's a biggie."

"Sure. We'll just give them a budget. Besides, if they're like us, they'll have it way too long anyway. Do you think they'd get a kick out of me building them their living room tables? I could probably do three for roughly two hundred dollars. Besides, this way we can actually give them something besides a budget."

"If you feel like it. Do you have enough time?"

He thought for a few seconds and sighed. "No." Then he perked up. "Okay, I'll let Stephie pick out the legs and the table edge. She'll get a kick out of it."

Connor caught Chris's attention. "You could build them tables?"

"Do you like the ones in our family room?"

"Yeah."

"I made them. But I was thinking more in line with the one next to the recliner in the kids' video room."

Connor's eyes narrowed. "You made that one too?"

"Yeah." He joked, "Morgan doesn't like store made tables. She only wants custom ones."

She sat straight. "Don't give me that shit. You're the one that can't pick out a table."

He pulled her head to his and kissed her.

Connor breathed deep. "I feel like we just betrothed them."

Genna lowered her beer. "From what I can gather, they've been betrothed for a while, not to worry." She turned back to Chris and Morgan, "And we want to chip in on the furniture. *We're* not giving them the apartment. Or…" She looked at Connor. "we'll buy them a TV."

Morgan turned to Genna. "Did you see the apartment?"

"No. But she told me where it is. It's walking distance to everything at the school. I'm pretty sure it's close to where I spotted them."

"Oh my god, visiting them will be so much fun." Morgan grabbed Chris's arm. "I want to go to a college football game."

Genna placed her hand on Morgan's. "You're too funny."

Chris eyed Connor and pointed a thumb back at Morgan, "*I'm* nineteen."

"Morgan looked at Genna, "Can we stop them from buying furniture they'll regret in a year?"

Genna smiled. "Sure! With tact…"

They didn't leave until well after they initially intended, and three of them were feeling no pain. Connor motioned for the keys from Chris and the way Chris dug in his pocket, assured Connor his request was warranted. The two girls stood arm in arm, whispering, giggling, and waiting for someone to unlock the thing.

Connor watched the women whisper and sway. "What are you two scheming?"

Morgan raised her finger to her lips. "SH!…We're planning the break-in!"

Connor grinned and shook his head.

Morgan turned to Genna. "Wait! We don't have to break in. You *live* there!"

Connor whispered under his breath, "oh my god." He peered into the rear view mirror as they got situated, "Hey, you two have to be careful what you touch, okay? I don't want the kid thinking we're as adolescent as we're about to prove we are."

"Hey!" Genna tried to tap him on the side of his head, but hit the headrest instead.

Fifteen minutes later, Connor nearly pulled into the wrong drive but corrected last second. "Man, are you drunk?"

"No, chooch!"

Morgan looked at Genna. "What's a chooch?"

"Italian for doofus, I think. He got that from my side of the family."

The two girls hurried out of the car as soon as Connor put it in park, and ran across the other drive to the Blair side door.

Chris exited laughing. "You have to admit we have the best times at that place."

Both guys followed the ladies into the house, and Chris headed right for the fridge. "Shall we have one more?"

"Why not. I doubt the ladies are done."

Chris opened it and grabbed two beers and they headed toward the family room.

Three minutes later Morgan came down the hall and turned into the room holding her hand over her mouth as Genna followed behind her. "We're pretty positive they're lying."

Connor was in the middle of a drink and gulped and coughed, "No way! Really?"

Chris pointed to the kitchen. "Go get yourselves a beer."

They both disappeared into the kitchen and came back moments later, laughing. "Yep, we're pretty sure."

Connor raised both hands. "I don't want to know how. Your word is good enough for me."

Morgan and Genna continued whispering and giggling. Chris leaned back, smiled and shook his head lightly. "Too funny! Them lying little bastards."

Genna pointed her finger. "No telling them we know, hear me?"

Chris looked up. "Are you kidding? I'm proud they can at least lie as good as we did when we were their age. But I do love how kids are sure we're dumber than they are, strictly because we've been here twice as long as they have."

"Hey, thank God, or they'd ask too many more questions."

They all nodded at Connor and relaxed as they finished their nightcaps.

~~~

Jake stretched his elbows out wide and ran the backs of his fingers over the sides of his eyes, then raised his arms straight up, rolled toward Stephie and kissed her mouth. She was still asleep, but that wasn't a concern, nor was it stopping him. He slid his arm under the covers and caressed her warm body, then slid his hand down her back until he found her bottom, and promptly gripped a handful.

She took a waking breath and he felt her arm slowly wrap around his neck.

"Good morning!"

He buried his mouth in her neck. "I'm pretty sure it's not morning yet." He ran his hands up the back of her neck and through her hair. "Hey, where's my phone?"

She sung her reply. "I don't know." Then stretched her arms straight on each side of his head. "I may have accidentally shut it off and put it in my purse."

"You may have, eh?"

She sung her response. "I may have…"

He shook his head, pulled her into him and sealed his open mouth on hers. After a long loving kiss, he gave her a peck and asked, "Can I do something I've fantasized about?"

Her entire body reacted to his request. "If it's me, you know you can." Her voice lowered. "You can have me any way you want."

Her eagerness to have him fulfill his fantasy touched his soul. He filled with emotion. "I love you."

She sighed from her well of emotions. "I love you so much."

The room was amazingly dark and they were tranquilly oblivious to the rest of the universe, and it to them, with no idea of the time and completely shut off from any outside distraction. He moved tenderly on her, and her movements seemed to follow his. "Does this feel good sweetheart?"

"Oh Jacob! Yes!"

They each enjoyed their height of passion, and then he collapsed onto her and lay there for an extended minute. He surrounded her as tenderly as he could, as they lay in silence in the darkness, and the sensation of being covered by his muscular masculine presence made her feel blissfully protected and completely loved. She was amazed at how wonderful it felt being under him, with his large shoulders surrounding her. There was no place better than where she was at that moment. He slid to her side, still covering most of her, and pressed his lips to the back of her head. She stayed on her stomach, not wanting to move, feeling his stomach expanding for air; emotionally overflowing from their continually increasing connection. She finally whispered, "Jacob?"

"What, love?"

"I love this."

"So do I."

She could still hear his breathing. "You make me feel very…"

He waited for a moment. "Very what sweetheart?"

"It's hard…" She hesitated, struggling to find the words. "…very much on the outside, like I feel on the inside."

"What do you mean?"

She sighed. "It's weird."

He kissed the back of her head. "No it's not. Nothing's weird. And I want to know." He slid the back of his fingers gently over her back and bottom. "Do you like how I make you feel?"

She moved tighter against him. "It's scary good. You make me feel like it's alright to be who I am. You make me feel like it's completely alright to be different."

He replied with a hint of indignation. "Who's definition?"

"A lot of people's definition."

"You mean the typical seven year old's definition?"

Her reply was playfully admonishing. "They're not seven."

"No. Not physically. You think I meant those who are physically seven?" He repeatedly kissed the back of her head. "No. The physical seven year olds aren't the problem. They seem to know they're seven. I was referring to those who are mentally and emotionally seven and that includes everyone who thinks like a seven year old, all those too lazy to think on their own, and all those who have other people think for them." He softly stroked her hair. "But those who cry like seven year olds are seven. We all hear them. They cry loud and often. But very few cry for any other reason than they're told to cry. They're told what to cry about and they're told how loud to cry. Adults try hard to ignore them, and for the most part, they do. But usually, all that does to an immature seven year old is make them uncomfortable, so they cry louder." He hugged her a little tighter. "Don't be concerned with the cries of seven year olds. Just recognize them for what they are. Cries of seven year olds."

He wrapped his arm a little further around her and pulled her under him. "But tonight, let's forget the children and just enjoy how phenomenal it is to be with each other."

Her breathing had increased and he held her until she finally breathed deep and relaxed. He could read her like he had known her since they were five ... exactly like he's known her since they were five. He knew she was extremely intelligent, but life had left her slightly more psychologically insecure than him.

He pulled her closer still, hoping his words and his caress could somehow transfer some of his surety to her, but her frailties and uncertainties were so beautiful. Her intelligence perfectly contrasted her confusion. Her femininity perfectly contrasted her gender. Her contrasts were part of who she was, and she was more beautiful than anyone he had ever known.

He felt her relax in his arms and listened to her soft breathing, then gently kissed the back of her head. *Thank you Almighty, for such a perfect gift. ...Such a perfect perfect gift.* He kissed her on the back of her head, and shut his eyes.

Light came peeking through the curtain and woke her, but she laid there with her eyes closed. *What a night! What an insanely perfect night!* Pictures of him flashed behind her eyes, like she had taken pictures with her brain. She tried to purposefully record them, hoping she could keep them forever. She didn't want to forget a moment of the joy of yesterday or last night. She covered her head with her pillow and backed up into him. He moved just enough to pull her closer and her breathing quickened immediately. *He feels so good!*

She couldn't relax though. She wanted to be up. She wanted to play. She smiled and backed up tighter to him and started slowly squirming against him. He couldn't see her wide grin, even if he was awake, but she was having fun.

He broke the silence with a low admonishing voice. "You know, that'll get you in trouble…"

His voice tickled her to her soul and she wiggled deeper. "You don't scare me."

He poked her hips and she jumped and let out a play shriek. He then pulled her over and rolled onto her. She met his eyes, smiling. "You're not so tough. I can take you if I wanted. I can kick your ass in video games, and I can kick your--"

"Will you shut up?"

He leaned forward until his open mouth met hers and she breathed in and sighed, wrapped her arms around his neck, and happily obliged. They kissed, cuddled, and caressed, but Stephanie had a plan for the morning. "Let's go take a shower."

He paused for a moment as her statement registered, "Sure." then jumped up and headed to the bathroom.

She went to her video bag, pulled out a jar of peanut butter and a spoon, and followed. She opened the jar, scooped a spoonful, and gave it to him.

"Thanks, I'm starving!"

He gave her the empty spoon and she scooped one for herself and then gave him another.

The shower quickly steamed the small bathroom and he pulled the curtain back. She resealed the peanut butter and they each stepped in, reached for half of the soap and started lathering, kissing and playing until they were both completely excited again.

She looked up at him with one squinted eye as the water ran down her face. "I have a surprise for you."

"What?"

"Not in here. Out there."

His hands slid over her without intention. "Oh, okay."

"I have another outfit for you too."

"You do?" His eyes brightened. "You looked gorgeous yesterday,"

She stopped. "Do you think?"

"Steph! Seriously. I never saw a girl as pretty as you. Your Halloween dress was frigging hot too." He nodded slowly. "I liked the dress you wore when we went dancing too." He smiled at her. "I really like your birthday suit too." He brought her into his arms and reached around her and soaped her bottom. "I really like this here too."

"Well, I want to dress it up before you're allowed to have it again, so just calm down."

He soaped his face and hair. "Want me to go get us breakfast? I'll hurry."

She felt an uneasy pang. "No, you're not leaving."

She shut off the water after they rinsed and he grabbed them each a towel. "Want your surprise?"

"Sure!"

She secured her towel around her. "Follow me!"

"Anywhere."

She opened the bathroom door, went over to the video game bag, pulled out a box and posed.

His eyes lit. "Cereal, my other favorite thing to eat."

She walked to the cooler, dug under the ice water, lifted up a container of milk and raised her eyebrows. "Did I do good?"

He laughed out loud. "You did great! Breakfast!" His stomach grumbled. "You wouldn't happen to have a bowl in there, would you?"

"Of course. You eat. I'm going to go get ready." She went over to the cooler, and pulled out two small containers of orange juice, then went back to the video bag, removed a plastic bag, walked over to him and dropped a vitamin in his hand. "There's bananas in there too. Be right back."

When she came out of the bathroom a while later, he was lying with his head propped up, in only his PJ bottoms, and when he saw her, he kicked the covers off his legs, turned and sat on the edge of the bed. He stared at her with an enormous grin. "Damn! You make my heart beat and I can feel it. You look...delicious!"

What was white yesterday was an amazingly feminine pink today, topped off by a high ponytail, tied with a matching pink ribbon.

He stood, surrounded her in his arms and kissed her softly. And as the kiss lengthened, it grew more and more passionate, and the more passionate the kiss became, the more she melted. She stared at him as he laid her on the bed. He could see her anticipation and her actions registered deep inside him. He wanted nothing more than the intimacy he knew she was feeling and this amazing connection filled his soul with pleasure.

He knelt beside her and studied her as he gently placed his open hand on the nightie. She stared back at him as if she didn't know what to do for him, and her look of complete surrender fed his desire. He moved his gaze down her delicate form, and then back to her eyes and realized she was staring at him, and the intensity of her soft stare let him know she was happily and eagerly waiting to make love to him.

He lovingly confessed. "Do you have any idea what you do to me, dressed like this?"

Her breathing intensified instantly. "What?"

"It makes me want to adore you." He inhaled deeply. "It makes me want to taste and kiss every inch of you, not that I don't anyway." He kissed her lips. "Are you going to wear stuff like this to bed when we have our own apartment?"

"Do you want me to?"

"Yeah!" He thought for a second. "But you can wear nothing too, if you want."

"Okay!"

They spent the rest of the day comfortably tangled together, kissing more than talking, making love and eating cereal and peanut butter. He broke one of their contented moments of silence. "What're you thinking about?"

"The time you called me Stephanie Harrison instead of Stephanie Blair."

He felt a slight twinge and his mouth dropped open. "You acted like you didn't hear me."

"I heard you."

He didn't know if he should apologize or disclaim it, though he didn't want to do either. "Did it upset you?"

"Upset me?" She didn't know how she could even explain the unexpected joy the name brought her. "No. It didn't upset me." All she could think at the moment was how she'd like it to be her name, but was suddenly afraid to reveal that much. "No....Not at all." But the emotion of the last day had her yearning for a commitment that exceeded even her insecurities, so she solicited the answer to a less dangerous question. "Do you think we should look for other apartments when we get a chance?"

"Yeah, definitely." He was never more sure he wanted to find an apartment for the two of them. "We definitely need to find something."

"We do, don't we." She wrapped her leg over his, and hugged him. "We definitely do."

~ ~ ~

The same light that woke her yesterday woke her again. But this time, her heart dropped, realizing the second most idyllic night, and the most perfect two days of her life were coming to an end. She sighed, pulled the pillow over her head, and backed up tight against her love. She tried to fall back asleep, but an uneasy feeling prevented her from achieving the goal; the time. She wanted to believe it was early, but her senses quietly argued, and the more she tried to force herself to believe it, the more her senses told her it wasn't.

The thought of going home and Jacob going into his own house upset her more than she knew it should, but she couldn't help it. She hoped for so long to feel the way she felt these last two days with him, and the notion of being separated from him dominated her thoughts, and those thoughts were distressing. She had very often in her life, been afraid to feel pure happiness but she felt it now and it scared her. She remembered hoping she would be normal some day and how silly a hope that ended up being, though she wasn't complaining at the moment, but because she was who she was, she thought only of him separating from her, like she did when they reached high school. Her heart dropped further as those memories came tumbling back.

She knew the thoughts weren't necessarily reality. She was smarter than that. She knew. She was intelligent enough to know. *Then why am I so afraid?* She started getting mad at herself for being this feminine and then became upset because she wasn't as feminine as she wanted to be. What a bizarre feeling, to always feel stuck between both. She curled up slightly. *How long can I have him, being less than he could get; less than he deserves? He's everything anyone could want, and I'm half of anything anyone would want.* She tried to reason with herself. *If God gave me only these two days, I would have happily agreed and thanked Him.* She inhaled slow and deep. *Wow, what a two days.*

She laid in silence, fighting then reasoning with herself to the best of her ability, waiting for Jacob to wake. Finally, he pulled her into him. "Good morning."

"Morning." Her heart overrode her anxiety and bliss temporarily overrode despair. She breathed deep and snuggled into him.

He kissed the back of her head as his words mixed with sounds of having just woken. "How are you?"

She covered any residual anxiety. "Good. You?"

"I feel great. I feel better than I ever did. This was a great vacation. Do I look a little pale though?" His voice increased. "I feel...*drained.*"

Her inner argument faded and her mood rose with his declaration, as he squeezed her to him.

"Have you been awake?"

She spun to face him and he wrapped her in his arms. She inhaled then sighed. "For a little bit."

His mood turned completely playful. "Why didn't you wake me? We have to fool around." He climbed on top of her. "Don't you agree?" He didn't give her a chance to answer. His mouth was on her as soon as the words left him, and once again, his masculinity overwhelmed her until she went blissfully limp.

As they made love, she strained to register every taste, smell and feel like they would be her last, and she kissed him like she was never going to be in his arms again. Who could say she was wrong? All the last two days did was create a yearning for him, beyond her wildest understanding, and she made love to him like it would be the last time they ever made love.

He struggled to catch his breath. "Wow! We have got to get our own apartment." He rolled over on his back with his arms extended out to his sides, touching the headboard above him; his chest expanding to its limit with every breath. "You might kill me, but I'm going to have to take that chance."

His words were soothing, but her thoughts were influenced by years of inner confusion. She knew she had a new fight to deal with inside her and she was all too sure the winner wouldn't be decided by anything but time. She buried her face in his chest and wrapped her arms around him, trying to memorize everything about him. She tilted her head and pressed her nose to his chest, trying desperately to memorize his scent.

He quietly noted her actions and they were telling him she loved him completely and that message reflected in his wide contented smile. They had sealed their relationship these last two days; of that he was sure. He bent his neck to its limits and kissed the top of her head. "Ready for a shower?"

She squeezed him tighter. He waited for her to release him, and when she didn't, he poked her sides. "Come on! Let's take a shower."

He pried himself away from her and went into the bathroom. She heard the shower spit its first thrusts of water and sighed. *I might kill him...he will kill me.*

His muffled voice blended with the noise from the water. "Sweetheart, come on."

They soaped, washed and caressed each other for an extended warm shower, each stealing kisses continuously, and she quietly sighed constantly. So far, the start of today was nothing more than a fuzzy illusion

He discreetly watched her dry herself; trying hard to control his grin. Her obvious disappointment their vacation was ending, secretly tickled him to his core. She was miserable, which meant she had a great time, and the only other message he registered from her misery was; they were going to do this well into the future. But it was time to snap her out of her funk. He grabbed her as she straightened her bra and plopped backward onto the bed with her on top of him. She sighed and collapsed in his arms.

"Are you alright?"

Her voice finally mirrored her dejection. "I can't believe we have to leave soon."

Her disappointment increased his fervor. "I know. But didn't you have fun?"

Her reply sounded more like a plea. "Jake! It was the most incredible thing…
ever! I don't want it to end. I don't want to go home." She looked into his eyes,
with soft mesmerizing eyes. "Can't we barricade the door and stay here until they
smoke us out or something?"

Her words tickled him. "You want our mothers to see us on the five o'clock
news?" He started laughing. "Your grandmother would have a heart attack if she
saw our faces splattered all over the TV." He thought for a second. "I do think the
idea of us on TV because we've been fumed out of a hotel room is pretty damn
funny though."

She now sounded resigned. "Oh Jacob." Her mouth twisted and the air in
her lungs escaped.

The long deep kiss that followed offered him a tremendously exhilarating
contentment, but for her, only a yearning for this connection well into the distant
future.

His enthusiasm filled his voice. "Come on! Let's go start the rest of our lives."
Each of his declarations gave her sparks of expectation but none were quenching
the depth of love she now felt. He had given her countless commitments over the
last two days, but no matter how many there were, she was amazed at how much
she needed the next one.

Leaving the room seemed surreal. She was sure they just arrived and they
already had to leave? Were the last two days all imagined? The elevator, the lobby,
the cold air; she wanted no part of any of it. All these things were getting in the
way of a spectacular two day dream she didn't want to end. She came out of her
daze and eyed Jake as he turned the car out of the parking lot. "I know we just
spent two and a half days together, but is it okay if we spend the rest of the day
together?"

He smiled. "I was going to ask you that."

She turned her whole body toward him. "You were not."

He glanced at her. "Yeah. I was."

She breathed in deep and her eyes turned glassy. "That's the best thing you
said to me these last two days."

He shook his head and sighed. "What? Did you think I was tired of you or
something?"

She semi-sung her response. "I don't know."

He reached for her hand. "You're an idiot. Your house or mine?"

"Mine?"

"Okay."

She slid her other hand on top of his, and held his with both hands.

~ ~ ~

Genna noticed Stephanie's car parked in front of the house as she pulled into the driveway, and walked into the house, hoping to find her home from her short excursion. Seeing her and Jake cuddled on the loveseat, as she walked into the family room, was an added surprise.

"Hi."

Steph rose from Jake's embrace, "Hi Mom."

"Hi sweetheart." They hugged tight as Jake stood to greet her. Genna looked up as she hugged Stephie. "Hi other sweetheart."

"Hi Mom B."

"How was your trip?"

"It was fantastic, Mom. We had a great time."

Genna subtly eyed Jake. He couldn't hide his telltale grin and it delighted her. "Did you have a good time too?"

"The best, Mom B. It was better than we both thought it would be."

She gave him a hug and kiss hello. "That's terrific. I'm glad you both enjoyed it. Are you eating dinner here tonight?"

He raised an eyebrow. "Sure."

Dinner was serene. The four of them sat and quietly enjoyed each other's company with light and loving conversation. Genna watched her two children as discreetly and intently as possible, and tactfully watched as Jake helped clear the table and stack everything next to Stephie at the sink after dinner. "Go relax, both of you. I got the rest of this. Go sit in the family room. I'll be in in a minute."

They washed their hands together and disappeared toward the family room. Genna walked in a few minutes later, sat in her corner of the sofa and picked up her book from the end table. Connor was already sitting in his corner of the sofa, half watching a comedy rerun and her two children had resumed their cuddle position on the loveseat, noticeably in their own private world.

She wanted to talk to them and enjoy the obvious love they were sharing, but since she knew their secret, figured leaving the subject alone might be the best gift she could give them tonight. She quietly smiled and tried to concentrate on her book. She read the same paragraph four times and still had no idea what it said.

Stephie leaned toward Jake and whispered something inaudible to Genna then turned to her mother. "We're going to go play a video game, okay?"

Genna looked up from her book, "Of course. Have fun."

They stood and wandered toward Stephie's bedroom, hand in hand.

Genna waited until they shut the door before turning to Connor. "Any doubt in your mind?"

His face lit up. "None now. How cute is that though. Remember when we sat so close you would have had to pry us apart with a crowbar?"

She looked at him with raised eyebrows and a playful grin. "Want to go play a video game in our bedroom?"

He let out a soft laugh. "Yeah!"

CHAPTER SEVENTEEN
ACCLIMATION

Chris continually watched the bar door and when Jake finally opened it, he smiled and gave his typical low greet, "Jacob." and pulled out the bar stool next to him.

Jake allowed his eyes a moment to adjust to the change in light, and spotted his father. "Hey, Dad."

"Son." He caught the barmaid's attention as she walked past. "Alicia, lite beer for the boy and another for me when you get a chance."

"No problem Chris." She glanced at Jake as she walked away. "I'll need to see ID."

Jake placed his wallet on the bar and sat next to his father, as he scanned the room. Chris watched him with a satisfied smile, then put his hand on Jake's back. "I've been waiting for this for twenty-one years, my friend."

Jake glanced at him, curiously confused.

Chris patted his back. "I know it sounds strange, but I always looked forward to sitting at a bar and having a beer with you." He smiled. "So shoot me."

Jake leaned a little toward his father. "I'm still getting used to even being in here and ordering a beer. Am I like a grown-up now?"

"Yeah, but don't tell anybody." Chris lightheartedly glimpsed at him. "They'll start expecting shit from you."

Jake smiled and tried to relax. They sat for a while casually talking, sipping their beer, and watching a game with no sound. Jake scanned the room again. He had never had this view of Logan's before. "This is pretty cool."

"I think so." His father smiled. "Do you like cinnamon?"

"Yeah."

"Did you drive here?"

"No, Steph dropped me off. She said she'd pick us up too if we need it."

"Oh, she's a keeper. But I got my truck."

"I'll come get it for you tomorrow."

"You're a keeper." Chris put his arm behind Jake and squeezed his neck.

Jake eyed his father. "So, what do you want to talk about?"

Chris glanced at him, making a casual face. "Nothing special. I just wanted to have a beer with you."

Alicia stopped in front of them but kept her eyes on Jake. "You two need anything?"

Chris smiled as he noticed her full attention on his son and answered for both of them. "Yeah, two shots of cinnamon."

"No problem."

Alicia came back with the bottle and two glasses and poured them each a shot. "So how do you two know each other?"

"He's my son. Jake, Alicia. Alicia, Jake."

"Hi!" She eyed him up and down. "Cute."

Jake turned slightly red. "Thanks." He didn't know how to respond. "You too."

She walked away smiling.

Chris sipped his beer. "You know, now every time I come in here she's going to ask where you are."

"She will not."

Chris shook his head. "Ah, to be young…" He lifted his shot and sipped it. "So how's Steph?"

"She's good."

"Anything new?"

Jake thought about the school trip. "We're done another semester."

"How'd you do?"

"Good. Finals were tough though. I hate taking tests. But I really hate finals."

"I don't blame you. I wasn't a big school fan."

Jake looked around from his new vantage point. "I always liked this place."

"I should call your mother and tell her to stop by."

"Where is she?"

"Out shopping."

Jake turned his head toward his father. "Can I ask you a question?"

Chris turned slightly and rested his hand on the back of Jake's chair. "Sure."

"Is mom alright with me and Steph?"

Chris thought for a second. "Well, there's two ways to answer that question, so I think I'll answer two ways. One, you should never give a damn who thinks what…even your mother. But I appreciate where you're coming from. Life's a lot easier if she's on-board. And two," he took another drink. "I think she finally is. She knew what her confusion was. It was literally the bullshit she was raised with, and she realizes it. She just needed to file the bullshit away. And I think she finally has. She may not have it all away yet, but I think she's finally good with it."

Jake's voice begged for confirmation. "Are you sure?"

He nodded his head. "Yeah. She said some things a few days ago that make me sure. It's funny. Everything she sees says it's okay and everything she's been taught, from the time she can remember, says it's not. Meanwhile a fair percentage of those harping against it are doing all the things they're telling everyone else not to do…and more. I can separate those things easily. But it's not that easy for everyone. But yeah, I'd say she's alright…and she'll get better." He eyed Jake and smirked. "What can I say? Some people swallow more bullshit than others."

"Did she tell you me and her talked?"

Chris turned and reached for his beer. "No. When?"

"One night when you were finishing your last job."

"How'd it go?"

"I pretty much told her the same thing."

"Jacob, my boy…" Chris held up his beer and grinned sarcastically. "Shit plus two equals eight." Jake smiled and they drank together."

Chris continued before his glass reached the bar. "But I have to tell you son, she is a sweetheart."

Jake responded immediately. "So is Stephie."

Chris looked up at the TV as he rotated his glass on its coaster. "I meant Stephie."

Jake quietly smiled.

~ ~ ~

The sun was out and it was a beautiful day, but Stephie couldn't see it. She couldn't shake the uneasiness she had since she woke and the feeling was muddling her view of everything else. She turned onto the street which led to her house but quickly made the next left instead of going home. She needed to take a drive and be alone to try to figure out why she felt so uneasy. Then she remembered. She was afraid to be completely happy. She had never been completely happy in her life and the feeling scared her.

She had never had a dream come true and though these last few months and days were that dream, she was afraid to think they could last. Were people like her allowed to be completely happy? So many people spoke against her happiness without ever meeting her. So many said she was an offense to even a God they swore loved everyone. Whole countries and whole religions condemned her, without even knowing her name. It almost felt like she would be doing something wrong if she thought she was allowed to be happy, and the confusion made her feel like her heart would explode.

She tried to reason with herself. She was a good person. She never harmed anyone. She never even spoke badly about anyone. After all, she knew how far from perfect she was. Was she allowed to be happy? Would a God, who she faithfully prayed to, really make her the way she is so He could condemn her forever? Would any being, no matter how great or small, create something just so He could hate it? Was she allowed to be happy or should she wait to be crushed for no greater crime than being exactly who she was?

She picked up the phone, with her heart about to break and her eyes welling, and dialed the only person she knew, who could possibly offer an answer.

"Sister."

Her smile forced a tear out of her right eye, and the lump in her throat made it difficult for her to reply. She forced one. "Hi."

Vicky read her greeting. "Are you alright?"

The words made the tears flow. She didn't know what to say. "Hi."

"Hi hon. What's wrong?" She could hear Vicky's concern raise in his voice. "Are you alright?"

"No. No, I'm not. And I don't know why." She swallowed past the lump in her throat. "…And I need to talk to the only person who could possibly understand what I'm feeling."

"I'm here for you. What's wrong?

"Have you ever been happy?"

Vicky's voice softened. "I don't understand."

"Have you ever been completely happy?"

"Was there a problem with your vacation? Did Jake break up with you?"

Stephie quickly replied, "No. No. Not at all."

Vicky hesitated. "I don't understand."

She breathed deep. "Are people like us allowed to be happy?"

His voice turned solemn. "I don't know what to tell you. It's tough being abused for half your life and think about being completely happy." He paused. "I don't mean just physically abused, but it's all abuse. It's on the radio and in the world news every day. It's the kind of abuse where they swear they don't mean anyone specific, but they specify. It's tough being told you aren't equal in a country where the single most important idea is everyone's equality. It's tough hearing how you're a freak…and feel normal and have hope. It wears on you on a good day and makes you stay in bed on a bad one. Most of us hide who we are during the day because we're afraid of the abuse. Most of us are too busy worrying about surviving to think about being happy. But you and Jake give me hope. You make me feel like it's okay to dream, even for who I am. Has Jake hurt you? Has anyone said anything to you that hurt you?"

"Vicky, I just had the most prefect two days I could ever imagine and believe it or not, I'm afraid to be too happy. I've never felt what it's like to be completely happy, and I'm wondering if I'm allowed to dream and hope, or if I'm just really condemned for being who I am. And for some reason I'm scared a person like me isn't allowed to have dreams like a normal person, so I need to ask you…are we allowed to be happy?"

She heard him take a breath into the phone. "I don't know what to tell you. Secretly, *you* are my hope. Secretly, you're who made me think it's okay to go for complete happiness. You asking me that question makes me less sure. I mean, I could tell you you're allowed, but I'm one voice in an ocean of voices, and I've tasted enough hurt to say I'm not positive we're allowed. My own family shuns me. My own father disowned me. They made me. They didn't like what they made, so they threw me away. So I don't know what to tell you. I know *I* love you. I know *I* would allow you to have dreams and hopes and happiness, and I wish those things for you, but I... After that, I'm as lost as you." He paused for a moment. "But can I offer a thought that's helped me? I think maybe it'll help you."

Steph wiped her eyes and begged. "Please!"

Vicky inhaled. "Don't let what may happen tomorrow, ruin today or even yesterday if the day was good. It's scary to hope and dream. You may get your heart broken. Life might throw you a screwball that may hit you on the side of your pretty head. But I think it's okay to tell you, you can hope. Besides, hopeless isn't better." He went silent for a moment, then changed his voice. "...So, how was your trip?"

"Oh Vick, it was incredible! It was amazing. It was better than anything I could have ever dreamed." She smiled at a quick reminiscence. "And you are wonderful for teaching me what I needed to know."

Vicky asked lightly, "Everything was okay?"

"Oh Vick! I can't believe how much fun we had and how good it felt."

Vicky laughed into the phone. "Tell me about it. And I still think it's the best birthday present anyone ever gave anyone. Did he like it?"

"Eight times."

"AH!" Vicky laughed out loud. "Then what are you worried about?"

She answered meekly, "How big an idiot I am."

His excitement increased. "Well, get in line behind me!"

"How's Jonathan?"

"Great! Terrific! He treats me like a queen. No pun intended."

Stephie started laughing.

"Are you laughing at me girl?"

"I love you."

"I love you too honey. Better now?"

She inhaled. "Yes."

"Go tell your man you love him."

"He's having a beer with his father."

"Lucky him."

~ ~ ~

Stephanie lifted the last wine glass from the dishwasher and set it on the Christmas placemat on the counter. "We should invite Nana to come over tonight, instead of tomorrow. This way she can be here in the morning."

Genna glanced at her as she dried a holiday platter. "Would you go pick her up if she said yes?"

"Of course."

"Give her a call. See what she says." Genna held up a wine glass and examined for spots. "But tell her tonight is next door."

She took her phone out and dialed. "Nana?"

"Hi cipolline! How are you?"

"Good, Nana. You?"

"Great. What are you doing?"

"Setting up for Christmas with Mom."

"What can I do for you?"

"I was wondering…we were wondering if you felt like coming over for Christmas Eve at Chris and Morgan's, instead of coming over tomorrow. I'll come get you."

"Cipolline. That's sweet but you young people have fun. I'm staying overnight tomorrow. That's good enough for me. I can't party like I used to. I'll see you tomorrow around noon though."

"Ok, but if you change your mind, call me."

"I will."

"Love you Nan."

"Love you too."

She hung up the phone. "It's just the six of us. She'll be over tomorrow at noon though."

Genna removed the china from the dishwasher and piled it on the counter. "Okay. I'm glad you asked though. I like the way you try to include her. You're a good kid."

Steph appreciated the acknowledgement, but she really did like Nana's company. Her stories about the things her and Pop did were untoppable as far as she was concerned.

They carried everything into the dining room and started setting the table. "So when are we heading next door?"

Genna placed the utensils next to the dishes, and reached for the napkins. "Morgan told me around six thirty."

Stephie paused and looked at her mother. "Do you mind if I go over earlier?"

"Of course not. It's your second home. I understand." Genna glanced up from folding a napkin. "So how are you and Jake getting along?"

"Fantastic. Our relationship is better than ever. I mean, it was always great, and now…it's better than great."

Genna softly widened her eyes and breathed deep. "You're happy?"

"Happiest I've ever been."

"That's my Christmas present."

Stephie looked at her.

"Nothing makes me happier than you happy. Nothing."

They finished setting the table together, then Stephie went into the family room and sent Morgan a text. *I can come over and help you set up if u want.*

Her phone beeped with Morgan's reply. *Come on over!*

"Mom. Mom H needs my help. Are we good here?"

"Yeah sweetheart. Go help her."

Steph skipped across the drives and into the Harrison kitchen door and shivered. The outfit she had on was cozy inside but the cold wind went right through it.

"Hi!"

"Hi! Cold outside?"

"Freezing," She scanned the room. "Whatcha need me to do?"

"I was just washing these glasses and plates."

"I'll dry."

Morgan smiled as they worked next to each other. "This is the first time we did something, girl to girl."

Stephie nodded. "I know."

Morgan turned to her as she picked up a plate to dry and kissed her on the side of her forehead. No words were exchanged, but Stephie felt like Morgan just said more to her than she ever said.

Morgan broke the next momentary silence. "What time is Jake done work?"

Stephie smiled. "He told me he'd be home between four thirty and five. I hope they don't ask him to stay. Is Mr. H. home?"

"He should be outside stacking wood for tonight. I told him to take care of the fireplace."

They spent the afternoon cooking and laughing together, talking about life and school. When Jake opened the kitchen door, they both greeted him with a big "hi!"

"Hi! What're you two doing?"

Stephie walked up to him. "Preparing for the party."

"Really!" He kissed her.

"Yeah! We're having fun. It's the first time we ever did anything alone together."

Jake grinned ear to ear. "That's great."

Stephie hopped slightly. "Hurry up. Go take a shower so we can start the night."

Twenty minutes later, Jake walked back into the kitchen and sat at the table facing the counter. Morgan turned to him with a big basket of chips in her hand. "We're almost done." She handed the basket to Stephie. "Thanks for all your help. Go relax. I got the rest."

"Are you sure?"

Morgan smiled at her and nodded. "Yeah."

"I had fun."

Morgan met her eyes. "So did I."

They walked into the family room and Chris lit up when he saw her. "Hi sweetheart!"

"Hi Dad H!"

Chris finished setting up the fireplace and lit the fire, and in minutes, it added a beautiful yellow light to the room. The only other lights lit were Christmas decorations. There were snack bowls and dishes on every table and a beautiful buffet on the folding table.

Jake sat on the floor against the arm of the loveseat, facing the fire and Stephie waited for him to get situated, then sat in front of him with her back to his chest, and when she was comfortable, he wrapped his arms around her. That corner of the floor had become their new place when the six of them were together. Connor and Genna finally showed up and before long, everyone was eating, drinking and laughing, with the crackling fire serving as a cozy backdrop for the occasion.

"Jacob and I had an idea. Can we open our presents together? We were thinking at our house tomorrow for this Christmas and next year when we switch houses for the two days, we'll open all our presents over here?"

Jake chimed. "We'll take everything over tomorrow morning for you."

"It'll be our job to transfer the presents each year." She leaned back against Jake and felt his arms surround her.

Chris gave Morgan a small nod for his half of the consent. Morgan received the acknowledgement and turned to the kids, "Sure, if it's okay with Genna and Connor."

Steph's voice increased. "Every other year, each house?"

Genna glanced at Connor and hesitated, and he offered silent approval with a soft smile. "Sure. Why not."

Chris and Jake ended up in the kitchen together during the evening and he whispered to Jake. "When did she start calling you Jacob?"

He didn't realize his question was loaded until he saw the answer on Jake's face. "Not too long ago, but I don't mind. She can call me anything she wants."

Chris understood, and quickly joked. "Yeah. Beats the shit out of *asshole.*"

Jake snickered. "Mom does like calling you that every once in a while."

Chris glanced at him with a smirk, "Yeah, you'll hear it soon enough."

He opened the fridge and grabbed the ice tea pitcher. "I'm sure I will."

Jake walked back into the family room and stopped at the food table. He picked at the chips and turned to his mom, "Are we opening any gifts tonight?"

Morgan glanced at Genna and they both froze. She eyed Connor and then looked back at Jake. "Nope."

Jake squinted back at her, semi-stunned. "Even a small one?"

"There are no small ones this year."

"No?"

Connor replied for her. "No."

Jake stared at Stephie and she met his eyes. "How come it looks like they're all in on this?"

Chris answered Stephie with a deep slow voice. "Because we are."

She laughed. "I love when you guys do things together."

"Then you'll enjoy tomorrow."

Jake sat on the floor and Stephie moved back against his chest and stole an olive off his plate.

"Sweetheart, did you ever call and make reservations for your birthday?"

"Yeah, Mom." She turned to Morgan and Chris. "You're coming to my birthday dinner, right?"

Morgan put down her glass. "I haven't missed one of your birthdays since I've known you. I'm not missing this one. What are we doing?"

Chris butted in, "Logan's?"

"No, not Logan's!" She shook her head and rolled her eyes at Chris. "Sakana!"

His voice and his smile playfully teased, "Raw fish?"

"Yes!"

"Them not cooking the stuff and still charging you that much? ...It's a disgrace! I'd make them cook it if I were you."

Morgan and Genna replied in unison... "Idiot!" and all three ladies laughed.

Chris held out his arms. "What? They're bringing your dinner to you and they forgot a step. I'm telling them to take mine back to the kitchen and cook it a little longer."

Stephie studied him. "You do realize, half of sushi is cooked, right?"

He tilted his head and looked at her and she lit up. "I'll go eat your damn raw fish with you."

"Thank you! They have other food too, you know."

Jake whispered in her ear. "He loves sushi."

She playfully scowled at Chris and his soft smile confirmed their special relationship. "Don't tell her that. Sometimes you have to pretend you don't like something, so they think you're only doing it because you love them!" He turned to her again. "Who's going?"

"Us seven and Vicky and Jonathan."

"Perfect. When?"

"On my birthday, so I can have a beer and sake. I'm the last one to reach drinking age."

Chris narrowed his eyes and the least little smirk appeared. "Want a beer?"

She thought for a moment. "Sure."

~ ~ ~

Stephie and Jake spent Christmas morning together between both houses, stealing alone-time where they could, helping where they could, and making plans to continue their search for an apartment. Genna finished setting up the buffet and joined them in the family room but they weren't waiting long before they heard the kitchen door open, and Morgan's voice. "Hello?"

"Merry Christmas. Come on in."

Chris led Morgan toward the family room, but his head turned as he passed the buffet set-up in the dining room and rubbed his belly. He pointed over his shoulder as he approached Genna. "Is that food for anyone?" Then he hugged her around her waist. "Merry Christmas, mother of my two children."

Genna eyed Morgan behind him. "He really is an idiot."

"And he's all mine. You can't have him." They both laughed.

Stephie stood and led Jake toward the dining room commotion and waited her turn to hug Morgan. "That really is the family term of endearment, isn't it? Jake and I say it."

"I guess we've taught you well."

They eagerly attacked Genna's breakfast buffet, and after they ate, Genna placed her plate on the coffee table and took charge. "Okay, let's open presents. Oldest first." She looked at her mother. "Go ahead Mom."

Lorraine lifted a card from the Christmas bag she had next to her chair and held it out toward Stephanie. She eyed the two of them. "This is for both of you."

Steph moved to an angle Jake could see and opened the envelope. She unfolded the piece of paper and read the word *Lease* at the top, but she didn't fully understand. Jake squinted, "Is this a lease for an apartment?"

Stephie glanced at Jake then turned toward Lorraine. "Nana, is this a lease for an apartment?"

"Yes, it is. I heard you two couldn't find one near school, so I searched a little and found a cute one right on the other side of Main Street. It's a two year lease, starting January first."

"I don't understand." She turned to her mother. "They're really expensive."

Genna replied in a soft voice. "Sweetheart, it's paid for. She paid the rent for you for two years."

Stephie instantly started crying. She covered her face with her hands and cried, and the three other women started crying.

Jake stood to hug Lorraine and say thank you, but everyone was focused on Stephie. Lorraine spoke, "Is that alright?"

Stephie went over to her grandmother and wrapped her arms around her. "It's unbelievable. But you do too much for me. You don't have to."

"But that's why I do it. Because I know in your heart you don't think I have to. If you demanded things, you'd never get them. You get gifts because you love me without them, and that's why it's so enjoyable to give you things."

She reached for another envelope from her bag and handed it to Stephie. Stephie gazed at her in amazement, opened it and found pictures of the apartment. She sat next to Jake so he could see; the second floor of a townhouse, down a quaint side street in the town. The front looked pristine.

She looked at Lorraine. "Oh Nana, this is unbelievable. When can we see it?"

Lorraine quietly enjoyed her grandchild's joy. "Not until the third. I'll give you the details where you pick up the keys and everything, later."

Jake finally hugged and thanked Lorraine, but Stephie could tell he was still confused, and Chris echoed her thought before she could speak. "I don't think Jake understands either. Jake, your rent is paid for, for the next two years. You can live on campus without dorm debts."

"Yeah, but I can't live there for free."

Lorraine's joy showed on her face and her voice reflected loving authority. "Yes you can, and you will. This is for both of you, equally. This is my gift to both of you."

Morgan hugged Lorraine. "What a wonderful and generous gift. Thank you from the bottom of my heart."

Lorraine touched Morgan's cheek and smiled. "It's my pleasure."

Genna wiped the last bit of moisture from her eyes and looked at Morgan. "You go next."

Morgan handed them a card and Stephie passed it to Jake. He opened it, read the card out loud, removed the credit card from inside and held it up. "Thanks! Gas card?"

"Nope. Furniture debit card. You two have to buy something to sit on."

Stephie immediately hugged and kissed Morgan as Jake asked, "Can we buy a decent sofa?"

Chris answered, "Relax. We're not done. This is my personal gift to the two of you."

Chris handed Stephie a card and she read it out loud. "One trip to the local lumber store for table legs and table tops--enough to build two end tables and a coffee table. Your choice of color too."

She jumped with joy! "Are you going to make me tables?"

"Yeah." He started chuckling. "But you have to pick out the legs and the top and show me what edge you want. Both of you have to come with me, okay?"

"Oh my god. I'll keep them forever!" She hugged him the longest and tightest.

He held her and whispered in her ear, "I love you."

"I love you too."

Genna glanced at Connor. "Okay. Dad B."

The kids looked at him.

"I was going to give you a gift card for a TV, but after seeing that hug, I think I'm going to try to build you one first."

"No Dad, please don't."

They all laughed.

"Hey! Alright. Here."

He handed them their last card and she opened it and held it up, then stood and hugged and kissed him on the lips. "I love you Dad."

"I love you too, sweetheart."

They all hugged and kissed and Jake spoke, "I can't tell you how great I think everything is. This is overwhelming. I can't believe it. Thank you so much." He went around and hugged everyone again. He hugged Lorraine tight. "Your gift is overwhelming. Thank you." He kissed her.

She reached up and stroked his cheek. "You're a good boy."

Genna took control again. "So, what'd you get us?"

Stephie held out her arms. "Almost nothing compared to what you got us."

Morgan sipped her coffee. "Oh relax. It's not a competition."

Stephie handed all three ladies, what looked like identical packages. "You have to open them together. They're all the same."

All three opened their gift and held up an eight by ten framed picture of the two of them, standing arm in arm. Stephie in a cute gray sweater dress and Jake in a nice blue button down shirt and black pants.

"Do you like it? It's the first official picture of Jacob and Stephanie."

"Good job! This is a great present."

"Well done!"

"And we made you each a smaller one for your work or wherever. We framed them ourselves."

When everyone had opened their last picture, Morgan eyed Jake. "What did you get each other?"

Stephie answered, "Nothing." She looked at all four parents, who were each staring back at her. "We decided we needed our money for more important things, like a sofa and a frying pan. And I would have hit him over the head with any frying pan he bought me for a present."

Chris started laughing. "I like her."

"I wanted to buy her something." Jake raised his voice apologetically. "She asked for an unsmelly sofa."

Morgan lit up and nodded. "That's how Chris and I started out. My Aunt Rose bought me a thirty five dollar plastic sofa at an auction, because we were sitting on folding chairs in our first apartment. Do you remember?"

"Yeah." Chris shook his head and smiled. "How come the toughest times become the best memories?"

Stephie spent the rest of the day helping Genna, taking care of Lorraine, whispering into Jake's ear about the apartment and trying to finally accept the idea she just may be allowed to have the same hopes and dreams as everyone else.

~ ~ ~

The day after Christmas was a lazy day prearranged for recovery and relaxing. It was cold but calm out and another natural masterpiece was being painted. Morgan knocked on Jake's bedroom door on her way back from the bathroom. "It's snowing out."

The bedroom door opened almost immediately and Jake stepped into the hallway. "Really?"

Stephie rushed between Jake's arm and the door jam and then past Morgan, heading for the family room sliding glass door.

"Been snowing for hours."

Jake turned and headed to his mother's room. He couldn't see Stephie and she couldn't see him, but they were both staring at the pristine white crystals covering the back yard like a pillowy blanket. Steph rushed past Morgan again in the family room, and headed toward Jake's room. Morgan watched her hurry by and softly shook her head. *You'd think they never saw it before.*

Steph turned the hallway corner as Jake reappeared and she jumped up and down. "Snow football!"

He smiled. "That's what I was thinking."

"Oh! It's been so long since I kicked you're A in snow football."

He snickered. "When did you *ever* kick my A in snow football?"

She ran into his room and grabbed her shoes. "Always."

"You're delusional." She was giddy and it delighted him.

"And in about an hour."

He pointed at her. "Out back in fifteen."

She slipped on her shoes and ran past him, "I'm so going to put a hurtin' on you." grabbed her coat and headed out the kitchen door.

He turned back into his room and pulled his work boots out of the back corner of his closet, with a smile as wide as could be.

Morgan returned to her seat in the family room. "Your kids are going to play football in the snow out back."

"I heard." He scanned the yard through the sliding glass door, from his seat. "Kids are great."

Stephie burst into her kitchen. "Mom! Dad! …It's snowing!" She ran to her room and heard the "Hi!" follow her from the family room. "…We know! It's been snowing!"

"Jake and I are going to go ruin his back yard."

"Have fun!"

It had been a long time since they played this game and it brought back memories as fast as she dressed, and when she was done, she looked like she gained ten pounds. She could barely move. She walked out her side door and through the back yard gate behind Morgan's car, and saw Jake standing there tossing a foam football into the falling white flakes and immediately ran toward him. He waited until she was almost in arms reach before dodging left. Her right hand reached out for him as she passed him and then she turned and chased him into the middle of the yard. He was now twenty feet from her and as she walked toward him, he tossed her the ball. "So, what are the rules?"

She tossed it back to him, "Whenever I have the ball…" and then caught his soft throw. "I automatically get seven points," She tossed another wobbly pass back. "and whenever you touch the ball," She caught it again. "…you get three points." She tossed it over his head and started chasing him. "Just like football!"

He laughed and dodged her again. "You mean you don't ever want to touch it?"

"No. You have to give it to me automatically after every time you touch it." She frowned as she missed him again. "…And you have to let me tackle you."

He held the ball and looked at her. "You know, I normally would have told you I don't like the rules, but right now, I still think I can whoop you, even with your completely one-sided rules. Move down there. I'll kick off."

She hopped and skipped backward. "I'm going to crush you!"

He threw the ball high toward her but it landed in front of her and she barely picked it up before he reached for her. She shrieked as he wrapped his arms around her, flopped backward with her in his arms and rolled around in the snow. "You're cheating!"

"How am I cheating?"

"You're not letting me win!"

Morgan moved next to Chris on the sofa and he wrapped his arm around her. She chuckled as she watched her two kids play together. "I have to text Genna. She needs to see these two." She held her phone. *The kids r playing in the snow out back. U should be able to see them.*

Genna reached for her phone when it beeped. *Thanks.* She turned to Connor. "The kid are playing out back."

Connor walked to the sliding glass door, and softly laughed. They were both running around, covered with snow. "They're a riot. Kinda makes me want to go out and join them."

Genna met him at the door, wrapped her arm in his and rested her head on his shoulder. "I'd rather watch them and then take a walk."

She moved between him and the glass door and he wrapped his arms around her. "I wouldn't mind taking a walk later."

They stood arm in arm, watching their children play.

~ ~ ~

Stephie tossed and turned the entire night but when the alarm went off, she popped up, completely awake. Her heart immediately raced. She picked up her phone and texted, *Jake.*

A minute later her phone beeped, *yeah?*

She dialed him. "Yeah?"

He laughed. "I take it you're a little excited?"

She started hyperventilating. "What do you think? I want to be at the office when they open."

"I figured. I'll be ready in twenty minutes. Bring the thin bottle with you."

Her heart jumped. She knew exactly what he meant, but suddenly craved hearing more. "Really?"

His reply conveyed playful dominance. "You heard me."

His words were always her strongest aphrodisiac, and that fast, her thoughts went from the apartment, to anointing the apartment as theirs. She breathed deep. "See you in thirty."

They pulled up to the office twenty minutes early and found a parking spot with a view of the door.

Stephie couldn't control her excitement. "Let's go see if anyone's there."

And her excitement produced the usual soft smile on Jake. "Sure. Let's go check."

They walked to the door, found it open and went in. Twenty minutes later, they walked out with two apartment keys in their hands. "Jake!" She jumped in front of him, and held up her key, then skipped back to the car, waving it.

"You're too funny. Did you bring the little bottle?"

It was the only thing she purposefully packed. But she also had something special on under her coat, for the occasion. A few minutes later, he unlocked the apartment door for the first time, and they walked in with their mouths open. Stephie dialed her grandmother.

"Hi cipolline."

"Nana, we just walked in. It's incredible! It's so new and beautiful and clean."

Lorraine chuckled. "I knew you'd like it. I thought it was special too."

"Oh Nana. It's fantastic. Thank you."

"You're very welcome…but I expect your grades to stay exactly where they are."

"I have no intentions of letting you or me down. I'll show you how much I appreciate this. So will Jake. He wants to say thank you." She handed him the phone.

"Grandma Lorraine, thank you so much. I'll show you how much, by my grades too."

"That's all I want. And you're welcome. Enjoy your day."

"It's already a great day."

"I'm glad you think so. Bye bye dear."

"Bye Grandma Lorraine."

Jake dropped the video game bag she insisted he bring in, then pulled her into his arms, and gave her a long deep kiss in the middle of their new living room. Her arms wrapped around his neck and when their lips parted, she lit up. "That was our first kiss in our apartment!"

She jumped up and down in his arms, making Jake giggle. "I've never seen you this wound up."

"We have an apartment!"

He laughed a little harder. "Yes."

She ran into the kitchen. "Together!"

"I know."

"Look at this place!" She spun in a circle. It was cozy, pristine, clean, and contemporary, which was Lorraine's taste and had become Stephie's. She secretly loved the way Morgan and Chris had styled their house, and though she couldn't pick things out yet, knew what she liked when she saw it, and she liked this.

She ran down the small hallway to the next door. The bathroom wasn't much bigger than the other apartment but this was newer, prettier, and cleaner. "Jake, look at this!" He was right behind her and placed his hand on her hip, peering over her shoulder.

"It's really nice." He shook his head. "I can't believe your grandmother did this for us."

She ducked under the arm he had propped on the door jam and went to the next room. It was small, but it seemed to be a bedroom or a large closet without clothes rods. Then it registered and she crossed the hall and into the bigger bedroom on the other side. "Jacob?"

A moment later, he filled their bedroom doorway and watched her point to the small room across the hall. "There's a place where we can set up a desk for homework! ...Or your weights! ...Both!"

She slid past him, hurried back into the living room and spun slowly, memorizing every wall. He came up behind her and slipped his arms around her waist. "Do you like it?"

"Oh Jacob! I can't believe she would do this for us. It's amazing."

He let out a contented sigh. "It sure is."

They kissed in the middle of the living room; both aware that there was no one to be concerned with; no one who could interrupt. They were in their own safe world where they could be exactly who they were and with exactly who they chose. She let go of him and removed her coat, and his silly grin appeared immediately. His gift, more precious than gold, stood there, dressed in gold. She was wearing the shiny gold skirt and matching halter top she had on when they went dancing; sheer black thigh highs and all.

"I hope this is okay." She looked up at him. "I had to wear it. I can't look at it in my closet without being disappointed we didn't finish the night like I wanted." She smiled. "…but we can fix that today."

He stepped closer to her, and with his grin still in place, slid his hand under the back of her short skirt. She whispered softly, "What room do you want to make love in first?"

He whispered back, "Right here, but don't worry. It won't take us long to cover every room."

Her heart fluttered. "Promise?"

He reached for her hand and led her down to the carpet. "Oh, I promise."

She studied his eyes as he gently caressed her and whispered, "We're sleeping here tonight even if we have to sleep on comforters."

She slipped her arms around his neck. "Tell me about it. I need to wake up next to my alarm clock."

They kissed and caressed and made love in the middle of the living room.

The day was busy. They made four trips to the apartment, bringing everything that would fit in the car, and their sofa was delivered between trips two and three. The sun was setting as they unloaded for the fourth time, and he gently removed the TV from the back seat as she watched. She had a flashback. "This reminds me of our first time moving together."

He gripped the box awkwardly as it finally cleared the door opening. "Except we don't remember it."

"Yeah, but with our mothers telling the story so many times, I kind of feel like I remember it."

"That's funny. So do I." He jokingly smirked as he turned toward the door with the TV in his arms. "I do remember I carried more than you that day too."

She smacked his rear. "Ass."

They scrounged through loved ones' basements and attics to find pictures, forgotten furniture and anything that could help them make their place feel like home and within a week, the few pieces of furniture they had bought or borrowed were in place. Chris delivered the living room tables he made them, and the dinette table and chairs they claimed from Lorraine's basement. And everyone they loved had been invited and had stopped by for a visit.

Chapter Eighteen
Confirmation

Morgan reached for the light on her end table and turned it on while Chris dressed for work in the dark. He glanced at her. "What are you doing up?"

She yawned, "I can't sleep."

"You feel alright?"

She sat up. "I miss the kids."

He nodded and smiled, "So do I. Just when they stop being a pain in the ass… they're gone."

Her voice reflected her longing. "I want to see them." She rose out of bed and headed toward the bathroom, detouring enough to give him a kiss. "Mind if I text them and ask if they want to meet at Logan's tonight?"

His eyes followed her into the bathroom. "Of course not. When do they start their next semester?"

"Soon I think. The nineteenth or twenty-second. Somewhere around there."

He pulled his sweatshirt over his head. "Let's invite everyone and see if we can make it a party. …And see if Vicky and Jonathan want to come."

"Okay."

"Text me during the day and let me know what's going on." He waited for her to reappear and kissed her goodbye, then turned toward the kitchen for his work boots and coffee.

She grabbed him and kissed him again. "Love you."

He reached around her and gently squeezed her ass. "Love you too."

She dialed Stephie on her way to work. "Hi, love. How are you?"

"Hi Mom H! Good! We start school in a few days."

"I know. It's why Chris and I were thinking about a small party tonight at Logan's …before you get busy again with school. We were going to invite your mom and dad and Vicky and Jon too. What do you think? Do the two of you want to meet us there?"

"Sure!"

"I'll call your mother. You call Vicky? Then we'll text to confirm."

"That sounds great, and Jake and I will be there, no matter who else comes.

"Okay love, see you there around seven."

Steph waited till ten to call Vicky.

"Hey girl."

"Hi Vick. How are you?"

"Good. You?"

Steph smiled. "Good."

"What's new?"

"Morgan called me this morning and asked me to ask you if you and Jonathan feel like meeting the six of us at Logan's for dinner and drinks tonight. It's a neighborhood bar. Nothing special, but it's decent. I'm not sure if my parents are going. Morgan's calling my mom, but it's Jake's parents who are asking, so obviously they're going."

Vicky's voice changed. "Jake's parents are asking me if I want to have drinks and dinner with them?"

"Yeah. Them and us and maybe my parents." She started selling. "They're a lot of fun."

"I'm actually kind of dumbfounded. They asked you to ask me?"

"You and Jonathan. Or just you if he can't make it. You feel like?"

"Hell yeah! Your parents invited *me*?"

Stephie leaned back and her smile grew. "See what happens when you don't see your adopted parents enough?"

"Oh honey, I am thrilled."

"Don't be. The place isn't that special."

"Oh, it will be for me."

"I'll text you the time and directions. Ask Jonathan."

"Will do, honey! See you tonight."

"Love you."

"Love you too."

The texts went back and forth and by two in the afternoon, everyone was going. Morgan typed the last text. *Harrison - party of 8. 7ish logan's. c u there*

Stephie and Jake waited in the car until they spotted Chris and Morgan, and walked into Logan's right behind them. The four of them quickly rearranged three square tables and enough chairs for everyone. "I just talked to my mom. She and dad are a minute away and Vicky and Jon will be here in ten."

Morgan lit up. "Perfect."

"Oh Hi." Alicia walked up behind Stephie and spotted Chris and Jake. "Hi Chris."

"Hi Alicia. This is my wife Morgan."

She met Morgan's eyes. "Hi."

Chris continued, "You remember Jake."

She gazed at Jake and smiled. "Yes." Her voice changed. "I remember."

Jake greeted her tentatively. "Hi."

She perked up. "How've you been?"

"Good. You?"

"Good."

Chris regained her attention. "Bring us two pitchers of lite and six glasses to start?"

She looked at Chris, "Sure" then turned and walked away.

Stephie stared at Jake and playfully scolded him. "Who was that and why didn't you introduce me?"

Jake stammered and Chris laughed. He pointed to his father. "I was just in here with him. You dropped me off. And she was the bartender, that's all."

"Hi everyone." Genna and Connor walked in and claimed two seats.

Morgan kissed her on the cheek. "Hi. You're just in time to save Jake's life." Then Morgan chuckled at her own joke.

Stephanie defended herself. "I'm not mad. He's an idiot, but I'm not mad." She playfully smirked and gave Jake a kiss. She made silent plans to give Jake another when she saw Alicia close by.

"Hi, everybody."

"Hey Vick! Hi Jonathan."

Vicky sat across from Morgan and next to Chris on the one end. Jon sat next to Vicky and across from Stephie, and Jake sat next to Stephie and across from Genna, with Connor at the other end. Alicia came around again and took another drink order and the party was underway.

They ate, drank, joked and enjoyed each other's company, and the entire time, Vicky seemed fascinated with Chris, and constantly initiated conversation with him. He was amazed at Chris's ability to accept his children, even though he seemed so rough and blue collar. While everyone talked and joked, Vicky leaned toward Chris. "I think it's awesome you invited us."

Vicky's words caught Chris. "You're welcome to join us anytime."

Vicky continued, "I'm so happy you're so cool and I love that you love your son...both your children."

Chris instantly replied. "What's not to love?"

Vicky exhaled and his chin lowered as his brows rose. "Ask my father."

Chris's voice casually projected the confidence of his persona. "I already asked mine, and He said *love everyone*. And once He gives His edict, all other edicts pale in comparison."

Vicky breathed deep. "You're a very impressive man."

Chris shook his head slightly. "Not really."

Vicky affirmed. "My father couldn't tie your shoes."

Chris inhaled. "They're work boots. No shine. Only mud." Chris raised an eyebrow, smiled and turned slightly to him. "Hey, would you like to have a beer with me someday?"

Vicky's eyes widened further. "Me?"

Chris smiled, "Yeah, you and me."

Vicky's eyes welled and his mouth opened slightly.

Chris continued the invite. "Do you watch sports?"

"I like baseball."

"Perfect."

~ ~ ~

Jake's phone started beeping in the pitch black and she jumped him in the dark. "*School!*"

He laughed. "You're an idiot."

"That's why I'm going to *school.*"

"But if you keep straddling me like this, you're going to be late for *school.*"

She leaned down and gave him a big kiss and that fast, jumped off him and with another bounce, bounced off the bed. "You coming?"

She heard him answer as she left the bedroom and entered the bathroom. "Of course."

She pulled the shower faucet on, then gave a slight shiver and rubbed her upper arms as she waited for the steam to circulate around the small room, and Jake pulled her into his arms as he came in behind her. She looked over her shoulder at him. "I can't believe how great this is."

"I know." He kissed the back of her neck, "This is crazy." then pulled the shower curtain aside for her. She glanced at him as she stepped in. "We're going to walk to class."

They took turns under the warm water and began soaping each other. "We have to claim our lunchroom table."

She wrapped her arms around him, and rubbed against him as she washed his back. "I know."

He slid the soap over her bottom. "But not a library table. We have to have a permanent lunchroom table, but it's completely uncool to sit at the same library table."

She spun back around and rubbed her back against his front. "I agree completely...jackass."

"Hey!" He poked her sides. "It's idiot, to you."

He spun her around and kissed her. "Do we have time to fool around?"

"Sure. But we have to hurry." They both soaped each other and both enjoyed the other's immediate reaction.

"I like this. We've never done this before school." They each worked the soap into a lather.

"We have to hurry." She studied his eyes and smiled deviously. "Whoever is last makes dinner."

He wiped the water from his face. "You really don't want to train me to be fast."

"But a girl can give her boyfriend some quick relief every once in a while, can't she?"

His grin appeared. "I can't argue with that." He kissed her and pulled her into his arms and playfully rubbed against her; the soap lather between them providing all the sensation needed to accomplish their intentions. She lovingly met his movements, and moments later they both moaned in pleasure.

"You're making dinner."

"Hey, that's not fair."

They re-showered and did their best to tease and torture each other until they finally left the apartment. Once they were outside, he reached for her hand and they traced the path they had established the week before. They eventually split since their majors and classes were in different buildings, but they had already set a plan on where and when to meet.

Stephie reached the cafeteria first and scanned the room. A group of students were already sitting at the table they had picked. She took out her phone, *Meet at the door. R table is taken!*

A whisper came from behind her, "Okay."

The room was crowded where they thought it would be empty and empty where they thought it would be crowded but they found a table. Stephie was still surveying the room, when Jake sat down. "I hereby claim this table for second period."

"Are you sure?"

"Yeah. Sit."

She sat down, still looking around. He watched her and smiled as he opened his backpack. "Would you knock it off."

"Hey! This is important."

"No, it's not." He gave her a glance as he reached into his back pack for a textbook. She stuck out her bottom lip like she was going to pout and he laughed and opened his book. "How was your first class?"

She shrugged. "Jury's out, but I'll get used to it."

"I'm sure you will."

"How was yours?"

He kept his head down, pretending to read. "Good! The professor's hot."

She flicked her pen at him and that fast reached for it. "Give me that back."

After getting situated, he pulled an apple from his back pack and bit it, then reached back in and took out a banana and two cans of soda. "I brought you breakfast."

She glanced up from her textbook and smiled. "Thanks. Did you make this yourself?"

"Yes, and since I'm making dinner tonight too, if you don't finish your banana, you can save it and add it to yours."

She wanted to say something clever, but all she could think about was the idea they were going home and having dinner together.

~ ~ ~

Their first year at the new school passed quickly and they met everyone's grade expectations, including their own. They made the apartment their home and were happily getting used to their new school and living together. They each took two summer classes to lighten their regular semester workload and both found part time jobs fairly close to the apartment. By their third semester, they were well entrenched in their new lives, and casually making tentative plans for the rest of their lives.

Stephie walked up to the group standing in front of her closed classroom door and waited patiently for the classmate in front of her to walk away, so she could read the message attached. She took her turn and read the professor's note on the door, canceling class, and happily set out toward Jake's building and classroom. She found a bench down the hall in the opposite direction from how he would leave to meet her, planning to surprise him, and sat and opened a textbook. She quietly read until the class let out and as she prepared to sneak up behind him, she watched him walk out laughing with a very pretty blonde who was obviously having a hard time not touching him.

Her heart dropped. What was a plan to surprise him, instead became a scene from her worst nightmare. She stood there, in shock, motionless. Her deep breaths…her only movements. What had been a period of blissfulness had come to an abrupt and unexpected end as she once again contemplated her chances of happiness for the first time in a long time. She stood there for an extended time, trying to rationalize feelings she remembered all too well. She knew he would expect her home by a certain time, but she wasn't sure she would be functioning by then, or any time soon, so she quickly texted, *Held up in class. Don't wait for me. Be home soon.*

She didn't know what to do or where to go. She went back to the bench, and sat and stared at the open classroom door. She stood up to walk home twice, but did nothing more than make a circle in the hallway and sit back down.

She finally stood and began the slow walk home. Her mind an accompanying enemy and her heart weighing far more than it should. No matter how well things were going, she never felt completely sure she was everything he could want or get; not ever fully sure he wasn't with her because he was too wonderful and kind to leave her.

She didn't want to be moody all evening, and all her mood did was give her something else to be mad at herself about, but she couldn't help it. Nothing she could think of removed the picture of the pretty blonde from her mind. He finally looked up from the textbook on his lap and squinted as he always did. "What's wrong?"

With those words she turned to him and fell apart, crying. He rushed over to her and braced her like she was going to crumble to the ground. "Sweetheart! What's wrong?"

She lowered her head, still crying. "I love you."

He tried to meet her eyes. "I love you too. What's wrong?"

Through her tears, she composed herself the best she could, "I love you so much, and for so long, that I want you to have everything you could want, and everything you haven't even wished for…even if it isn't me." She so craved his happiness that she convinced herself long ago, she wouldn't stand in his way for whatever he desired, and was now scared to hear if he had reached that point. It would break her heart but she loved him more than she loved herself. She wasn't jealous; she was resigned.

His pain reflected in his voice, "Oh god Steph! Your words are pure love," and a strange sad smile broke on his face. "But you don't understand. You're what I wish for. You're the only thing I wish for."

"But you can do so much better than me." Her own words made her cry harder. "I can't give you babies. I saw you with that girl leaving your class. She's a real girl, and she's really pretty." She looked at him through tear filled eyes. "It's okay if you need more than me. I really love you that much."

His eyes welled, and with tender exasperation, replied, "Oh god Steph! Don't you understand I love you completely? Why is there *any* doubt in your wonderful perfect being? Everyone spends a lifetime searching for their perfect match, their perfect love. The person they hope to spend the rest of their life with. Most fail. But I have you. I didn't fail. God smiled on me and gave me *you*. From when I was still a child, He gave me you. No sweetheart, there is nothing I want *but* you. I need to die in your arms, to consider this place and my time here special. And if I have nothing else…nothing else when that day comes, but your arms around me, I will die a fulfilled and happy man."

Though his eyes were filled with moisture, a faint grin appeared on his face. His voice turned playfully scolding. "I had all intentions of making my proposal to you, some kind of cute and big deal…"

She felt her heart pound and she gasped for air.

"And I've been working on it for a long time in my head, but sometimes a man needs to weigh far more important things than a cute plan and a surprise…"

She started trembling and crying for a completely different reason.

"And today, I need very badly to wipe from your mind any doubt, any inkling of a fleeting thought that you're anything but my definition of everything I need or want."

He reached for her hand and led her to their room but instead of going toward the bed, he led her to the closet door, let her hand go and knelt at his shoes. She stood there trembling. He reached into one of the work boots in the very back corner, pulled out a small plastic bag and stood up. Her heart pounded as she covered her mouth, quietly sobbing, and hoping. He turned to her and knelt on one knee in front of her, and looked up at her…and she started crying all over again.

She watched single tears fall from his eyes. "I believe I mentioned I was trying to think of a clever way to propose. Instead we'll laugh at where I gave you this." He opened the small felt covered black box he had taken out of the plastic bag and removed the little gold diamond ring inside, placed it on her trembling hand, then looked into her eyes. "Stephanie Blair, will you marry me?"

Her legs trembled for the force of her tears. She felt so unworthy of him; her definition of a perfect person and a perfect man, but she also knew she would not wish to survive without him. Only he sustained her and gave her life meaning. She composed herself, and motioned him to come up and hug her, and to the best of her ability, as he did, she whispered through a broken voice and the lump in her throat, "I need you. I need you so much. I tremble at the slightest thought of losing you. You are my life and the love of my life. I have dreamed and fantasized about this day. Of course I want to marry you. You have been my love since I was too young to even understand love. But now that I do, I only have love for you. Please marry me."

His hug lifted her off the ground and they kissed more passionately than they have ever kissed, and then he answered, "Yes! Please marry me?"

She whispered in his ear, "One thousand times, yes!"

EPILOGUE

The sale sign had been marked *sold* for roughly six weeks, but Danielle never asked about it, so her mother saw no need to explain the possibilities associated with its implication, but when Danielle heard the low resonating hum build while she played with her new kindergarten schoolbag and lunch pail in front of the TV, she stopped for a moment to listen.

The hum grew increasingly louder until it permeated the entire house and as it grew, she stood and went to the front picture window next to the chair her father occupied, to investigate. Out of the right corner of the window and into her vision came the enormous silver truck. It made an awfully loud groan and slowed as it went from the right side of the window to the left, and then seemed to stop just out of her sight. She ran to her mother, "Mom, I think something's happening next door."

"Oh, really sweetheart?" Her mother looked out the nearest window facing next door. A car was now parked in the accompanying driveway. "What do you think it is?"

Danielle put her hands on the windowsill and watched. "I think we're getting new neighbors."

"You do?"

"Yeah!" She paused for a second. "What if there's someone my age?"

"Well, just in case, I think we ought to go make her or him feel welcomed, don't you?"

"Yeah, Mom. We should, shouldn't we?" Danielle looked up, and saw the curious but pleasant smile on her mother's face.

"Go tell daddy and let's go say hi, okay?"

"Okay!" Before she turned or took a step she yelled, "Dad! Dad!" She continued as she ran back to him. "Mommy said we have to go check out our new neighbors."

The child ran to the side of his chair and pulled on his forearm, "Dad, I think we have new neighbors and mom told me to come get you so we can say hi."

He looked up from his computer, quickly looked down and clicked save, and gently shut it. "Okay sweetheart. Go tell mommy I'm ready."

The little girl ran out of the room, toward her mother. When he stood, he saw a second car pull into the far driveway next door. "Sweetheart, they're here."

Danielle impatiently watched her mother place the last glass in the cabinet, then reach for her hand. They walked to her father at the front door, and the three of them went out together. She could see the woman leaning inside the open back door of her car as they approached, and a moment later, out stepped a little girl, but Danielle, more timid than her father, never let go of her mother's hand as they walked together toward their new neighbors.

The little girl noticed them coming toward their new driveway and backed up against her mother's leg, and the woman paused as her child changed her attention from the back seat, to the sidewalk. She began stroking her daughter's hair and looked down to see her reaction to the approaching girl holding her mother's hand. "Look Jennifer. I think they're our new next door neighbors."

Danielle smiled as she watched the little girl lean against her mother, then looked up at her mother and father as her mom broke the silence. "Hi. Welcome to the neighborhood."

"Thanks." The woman smiled warmly and continued stroking her daughter's hair.

"We're the Harrisons. I'm Stephanie and this is Jake. And this is Danielle." Stephie and Jake extended their hands.

"Nice to meet you. I'm Kaitlin and this is Jennifer." And from around the corner of the house and the other side of the car they heard, "And I'm Scott."

Jake turned and continued to extend his hand. Scott took it, and they shook. "It's a pleasure to meet you. Welcome to the neighborhood."

Danielle watched, then looked at Jennifer and held out her hand. "Hi, I'm Danielle. Welcome to the neighborhood."

Jennifer looked up at her mother, then reached for Danielle's hand. "Hi, I'm Jennifer. Welcome to the neighborhood."

The four adults laughed softly.

Kaitlin looked down at Jennifer and with the gentlest push suggested, "Why don't you show Danielle your new house?"

The little girl looked up at her mother and then Danielle and without a sound, started running toward the front door. Danielle looked up at her mother and Stephie softly nudged her, "You can go." And that fast, she started running to catch her new neighbor.

THE END